XIAXAN FOX

Xiaxan Fox

An orphaned princess battles across realms to reclaim her kingdom.

Born under a calamity star, Princess Jenaso 'Joi' of Letoura survived the massacre of her family and the burning of Tennaba. Taken in by the neighboring King of Meideon, he raises her as his daughter alongside his two sons.

Years later, at a pre-coronation event, revealing her identity has old enemies once more after her, not to mention all the suitors for her hand. To secure her safety, she escapes with a Xiaxan fellow trainee and secret admirer, Prince Sohar of Greyad.

Across five realms, she battles her family's enemies, old and new, with magic and sword but must decide whether to pledge her life to her kingdom or follow her heart.

Xiaxan Fox

by Sevannah Storm

This is a work of fiction. The characters, incidents and dialogues in this book are of the author's imagination and are not to be construed as real. Any resemblance to actual events or persons, living or dead, is completely coincidental.

Also by Sevannah Storm

The Blood of Legends Series

The Huntress

The Healer

*

The Gifting Series

Soul Forged

Fate Forged

Sun Forged

War Forged

Star Forged

Shadow Forged

Earth Forged

Lust Forged

Fire Forged

Time Forged (Coming soon)

*

The Space Hunter Chronicles

The Shikari

The Justisaar (Coming soon)

*

The Qaldreth Warriors

Sol Survivor

Dark Survivor (Coming soon)

*

Standalones

Xiaxan Fox

Ire of Silver

The Lady and the Assassin

The Crucible of the Eternal

*

Plump Playwright Series

Plump Jane

Seducing Amelia

Loving Finley

Keeping Tessa

Kissing Navy

Sea of Turmoil
The Sea of Sisters
Orth
Birson Westlands
Meidcon
Raica
Temple of the Divine Reston
Greyad
Letoura
Brat's Pass
The Wood of Yellowsong
Cithedele
Hornook Mountains
Ta
Tessara
Swamp of Pestilence
Derensberou
The Crystal Sea
Seit
Rendar
Sersem Mountains
Drem
Manorio
The Yearning Sea
The Gulf of Lost Hope

Chapter One

Sacrifice

Swords clashing and wailing women echoed in her ears. In the supposed safety of her bed, Joi lay frozen, staring at the flickering shadows spiking her fear. A hand on her chest drew a scream from her, and she fought the blankets entangling her feet. Her father leaned over her to grip her shoulders. Dark-brown oil dribbled down his forehead, and his pristine hair now framed his worried face in a black sweat-matted halo. She squeaked when it dripped red onto her silk blanket. It had the thickness and color of blood. Gasping, she flicked her gaze to her father's wounded temple.

"Da?" She scrambled to her knees and wrapped her arms around him as best she could. The sting of smoke and the earthy scent of sweat mingled, assaulting her nose. He was here; she could breathe. In his arms, she had nothing to fear.

"I love you, little one. I need you to be strong for me. Can you do that?" His voice broke, and he sucked in a shuddering breath.

Strong? She would try, but her brother Jeiram was the fiercest. She nodded, agreeing to anything to wipe the sad expression from her father's gold eyes. He removed his carved token, a gold disc with flames crafted in the purest ruby, then tied it to her sleep garments. With a grimace, he slipped off his gold medallion—a ruby in the center—and looped it over her head. The weight of it pressed down on her chest as heavy as his hand had been. Warmth burst through her as the medallion pulsed a greeting. She had seen it do the same for Da, but never for Ma.

"It belonged to my mother," he said before kissing her temple. "Now go with Ayo, she'll take you somewhere safe."

"Da?" Joi reached for his fingers, not liking the cold shivering over her. "You won't come to find me, will you?"

He squeezed her hand, his skin damp and overheated.

"Oh, my bright girl, you're too observant for one so young. I'll be with you always, here and here." He touched the token and the medallion. One more hug, and he left her, his disappearing back forever burned into her memories.

"Ayo?" Despite the unhindered tears flowing down her cheeks, Joi tried to smile at her nursemaid who grabbed a rucksack she had hidden under the bed. With a shake of her head, Ayo took Joi's hand and jerked her to her feet, then kneeling to pull on her slippers.

"Come, Princess, we must rush. The king has organized an escape route via the river, then by horse to Meideon. There, King Buro will take care of you."

"Meideon?" Joi asked as she ran after her favorite servant. "I don't want to go there. I want to stay and fight. Da needs me."

"Don't be silly, Joi. You can't wield your eating dagger, let alone a sword. Your magical energies haven't risen yet. Please, you can help your father by being safe. He won't have to worry about you."

Joi said no more, running as fast as her little legs could carry her. Ducking under Ayo's outstretched arm holding the door open, she paused, unable to blink. Ice drenched her cheeks, and her tears burned paths down to drip off her chin. The scene greeting her was brutal. The once beautiful and serene gardens of the royal court were in chaos. Blood splattered the white blossoms of the Snowthistle trees and battle scars marred the gray bark, looking like her artwork and messy handwriting. The bodies of wounded and dead soldiers carpeted the ground like the reenactments of the Battle of Heaven's Fire. Some wore the familiar Letouran armor, others wore black-and-silver cloaks. She tried not to look at their faces with their unseeing eyes open as if they watched her. And no matter how hard she focused, she couldn't see their chests rising and falling.

One man stood in the middle, his black cloak dipping into a pool of blood beneath his boots. Joi shuddered, nausea roiling in her belly. She gagged and held a fist to her mouth as if that would silence her sobs.

He extended his fingers to point at her. "Ah, young Jenaso. I will slay you now and end the curse of Letoura." His eyes glowed as black smoke swirled around him.

Joi clung to Ayo's hand. Shivers skittered along her skin as the man called on his energy. Fear possessed her, freezing her tongue.

Scooping Joi into her arms, Ayo ran, dodging bodies, weapons, flames, and panicked horses. She crept through the palace servant's hidden entrance before darting across the fragrant herb fields toward the river. Ayo gulped for breath, her speed dwindling as she hugged Joi tighter, but Joi's focus remained on the palace. And with reason—the man appeared through the archway as Ayo lowered them into an awaiting boat. The boatman nodded in greeting and dipped his ores into the silent river, paddling them away from the dock.

The hull glided through the water slower than Joi liked. She hadn't run, hadn't fought the attackers, but she couldn't breathe. Something terrible had happened, tearing apart her world. Would she see her parents and her beloved Jeiram again? A different yet familiar darkness settled inside her. It wasn't magic-born, but it hurt, squeezing her chest. Was it fear? Like when Jeiram had broken his arm? She had been so scared for him.

Joi didn't dare blink as she focused on the bank, ignoring the burning buildings, the screams of metal, of death, and the sour stench of fear in the air. Her world was collapsing—everything she knew ripped from her. That man with his cold gaze and his wicked laugh was a stranger. She had never seen him before and didn't understand why he hated her so. He wore the robes of a Drem, but no realms were at war. It didn't make sense.

They were in the center of the river when the man reached the riverbed. He held up a hand with black smoke streaking from his fingertips. As unskilled as she was, Joi knew when the black smoke touched them, painful death would be their fate. Brother Jeiram had taught her one skill—she had pestered him for weeks until he gave in—but neither had known how much she would need it.

Joi stretched out her hand, palm forward, and swirled her other hand over her forearm. The boat swayed, and she sucked in a sharp breath. She must stay focused unless she wanted to explode things—which she could if she wasn't careful. She was eleven years old and not as strong as Jeiram, who had many tutors. Joi had yet to officially start her studies.

The smoke skipping over the water's surface braced her with fear. It rolled over the water too quickly. She reached out her hand again, swirling, gliding her stiff fingers, willing the magic to form with her eyes closed in concentration. Oily nausea filled her belly as the black smoke touch her, brushing against the fire burning within her. At her failure, her shoulders slumped with dread fluttering her heart.

When she opened her eyes, her light blue magic swirled over them, forming a dome of protection. The black smoke coated it, mottling the pure blue in some areas where the dome wasn't at its strongest. That worried her as her energy drained from her, tremors shaking her limbs and chattering her teeth.

"I cannot hold it." She cast a desperate glance at Ayo.

The water splashed on either side as the boatman dipped his oar in with valiant efforts to gain distance. The night fell silent the farther they traveled. No wailing crossed the gurgling river, despite the burning city shining as a nightmarish backdrop.

Ayo fought for breath, having carried Joi longer than she was able to. "You won't die, I won't let you." She grabbed Joi's outstretched hand, closing her fingers over it.

The dome disintegrated under the black magic's forceful onslaught. Tossing Joi to the bottom of the boat, Ayo threw her body over her, crushing her. "No energy can control water, and it's for this reason, it remains neutral. The closer you are to it, the safer you'll be."

A loud splash preceded the violent rocking of the boat. The boatman abandoned them. Hot anger gripped Joi, overwhelming her fear that the man would do such a thing. Part of her understood. His life, his family, was in danger. Nonetheless, the coward! She forced herself to focus on Ayo's words, instead, willing the fury to fade.

"Does that mean a wet person can't be harmed?" Joi drew in short gasps of air, struggling to breathe under the weight of her servant and friend.

"To some extent..." A cry escaped Ayo—pain and sadness twisted her face.

Cold dread slithered along Joi's skin. Something warm saturated her garments, and the metallic scent of blood surrounded her. It mingled with the familiar fragrance of her beloved servant and the memory of Da's hug.

"Ayo?" Joi's voice was a whisper, scratching her throat.

Brushing the hair off Joi's forehead, Ayo's face paled ashen despite her smile. "Find King Buro, Joi. He's waiting for you. Nateo will ensure you reach Meideon. Be safe, Princess..." The light in her eyes faded, and her body went limp, crushing Joi further.

She cried out, her hands grasping Ayo's shoulders in desperation, fear, and something more than the weight squeezing her chest. It seized her lungs, hindering her ability to breathe.

"Ayo," she chanted, sobs tearing through her as she shoved against her servant's body. "Ayo…"

Joi's tears dwindled as time passed. She lay there with the gentle rocking of the boat against the city's dying cries. With Ayo not stirring and her eyes not opening, she must have moved onto the next life, to a glorious life with the Divine. Joi scrubbed her own face, fighting to keep the next wave of tears at bay.

She was alone.

"He's given up, Princess." The boatman's voice startled her, and she jerked, tightening her fingers on Ayo's cooling arms.

Joy and relief flooded her with fresh, grateful tears. He hadn't abandoned her.

"The king's man is waiting for you at the bridge," he said. The boat dipped, a violent tilt threatening to topple her as he pulled himself into his craft. "You best climb up and wash your face."

She obeyed, wriggling out from under Ayo's body, swaying the boat with her efforts. The boatman steered them toward a mounted rider's shadowed form. Joi splashed her face and used the sleeve of her soiled sleep garments to dry off. With an unnatural fear trembling her hands, Joi searched for her imperial token and medallion. Only upon finding them did she draw in a steadying breath. Stroking Ayo's curls one last time, Joi raised her arms for the boatman to lift her onto the muddy banks.

The mud squelched beneath her slippers, soaking through the silk and cooled her feet. She scanned the area—the sturdy bridge remained untouched, but the surrounding city echoed with the wails of the dying and the spicy stench of charred buildings overwhelmed her senses.

"I will not bow, Princess Jenaso—it might draw attention. I am Nateo, sent by King Buro to hurry you to safety." The tall man drew closer on soft heels, leading his horse behind him.

"My maid…" She cast a glance at the boatman. She couldn't bear to say Ayo was dead, but Joi couldn't abandon her body either.

"I will cast her into the seas, and may the Divine bless her for her sacrifice." The boatman gathered Ayo's cloak around her as if to shield her from the cold river breeze. Such a simple gesture made Joi believe the man would do as he vowed, that she could trust him to honor her friend.

"Thank you, sir." She faced Nateo and held up her arms.

He glided forward, and with ease, lifted her onto the front of the saddle. Launching himself behind her, he looped an arm around her to keep her close and gathered the reins with his other hand.

They darted through the panicking populace. Fear and disbelief stained with sorrow contorted the survivors' faces. Relief added to the guilt eating at her. The solid chest of Nateo was at her back, surrounding her in a feeling of safety. His sword rested on his hip, and she assumed he knew how to use it. Not that she wanted him to kill anyone for her, but it eased her heart that he could if he needed to.

An image of the black sorcerer came to mind, and she shivered. Joi hoped they didn't encounter him again, because even with his sword, Nateo would not be able to thwart that evil man's magic.

Once they left the burning city behind, the scenery flew by, blurring the foliage into a steady silver. She rested her head against Nateo's shoulder, no longer gripping his arm hard enough to bruise him.

"I cannot call you *Princess* on our journey. We will travel for the next week. My king asked if I may address you as something else; whatever you prefer."

"Ayo called me Joi."

"Very well, Joi. From this day forward, you are King Buro's long-lost niece. You will remain hidden for a year or two, then he will announce your existence at court as Princess Joi of Meideon."

"Yes," she said, assuming it was what her da had organized for her, allowing him this one last time to influence her life.

After that, she would decide her own destiny.

Chapter Two

Gaining a Daughter

Exhaustion pounded at his vision, his temple. Buro hadn't found rest, not with the impending arrival of his new ward, Jenaso. The message crows kept him informed, and when Nateo crossed the borders between Letoura and Meideon, the crushing weight on Buro's chest lessened. Yet, he wouldn't know peace until she was here in the palace.

Amid heated debate on the productivity of the jade mines and fishing ships, Buro's ever-vigilant guard, Tei, informed him of Nateo's arrival. Buro leaped to his feet, chasing his advisors out of the throne room. His boots thumped on the cobbled stones as he ran pell-mell along the underground passages, trusting Tei to follow. Buro did not fear for his life, for they were not at war, nor would harm befall him within his palace and the beloved city of Ethrielle. With Tei present, the risk to Buro's life was minimal.

Nateo had circled the city to ensure no one saw him enter from the direction of Letoura. This left Buro waiting, pacing on the eastern side of the palace. His cloak and robes billowed from behind him. Each violent stride aligned with the reverberating thunder from the approaching storm. The wind was as turbulent as the emotions roiling within him, with icy fingers as sharp as the fear piercing his usual serenity.

Sorrow's darkness embraced his heart. He and Kura became friends when they had wrestled on the ground over the charms of a palace maidservant, of all things. Just remembering that day decades ago, a smile formed—a burst of warmth rolled through Buro's chest despite the chilling wind lashing at his cheeks. They had received severe chastisement and were sent to work the mines for a week. It took *that* long to travel to the Bowels of Abarat. Harsh words and scuffles soured their journey, but the seven days of mining stone and precious gems under the sweat of their brows strengthened their friendship. The test of time proved their loyalty to each other. This was why Kura chose Buro to care for his precious daughter.

The thunderous hooves of the horse galloping across the bridge paused Buro's pacing. He rested his hand on the cold ivory hilt of his sword—his grip soft but possessive, like a lover's touch on his hip. Nateo drew his horse to a halt with a strong arm wrapped around the sleeping girl. Keeping her clasped against his chest, he slid out of the saddle.

Buro darted forward, determined not to wait, that not a raindrop would land on her. He had promised Kura he would keep his daughter safe, and by the Divine, Buro would. The crows told him of the massacre. How the royal blood spilled down the palace steps, staining its beautiful white stone floors. The city shook with wailing as Letourans saw the same fate as their rulers. Unlucky visitors were unable to escape the slaughter.

If such a massacre occurred on Meideon soil, his people would demand justice for their loved ones, and as their king, he had no other recourse but to confront King Rumoc of Drem. Despite Drem being rich in minerals and silver, Rumoc wouldn't offer recompense for this incident. They were an arrogant people, indicative of Rumoc himself, who believed he was above natural law.

There had been whisperings of such a decisive plot, but hope had prevailed. Although, Kura, ever the strategist, planned accordingly. Seven days after his death, his daughter was, at last, safe. Buro gathered the girl from Nateo's arms, giving him a nod, before rushing into the palace through the hidden tunnel. Buro hoped her brother and the heir-apparent made it out as well. To lose him too would be brutal for the young girl. He tamped down the sorrow welling in his chest, at the loss of Kura and his beautiful empress, Eria. His hold tightened on their last essence asleep in his arms.

"Did she choose a name?" he asked Nateo, who followed him from the servants' entrance into the hidden tunnel.

"Joi, my king." Exhaustion roughened Nateo's voice.

"A simple name, perfect. You did well, Nateo. You have my eternal thanks and the appropriate reward."

"A reward is not required, my king. To save her was thanks enough." Nateo trailed Buro into the stone foyer and her new chambers. "I cannot say when last I had such a delightful trip. Despite what she must have endured, she was polite yet inquisitive, peppering me for stories on the Meideon royal family. I admired her unexpected intelligence and her quest for knowledge even more so."

"Truly? I'd received whisperings of such...I will steer her toward the scholars. Perhaps they would serve as a distraction during her mourning."

"Wise as always, my king."

"You and Tei serve me well, but I need you to become her shadow, Nateo."

"As you command, my king."

Buro grunted as he placed the girl onto her bed, pulling the blanket over her. She snuggled into the bedding, cupping a hand under her cheek. He took the time to assess her—her small, pale face with the dark, slashing eyebrows of the Letoura. A thick braid trailed behind her, black as a moonless night. Her cheekbones were high, adding an ethereal air to her features. Her pointed chin was the elegant ending to her angular jawline.

"She received the blessing of Eria's beauty despite having been born under a calamity star," he said, brushing a curl off her temple. "Nothing must harm her, Nateo. I cannot fail her father."

Stepping back, Buro untied the drapes to obscure her, not a usual task he performed. It was strange to do so now, but determination spurred him to protect her against anything, even from a stray insect.

"Da?" Kylen made no sound as he scampered toward the bed. "Is that her?"

King Buro had shared the possibility of a sister with both his sons, needing them to protect her when Nateo couldn't. Both had large hearts, something Buro valued the most. Honor and integrity flowed in their veins as it had done for the Meideon royal family for generations. For these reasons alone, he could trust her to their care.

"Yes, this is Joi." A smile curled Buro's lips as his son parted the drapes to peer at her.

"She is beautiful," he said with a scowl. "Brother Mion and I will need to train harder. They will come for miles to see her."

Buro grinned, and he shared with Nateo the pride warming his heart. Such moments proved his sons would grow into honorable men. "She will train alongside you, my son. We cannot protect her all the time. Evil is persistent, and many a noble heart is lost to its allure."

"Da, may I remain here in case she awakens afraid?"

Buro studied his oldest son's features, his determination an echo of his own. With a nod, he and Nateo retreated, leaving the young addition to his family in the care of his eldest pride.

"Kylen's request to stay is good, my king." Nateo closed the carved wooden doors behind them. "Should the prince form an affection for her?" He hurried after Buro.

"She's the last of the Letouran royals, more than suitable as a consort or empress to my son." Buro veered left then right, down the many passages—a maze if one did not know the way. Having played there as a boy, he knew it by heart.

"Please excuse my presumption, but perhaps you should raise her as the empress you want?" Nateo paused outside Buro's chambers.

"You do not like the insipid females sent to entice my sons?" Buro flashed him a smile. "Not all find battle women appealing, but yes, I agree. Your presumption is forgiven."

"You are gracious, my king." Nateo bowed, placing his right palm over his heart.

"Now find your rest. I will have Lanz guard the young ones."

"Thank you again, my king."

Buro watched Nateo stride down the wide passage before disappearing around the corner. Yes, Nateo was wise to suggest such. Buro should mold her into the empress he needed—no matter whether it was Meideon or Letoura she would reign over. Nodding, he entered his chambers, for once void of servants. With a smile, he undressed—yet another rare task, one he strangely enjoyed and in absolute privacy too. A portent of good things to come.

Chapter Three

Brothers-in-Arms

Five Years Later

JOI SPUN ON THE spot, sweeping her right leg behind her, absorbing the blow from their connecting swords. Sparks flew, gold and silver, as the blades kissed along their edges. With another spin, she swung the sword out in a graceful arc, to attack from the other side. Sohar raised his blade, meeting her downward slash again. Hers slid down, hooking on his hilt as their gazes met across the touching steel.

Defeat wasn't easy for her. Flipping backward so her foot collided with his chest, she dislodged their blades and sent him stumbling. She landed in a crouch to absorb the force. Gripping her sword with both hands, she raised it in front of her face in case he caught her off guard. Arching a brow in query, she taunted Sohar with a smirk.

"You are well-matched." Mentor Selat clasped his hands behind his back. He strolled on to observe another sparring pair.

She spared him but a glance. She didn't believe they were well-matched, with herself the lesser. Xiaxan required stamina, focus, strength, and self-discipline. It wasn't easy to manipulate air to gain height and range in battle. Using weapons such as spears, swords, and daggers, meant extending her perception of her physical limits.

Joi could recall the day Sohar, the Crown Prince of Greyad, arrived for Xiaxan training—the young man with white hair as striking as any she had ever seen. His unspoken displeasure was evident to all, that a girl was a trainee alongside him. He had never voiced his opinion nor given her an advantage due to her gender. This was why she preferred to spar with him, despite his obvious disapproval. Over the years, she had grown to respect him. His steadfast attitude, his strength of justice, his applied wisdom—all served to alter her assessment of his character.

"Too much Redanta last night?" she teased, then chuckled when his snort crossed the gravel training circle. "Not up to the challenge?"

"Joi-Joi," he said, reprimanding her for attempting to distract him.

That she adored his name for her was something she didn't share with anyone. She loved it when he called her "Princess" too. Perhaps any name spoken in his rumbling voice pleased her.

He lunged for her, crossing the distance in a single bound. His sword led his charge, the tip of which came perilously close to her cheek. The cut burned, but she didn't dwell on it. Diving into the strike, she threw a punch, connecting with his sternum, before spinning to the side of him to tap his temple with the hilt of her blade. That was the plan. The punch landed, but the sidestep forewarned him. He twisted out of the way, bringing his blade around in a smooth arc.

She rolled forward, missing the sharp edge by a finger's width. Dropping her blade, she braced herself on the palms of her hands and kicked up, connecting with his hip. He stumbled and grunted, the only indication she hurt him.

"Too much Redanta isn't good for you. I'll have my maidservant water yours down." Joi wagged a finger.

Sohar dropped his blade, grabbed her hands, then yanked her off the ground, pinning her against his chest. He spun her at the last moment so the length of her back rested along the front of him. His arms were tight, holding her in place no matter how hard she struggled. The brush of his lips across her cheek and the heat spreading from the gentle touch made her stiffen.

"You lose, Princess." His breath feathered across her ear, spiraling shivers down her body. An unknown reaction on her part, and since she didn't understand it, she ignored it.

"Using your greater strength against me is cheating, Mighty Sohar." She flipped her head to meet his crystal-blue gaze, her lips almost meeting his in the process. Joi chose to ignore that too, despite his touch lingering.

"Your taunts are not?" He didn't pull away from her, and as usual, no expression crossed his face. Sohar's focus shifted, trailing over her temple before lowering to linger on her parted lips.

"If you cannot handle distraction, then you have no place in battle," she said.

His eyes widened, and she could've sworn she saw amusement in their depths. Joi discarded that thought as soon as it formed. He was a stoic man. Even when drunk, he showed no warmth.

"You need to escape my 'greater strength' if surviving a battle is your intention." He lowered his arms, thrusting her away from him as he bent to collect his sword. "Women have no place in battle."

"Truly? No camp concubine to ease your...stiff muscles?" Embarrassment scorched her face further as the words tumbled from her mouth. She knew full well how her fellow trainees received attention from the ladies at court. Perhaps jealousy had torn those words from her? Not that she could recall Sohar's interest straying to carnal delights.

He said nothing for a long time as he appraised her face and quivering body in the white trainee's pants and tunic.

"Joi-Joi, come say that to me when you have eased a man's stiff muscles and without a blush, Princess." He cupped her cheek, brushing his thumb over the tiny scratch he had inflicted. She didn't feel the sting, just the hot texture of his skin. "My apologies. I won't hurt you again."

He abandoned her in the training circle, sauntering off with an arrogance that infuriated her. The urge to stamp her foot gripped her, but she was always under observation. The life of a princess.

Instead, she glared at his retreating back, his long legs striding away from her. Despite the scowl furrowing her brow, she lingered on his broad shoulders. Curse it, she didn't learn. How many times had she lost to him? Now she had to serve him every night with noodles from Pan's outside the palace gates. Da would keep her allowance if he discovered she had ventured there, never mind for seven consecutive days.

"Why do you taunt him so?" Her oldest brother, Kylen, paused beside her, pressing a white cloth to her cheek. As she had stated, someone *was* watching.

"I suspect it's his silence that irritates me."

"Need an escort?" Ky asked, and she threw her arms around him, squeezing him tight. He grumbled about it despite hugging her back. "Da would punish us both if he found out I let you go without additional protection."

"I don't see why—Nateo is more than capable."

"True, but I will escort you regardless. Pan's noodles are the best." Ky pulled away to rub his belly, wrinkling his white tunic.

"Ah, so your ulterior motive is your stomach? Why don't I bring you a bowl, as well?" She scooped up her blade and slid it into its scabbard at her hip. "I'll do that anyway. My maidservant will bring it to your chambers."

"I *should* escort you." Ky raised his chin, a clear indication he was intending to be stubborn about this.

"No, Nateo will, and if you say one more word, I'll sneak out...alone." Joi patted his shoulder and strolled away, each step full of dread, expecting Ky's voice to halt her. As the crown prince, should he command her, she would have to obey. When she reached the training arena's gate unhindered, she released the breath she held.

"Lost again, Princess?" Nateo fell into step beside her.

She grunted in response, unhappy that everyone knew her business.

"As usual." She slanted a glance at her omnipresent companion. "I don't understand why I cannot best him. I mean, you've trained me, showed me your finest techniques. I've learned the same lessons as he did, endured the same trials of combat. I'm baffled."

"Your passion is your downfall." He chuckled. "I wouldn't change that for all the jade in Meideon."

"Curse it, Nateo. How can someone be so unfeeling?"

Nateo answered with a shrug, and Joi huffed.

"Greyadians endure much, having to battle Orthians daily. I suspect a tight control over their emotions ensures decisions aren't made that would jeopardize their soldiers or their realm."

She grunted. Covering Greyadian culture in her studies was simpler than dealing with it. No matter how she taunted Sohar, he remained aloof. Perhaps an event had occurred in his past to harden him more than he needed to be? In the years she had known him, she could count on one hand the number of times he had smiled and not just a token smile, which was a brief lip curl.

Nateo gestured to the south. "Pan will deliver a few bowls to the palace gates, so we need not venture out."

"You expected me to lose?" Joi gasped, more hurt than she cared to admit. She bit her lip, hard enough to draw blood, the metallic liquid drenching the tip of her tongue. Curse these feminine emotions which had fluctuated violently in the last few weeks. She would summon the royal physician, but then she would be a topic for discussion within the hour. They would have her dying of some sort of malady, ancient and unknown, which would then prompt a visit from Da. To say she had endured such an occurrence before would be an understatement.

Her seventeenth birthday drew near. Few knew her true age or her Letouran identity. According to the annals and scholars, her arrival as the king's long-lost niece was two years after the slaughter of the Letouran royal family. During the years between her escape and her official arrival, Nateo and Ky were her only companions. It was Ky who held her when she awoke screaming, and when sobs racked her little body. She had at least three more years in the world's eyes before she reached "eighteen" and was old enough for marriage. When in truth, she would be twenty. A small lie but worth it, or so Da said.

Did that make her older than Sohar? He had trained first under Greyad's generals before venturing to Meideon to learn from the Xiaxan mentors. She hoped he answered her next time she asked him his age.

"I thought you would win this time, Princess. You're holding back, scared to harm him. He has no such fear." Nateo brushed his forefinger over her cut. It stung at his touch, but the pain was minimal compared to the trials by combat. "Besides, if you'd won, Pan's noodles would be a celebratory meal."

"True—any excuse for a bowl of his noodles." She looped an arm around Nateo's waist. The fact she could show her affection was a hard-fought battle. In the beginning, embracing Ky or Nateo had been as unpleasant as hugging a dead tree. "I'll run to the gates to collect them, and yes, I promise not to leave the palace."

She darted forward before Nateo could stop her. She was smaller than her brothers, but she made up for it with speed. Laughing as she closed the distance on untiring legs, she drew to a halt with sufficient force to raise a cloud of dust.

"Princess," two guards chimed as they knelt.

She waved dust from her face. "You may rise. Has Pan delivered the noodles?"

"He crosses the bridge now, Princess," one guard said, resuming his position alongside the iron gates.

"Do you require assistance?" the other one asked.

"Go meet Pan and assist him," she commanded, clasping her hands behind her back as she waited.

The guard hurried away from her vantage point, and she watched the argument play out. Pan was adamant he didn't need assistance, and the guard seemed determined to obey Joi. He jumped into the air, a few feet off the ground with a loud squeal. Old man Pan had hit him with a red bolt of energy. She smothered a chuckle, amused yet intrigued. Red energy? She had never seen the like, but she wasn't well-traveled. She would ask Nateo later.

"Evening, my princess." Humor danced in Pan's dark eyes. "I brought extra bowls."

"Were the gold coins sufficient to cover it?" She dipped into her secret pocket, but the man's gnarled fingers gripped her wrist to stop her until the guards yelled at him to remove his hand. With a chuckle, he did so.

"I meant no disrespect, Princess. Lord Nateo was most generous."

"Touching royalty is punishable with the loss of a hand. Doing so will affect your ability to make delicious food. Therefore, I decree there was no offense committed." She flashed a look at the guards, who assumed their positions with stiff vigilant postures.

She bent to scoop up the basket, grunting under the weight of it. Yet the aroma rising to greet her made her draw in a deep inhalation of appreciation. Mm, her mouth watered, and she drooped her shoulders on a sigh. "Thank you, Pan. I'll see you tomorrow."

When he didn't respond, she found him staring at her chest with shock hardening his weathered features. Joi glanced down, releasing a sigh at finding her tunic wasn't gaping. Her medallion had slipped out with the ruby catching the last rays of the setting sun.

"The Medallion of the Scarlet Mirrors." He raised a trembling hand as if to touch her. The guards squeezed between them to prevent a second offense. She lowered the basket to the paved road and passed around them.

"You know my medallion?" She tamped down the excitement skittering along her senses. The ruby pulsed warmth through her chest. It went fiery hot if she was in danger, but she didn't sense evil from the old man.

"Yours?" His bushy eyebrows arched up, crinkling his wrinkled forehead.

Faded memories flashed of her father's beloved face as he passed the medallion onto her. She had often tried to capture that moment when his eyes had softened, portraying his love for Joi. "Yes, my father gave it to me." She cleared her throat, holding back the burn of pointless tears.

"Your father?" He glanced around, his gaze settling on the observant guards before shaking his head. "I've heard tales of this medallion but never seen it."

"Oh? I'm interested in hearing these tales, Pan."

"May I, Princess?" He gestured to the medallion, his fingers twitching with eagerness.

She lifted it off her chest, making it easier for him to hold.

He gripped it between his gnarled hands, yanking her closer to him. Throwing out a hand to warn the guards to stand back, she let the old man run a trembling fingertip over the wording circling the ruby. "A mirror of souls, a seal of minds."

"Is that what it says?" She took it back from him to trace the lettering carved into the gold, trying to read the letters she had given up on years ago. The ruby glowed its welcome, pulsing as it flooded her hands with warmth. In Pan's clutches, it remained cold and lifeless.

"It's meant to react to your blood, Princess." His face altered into one of awe, not that she understood why. "An honor to meet you, Princess Joi." He bowed with his right palm over his heart.

"Wait, Pan, I'd love to hear of these tales. Tomorrow night?" She could command him to tell her, but kindness cost her nothing. She found kindness and respect brought loyalty. Someone in her situation needed loyalty more than subservience.

"It is a pleasure to serve." He flashed a toothy smile, cracking his wizened cheeks in the process.

"I will have a few bottles of Redanta waiting," she said, and the light in his eyes told her she had offered wisely.

Pan left her with an energetic bounce to his step.

Shaking her head, she faced the guards. "Thank you for protecting me. Your presence has brought peace to my heart." She collected the basket, ignoring their surprise, then straightened her shoulders. Open praise also garnered support.

One guard hesitated, lifting his gaze from the ground to her face. "Please excuse my presumption, Princess, but it is not safe to come to the gates yourself."

"Your presumption is forgiven." Joi blessed him with a small smile. "I have lost again to Prince Sohar, and this is my burden to bear."

"Prince Sohar is most impressive," the other guard chimed in.

She walked away, not needing to hear from the palace guards what a disappointment she was. She headed to Sohar's chambers, wanting to be done with this debt. Along the way, she replayed the incident with Pan and her medallion. The annals were void of information, so the scholars labeled the medallion's engravings a mystery. Yet a wizened man called it by its name. He could be fabricating it, but something within her knew he spoke the truth.

Medallion of Scarlet Mirrors. A strange name, to be sure—and the writing made no sense either. *A mirror of souls, a seal of minds.*

Shrugging her interest away, leaving it for tomorrow, she knocked on Sohar's door and entered only when he granted her access. Joi wasn't surprised to see he had a visitor, her brother Kylen, nor to feel Nateo's presence at her back. He had been with her the entire time, hidden, as was his custom. Having made a vow to Da to keep her safe, he did so with breathtaking diligence.

"Good timing, Joi-Joi." Sohar gestured for her to place the basket alongside the table. He had bathed since their sparring. His unbound white hair cascaded around his angular face like silver rays of pale moonlight. Ky had bathed as well, and she grimaced, realizing she hadn't. Now conscious she might not smell as fresh after a day of training, she smothered an outward cringe.

Thank the Divine, Pan's noodles overwhelmed any odors with its mouth-watering goodness. Yet when she served a portion of it to Sohar, her stomach roiled. The thought of food made her gag. Meeting Pan was fortuitous after deciding a long time ago to cease the search for the medallion's origins. Her mind was in turmoil, and a heavy feeling pressed on her soul, as if she plummeted into darkness. The idea of sitting there and pretending a cheerfulness nauseated her. Hiding her reaction, she dipped her chin to rest on her chest. Without looking at them, she served Ky, breathing through her mouth.

She rose to her feet, the last bowl in hand, then offered it to Nateo. "Rest well, and there's no need to follow me, Nateo. I'm returning to my chambers for the evening."

"No Redanta?" Sohar asked with widened eyes. Her departure no doubt surprised him.

She shook her head and left his chambers. It was too late to order a bath. Besides, she preferred a swim in her fountain. Deeper than a tub, its cool waters would wash away the stress of the day, and perhaps bring clarity to her chaotic thoughts.

19

Chapter Four

Fragments

Joi slipped the medallion off and handed it to Pan who sat across from her in her chambers. They were as alone as was possible, with a disapproving Nateo hovering at the door. She had tasked her maidservant to deliver the noodles to Sohar for the remaining days of the wager—a violation of the terms, but Joi couldn't bring herself to feel remorse. This was more important, and if need be, she would explain it to Sohar.

The old man gathered the medallion in his shaky hands, the precious gift it was. Joi smiled and poured Redanta into his cup, placing it within his reach. She sat back on her heels and waited, patient now that he was here. The day had gone by in a blur since she had foregone the training field to visit with the scholars. Mentioning the name of the medallion and its carved words excited them. She hoped they found something within the annals, another clue, another step toward understanding her legacy.

"I'm sorry about your father, your mother too." Pan's tone held longing, sadness, and familiarity, as if he had known her parents well. "He was a great man, a revered king. She was a renowned beauty but allow an old man to say, you surpass her."

Her heart paused then leaped and danced. "You know who I am? You've seen my mother?"

Pan's dark eyes filled with warmth. "Forgive me. I forget you know not my history. I was once called Panzan."

Nateo, from the hidden shadows where he stood sentry, gasped, then hurried forward to kneel beside Joi, awe, and interest warring for supremacy on his chiseled features. "How is this possible? They say you died in the Battle of Heaven's Fire."

"I should have." Pan's lips twisted into a grimace. "My son died that day. Despite my skills, my knowledge, I could not save him. Life lost all meaning." He glanced at Joi, and a sad expression softened his face. "News of your family's massacre reached me, and with it, despair. I'd failed your father, yet again. My oath meant nothing to me, my honor in tatters. Had I been there, your family might have survived."

He peered into the untouched cup of purple liquid, its fruity scent tainting the air. "I drowned my sorrows, spending your father's blessings on wine. I lost everything, and I never thought I'd receive another chance...at redemption." He offered her the medallion, and she accepted it, looping it over her head to let it find its usual resting place. "Revive, oh, river of life and love. Revive."

When he spoke those lyrical words, a fleeting memory came to mind of her father activating the medallion. She recognized the words as power-filled. Which power and to what purpose, she did not know. If only she recalled the memory before...yet, learning one phrase didn't mean she could wield its power.

Her ruby pulsed once, then burst into light—splintering red diamonds on the surrounding surfaces. Joi gaped at Pan, as she fought the urge to yank the medallion off her. Red smoke spiraled out, and before she could react, it coiled around her chest, forming a translucent armor. Fire followed suit, burning her where it touched her. Fear and panic gripped her heart but not pain. What was this? She threw a pleading look at Nateo, not knowing what he could do to rid her of the heat, the intensity.

"The Scarlet Fox is your legacy," Pan said. "Only the royal family of Letoura has the strength to wield it. Many have tried, including the Drem, with the blood price for their ambition."

At his words, Joi's breaths became shallow with panic. What did this all mean? But the heat wrapped her in a familiar comfort reminiscent of her father's last embrace, and she calmed.

Nateo touched the red ribbons of smoke, gasping as it lashed out and curled around his finger. He scowled as he yanked his finger back, popping it into his mouth, as if her tendrils had scorched him.

"Does it harm you too, Princess?" Nateo's concern replaced his previous awe. Before he touched the translucent armor, she thought she had seen the lust for power harden his expression.

"It *was* hot, but now the heat is bearable." Relieved, Joi smiled at Pan, grateful for this progress. She would take this to the scholars tomorrow. "What did you do? Awaken it?"

"No, I asked it to awaken your latent power." He raised his cup for a sip.

"You did?" she squeaked. She squeezed her eyes shut to focus and bit hard on her lip. Testing her lacerated lip with the tip of her tongue, she tasted blood. There! If she listened hard enough to the magic tingling in her body, she found heat swirling inside—in her belly and heart—weighing on her lungs, snatching her ability to breathe.

"Say after me: source of life, cleanse me." Pan's gravelly voice cut through her rushing thoughts.

Joi cracked an eye open to study him. After his last instruction to the medallion, she was wary to command it, expecting it to burn her. He didn't say it again, simply waited for her to comply. Squaring her shoulders, she muttered the words. Fire burnt her lip and her cheek, and she knew, deep within her, it healed her. Delight flooded her, merging with breathless ease to the fire coursing through her.

Ideas pricked at her mind. The possibilities of the medallion... "If I need to heal someone else?"

Pan hesitated, his fingers tightening around the cup. "Source of life, heal through me. I must warn you, Princess Jenaso, to do so might cost you your life force. The greater the wound, the greater the drain on your power."

"Princess Jenaso?" She gasped, sorrow piercing her unguarded heart. No one had called her that in years. To dispel the sadness since she could do nothing about it, she shook her head. Brief images blurred her vision—her father's blood-stained face, Ayo's pale one, and the Drem's dark one—and her family's murderer. "You called this *my* power. It's not the medallion doing this?" Joi waved her hand at the swirling red spirals of smoke. It coiled around her fingers in a loving caress.

"All members of the royal family carry the Scarlet Fox. Should one die, that power shares itself across the remaining members. You carry half of your family's power." Pan raised his cup in salute.

"Half?" She grabbed his arm, sloshing Redanta onto the silken tablecloth and staining it. "Jeiram is alive?" She flashed Nateo a huge smile as uncontrollable hope erupted out of her.

The tendrils of smoke swirled outward in reaction to her emotions. This time its caress didn't burn a cringing Nateo. He blessed her with a relieved smile even as his shoulders slumped.

"It appears so, Princess." Pan helped himself to the Redanta carafe. "Now, about your training—"

"To use my powers?" She trembled with unbridled eagerness. To learn how to use this Scarlet Fox was to be one step closer to realizing her legacy.

"Yes, as a Cento mentor, I need to train you with due urgency." He downed his wine then hiccupped.

"Cento." She tested the word on her tongue as she watched the retreating tendrils in dazed amazement.

"The use of the Scarlet Fox." Nateo took the carafe from Pan before he finished it. Nateo poured a little into his own cup then downed it. "We long believed we lost this knowledge. I will cancel your current lessons. This night, I will petition King Buro for permission and a pass."

"We need to move Pan into the palace." Joi leaped up to pace, too energized to sit still.

Pan shook his head, toying with gray strands from his bun. "No, I remain with my shop. Your training should be in secret, Princess. The Drem have ears everywhere."

"I'll see Da now if you don't mind, Mentor Pan." She glanced between Nateo and Pan. "The sooner I ask, the sooner we can start." Da would say yes. She knew he would. Asking him would grant her an audience with him, and perhaps she could steal an hour of his time.

"Your training will be in the evening which means you must attend your current lessons. There must be no reason for anyone to question your behavior." Pan yanked the carafe away from Nateo, tossing him a glare in the process.

"Princess, this is too much to ask of you." Nateo looked concerned, and in the silence, she agreed. This would be an additional burden on her body and mind.

"There are ears among the trainees," Pan said. "Although I hear things in my shop, I had not heard that you were Princess Jenaso. Our king is an excellent strategist to have kept it secret this long." He clambered to his feet with his knees making strange cracking noises. "To hide the Fox, say this: The power of night rest upon the light."

Joi repeated those words, and once again her medallion was but a piece of jewelry.

"I will see myself out. Lord Nateo, I request a secluded area to train. Perhaps an empty consort's palace?" Pan swayed on his feet before righting himself.

Nateo bowed his head. "I will arrange it, Lord Panzan."

"Pan will do. I sacrificed my title along with my honor." The old man ambled out, disappearing into the shadows.

"Would you like to discuss this, Princess? Before we see the king?" Nateo stood, and she followed him up.

"I'm sorry it harmed you." Joi looped an arm around his waist as they left her chambers.

Was this possible? Had Pan spoken the truth? She hoped he had since the existence of the Scarlet Fox was undeniable. When she clasped the medallion, it vibrated against her palm. It was dormant now, but no longer extinct. Crossing the courtyard, she raised her face to the night's sky. The bright consistent stars grounded her thoughts.

"A minor burn, quick to mend."

It didn't sit well with her that the tendrils hurt him. Harming those she loved would never be acceptable. Nateo's continued silence worried her. Not that he spoke incessantly, but what he witnessed should have raised questions or, at worst, concerns. It did for her.

"I don't like your silence." Joi squeezed his waist.

He dipped his head to meet her gaze before casting his focus skyward. "I worry. Double the training will exhaust you."

She grinned to show him she was less concerned about her upcoming schedule and more excited about what she would soon learn. "I'll do less sparring and more written learning. I've done so before, and it didn't draw notice. Besides, now that I know more, the annals might reveal their secrets."

"True." He smiled. "I am relieved." They climbed the steps to her surrogate father's palace.

"Summon King Buro's personal guard, Tei." She used her authoritative voice. She hated it, but the guards and a few servants could not respond without hearing it.

"Very well, Princess Joi." The guard rushed into the palace. The other guard blocked the passage in front of them, an additional obstruction.

"Princess, this is a surprise." Tei hurried toward them with the returning guard on his heels.

"Evening, Tei. Is my father free?"

"Judging by your expression, this is urgent." He gestured to the guard to allow her and Nateo entry.

"He's not with a consort?" Joi chewed on her lip, hesitating. She was impatient to share the Scarlet Fox with her da. If he was busy, then she would wait, but see him she must.

"The king is free at present," Tei said, cryptic in his responses, as expected of her father's trusted guard. He knocked on the iron doors before announcing her presence. Entering at the sound of the king's command, Tei ushered her in.

"Stay, Tei. You need to hear this too." Joi caught his upper arm in passing.

"My little girl." Buro held out his hands to grasp hers.

She smiled, the warmth of love for him welling inside her. How blessed could she be, having had the love of two fathers?

Buro chuckled, touching her cheek briefly. "Not so little anymore but still stubborn. I worried your continued loss to Prince Sohar would diminish your reputation. Adoration greets you, no matter what you do."

Adoration? What was Da talking about? She was but a princess whose worth was in the alliance she formed for her realm. Fidgeting, she tapped her booted foot, but stilled when her nervousness echoed through the chambers. "Someone in my position should not take loyalty for granted, Da."

He studied her with his head tilting to the side. The unbound freedom of his long hair cascading down his back was a rare sight.

"There is something different about you. You feel...strong, powerful—you pulse with energy." Buro turned to Nateo with an arched brow. "What say you, Nateo?"

Nateo dipped into a stiff bow, his hand across his heart. "I present to you, great and illustrious King Buro, Princess Jenaso."

At this announcement, Buro's lips formed a firm line, a sign of his displeasure. Joi chuckled, throwing her arms around her da. She kissed his chin before stepping back. "I never forgot my identity, Da. It was silly to expect me to forget who I was."

"True, but the sorcerers assured me you would have no memory of it."

"They lied." She softened those words with a smile. "Tomorrow, I'll ask Mentor Panzan why it didn't work." Buro jolted as if she punched him. Delighted by his reaction, she laughed—doubting anything surprised him. "I start my Cento training in secret—with your permission, of course."

"I don't want you to." Buro gathered her hands in his again. "I don't want you in harm's way. I don't like that you to need to defend yourself. I want you happy, safe, with children running through your palace."

"Children? Me?" Joi teased. "The Drem haven't forgotten, Da. You know this in your heart. Jeiram and I need to seek justice to end this feud."

His grip on her hands tightened. "Jeiram's alive? You know this how?"

She lowered her chin to stare at the floor, joy at this newfound information still overwhelming her. "Pan says I hold half the power."

"Half?" Buro asked, his eyes widening. "You *must* train. To contain so much will endanger you. Permission granted. Nateo, see to it." He spun Joi around and directed her to his strewn pillows. "I assume you cannot reveal the Scarlet Fox during sparring, so let's discuss how to conquer young Sohar without it."

Chapter Five

Self-Preservation

Concern furrowed Sohar's brow as he stared at the spot where cheeky-yet-adorable Joi always stood. She was missing for the fourth day in a row. Worrying about her clenched his jaw. She wouldn't hide because of the lost wager. Nor was she one to sulk as other women did. If she became angry, she lashed out, which was something he had experienced on previous occasions. Although, she had yet to harm him.

This was why he pushed her. She held back, not prepared to injure those sparring with her. This was an injustice to her and her training partners. Joi needed to learn the sounds her attacks made, the impact as they connected with soft tissue, or when breaking bones. She needed to unleash her strength to survive any attack. King Buro must fear for her life, which was why he allowed a woman to train under his Xiaxan generals.

Despite the common nature of magic, only a select few were lucky to receive Meideon's Xiaxan training, which was either due to a fortuitous birth or at the recommendation of someone of good report. Once a century, an individual not of nobility would be born with an unusual capacity for magic. They too would receive training and an immediate inclusion in the Meideon army.

As the niece of the king, Joi's enrollment wasn't suspicious, simply that women were rarely Xiaxan trained. No matter how he pried, Nateo and Kylen revealed no details about the mysterious and beautiful princess other than what was openly known.

Swirling his blade in his hand, Sohar's focus rested on the gravel where her feet had once been. What was this sensation crushing his lungs? If he didn't know better, he would say he was experiencing a new emotion. Was he missing her? Swishing his sword again, he finished the move by sheathing it in its scabbard down his back.

Her maidservant delivered the noodles, and that was reason enough for him to seek out Joi. A violation of a wager was a serious offense. He would wait until the moon was at its zenith, not wanting palace gossip to reach his father's ears. A Greyadian must remain stoic. To feel was acceptable, but to reveal one's emotions was not. Therein lay his dilemma.

Joi invoked a myriad of emotions within him, and numerous times he had lapsed. Without his permission, his impassive features morphed into a grimace, a smile or, Divine help him, a chuckle. No one could have anticipated his Final Contest would be a tiny Meideon princess with exquisite golden eyes.

Each young Greyadian was to endure and succeed a mental test—a rite of passage of sorts. Tailored by the Divine, the challenge of one's control and inner strength often occurred in battle. Women did not pass their tests with battle prowess, for theirs were of an emotional nature. Lust, greed, perhaps even jealousy. Not that he could confirm this since Final Contests were personal and rarely spoken of.

He entered his chambers, nodding a greeting at his personal guard, Mazza. Sohar stripped off his trainee pants and tunic, tossing them onto the floor as he climbed into the bath. The heated and scented water eased his tired muscles, but despite this, he had an underlying sense of dissatisfaction. Sparring with Joi brought him excitement, and without noticing, she had slipped past his defenses.

He looked forward to seeing her, to sparring with her—both physically and verbally. He found himself wondering what she did in the evenings when she wasn't drinking Redanta with him. Lately, he had noticed the curve of her neck, the rise and fall of her breasts, and the soft plumpness of her lips. Divine help him. She was too young to justify the thoughts he had of her.

Her maidservant delivered the noodles once more, and with disappointment eating at him, he lost his appetite for the flavorful meal. Groaning, Sohar pushed the bowl away and pulled the Redanta carafe closer, preparing to settle in until it was time. The wine relaxed him further, lowering his mental guard, as well. When he spent time with Joi, he ensured his wine was weaker. Warmth blossomed in his chest as he remembered her teasing threat to water down his wine. If she only knew he did so as a precaution.

He couldn't afford to lose control around her.

Sighing, he watched the moonlight crawl its way across his wooden floor. When it reached a certain point, he rose, slid his feet into his slippers, then flicked a cloak over his silk garments. Thankfully, his long legs carried him swiftly to her palace. His knock was soft, not willing to wake her if she had retired for the evening. At her permission to enter, he did so with more eagerness than he had a right to feel.

Having been there before, he searched the strewn pillows and lower table where she entertained. This time, a splash from her fountain drew his attention. Breaking the surface, her pale face rose from the water then her linen-clothed shoulders until her entire form dripped onto the floor. The fabric clung to her like a second skin, revealing more than hiding what made her different from him.

In the silence, his breathing altered. Sohar absorbed every curve and indent of her feminine form, somehow knowing he would recall this memory in the future. He had known her to be exquisite and had fought her sensual allure. He was her fellow trainee, and she was far too young for him. He would not dishonor her with salacious thoughts—no matter how they tormented him in his slumber.

Joi peeled on a robe, cinching the sash tight before padding toward him. "I'm pleased to see you, Sohar."

"Oh?" He waited for her to explain her wager violation. She gestured to the pillows before sliding onto the closest pile. Accepting her offer, he joined her on the rug.

"Information of my family has come to light. I'm hoping the scholars can help me piece it together."

"This is good news." Relief coursed through him. She wasn't avoiding him on purpose. He hadn't done something to push her away, even though that was what he needed to do. Admiring her face, unable to resist doing so, he lingered on the shadows under her eyes. She looked thinner and exhausted. "You're overdoing it, Princess."

Joi winced, and heat pierced his chest, hating that he had inflicted pain on her. She ran a hand over her face, a visible indication of her exhaustion. The sleeve gaped, displaying intricate scarlet lines under her skin. They swirled from her wrist and up her forearm with magic he didn't recognize. He traced one with a fingertip. She gasped and jerked away from him, yanking the sleeve of her robe down as if cloth could erase his memory.

Not liking that she hid this from him, he burst forward to crowd her, capturing her hands in his. He held on tight since it was her nature to fight him. Even kneeling, he was still taller than her, forcing him to dip his head to meet her golden gaze. When he had her attention, he slid his hands up her forearms, taking the sleeves with them.

"They're beautiful," he said, but didn't release her.

Each realm had its own magic color determined by the soil, air, and ancestry which affected the ability to absorb the life infusing all things, and none of them were scarlet. Only white magic marked a Greyadian's skin, shimmering and glowing under the surface. She struggled, drawing him from his thoughts. He was angering her by trapping her, forcing his will upon her, and in doing so, due for a beating if he allowed it.

He hooked her attention again. "Joi-Joi, please, if you need me, you have but to ask."

"I'm in no danger, Mighty Sohar." Pink splashed across her cheeks, but she didn't look away. "This is my legacy."

"You are Meideon." She was more than that. Her brothers, Kylen and Mion, did not have her ebony hair and gold eyes. No one at the palace did.

"I am told I resemble my Selion mother," Joi said.

Selions had yellow hair. Perhaps it was her delicate face she was referring to? Sohar accepted that her mother was as beautiful, but it didn't explain why Joi wasn't telling him everything.

"Do you not trust me?" He softened his voice to lessen the harsh question when volatile emotions burned in his chest, begging for release. Horror, dismay, and sadness threatened to contort his face. He fought to keep his expression neutral.

She winced again and shook her head. "It's not a question of trust. I do not know enough to share."

"When did these lines form?" He feathered his fingers over her skin, marveling at the softness. She was cool from the fountain, and a hint of jasmine lingered in the air. Water rivulets ran down her cheeks and neck to saturate the toweling robe, mesmerizing him. Did she not feel cold?

"Two days ago. It has the scholars in a panic." Joi flashed a smile.

His heart twisted with a painful need. He would never reveal to her how much he adored her smile. Releasing her arms, he leaned back on his haunches to study her. As each minute passed, what he had to do solidified into a certainty. He brushed his fingers from her temple, down her cheek to her jawline. The cut he inflicted had vanished which meant she had seen a healer, but its disappearance didn't remove the guilt he felt at having harmed her.

"Evening, my prince," Nateo greeted from the doorway.

Sohar nodded and admired Joi one last time. He had to leave, to return to Greyad. Staying tested his control, his stoicism. A Greyad never showed emotion, and with Joi, he longed to share in her appreciation for life. Leaving might shift his Final Contest to that of a battle. He had to try.

"Take care of her, Lord Nateo." He lingered his gaze on her tempting lips, trying to memorize the curve and plumpness of them. He rose to his feet and left. It took every ounce of his strength to not look back and accept his decision. His father wouldn't expect him to return so soon, but what choice did Sohar have?

He paused, pressed a palm to the smooth-stone pillar outside his palace, and raised his face to the starlit sky. He drew in a long steadying breath and squared his shoulders.

He would miss her.

Chapter Six

Almost Time

Rumoc, Master and High Emperor of Drem, studied the old man in the mirror's reflection. Lines cracked around his eyes and mouth—few were from laughter. Sadness and time scarred his face. His heart had long since frozen, harder than the ice on the Selion Mountains. He was once a beloved prince, revered for his appearance, his kindness. Rumoc could not recall the last time he had shown anyone mercy, not even to his first consort.

Gray streaked his once umber-colored hair, and the brown of his eyes reflected shadows of his former self. In his youth, he had fallen for a forest maiden. Their beauty was renown, sought after, but to find one was a blessed occurrence. Or so his father had said. Sister Luck had smiled on him when he stumbled upon Eria late one afternoon.

Rumoc recalled, with vivid clarity, how the sun's gentle rays bathed her yellow hair, setting it ablaze. Her green-blue eyes vacillated, undecided on a color. She was younger than him, and in her innocence, begged him not to reveal her existence, trusting his honor. And he behaved with honor.

A smile curled Rumoc's grim lips when he remembered his first words to her were charming, a skill he had perfected by then. *What will you give me for my silence, oh-an-gel-of-the-forest?* He had lived for months in the small village Witon, ignoring his father's demands to return to the Royal City. Every day he met with her and had fallen for the sweet woman. Oh, what a fool he had been! Excited to share his swollen heart, he had invited his best friend, Kura, to meet her. In disbelief and devastating shock, they fell for each other. Their love had formed in an instant, like a blossoming Gyqio orchid that bloomed only once in its life.

She defied her caregivers and abandoned her culture to marry Kura, a union blessed by the stars and ancients, or so the Letouran soothsayers proclaimed. Rumoc tried to feel happy for them, hiding his pain and anger. Over the years, his visits to Tennaba dwindled as resentment encased him until his heart beat a black, seductive poison.

He blamed her for the assassination of his father and his two younger brothers. It did not exempt her that their deaths were by his own hand. She altered who he was at a fundamental level, and love, regret, compassion, and forgiveness were meaningless words. Silly sentiment weakened a king and drained his power. He was wiser now.

Rannic, his only son, rushed into the throne room and prostrated himself before him. Rumoc frowned, pleased and angry at the disruption to his dark thoughts. The black poison in his heart thrived on hateful emotions, more so when they were his own. Irritation swept through him, and he grimaced. His son was a weakling—a result of his mother's upbringing. Extensive training under Drem's generals hadn't wiped the whine out of his voice. His son—the incompetent imbecile and the future of Drem.

"We found him, Father," Rannic said into the carpet where he buried his face.

Rumoc gaped—the words that tumbled from Rannic's lips were too unbelievable. He glanced at his advisor and confidant, Lorva, waiting for his nod of confirmation.

"Truth?" Rumoc gripped his son's shoulders as excitement and hope rivaled his ever-present hatred of the Letourans.

"Yes, Jeiram is alive and well. King Velisand took him under his wing."

Rumoc scowled. That meant Jeiram was untouchable. Drem could not wage a war with Seit and hope to survive. A victory against their armada was impossible.

"Could that mean Jenaso escaped with her life?" Rumoc met the black eyes of Lorva, who had informed him the girl had drowned. Ah, his own man was untrustworthy and betrayed him as had everyone else in his life. Why was he surprised? He paced in front of his stone throne, satisfaction and a deep, renewed hope calming his anger. "Which king had Kura trusted?"

"King Kura was well liked," Lorva pointed out. Rumoc glared at the man, not needing the reminder that Eria had chosen the arrogant swine over him. "As I recall, her nursemaid took the princess eastward upriver."

"East? Meideon?" Rumoc nodded. Yes, it would be Buro to whom Kura would entrust his daughter too. Anger surged through him. "Why have we not heard anything? What do we pay for?"

Lorva clasped his bejeweled hands in front of him. "The only new addition to the royal family is their cousin, a girl two years younger than Jenaso."

"Age is relative and can easily be falsified. What of her appearance? Does she have black hair with the golden eyes of the Letouran royals?" Hope further stirred Rumoc's senses.

"My Illustrious King, gaining access to the inner palaces has been a struggle. We have not received an actual description of this girl except to say she is beautiful."

"Ah, Eria, did you pass your seductive appearance onto your daughter?" Rumoc rubbed his chin with his thumb. "Rannic, get me an exact description. Let's make certain before we annihilate another royal house."

"They deserve it, Father, for choosing the wrong side." Rannic kept his nose to the rug.

"I have another suggestion, My Eminent One," Lorva said. "Don't wage war on the Meideons. After all, they're renowned for their Xiaxan battle strategies. The cost to our legions would be extensive. Why not match Rannic with her, and should she meet with an accident, who would gainsay you?"

"If I could not have Eria then Rannic should have her daughter? As in, allow him to bring Eria's seductive witchcraft into *my* realm?" Rumoc pressed his lips together, clenching down on the rage building within him.

He had once been a mild-mannered man until obsession over Eria gripped him. Some days he wasn't certain if he had a sound mind—so many voices and thoughts whispered, taunting him. Lorva's idea had merit. Rumoc raised his face to the black stone vaulted arches high above him. In the bowels of the palace below him and toward the Gulf of Lost Hope, who would see her body splatter the jagged rocks?

Casting a final glance at his reflection, where a bright smile dented his cheeks, he faced Lorva and nodded. "In three years' time, we will suggest an alliance."

"I don't want to marry her," Rannic whined and dared a disrespectful raising of his gaze. For this he received the back of Rumoc's hand, smearing blood from his cut lip across his face.

"You'll marry whomever I choose. Besides, you haven't seen her yet. You will change your mind, I promise you, my son." Rumoc smiled as his gaze settled on Lorva.

What to do with him? The Needles of a Thousand Cries? Too time-consuming. The venom of an Ilutar scorpion? Excruciatingly painful with death a mere hour later. Exile to the barren wastelands of Orth? Yes, that was an option, but Rumoc wanted to strip him of his powers first. A delicious and painful experience. For that, he would have to ask Ninlassa for assistance. His lip curled in distaste at having to speak to that detestable woman.

Rumoc approached Lorva to rest his hand on the older man's shoulders, his black, silk tunic shot with silver thread. An expensive garment. The man's braided hair fell down his back with silver beads interwoven into the brown strands. Lorva had always been a man who valued his blessings.

"Why? Why lie to me?" Realizing he sounded like his pathetic son, Rumoc straightened his bearing. "Have I not rewarded you for your service? Did you find fault with my blessings?"

"I truly believed her dead, my king. By the time I found her, I'd enhanced my magic's potency with the souls of her parents." Lorva bowed his head. "She would not have survived such an assault."

"You didn't follow the boat to be certain?" Rumoc tsked before palming his bejeweled dagger, twirling it before sinking it into Lorva's neck.

His crimson blood gushed out, tainted with the black energy of the Drem, yet Lorva made no noise, accepting his fate. No anger, fear, or sorrow entered his eyes. As the body crumpled to the floor, Rumoc dropped to his haunches to yank out his dagger. He wiped the blood on Lorva's silk sleeve.

Rumoc met his son's gaze. "Search his chambers. I want to know what other lies he's fed me."

"Yes, Father." Rannic rose to his feet and scurried out. Guards entered, bowed, then removed Lorva's body, his blood trailing behind like the tail of a comet.

Rumoc slid his dagger back into its hidden scabbard on his forearm. He dared not mourn the loss of a good servant. Had Lorva's duplicitousness reached other's ears, it would have brought mockery on Rumoc's shoulders.

"Bring me Saith," he commanded the guard who was replacing his stained rugs. "I need a new confidant."

Rumoc chuckled before staring at his reflection in the mirror.

CHAPTER SEVEN

FINAL CONTEST

Three Years Later

AFTER UNFOLDING THE LETTER he received from Prince Kylen a few months ago, Sohar reread it. Why, he did not know, since he had the cursed thing memorized. He ignored the paper's worn edges, a physical indication of his obsession. Ky's request was simple: escape the palace and hide Joi in Greyad for as long as needed. Surrounding her with Greyad's trained soldiers would protect her from assassins and the Drem.

Simple. Sohar stared into the flickering flames of the fire burning the yellowwood with a voraciousness he admired. No hesitancy, no political machinations, just pure hunger.

Joi-Joi. Her face formed in his mind's eye as perfect as his memory could retain it. Over the past three years, the exact shape of her nose was beyond his recollection. As was the arch of her eyebrows, but he recalled her plump lips and golden eyes with clarity.

The sight of her drenched form still haunted him. He did not struggle to remember the linen clinging to her, the water rivulets forging paths down her pale skin, and tiny droplets dewing on her eyelashes. If only time and distance had faded that as well, or the Divine had seen fit to send him another challenge other than Joi as his Final Contest.

Folding the letter, he slid it into the pocket inside his leather armor. They would reach Ethrielle, the Royal Seat of Meideon, by sunset tomorrow. He would see her again. Sohar scowled, dreading the reunion as much as he yearned for it. How had she changed? She would be eighteen soon which meant marriage requests would be forthcoming. Judging by her beauty, she would have the pick of the realms.

He hid a chuckle within a cough, not envying Ky dealing with it, his friend's pseudo-grumpy face coming to mind. Having seen the affection Ky had for his younger cousin, Sohar was wise to his antics with his grumpiness a ruse. Ky had once explained why King Buro allowed Joi her preference for physical affection. To touch a royal without permission was a crime, yet she openly hugged her loved ones.

When Joi arrived at Ethrielle, nightmares plagued her as she mourned the loss of her parents. Ky spent nights comforting her, and no one had the heart to deny her the affection she needed. Knowing Joi well, that she hugged King Buro was believable.

She never hugged Sohar, a regret he held close to his heart. Their relationship was one of mutual respect, and because of this, he hadn't revealed how he felt about her. He released a deep sigh, dreading this upcoming season in his life. In his youth, he had hoped his Final Contest—the greatest test every Greyadian must face—was an Orthian raider or warrior. Succeeding in such a public display would bring honor to his father since most contests were a fight to the death. As far as he could see it, he had two choices: kill her or forget her.

Everything within him rebelled against both options. Anticipating chaos and a testing of his control—as was the case when he was with her—he hoped he passed with Joi finding her rightful place in his life: a memory. That was all he could ask for, a lifetime of loving her from afar. At least, she would be alive and well. As Crown Prince, his life wasn't his own, and neither was his heart. Everything in him should belong to Greyad.

Mazza, ever the servant, even with the high honor of Sohar's personal guard, offered him Kelenian wine. "What has you sullen, my prince?"

"Are my emotions and my inner turmoil evident?" Sohar grimaced, fire burning in his chest with self-directed anger. They hadn't arrived in Ethrielle, and already he was failing.

"It is visible to me. I attended to you during your Xiaxan training, and I assumed your Final Contest is Princess Joi?" Mazza sat down on the closest log.

Sohar's shoulders slumped. "I am unable to resist her, Mazza. My emotions fluctuate when I'm around her. No matter how much I strengthen my resolve, my reactions spiral out of control. I ran away like a coward." He gripped his cup with enough force to warp the metal. "Not my proudest moment, Mazza."

"Nevertheless, a wise decision, my prince. Better to face your opponent with strength than from a position of weakness."

At his words, Sohar grunted, acknowledging the old battle proverb.

"Are all Final Contests as complicated? The scrolls remain cryptic on this, as you know." Sohar tamped down a groan, a verbal reflection of his frustration. It was rude to ask another Greyadian about the strongest test of their self-control, but curse it, he needed guidance.

"May I offer my untutored opinion, my prince?" Mazza refilled his cup with efficient grace.

"Please do." Sohar raised the wine to his lips.

"You have two paths, and if you forgive me for my daring, I've given your Contest extensive thought. Remain a strong Greyadian, firm against the temptation the princess poses. In doing so, you sacrifice any delight this world can offer you. Such men are mired by their own bitterness."

Mired by bitterness? He scowled at Mazza's exaggeration. "Or?"

"Marry her, my prince," Mazza said. Sohar jerked as if punched. "Embrace all she brings to our realm, all she means to you."

"Lose control daily? Fail my Final Contest?" Disbelief riveted him that Mazza would dare suggest he abandon his honor and his responsibilities.

Mazza raised his palms. "All assume that to succeed, one must dominate or kill one's Contest. You cannot kill the princess, nor do you want to. My grandfather mentioned his once—he had chosen to marry his Contest instead, a woman who harangued him since childhood. They were a happy union; my grandmother brought far more blessings to his life than he had foreseen."

Marry Joi? Sohar exhaled, fighting the burst of excitement warming his heart. "I value your courage for speaking from your heart, Mazza, but my father expects dominance, and as his firstborn, I cannot fail him."

"This is true unless she is of impeccable lineage." Mazza hefted a fire poker, twirling it as he spoke. "What do we know of Princess Joi? The Meideons claim she is a relative but, forgive my presumption, she has the look of a Letouran royal."

"Letouran?" Sohar sat up, his interest piqued. "No one has seen a royal since the massacre." Should such a person come forward, the crowning would be immediate and the sections of Letoura returned to them. There were five realms, and each remaining realm had assumed a quarter of Letoura as curators.

"Two years after the massacre, King Buro inducts an unknown relative into his family without suspicion?"

"It could be a coincidence, Mazza." Sohar wished it was.

He needed Joi to be a cousin, not the heir to Letoura. If she was the queen, marrying her would bring war to Greyad, and even though they were at peace with Drem, it was tremulous. At best. Pain, sharp and forceful, lanced through his heart. He clutched his chest, dropping the half-drunk cup. The blue wine soaked into the yellow grass, glazing it green. He rubbed the throbbing ache, wishing he could understand why she invoked such emotions in him.

If she was Princess Jenaso, she must have suffered. He didn't like knowing she had witnessed the massacre. His heart cracked as he imagined a younger version of her sobbing in Ky's arms. He had said she mourned her parents, so that hadn't been a lie.

"Her eyes *are* gold, my prince." Mazza scooped up the cup and replaced it with a clean one, refilling it to the exact amount it held before the spill.

"No." Sohar shook his head, denying the truth, even as it settled like a lump of iron in the pit of his stomach. Yes, her eyes were a breathtaking gold. No, not his Joi-Joi. She said she didn't know her legacy despite the scarlet swirls entwining up her arms in an intricate design. "Scarlet Fox." He gasped, now seeing them for what they were. The darkness dampening his heart slumped his shoulders farther. The more he learned, the more he couldn't claim her. "To marry her would bring more war to our borders, Mazza."

"True, my prince, but you wouldn't let her go into battle alone. You care too much," Mazza said, stoking the fire until the heat of it scorched Sohar's knees. He did care too much, and should the time come, he would stand alongside her fighting the Drem. At what cost?

"I cannot marry her, nor can I kill her. I need to reinforce my control and dominate the temptation to succumb to her charm. Does my father know?" Know how he was failing him? Bringing strife to the realm? Losing his Final Contest? Forsaking his heart?

"He suspects something happened during your training and tasked me to investigate. I informed him your brothers-in-arms were not forthcoming."

"You lied to my father?" Many deceived him, but he hadn't expected honorable Mazza to be one of them.

"No, I did ask a few subtle questions, but they revealed nothing." Mazza bowed his head. "I am your personal guard, my prince, and should your safety require it, I would lie, kill, and die for you—without hesitation."

"A diplomatic answer, my friend." A smile threatened to slip past Sohar's control. "Joi-Joi mentioned she looks like her mother. Queen Eria was a Selion forest maiden, and since Joi does not have their yellow-gold hair, then I must assume she is not a Letouran royal."

"Regardless, my prince. Her eyes are gold, and for this alone they will crown her."

"True," Sohar said. "There are ways to alter one's eye color."

"You do not want her to claim the throne?" Mazza gaped.

"Should I marry her, Mazza, she would need to divide her time between Greyad and Letoura. In which palace will we live?"

Mazza graced him with a gentle smile. "Does this matter when her heart is the reward?"

"Ah, Mazza." Sohar relaxed his control enough to chuckle. "You're a romantic. I am surprised and disappointed."

"I may be, my prince, but what is there to life if not to love and to love well?"

"True. I suggest we seek solace in our dreams and see what tomorrow brings." Sohar rose, gathering his gray cloak around his armored form as Mazza scurried ahead of him. Gesturing to the prepared tent, Mazza hurried inside to hold the entrance drapes open. Sohar ducked in and stood still in the center of the cushion-strewn carpet. Mazza removed his boots and armor and unraveled his hair to run the comb through it before leaving for his own bed.

Sohar sprawled onto his back, sliding his hand behind his head. He stared at the tent's ceiling, recalling the face of the woman who haunted his thoughts and dreams, claiming them as her own. He allowed himself the luxury to imagine asking for her hand. The expression on her face, her greeting him with a hug. His heart swelled...a hug would make this all worthwhile.

A full smile broke across his face, the feeling of it exquisite and sinfully delicious.

Regardless of his welcome, he would claim a hug, even if she scolded him for his audacity.

Chapter Eight

Change is Constant

Gliding her hands around each other, Joi summoned a ball of scarlet energy. Diving deep inside her mind, she called the power from her core, ignoring the faint trails of blue energy in the ground beneath her feet. She hadn't toyed with her birth-magic since her days with Jeiram. As the red ball grew in strength and size, she rolled with her arms and shoulders. Her knees trembled under the strain, but she gritted her teeth with determination. The bigger, the better—Pan would lose the wager and teach her his family's secret ingredient for his noodles.

"Well done, Princess," Nateo cheered from the side.

Digging her feet into the gravel, she cried out as she searched deeper within her, summoning the last vestiges of her soul. The ball grew, and with delight, she glanced at Pan just in time to see his walking stick descend. It connected with her elbow. She yelped, sucking the energy back into her. The sudden surge had her reeling with dizziness. She stumbled but caught herself from throwing out a steadying hand.

"Fail." He chuckled. "The true wager was to admit defeat, Princess. To waste one's being on a ball of red smoke is pointless, do you not agree?"

"I *can* do it," she said, rubbing her stinging elbow. She had been so close. Never had her ball been this big.

"Yes, you can, but should you?" He shook his head as he ambled away from her to lower himself onto a stone bench. "Some battles one should not choose to fight. Some battles require strategies other than blindly running in. Have I taught you nothing?"

She nodded. "My apologies, Pan. I struggle to curb my recklessness." Over the last few years, her impetuosity had lessened. Yet there were those times when stupidity and bravery walked a fine line. Pan was quick to point those out to her, to force her to strategize before she acted.

"Of that, we agree. You are ready, and in time too, if a young man claims you. I can teach you no more. Your training now falls into the hands of experience, and trust me, Princess, it is a merciless taskmaster."

Joi squared her shoulders and raised her chin. "I will not disappoint you, Pan."

"You will—to expect anything else will be the true disappointment. We are comprised of all the elements, and as such, are fallible." A warm smile cracked his cheeks.

"Fine, I'll try not to disappoint myself." She sent him a wink.

"A noble endeavor." He clasped the head of his walking stick. Crafted of dark wood and carved with a lion's head, it was a gift from her. "Now, you best prepare for this evening's festivities."

At the reminder of the changes her life would soon take, she couldn't stop the frown from furrowing her brow. Bowing to Pan with a hand over her heart, she faced her fate and strolled to her palace.

"How many have arrived today?" she asked Nateo as he slid into step beside her.

"Many, but more specifically, Lord Aoni and Prince Rannic."

"He would dare?" She gasped, throwing a glare at Nateo.

"Which one?"

"Either. I should skin Aoni alive for touching me, and I should kill Rannic for his father's sins." Her strides lengthened as a revenge-fueled fire burned through her. Scarlet smoke coated her hands in anticipation of a battle.

"Shall I lure both into a secluded corner?" Nateo teased.

Her lips twitched, and her shoulders slumped as she gave in to the smile. She curled her fingers into her palms, suffocating her energy. "Point made, Nateo. They deserve a flaying first. I will endeavor to endure their presence." She passed through the iron doors he held open for her. "Any news from Sohar?" Keeping her face dipped hid her flushed cheeks—not that she cared if he partook of the festivities. Deep down, she wished he was among the hoards interested in marrying her.

"No, my princess, but I have been by your side this day. He might arrive without me knowing."

Forcing a shrug and a smile, gratitude welled within her when her maidservant rushed forward to help remove her boots. Opaque drapes divided her chambers into separate compartments. A quick peek revealed the dark blue garment lying across her bed—the Meideon ceremonial gowns only for special occasions such as family birthdays and visiting royalty. Joi glowered at the garment as if it would kill her to wear it.

This evening was the celebratory event for Kylen's coronation scheduled tomorrow morning. Da felt it was time to abdicate his throne and to live a simpler life. He had said something about learning how to fish and finding a woman not needing to please him for power, one who would love him as Ky's mother had.

Joi couldn't fault him for such a longing. Her "coming of age" was reason enough to open the gates to every nobleman eager to catch her eye.

"You may collect the princess in an hour, Lord Nateo." Her maidservant gestured to the steaming tub alongside the fountain. Joi grumbled, having preferred a quick dip in the cool waters of the fountain than the petal-coated tub.

By the end of the hour, she decided this event had tortured her enough. The bath helped ease her stiff muscles, and something in the water made her skin appear paler. It was that or a marked lack of sun in the last year. Her maidservant washed and oiled her hair until the black strands glistened. No wonder the palace consorts were so miserable. To endure this daily would drive a woman insane.

The dark blue silk gown wrapped around her, tight enough to alter her breathing. The deep V of the outer gown crisscrossed over three layers of intersecting scarves in alternating shades of blue and white. A wide belt in the same dark blue silk, and lined in gold, hugged her waist, cracking a rib or two. Tiny blue slippers adorned her feet which were visible only when she walked, peeking out from the yards of fabric forming the skirt of the gown and a diaphanous cloak draped across her shoulders.

It didn't end there. No, her maidservant combed her hair until it fell down her back in a silk curtain, the tips brushing her backside. Joi hadn't realized it had grown so long since she kept it braided. The golden clip Sohar sent her for her last birthday pinned her hair away from her forehead and secured the shorter strands.

Well, she said Sohar, but she assumed it was a clerk who had chosen the gifts and had them delivered. Over the last three years, she anticipated the Greyadian gifts. Although, why she felt so was something she had yet to understand. He hadn't shown encouragement, a willingness to be with her, nor had he sought her out other than for the wager violation. Yet his gifts meant more to her than they should have.

Black coal lined her eyes, and pink oil painted her lips. The woman in the mirror's reflection was no one she recognized. Except for her eyes and hair color, there was nothing to tell her apart from the other court women. She shrugged, finding the reflection deceptive. This wasn't her, and since wearing ceremonial garments and silk gowns wasn't her first preference, her husband would only see her dressed so on specific occasions.

"My dagger," she said, yanking the draped sleeve back for her maidservant to strap the scabbard on. The girl hesitated long enough to draw Joi's scowl.

"No weapons allowed, for the safety of all, Princess."

"Oh, yes, I remember now." She pouted and shook her sleeve into place.

"Your medallion, Princess?" Her maidservant held up the jewelry so the lamplight caught the ruby's essence. "My king asked it to be visible."

"Truly?" Joi gasped, understanding the implication of that command. Tonight, all would know her true lineage. A daring reveal, especially with Prince Rannic of Drem in attendance. She took the medallion and stroked her thumb over the ruby. It pulsed in greeting, and she smiled in return. "Do we have any Redanta wine? Just one cup to relax me."

"Are you nervous, Princess? You look beautiful, and you will be well received." She bowed her head. "I will rush out for a fresh carafe. I won't be long."

Joi sighed as she slipped the medallion on, moving to stand in front of the mirror to ensure it draped correctly. It rested on the folded scarves like a third eye. Would Prince Rannic recognize it? She hadn't heard much about the young prince—her Cento training drew all her attention. There were rumors he was a handsome young lion, with burnished hair and black eyes. Court life taught her there was more to appearances.

In contrast, Lord Aoni was tall with sun-kissed hair and a charming smile. It was his eyes she disliked. They were a cold gray, with less emotion than Sohar's stoic, crystal-blue eyes.

When Aoni trapped her in the armory, his charming smile turned menacing, his ice-gray eyes wicked. He had used his skills and height to his advantage that day. She had bruises to show for her efforts to avoid him, despite blessing him with a bloody nose for his audacity which soured his mood further.

Only her maidservant and Nateo knew about the incident, and she had sworn them to secrecy. Not that she thought they would spread rumors. Da had a fierce love for her as the daughter he never had, and anyone caught offending her he dealt with harshly. It would also embarrass her to have it public knowledge, forcing Da into an awkward position. He would have to involve the court's councilors who would note all the details in the annals.

Joi hadn't wanted it to become palace gossip which made more of events than was true. This didn't mean she had buried the urge to make Aoni bleed again. She suspected it was Nateo, who had ensured the pompous lord never trained near her.

A knock penetrated her vengeful thoughts, and she assumed it was Nateo returning to escort her. At her command, the shape of the man who entered was not her beloved companion's. This man was tall and as copper-toned as Kylen, his hair a light brown too. The angular jaw and mesmerizing green eyes made her gasp. Joy burned through her, and the Scarlet Fox responded, swirling from her fingers, and coiling around her hands to her forearms.

"Second brother Mion?" She took a stumbling step and halted, waiting, *willing* the Fox to fade. She didn't want to harm him. The bright smile breaking across her youngest brother's face, one she adored, bounced her on her toes.

"Greetings, dear one." He rushed to gather her hands in his. "No, save my hug for later. I don't want to spoil how clean you look."

"I haven't seen you for four years, and now I can't hug you." She pouted. "When did you arrive?" She freed her hand to smack him on the arm.

Mion chuckled and gathered her escaped hand in his for a squeeze. "A few hours ago. My sequester would be ongoing if it wasn't for this festival."

Her maidservant entered, carrying a tray with a carafe on it. She bowed at the sight of Mion and scurried to the table. While she poured two cups, Joi took the opportunity to study Mion. She brushed a curl off his forehead, unable to remove the smile on her lips.

"I'm so happy to see you, Mion."

"It shall be a brief visit if the rumors are true. Many marriageable suitors have arrived to lure you away. I escorted King Velisand and his three daughters for the coronation."

"Are they as beautiful as they say?" She accepted the cup of Redanta from her maid-servant. "Is that why you couldn't visit?"

"Yes, and yes." Mion chuckled, gesturing to her to drink, to not wait for him. She did so, downing it at once, relishing the comforting burn of the tart wine. "Although, King Velisand is hopeful one of his daughters will appeal to Ky."

Joi smiled, now seeing the festivities as more than finding a match for her. As soon as he put the cup down, she laced her fingers through Mion's and rested her temple against his silk-covered shoulder.

"Shall we go?" She grimaced, dreading the upcoming festivities.

Adorned in the festive pale blue robes of a servant, her maidservant fell into step behind them as they left.

Nateo waited outside, bowing to Mion. "Welcome back, my prince."

"Lord Nateo," Mion said and the four of them strolled as one toward the grand hall. "There were red tendrils on your palms—care to enlighten me?"

Joi clapped—her excitement impossible to contain—and proceeded to update her brother on all he missed.

Chapter Nine

To Observe

Sohar coerced the shadows to absorb him, a difficult task for Greyadians with their white hair, yet it was a skill taught from childhood. He scanned the gathering royalty anticipating King Buro's arrival. The waiting area was a covered balcony, reserved for honored guests. As per anything to do with court life, there were protocols to follow. Despite kings in attendance, the announcement of King Buro had to occur first in his realm.

They had formed factions as they waited, each realm of Amuin keeping to themselves. The red-haired vibrancy of Seit, a realm known for their love of ocean life, extensive armada, and beautiful women were south of Meideon. Their magic, drawn from their land and seas, and depending on their dominant lineage, was green.

A single ambassador from the Selion Mountains with her flaxen hair glowing like the sun, stood alone with her maidservant. Squeezed between Drem and Letoura, the Selion forests called forth blue magic.

Meideon, Drem, and Letoura crossed cultures often which meant they were a mixture of black to brown hair, bronzed to pale skin. Meideon's magic was gray, Drem's black, and Letoura shared blue with the Selion Mountains. Drem was south of Letoura which dominated the center of Amuin. To the west was Greyad, the largest realm, and north of it, the broken deserts of Orth.

Gathered in a corner, the Drem stood out with their menacing looks behind false smiles.

Only Prince Rannic, as the son and heir to King Rumoc of Drem, was present, and as Sohar suspected, he planned on asking for Joi's hand. King Velisand and his three daughters represented the Seitians. Their fiery hair and lithe forms drew heated glances from the other realms. Velisand's High Consort Ressa wasn't in attendance with rumors abounding that she wasn't well. Sohar focused on the man, noting the dark circles under his eyes and the sadness tainting his polite smile.

Greyad's representation was inconsequential tonight—a fact that would draw notice and inflame gossip, but it mattered not. Prince Kylen had asked he come alone, and in this, his father agreed. His brothers could have attended if they were not out quelling the scavengers from Orth—a constant battle they fought to the north of their borders.

Prince Kylen arrived, weaving between the factions with easy charm. His cloak was resplendent as it billowed out behind his bold movements. Sohar grinned, confident in the shadows his inability to control his emotions would remain hidden. He was here to observe, and to ensure swift action should the Drem alter their countenances upon seeing Joi.

The sound of her light and lyrical laughter heralded her arrival. Excitement snatched his breath, and he allowed it to affect his heartbeat before quelling it. He shifted from shadow to shadow until he could see her, wanting a glimpse before the guests noticed her. She was at the bottom of the steps with her hand in Mion's, laughing at him.

Oh, Divine, she was the same yet lovelier than he recalled. Her dark blue gown hugged curves he had envisioned would form in the last three years. There was a strength about her, a confidence, new and breathtaking. Sparring with her now would challenge his skills, and he hoped she would show no mercy.

"It's time," Mion said, and Joi frowned, dropping his hand. She tucked her head down as expected of the women at court.

"Who invented this posture? Stick my thumbs into my belt and form a diamond with my fingers? My elbows fly out, making me look like a chicken or a surprised fowl."

"Shh," Mion hushed her, but there was humor in his voice. "You're a beautiful chicken."

"Beautiful? How can I look beautiful when my neck has swallowed my chin?" She laughed. "At least I can see the floor. Perhaps someone decided on this because the women were falling over these ridiculous gowns."

Sohar smothered a chuckle, pleased to hear his Joi-Joi hadn't lost her effervescence. Wait, he hadn't just thought of her as *his*? He scowled and forced himself to slide away, assuming a position with the best vantage point.

As she crested the steps, he focused on Rannic. With Joi forced to move among the factions, it wouldn't be long before he would notice her. Sohar listened to her charm the Seitians but kept his attention fixed on the Drem. He analyzed every nuance of emotion crossing Rannic's features. Curiosity softened the man's face since his interest was on the Seitian princesses anyway. Joi's intrusion only served to intrigue him. Rannic stiffened with his features hardening. His gaze traveled her form as if she were a common consort, and a calculating expression settled on his dark face.

Anger, bright and forceful, curled Sohar's fingers into fists, at Rannic's audacity, disrespect, and general demeanor. If Sohar had his way, he would kill the man where he stood.

Alas, he was to observe, and he had. Rannic's open aggression, with hatred lacing his every word, meant she was in danger as Kylen anticipated. They had foolishly hoped that King Rumoc would not pass on his hatred to his son. Rannic's tense posture and disrespect revealed his intention to follow in his father's footsteps and destroy any Letouran of royal birth.

Sohar's muscles tightened as Joi approached the Drem. New respect blossomed within him for she displayed no emotion other than welcoming—her walk was graceful, unhesitant, her greeting joyful and charming.

"Prince Rannic, it is a shame we have only met now. I'm grateful you were able to attend my first brother's celebration."

"Brother?" He delivered his question in a harsh voice. His companion leaned forward to whisper something. The prince jerked, and with a nod, faced her. A bright, insincere smile wounded his face, contorting his handsomeness. "Thank you for the invitation Meideon extended to Drem. It is unfortunate my father could not attend—meeting you would have pleased him."

The implication wasn't subtle, not by anyone's standards. Sohar glanced at Joi—she had picked up on it too. Her posture stiffened just the slightest.

"I can have the royal painter draw a portrait of me if it pleases you. With special emphasis on my eyes?" She blessed him with a bright smile. "I'm told it's my best feature."

Rannic paled under her offer, and she laughed in a breathless way that did things to Sohar's heartbeat. He rubbed his chest, hoping to ease the fluttering.

"I see my father. Please excuse me. Do enjoy the evening." She glided away to slip her hands into King Buro's. He kissed her temple, appearing as a doting father would have. Releasing her hand, he pinched her chin between his fingers to give it a playful shake.

She smiled and assumed her position which was behind Prince Mion as the youngest Meideon royal. The Festival Advisor rushed around, pleading with the remaining royals to find their places. Sohar slid out of the shadows to stand behind Rannic, planning to eavesdrop on their conversation. He waved his hand behind the prince's back and allowed his white energy to settle into the prince's black, embroidered cloak. Now he would hear anything said near the man without having to endure his insufferable presence.

"Your father expects you to request an alliance with the princess. Glaring at her will not make her favorable toward you." His advisor's disrespectful tone said much about Rannic's standing in his realm.

"We're surrounded by idiots." Spittle pooled on Rannic's bottom lip. "How can they not see who and what she is? She *is* Jenaso. I don't see why I need her to like me since I plan on killing her anyway."

"Fool." The advisor grabbed Rannic's shoulder as if to shake him. "You must marry her first. To kill her outright will start a war we cannot win."

"Don't call me a fool." Red splotched the prince's cheeks.

"Don't act like one," his companion spat, his patience non-existent. Rannic grumbled and gripped his imperial token, his stance threatening. "Many observe how you treat the princess, so gaining King Buro's or Prince Kylen's permission will require all your charm. Whatever little you have of it."

The Royal Announcer boomed King Buro's name and title, drawing their attention. Followed by the Crown Prince Kylen, Prince Mion, and Princess Jenaso of Letoura.

Gasps rippled through the crowded hall.

At the reveal, Sohar's determination solidified, and he nodded. The Fates had spoken. Any hope of her being a memory disintegrated. His fate merged with hers, and he needed to decide how embroiled—how invested—he wanted to be. For now, it was time to sow dissidence.

"I can *feel* your breath on my neck." Rannic spun to face him.

"Do forgive me, Prince Rannic. I'm too excited to see Princess Joi that I forget my manners." He forced a smile past his lips, knowing it would come across as youthful, as practiced. "I hope to marry her. I hear she's breathtaking."

"She's not Princess Joi of Meideon but Jenaso of Letoura, a woman not worthy of a Drem." Rannic's tone dripped hatred. His companion elbowed him in the ribs, and he grunted.

"I am delighted to hear you say so, Prince Rannic." Sohar clapped his hands in his "eagerness." "Should I bring home the Letouran realm, my father would be most pleased. When I'm crowned, I'll have more strength than the other realms combined."

"Is that so?" Rannic's eyes narrowed as he studied the cultivated vapid expression Sohar placed on his face.

"*And* I get her as a consort. I've heard she is stubborn. Showing her my dominance would be entertaining." He squelched the grimace threatening to ruin his efforts. Throwing that in had more to do with the rumors of Rannic's sexual preferences. He hoped to lure Rannic into revealing his intentions other than to woo her.

Rannic's eyes widened. "Indeed."

"Oh, yes." Sohar rubbed his palms together. The self-satisfied smirk he forced upon his lips was over the top but needed. He doubted subtlety worked on the young prince. "To be more powerful than my father? To have him bow to me? The thought of it is so exquisite, isn't it?" The calculating expression crossing Rannic's face almost had Sohar patting himself on the back. "You're announced, Prince Rannic. Before you think to do so, I claim the princess for Greyad."

"You dare to—" Rannic grunted as another elbow hit him in the ribs. He shot his companion a withering look. "Challenge accepted, Prince Sohar." With a wicked grin, he hurried toward the Royal Announcer.

Chapter Ten

Agony

A whimper escaped Joi, and she bit down on her lip. Any pain was welcome other than her current agony. Nateo slanted her a glance, then gestured to her maidservant to come forward. They crowded her, shielding her, and Joi lowered her cramped arms with a moan of pleasure. Court required specific garments and precise behavior. She had spent hours learning the etiquette—her posture conveyed secret intentions along with her body language. The first technique she had mastered was the chicken pose, with her face downcast. It covered most situations and conveyed her need for privacy.

"Thank you." She rubbed each arm. "I'm young and healthy. I don't know how the court ladies do this. It's preposterous to wear these cumbersome garments and walk like a frigid fowl."

"It's that or invite unwanted attention. It isn't much longer, Princess." Nateo glanced around the hall. "Everyone has welcomed you. Who you are and your marriage availability overshadowed the king's abdication."

A huff escaped her, and she contained herself, remembering she was under the scrutiny of the public eye. "I don't trust their fake commiserations or their offers of assistance. I will take nothing here at face value. Besides, they want to peer into my eyes to make sure I am who Da claims."

"Another hour or two will be sufficient. Is there anyone you wish to discourse with?" Nateo gave her his back to ensure no one caught her off guard. Such thoughtfulness. She squeezed his wrist in thanks. "High Consort Cerna would be suitable."

She straightened, enthusiasm coursing energy through her tired limbs. "Oh, I did not see her. Yes, Nateo, she would be perfect."

"I will escort you to her as soon as Prince Rannic has said his piece."

"Does he approach now?" She groaned, not in the mood to spar words with the imbecile. He hated her because his father did. Dipping her head with shame, she realized she was guilty of the same—hating him for his father. Not that destroying Rumoc could bring back her parents or restore the life lost to her. The fact he had slaughtered her family and the people of Tennaba with no repercussions, coated her vision with hatred and a red-haze of fury. The image of her father's face, bloodied yet filled with love, pressed against the back of her eyelids. She wanted Rumoc dead, or dying in agony, but if she had him to herself, at her mercy, what would she do?

What could she possibly do to the man to make up for her loss? She scowled as the tingling energy coursing through her body receded. Only then did she notice the red swirl rippling up her arms, having not felt them spark into life with voracious hunger, eager to soothe her violent emotions. Sucking in a calming breath, she curled her fingers into her fists, squeezing hard to smother the flames. She raised a trembling hand to brush over the pulsing ruby, as if to promise it retribution, asking it to be patient.

"Prince Rannic." Nateo bowed but did not place his hand over his heart. He reserved the formal bow for those held in great respect.

"Nateo, do let the poor man through," Joi commanded, boredom clipping her words. She assumed the startled-chicken pose as she raised her chin in an imperial way High Consort Cerna was fond of using.

"Poor man? I am Prince Rannic; my realm is most definitely not poor." The voice came from somewhere in front of Nateo's barrel chest.

She smothered a chuckle, enjoying ruffling the man's feathers.

"I meant no offense, Prince Rannic," she said, unable to bring herself to say *my prince*. "Should I not refer to you as *poor man*, Nateo will not let you pass."

Nateo edged aside, hiding his laugh with a cough, but a glance at his face revealed no humor. She bowed to Rannic, ensuring her expression remained serene. That was harder to accomplish than one of Pan's wagers.

"I will be bold in a sea of insincerity." Rannic tugged her hand from her belt.

Her skin crawled at his touch, but she dared not yank her hand away and most definitely, dared not rub her palm along the fabric of her gown.

"Insincerity?" She arched a brow, hoping he would be "bold" enough to get to the point.

"I aim to claim you as my princess, my empress, and high consort," he said, and with such arrogance the urge to smack him assailed her.

Pan would be proud of her control this evening, and her new ability to curb her impetuosity. It was temporary, but welcome all the same.

"I am certain my father would consider it an honor to receive such an offer." A darkness pooled in her chest and slithered to her stomach, coiling in dread. Until now, she hoped this would be the extent of their interaction. His announcement doomed them to whatever path Fate laid out for them.

"Father?" His tone of voice implied he knew full well why she had no father.

For that, she retrieved her hand with as much grace as she could muster, before hooking her thumb into her belt. "King Buro." She smiled, casting a glance at her da seated on the throne. "After the unjustifiable *massacre* of my family, he raised me as his daughter. I had eleven years as Kura's daughter, a wonderful father, and seven years with Buro as my da. It is rare such events bring blessings."

"Blessings?" A smirk curled his lip.

Her smile hardened, but she kept it in place by sheer will. A lump formed in her throat, and she struggled to speak. "I lost Jeiram but gained Kylen and Mion as brothers. You are an only child, I hear." She placed her hand on his sleeve as if to offer him her sympathy.

He covered her fingers with his, trapping her as he grinned. It transformed his face, this time not in a hideous way, but showing he could be charming if he chose to. "I'm sorry for your loss, Princess Jenaso."

His insincere condolences sounded genuine as if his father wasn't responsible for the slaughter of her family.

"Thank you for your kind words, Prince Rannic. I will offer prayers to the Divine for your safe return to Manorio." Despite her best efforts, hope laced her words, that he would be a better man than his father, or that he wouldn't pursue her out of an unjustified vengeance.

"*Our* safe return, Princess. I will leave here with you by my side. As Crown Prince of Drem, my intentions become reality." He flashed a charming smile.

Her skin crawled at his deceptive admiration. "You flatter me, Prince Rannic. I am no beauty, certainly nothing compared to the princesses of Seit." She gestured to the flaming beauties, and he glanced up with eagerness. "Perhaps you should pursue one of them in the hopes of securing a consort?"

"I had not heard you were a strategist—as wise and as lovely." Rannic bowed his head and left her.

Joi threw up a silent apology to the Seitians for their impending infliction.

"Well done, Princess." Nateo gifted her with a smile before nodding at High Consort Cerna. "Shall we?"

"I would appreciate it, Nateo. To have one decent conversation tonight would be a valued treasure." She strolled forward, with Nateo and her maidservant falling in behind her. Smiling at advisors, royalty, and scholars as she paraded around the room, she glimpsed a shock of white hair. Gasping, she faltered. Sohar? No, it couldn't have been him, although, she hadn't spoken to a Greyadian this evening. Was their representative not in attendance?

A sharp pain pierced her heart, and she glanced down, stunned at the burn of tears. Joi blinked—in hopes of dispelling the moisture—and drew in deep breaths, trying to calm her erratic heartbeat. Why she cared was beyond her. She should abandon all hope as he abandoned her three years ago. The bitterness of it still stung.

"Princess?" Nateo's concerned voice drew her attention, and she raised her gaze to meet his. "Would you prefer to make your excuses?"

"No, I am well, Nateo. I thought I saw someone I once knew." She straightened her shoulders, and in her best chicken pose, waddled to Cerna.

"Princess, has this evening been trying?" High Consort Cerna accepted Joi's offered hands for a squeeze. She peered into her eyes and pursed her lips in understanding.

"Not at all, Mistress Cerna. I fear these lamps are too bright."

"It's perhaps due to your evening lessons. Reading the annals by candlelight is never wise." Cerna smiled, and the pure joy of it was pleasant after hours of varying degrees of insincerity.

"You humble me with your consideration." Joi smiled in return, a natural one that didn't hurt her cheeks as much. "You are breathtaking tonight, Mistress." She admired the cut of the gown, the crisscrossing scarves also in a dark blue. One had a floral design which was a feminine touch. Gold adorned her ears, and an exquisite, bejeweled hairpin rose high above the crown of her head. Her Meideon brown hair fell down her back, sleek and controlled. Out of all the consorts, only Cerna had breached her walls.

Joi announced, after varying court dramas, she wouldn't tolerate deception or manipulation, and any consort caught doing such would receive a cold shoulder. Some had still tried, but between training and her evening princess classes, she hadn't the patience to deal with the drama. Boredom tended to do strange things to one's mind, so she couldn't blame the consorts for their manipulations.

She conversed for a while about the guests in attendance, the food, the appearance of her brothers, and last, on who would make a lovely addition to the court as Kylen's High Consort. By the end of the conversation, they were giggling like girls, discussing the merits of courtship and the value of a well-chosen gift.

"What do you plan to do once Da abdicates?" Joi asked when their laughter dwindled. Cerna's eyes glazed with unshed tears, but she smiled despite them.

"King Buro has granted me freedom. I return to my beloved home, to reunite with my sisters." With the grace of a trained consort, she fondled a gold earring. "I brought wealth and honor to my family. All I long to do is drink tea and watch the sunsets from our back garden."

"I will miss you, Mistress Cerna." Another squeeze of her hands, and Joi left, abandoning her to bid her da farewell.

Before the sun rose tomorrow, he would begin his journey. He placed his crown on the white silk pillow carried around by the Master of Coronations. Joy and sadness shared Da's face, but now, conversing with Kylen, only excitement remained.

"Joi, my girl, come bid me farewell for I fear my old bones will seek solace early this evening." Da's expression was warm and welcoming. She clasped his outstretched hands, flashing him a smile as he gathered her closer. "So many noble lords have asked for an opportunity to gaze upon you. I am pleased to say that finding you a husband now rests on Kylen's shoulders."

"As well as finding himself a consort, I'm sure," she teased.

"Oh, wisely said. Have any caught your eye?" Da scanned the hall, and since she had this discussion minutes ago, she gestured to the woman seated at a table, alone except for a hovering servant.

"The ambassadress, Lady Aenwyr." She dipped her chin to hide her smug smile as both men glanced at the woman she suggested. Having not conversed with her tonight, Joi couldn't say whether her demure comportment was a farce, but she was observant, polite, and her servant appeared well cared for. She was quite beautiful, as conventional of a Forest Maiden from the Selion Mountains.

Her flaxen hair was paler than expected, almost as if the sun and the moon spun silver and gold together. Sensing her regard, she met Joi's gaze, and her blue eyes glowed with inner peace.

"Intriguing," Da said. "From neither realm therefore not showing partiality." Kylen appeared riveted by her. There was no expression on his face, nothing to indicate his interest. Yet, Joi knew him well.

"I do not believe I've had the pleasure of speaking to her this evening. I will apologize for my slight." Ky bowed to Da, and with a nod, he strode across to the lady.

"I am impressed." Da squeezed Joi's hands.

"Not me—High Consort Cerna mentioned her. All blame falls on her shoulders," she said with a wink, to let her father know she was jesting.

"Noted. Suitable punishment will be forthcoming." He glanced at Cerna to give her a respectful nod. "I see this evening has been trying. Nateo, escort Princess Joi to her chambers and come see me when you have settled her."

"Da..." She gasped, not wanting to leave him just yet.

He pinched her chin. "I promise to send crows, my girl, and visit you if the urge occurs."

"At least visit for Ky's marriage ceremony." She forced a smile past the lump constricting her throat. This was goodbye. King Buro chuckled, kissed her temple, then nudged her toward Nateo. He bowed to the king, hand across his heart, before he followed behind her.

Chapter Eleven

Confrontation

Their footsteps back to her palace echoed through the crisscrossing passageways. Despite the evening shadows calling forth winehouse tales of evil spirits, she found the silence comforting. The cool night breeze whipped the ends of her hair and toyed with her multi-layered gown like fingers sifting sand. With no one to see her, she lowered her arms, grateful to rest them. With the constant ache in her elbows, she vowed to never assume the chicken pose again. Nateo and her maidservant remained silent as well, which Joi appreciated, as if they too basked in the serenity.

She was certain Nateo had many amusing observations he wanted to share with her, but she was too exhausted to indulge him. She climbed the steps to her palace and paused to admire the full moon casting its silver light on the rose garden before her. With a nod, she bid Nateo good solace and asked her maidservant to retrieve a few extra carafes of Redanta wine.

"I had them delivered while we were in the hall, Princess." She gestured to the four bottles on the table, visible through the opened iron doors.

"Wonderful. You can retire for the evening." Joi entered her chambers, desperate to tear off her gown. Undoing her belt, she released a long-drawn-out sigh, the vise around her ribs easing. Thank the Divine, she could breathe again. So many had stared and spoken to her, that a moment of peace and solitude would ease the tension in her body.

"But, Princess, should I not ready you for solace?"

"I can do so this night." Parting the gown to loop the scarves off, Joi tossed them over her armor stand. The dark-blue-and-white silken sashes contrasted with her well-oiled leather armor.

Alone, at last, she made swift work of disrobing her slippers, cloak, and gown. Moving into her sleeping compartment, she found her swim pants and tunic in worn white linen, spread across her bed. Her maidservant was worth her weight in gold. A dip in her fountain pool to wash away the sweet scent of the bathtub's petals, and perhaps by then, Kylen and Mion would visit.

"Did you miss me, Princess?"

Joi froze. She disbelieved her ears and spun on her heels to glare at Aoni, a man she hoped to never see again. "What are you doing here?"

She launched into the air, defying gravity with a horizontal dive, to reach her sword. Still in its scabbard, it rested on her weapons stand. Her transparent drapes swirled as if a gust of wind burst through her palace. Gripping the scabbard, she paused with her legs spread as a subtle warning, then she ripped the sword from its sleeve. Her infernal hair trailed her movement, but at least it draped her back again and didn't obscure her vision. Joi assumed the Xiaxan fighting stance—a lunge with her sword in front of her. She aimed the tip at his chest where his heart would be if he had one.

"I had a taste of you, and it isn't enough." He smirked, striding toward her, despite her physical warnings—her stance, posture, grimace, and fury. "You were the perfect princess this evening. I am impressed."

She narrowed her eyes at the thought he had spied on her, but then again, so many others had watched her this night. The rising tide of her anger gritted her teeth.

"I spared your life, Aoni. I will take it now if you persist." Although she said it, she didn't want to kill him. She just wanted him to stop pursuing her.

With a humorless chuckle, he ignored her warning and sidled to the side as if that would distract her.

"I warned you." A flick of her hand awakened the Scarlet Fox. It spiraled from her fingers to wrap around her forearms, revealing the intricate lines twining along her skin.

He froze, staring at the red smoke with wide eyes, almost with disbelief. Then with a smirk, he flicked his own hand. A gray spinning ball formed, burning smoke as if he held a lump of fiery coal.

"I don't want to hurt you, Joi, I want to marry you." Sadness poured from his green eyes. "I've loved you before you were Jenaso. Shouldn't that count for something?"

"Oh, Aoni. I apologize if I've misled you, but my heart remains my own." Red twirled on her palm to form a spinning ball. "Find a woman deserving of your devotion, and stop hounding me."

"You don't wish to spar with me?" he teased, palming his dagger.

"No, it's been a tiring day, and I'm expecting Prince Kylen." Maybe mentioning her brother would make him realize there wasn't time for this. Justice would be swift if Kylen caught him in her chambers.

"The Meideons are not your brothers," he said, stalling. For what? She did not know.

"They will always be my brothers-of-heart." There was no hesitation in her response. "Decide now, Aoni. Do you wish to die?"

He ran an admiring glance along her form, his expression intense. "I will save this for another day." At his words, he snuffed his energy.

Joi lowered her sword. "You're a stubborn fool, Aoni. Now that all know I'm Letouran, I cannot marry anyone. To do so is to curse him."

"I am without ties, Princess. I would devote my life to you."

His earnest plea struck a chord within her, and she sighed. Damn him, she didn't want to feel sympathy for him. She absorbed her energy as she stamped her foot, frustration presenting itself.

"If you can convince Kylen, then I will consider your request." Biting down on her lip, she tried to quell the rising hysterical laugh bubbling up her throat. "*Consider*. I make no promises."

"Truly?" Aoni's smile burst across his face, and he dropped his dagger back into his boot.

"Yes, but intrude on my privacy one more time and nothing you do will bring forgiveness." She scooped up her discarded scabbard and slid her sword in. He left her alone with a bounce to his step.

"Curse men," Joi muttered as she returned her weapon to its stand and lowered herself into the pool. The cool water did much to soothe her anger and the fire still simmering under her skin.

Chapter Twelve

Reunion

The happy stride of Aoni coming from Joi's palace startled Sohar. Fury gripped him, seizing control of his thoughts to such an extent he saw Aoni dying by his hands. Sohar's heart pounded in his ears, deafening him as he struggled to breathe, to calm himself. Grabbing the man by the shoulder, he slammed him against the wall, his knuckles whitening with the effort it took not to kill him. Kylen flanked him and placed a calming hand on Sohar's shoulder, but he shook it off.

"I told you to stay away from her," Sohar roared, his voice no longer his own. Gone, in an instant, were his Greyadian ways. And so, failing his Contest had begun.

"I didn't harm her. I love her." Aoni struggled under Sohar's grip.

"Love? What can you know about love?" Sohar pinned him against the wall, not caring that the back of his head bounced off it.

"I'll lay down my life for her. Is that not love?" Aoni threw a pleading look at Kylen who shrugged, uncaring that Sohar was close to ending Aoni's life.

Sohar stared at him. Aoni's words implied devotion. Perhaps the young man would lose interest while Joi was en route to Greyad. With a deep sigh, he released the poor bastard's robes, not bothering to smooth the crumpled silk.

"Does she return it? Does she love you?" A solid lump dropped into Sohar's stomach. He dreaded the answer but needed to hear it.

"She said her heart is her own, but I may petition Prince Kylen for her. She would consider my offer with sincerity." If his sparkling eyes and broad smile—at odds with the darkness tainting Sohar's heart—were any indication, this delighted the man.

"Prince Kylen, please allow Lord Aoni to petition you," Sohar said to Ky, who grimaced at his suggestion.

Sohar wanted a few minutes alone with Joi and to greet her without her brother's presence. Ky met his gaze, and with a slow nod, drew Aoni aside.

Not needing further encouragement, Sohar raced up her steps to tap on her door. At her soft command, he pushed the iron doors open and entered, closing the doors behind him. He scanned the room in time to see her slip on a toweling robe, the wet fabric beneath clinging to her back and shoulders. When he remained silent, she faced him, her drenched hair saturating the front of her robe.

"Joi-Joi," he said, unable to think of a proper greeting now that this moment had at last arrived. Her gaze met his, and a bright smile parted her plump lips, still pink from the festivities.

"Mighty Sohar." She darted forward but halted, glancing between the iron doors and him. "Where's Ky?"

"With Aoni." He closed the distance between them.

He caught her fingers with his and tugged her into his embrace, claiming the hug he had promised himself. Her touch was gentle but hesitant, then she clasped him to her, wrapping her arms around his waist. She rested her head against his silk-encased shoulder, saturating it with her hair while her warm breath feathered across his throat. He struggled to suppress a shiver that had more to do with her in his arms than his damp tunic.

"How have you been, Sohar?" she asked, but he couldn't answer her. Peace descended upon him, stilling his restless soul. Nothing mattered now that she stood before him. "Sohar?" She tapped his shoulder, and he released her, enough for her to lean back. This close, her skin was translucent with a flush of pink staining her cheeks. The gold of her eyes burned bright—alluring and hypnotic.

"I have been well." Why couldn't he form any thoughts? He frowned at sounding like an imbecile.

"I did not see you in the hall." She arched a black brow. "Were you late to the festivities?"

"I was there, Princess," he said.

She studied his face, and with a nod, pulled out of his embrace. His palms itched with the urge to yank her back, but for that reason alone, he allowed her to move away. She gestured to her cushions, and Sohar followed. Her wet feet pattered on the hardwood floor, the paleness of her skin and the sight of her dainty ankles indecent and as enticing. He stared at her tiny toes, memorizing the shape of them.

"I can't say how tired I am of fending off your suitors," Ky said as he burst into her chambers. "Aoni? You can't be serious, Joi." He lowered himself onto the pillows beside her. She shrugged and handed him a full cup before offering one to Sohar.

"What does it matter whom I mate?" she asked. "A man is a man, is he not?"

"You are not partial to any?" Ky scowled. "A preference would help...guide me."

"No, so choose according to what they bring to Meideon and Letoura." No emotion crossed her delicate features, as if they discussed the weather.

Where was the effervescent girl Sohar had left behind? Here sat a demure woman, unconcerned with the change Ky's decision will bring to her life.

"I must choose the next Letouran king? I think not." Ky's bottom lip almost pouted.

"Then wait until after I decimate Drem. I might not survive, so finding a husband for me now would be pointless." Using the edge of the robe, she dabbed at the water trickling down her cheek.

"You have settled on this path?" Sohar didn't like that she expected to die in the endeavor, but it was a possibility. He wasn't foolish to believe he alone could thwart fate or the will of the Divine.

"No, I'm angry and tired. Do not mind me, Sohar. Even though I seek to avenge my family, this path would gain me nothing but a blackened heart." Joi sipped her wine, licking her bottom lip before sighing. "Dealing with Rannic made me realize that, to halt this poison, I need to be the catalyst for change. If I continue to hate the Drem, so will my children, as will Rannic's descendants hate me." She refilled their cups then her own. "It is Rannic who will bring the fight to me. I plan on returning to Tennaba to rebuild the Royal Seat of Letoura. I'm hoping Jeiram will come out of hiding and join me."

"He's alive?" Sohar's gasp trembled his hand and threatened to spill his Redanta.

"Yes, and how I know this is best left for another time." She stroked the medallion around her neck. It pulsed a greeting, surprising Sohar who had never seen it do that.

"Joi, Sohar has requested you visit his realm for a while." Kylen placed his cup down, and she stared at him, her eyes narrowing with suspicion. Her face softened, and she nodded, forcing a smile.

"Trying to get rid of me, brother?" she teased. "Still haven't forgiven me for setting the stables on fire?"

He chuckled at the reminder. "That was an accident. You were sweet at that age."

"Sweet? Am I no longer sweet?" Her light laughter made Sohar smile. "You wound me, brother."

Ky huffed. "Nonsense. Now, regarding this adventure, let's allow Sohar the entertainment of sorting out your mischiefs."

"He can try." She eyed them both over the rim of her cup. "So, what's the real reason you need me absent?" She gave them each a pointed look, but her focus intensified when she held Ky's attention. There would be no escaping the question.

Sohar admired her skill as Ky succumbed with a grimace, rubbing his temple as if in pain. Having told Ky all that had transpired with Rannic, he understood the necessity behind the journey. Ky flashed a desperate glance at him, needing his help. Sohar had no intention of helping. Kylen would be crowned the Meideon king tomorrow morning. If he could not handle his younger sister, then he wasn't fit to rule.

"I'm inundated with offers for you, more than you realize." At his words, her gaze flew to Sohar's before returning to Ky. "I need to remove you from the palace until I have refined the selection. To remove the temptation, so to speak. Many want you for Letoura, and many want you for…you." He gestured to all of her. "Truth be told, I'm not certain you understand the magnitude of this, Princess. Commanding me to simply choose one is nonsensical, not when you plan to restore Letoura to its former glory."

Joi shook her head, tiny droplets spraying outward. "I'm not in danger here. Leaving makes no sense. What are you not telling me?"

"The Drem cannot be trusted. You of all people know this. Anyone could take you away and later claim you gave your permission." Ky pressed a fist to his chest as if he wanted to thump it. "I am your brother, king, and guardian. I will not allow any harm to befall you. I vowed it when I first laid eyes upon you after Nateo rescued you from a burning Tennaba." He pinched her chin as Sohar saw Buro do, and Ky's expression softened—filled with adoration and fear.

"Greyad is far. Why not the Town of Nieven?" She squeezed Ky's hand. "Isn't it better to keep me close for defensive purposes?"

Ky's shoulders slumped. "I have given this much thought for far too many sleepless nights. You are recognizable anywhere in Meideon, and Letoura would have you assuming the role of the queen before you are ready to. Greyad it has to be."

She knelt before Ky, gripping his knees. Sohar found himself mesmerized by the flitter of emotions across her face. "Brother Kylen, I am young and naïve, but please, do not overtax yourself on my behalf." She cupped his cheek with a smile spreading across her lips. "Be at rest. I live to serve the king, and should the king need my body, then so be it. In war and peace, I am yours to command. If the best man for me serves Meideon's interests, then I am content."

"Beautifully said, Joi-Joi." Sohar applauded, unable to hide how impressed he was by her words.

Kylen glanced at him before he trapped her hand with his and met her gaze with a smile. Sohar shifted on his cushion at Ky's brotherly adoration. He couldn't say if it was the emotion Ky revealed making him uncomfortable, or that a deeper, less filial adoration rested in his own heart.

She sank into her cushions, lifting her cup for a sip. "Just to the borders of Greyad then? Although, Sohar, I would love to see the Royal City, Rendar. All I have to feed my imagination is what my studies revealed."

"Oh, Princess." He allowed himself a small smile. "I feel my Rendar will be a disappointment to you. Nothing could compare to your imagination."

"Alas, my dear sister, keep in mind you will be under Sohar's authority. Should you need to travel across the Seas of Turmoil, then so be it." Ky flashed her a determined look when Joi gasped and opened her mouth to speak. "I command it," he said, his tone of voice ringing with finality as expected of a king.

Chapter Thirteen

Endings

Joi gasped, suppressing a shiver as her wet hair cooled her back. The formidable expression on Kylen's face had her realizing there was more to this. He was trying to protect her, again. That same look hardened his face whenever she hatched another fun event, one that would lead to discipline from Da. She tugged on her hand, and Kylen released it, looking startled he still had it trapped to his smooth jaw and cheek.

"I assumed they wanted Letoura, never myself. You don't think they would resort to kidnapping me, do you?" Her nose burned with unwanted tears. She had been too young when her father sacrificed his life to save her, too young to remember all the details, but not too young to forget the pain and love on his face. Later, the servants' whisperings revealed more to her innocent mind.

She knew who she was and played along with King Buro's plan to keep her safe. For that, she was grateful to him, and a more filial emotion had developed. She had brothers, and fellow trainees, all loyal to each other. Her life was rich with love, but it was temporary, fleeting. The Drem could succeed in their endeavors, yet until their final strike, her life went on. One which included a beneficial marriage, and if Fate was kind, one where she wasn't a token queen or consort.

Drawing in a shuddering breath, she spun on her knees to face Sohar. He studied her with an unusual expression—confusion. As if she baffled him. She tried not to stare back though. Of all her trainees, he was by far the most fascinating boy-to-man she had ever met. Tall, with flowing white locks, his crystal-blue eyes pierced hers, his brow furrowing even as his top lip curled in that half smile he reserved for her. Unable to stop herself, she traced a fingertip down, from his hairline to the bridge of his nose, wiping the crease there. Glancing away, she hid her interest and her scalding cheeks.

"Thank you for taking me under your wing, Mighty Sohar. Now that I am older, I will try to remember not to bother you with my incessant chatting." Her cheeks burst into hotter flames at the memories of his chastisements.

"That would be something to look forward to." His husky voice tipped her gaze to meet his. His small smile faded, and she mourned the loss of the warmth that had softened his features.

"When do we leave?" she asked Kylen as she patted Sohar's hand, clasping his knee before facing her brother and king.

"Now," Kylen said, surprising her again.

With her head quirked, she studied him. Why the haste? She hadn't bid Pan farewell...and would Nateo be coming with her? She slashed a look at Sohar before nodding. All these were details Ky would've thought of.

Sadness speared her heart, and she launched herself into Kylen's arms, burying her face against his chest, inhaling his sunbaked scent she had come to think of as home. "I'll miss you, brother."

Ky thrust her away from him, pinching his garment off his chest. "I don't think I'll miss you, sister. Look at my tunic. I'm soaked."

Joi laughed, unable to help herself. She leaned back to admire her handiwork, before nodding in satisfaction. "You're a bore, Kylen. Too serious, always over-thinking problems. Remember what Mentor used to say, 'the simpler the better.' Quit squealing like an offended pig—it will dry."

"Thank the Divine you are leaving," Kylen said, but she knew he didn't mean it. His eyes sparkled, and a smile twitched his lips. "I don't know why Mion gifted you with the pool."

"He said something about it being indecent for a Xiaxan warrior to swim in the public fountain. It brings dishonor to the name." She rose to assume her place on the decadent cushions. "Now you know my preferences for a suitable mate, brother?" She held his gaze, watching emotions flitter across his face, too fast for her to understand all of them.

"I know you, dear one. You don't like to share. For me, he needs to have the ability to protect you, and if he's more skilled than you, all the better." Ky flicked his attention between her and Sohar. "Someone with military strategy would be preferable."

Sohar laughed, the sound warm, rich, and unexpected, pinning her in mid-sip. "Who is more cunning than our Joi-Joi? I suspect she has a little fox in her."

Warmth engulfed her chest at his compliment, but more from his humor. She blinked at him, having never seen or heard him laugh before. The rumble, the burst of light across his face, was a delight to observe, altering his stoic attractiveness into that of a beautiful man.

Ky ran a finger on the table, using cups and carafes as landmarks. "Your maidservant will travel south with Sohar's servant, Mazza. A decoy will act the role of Sohar as you two travel west through Bray Pass in the Hokhoun Mountains. The fewer people who see your gold eyes, the safer for all."

Joi frowned. "Nateo?"

"He will guard Father on his journey," Ky said, and with a nod, she agreed, happy to part with her long-time companion if it meant Da remained protected.

"Pan bid me farewell yesterday. I didn't realize why at the time. He must have known about this journey." Fury stiffened her muscles, and the medallion pulsed out waves of heat. She snatched the cups and carafe to dismantle his "map," hoping the movements helped calm her. "How many people did you include in this scheme? Why exclude me, Ky? Why hide this from me?"

"Until Sohar arrived, I wasn't certain which plan would come into play." The scowl Ky blessed her with said he didn't need to tell her anything.

And curse it, he had the right of it. As king, his thoughts, decisions, and consequences were his alone.

"Mion has readied the horses and is at the servant's gate. I will await you there." Ky climbed to his feet. He shot a glance to Sohar, one she didn't understand, then left them alone. The air was thick with unspoken words and heavy with farewells.

"Joi-Joi." Sohar grasped her hands and trailed his blue gaze across her face. When he spoke, his voice was hoarse and thick with urgency. "Dress in your armor and take only what is necessary. The remainder of your possessions are with your maidservant who will join us in Greyad much later."

She freed her hands and rose before rushing into her sleeping area to find her armor laid out for her. Closer inspection revealed that most of her possessions were gone. Her maidservant's excellent deception impressed her. As Joi dressed, she watched him through the diaphanous drapes dividing her chambers. He kept his back to her, his broad shoulders stiff and his hands clasped together at the base of his spine. He studied a painting on one wall as if it fascinated him.

Joi strode toward him as she braided her hair, hoping to minimize the nuisance of it on the journey. She wore the black under-armor of a Xiaxan warrior—a high-necked tunic strapped tight around her torso with the billowing pants tucked into her leather knee-high boots. She tugged on her chest-piece, tying it on either side before buckling her sword onto her belt and a bejeweled dagger into her boot.

On her belt, she tied her family's token—the ruby-carved emblem glimmered in the lamplight. The sight of it added the weight of responsibility onto her shoulders. She *was* a Letouran royal. There was no escaping what lay ahead of her. The medallion pulsed as she slid a pouch of gold coins into the hidden pocket inside the front of her armor. One last flick of her hand draped her black-hooded cloak over her shoulders.

He faced the door, pausing to ensure she was trailing him. Keeping to the shadows, they meandered along pebbled sidewalks, dodging scurrying servants and the occasional lord out for an evening stroll. Thanks to her training, she wasn't breathless from the exertion. The fluttering in her chest and belly had another origin. Excitement tore through her, warming her chest. An adventure awaited, and the idea of spending an inordinate amount of time with Sohar added to the heat splashing her cheeks. She would have many opportunities to see him laugh again.

The sadness of farewells and the reasons for her departure roiled the pit of her stomach like coiling river snakes, churning up fear, doubt, and other insidious emotions affecting her confidence. She was capable. She knew she was. Pan and her Xiaxan training had seen to that.

"Beloved sister." Mion tossed the reins at Kylen before scooping her into his arms. "I've just returned only to bid you farewell." He squeezed, and she squeaked in response.

"Can't breathe." She gasped in a half-tease, and he lessened his grip. "I want to live those winehouse adventures, not just listen to them."

When they were younger, the two of them often escaped the restrictions of court life for the simple pleasure of storytelling. And the stories told at winehouses were enthralling.

Their entire monthly allowances went to those stolen memories. Often to Nateo's dismay, who had to sneak two drunken royals back into the palace.

"True, but live to tell your own, Princess. Promise me." He squeezed her again, this time a little longer. Joi endured, for she knew not when she would see Mion again.

"I wish I could, Mion, but it would be a hollow promise. I can foretell the future no more than you can control the weather." He scowled at her, his lips forming into an exaggerated pout. "Fine. I promise. It's a lie, which you know." She smacked his upper arm, and he dropped her to her feet, none too gentle, then pushed her toward Ky.

"Now remember, Sohar has my authority." Ky wagged his finger. "Don't give him any reason to dump you in the Swamps of Phaendor."

"What's with you two asking for promises I can't keep?" she mumbled as he yanked her into his arms for a quick hug then lifted her onto the closest horse.

Sohar pressed his palm to Mion's chest then Ky's before leaping onto his own horse, his gray cloak draping over its rear. With a nod, he kicked his heels into the horse's flanks as she did the same, and they broke into a gallop.

Trailing Sohar, Joi glanced back to memorize this moment. This was the exact bridge that had carried her toward Da and her new life at Ethrielle. Surreal yet symbolic, she couldn't shake the feeling this was the last time she would see her home.

Chapter Fourteen

Incompetence

The opulence of the guest chambers didn't lighten Rannic's current mood. As the Crown Prince of Drem, silk cushions and gold drinking bowls wouldn't impress him. However, its location close to the Seit princesses' suite of chambers did.

He glared at Saith, his father's new advisor. Disgust and disbelief warred within him. Having woken from a most pleasant solace, he did not want to hear the princess and Prince Sohar had snuck off and taken a caravan south-west to Tennaba last night. Now it would need hard riding to catch up—for he couldn't afford to lose track of the princess.

Sohar's suggestion to marry her and keep her realm for himself was a valid one. Rannic had every intention of stealing the idea, but hours spent in the lovely company of the Seitian princesses blinded him to the princess's whereabouts. Now she was in Sohar's clutches. Rannic had underestimated the Greyadian.

A mistake he wouldn't make twice.

"Curse it!" He ignored his servants who dressed him in his royal-blue silk pants and tunic embroidered with silver dragons across his chest. "Have the horses readied. We leave within the hour."

Saith hovered, looming in that arrogant way Rannic hated. "Should we not inform your father?"

"That we both failed? Are you insane, Saith? Do you wish to follow Lorva's fate?" Rannic balled his hands into tight fists as his servants yanked on his boots. "It has been hours since their departure. They should be nearing Railly. We have no time to lose."

His gaze rested on Saith's face, studying his expression—fear, avarice, and satis-faction were evident. Having seen the same emotions on Lorva's features, Rannic wasn't surprised. His father chose his advisors from the same bucket.

"We, my prince? Can we not fly?"

Rannic hesitated. Flying *would* be faster. The purer the lineage the more powerful the magic. His was undiluted Drem, and he had learned how to fly in the caves beneath Manorio. Should anyone see him fly, all would hear of it.

"Do not speak of it! We're forbidden to fly after the Battle of Heaven's Fire, as you well know. This isn't Drem where we can flout the rules without consequence. Besides, if we violate this law, news of our failure will reach Father. We ride, Saith." He spun on his heel just as his servants tied his thick fur cloak on and handed him his sword.

For the first time that morning, Saith's visage paled. "But...My Glorious Sire, my equestrian skills are so poor I'll slow you down. Take two guards, and I'll follow behind with your caravan and servants. It is imperative you find the princess."

Typical. Due to his incompetence, Rannic had to pay the price. He grimaced at the days lying ahead for him. "Very well, Saith. I will await you in Tennaba."

He left his palace, his black cloak trailing his long strides. Once the iron doors closed behind him, he pinned himself to the wall and slithered along it until he was under a shuttered window. His guards didn't question his actions. They knew better not to. They held back, allowing him time, and did not reveal his intent.

He peered through two rungs, eavesdropping since he didn't trust Saith to remain loyal to him. His father's advisor bellowed orders until the servants were too busy to observe him. Then dropping onto a pile of cushions, he removed from a secret pocket in his tunic a bronze-looking glass with a silver inlay. *The Mirror of Echoes?*

"My king, I apologize for the intrusion." Saith's voice softened to a groveling tone. "It is as you expected. He *is* incompetent."

Rannic didn't wait to hear more. Slamming the iron doors open, he darted into the palace to spear the advisor through the heart. His look of surprise soothed Rannic's bruised ego. He nudged the fallen body out of the way, jerked the mirror out of his hand then peered into it. His father's face shimmered in its reflective surface.

"It seems you need a new advisor, Father." He smirked. After all, what could his father do to him from across this great distance?

Father pursed his lips. "Curse it, Rannic. They don't grow on trees, you know. Regardless, where is the princess?"

"She is en route to Tennaba. I leave within the hour to trail her. Showing subservience to these arrogant upstarts has been an irritation. Once the princess is carrying my child, their honor code will force them to accept my offer. Her loss of innocence will be painful for her. I will make certain of it."

"I'm satisfied with this plan, Rannic. Tell me, is she beautiful?" Rumoc's face grew as he shifted closer to the mirror's surface.

Was she? Rannic doubted, and not for the first time, his father's sanity. "She is not as beautiful as the Seitian princesses, although her gold eyes are striking."

"That is interesting. I thought Eria had passed on her beauty. Never mind, you may proceed with your plan." Rumoc nodded. "I will send legions of our finest warriors to camp outside Tennaba. Within our curatorship, of course."

"Excellent. I will inform you if I need them." He waved his hand over the mirror, his black energy coiling around it to remove his father's image. He picked one of his servants at random. "You! You are in charge. I want my caravan in Tennaba within ten days. Later than this and you too will meet the Divine." He made a great show of cleaning his blade on Saith's silk tunic before sheathing his sword.

After choosing two guards, Rannic left the rest to escort his possessions. A comfortable trip for them, he had no doubt. Striding into the stables, he demanded three horses readied and minutes later, they were on the road to the town of Pers. From there he would travel to Carthives, Railly, Misondos, and the long, arduous road to Bontarmes. He would swap the horses where possible and perhaps, if Sister Luck was with him, he would reach the princess before she entered Letoura.

For this inconvenience and for every hour he suffered, he would remove a strip of skin from her, lash by lash. Then he would take hours with her to ensure she carried his child. Throwing back his head on a laugh, he hoped she showed as much spirit as she had last night.

She suggested he have the royal painter draw up a portrait of her? Her sharp tongue would be the first to go.

Chapter Fifteen

Blessings

Sohar caught himself gazing at her hair. Again. The sunlight filtering through the Wood of Yellow Suns kissed her face and transformed her hair into heated oru, a tar-like substance. He grimaced at his unflattering description, yet not knowing how else to explain the mesmerizing glow of her hair. On the other side, the reflection of the sunlight off the yellow leaves and mustard-colored grass made her skin look sallow. It didn't detract from her beauty though. He doubted anything could.

They had been traveling west for two days, stopping only to water the horses and rest for a few hours. He had avoided the towns Timouy and Cour, for secrecy's sake. They had to rely on the land to provide food, and on days when the bounty was scarce, the black bread with cheese her maidservant packed for them sufficed. Joi hadn't spoken much except for when courtesy required it. This surprised him. He had expected her questions to pepper their journey. A glance at her eyes showed sadness but not enough to curb her tongue.

Approaching on silent feet, he offered her an apple. She jerked, then flashed him a small smile, one he was grateful for. It was better than having her lost in her thoughts. She patted the neck of her horse nudging her in the hopes of a similar treat.

"How long do we stay off the roads?" She bit into her apple, her lips wrapping around the succulent fruit.

He shifted on his feet, choosing to scan the horizon than linger on her tempting pink mouth. "Until we reach the town of Vaeril. I have planned our arrival to coincide with the Festival of Forgotten Feathers." He circled her horse to check the saddle's straps. "I'd like to lose our followers in the crowds."

"Two shadows left the palace at the same time we did." She turned her apple, before sinking her teeth into it. "I'd hoped they were messengers. Vaeril is as good a place as any." She peered over the saddle at him, a crooked smile twisting her lips as she chewed. "I hear they have wonderful winehouses."

Sohar snorted. "We're not on a pleasure hunt, Princess."

"You'd suck the sour out of a lemon, Mighty Sohar." She pouted, shaking her head before feeding the remainder of her apple to her horse. "I can't see why having entertainment would harm us."

"It would lower our guard, and until we've lost our followers, there'll be no winehouses for you." His lips curled despite his determination to remain in control around her. "Knowing you, winehouses mean wine. I'm securing your safety, not babysitting a drunkard." Although, in truth, he loved seeing her intoxicated. Her relaxed inhibitions made her adorable.

She huffed. "Drunkard? I'll have you know I can drink far more than Kylen can."

"Of that, I have no doubt, Princess. I promise, at the first winehouse we encounter in Greyad, you can have all the wine your little self can handle." Stroking the horse's neck, he wished he could run his fingers along the column of her neck and through to the tips of her hair.

"On your allowance?" Her question startled him, enough for a chuckle to rumble up his throat. He glanced away to cough, hiding his humor.

"I'm the crown prince—I have no allowance," he said after a few minutes of wrestling with his lips to remain stoic. "Once in Vaeril, we're to replace the horses with fresh ones at the Token of Kings Inn. Should we become separated for whatever reason, I will meet you there."

Joi nodded before pulling herself into her saddle. "I think we need another name for me. Joi and Princess defeat the purpose of this adventure, Sohar."

"Very well, what name do you suggest?" He dipped his head to hide his smile which formed despite his best attempts to stifle it.

"Meila—it means beautiful seductress." She chuckled.

His gaze flew to meet hers. The mischief in their golden depths erupted laughter out of him. It was so sudden, he couldn't tamp it down in time. He turned his head, focusing on his own saddle, not wanting her to see his lapse. But, Divine, it felt good to laugh.

"Yours will be Ozu." She trotted her horse closer.

"I don't want to know what that means." One laugh was enough of a lapse for him to strengthen his determination. "You can tell me when I've drunk my weight in wine."

"Coward," she teased as he mounted.

"With you, *Meila*, it's best to be on my guard." He scowled at his words. He hadn't intended to reveal anything personal. "I never know when you'll surprise me," he said, covering his mishap.

"I'm sorry you hate surprises, *Ozu*," she mumbled before following behind his trotting horse.

Breaking into a gallop ended the conversation which pooled cold, dark sadness in his chest. He was wise to end their interaction when he had; to continue down that path was to soften his guard completely. The sly fox had a way of stripping him of his well-earned control, but the idea of failing his Final Contest bothered him less and less which worried him more. He couldn't be the only prince in Greyad's history to fail his challenge. Losing control could have two consequences: he would emerge victorious, having conquered the temptation of her or he would marry her—he knew not what his reaction would be.

Part of him could walk away from her now and end this internal torment. Another part of him wouldn't abandon her and wanted to claim her, or at least, see her happy. The sweeter of the two was to marry her, but that came with its own difficulties.

Glancing back every few miles to check on their pursuers was to see her pensive face, determined yet lost in thought again. On one or two occasions, when she caught him looking at her, she would offer him a sweet smile before dipping her chin. Odd. But Sohar didn't dwell on it. Perhaps she preferred the company of her thoughts instead of meeting his gaze or catching up to him for a word or two.

Exhaustion beat at him, with the addition of hours in the saddle forming a dull ache in his spine. The urge to stretch his limbs called for a rest. He chose a spot on the riverbank, under the curved roof of a massive boulder. His back was to the coarse rock so he could rest and be on guard for an intruder. He had tethered their horses, and with her cloak balled under her head, finding solace seemed swift for Joi. She hadn't said more than two words since they stopped.

Tomorrow they would reach Vaeril, where they would find a hearty morning meal and the next leg of their journey taking them west through the Bray Pass into Orth. Until then, he needed only to wait a few more hours. Standing to remove his cloak, he draped it over her sleeping form, kneeling alongside her to brush a black curl off her temple.

She was worth all this—the exhaustion, the hunger, the journey. He would offer his life for hers, and therein lay his dilemma, for his life wasn't his own. He tamped down those thoughts, having gone through them many times only to return to the same conclusion. Joi was all that mattered.

Chapter Sixteen

Attacked

Leading her horse behind her, Joi kept her head down and the hood billowing low over her eyes as they crossed the stone bridge into Vaeril. The town was a bustle—merchants called out their wares, and citizens hurried this way and that. There was too much activity for her to focus on a single curiosity. Ladies of the elite classes strolled, arms linked and giggling, as their gowns trailed in the dust. Their servants remained close, laden with packages and other purchases.

Colorful feathers in all shapes and sizes littered the cobbled streets. Erected every few feet towered a befeathered totem with little space left for any belated revelers looking to pin their wishes. She had never attended such a festival. Although her studies were thorough, covering all festivals across the realms, their arts, history, and commerce. In truth, she enjoyed samples of their cultural dishes the most.

Orth was once a tropical realm. Their earth magic was strong, even among those with diluted ancestry. The warlords enhanced their craft until they challenged the natural boundaries between order and chaos. In doing so, they had brought disaster to the land. Fissures opened from the bowels of the earth, killing all life around it. The warlords refused to cease their quest for power. In the end, it took the combined might of the realms, but by then, only deserts remained. Vaeril supplied provisions for the Meideon soldiers during the Battle of Heaven's Fire.

Chosen for their easy availability, they used feathers to offer tribute to the fallen, to their lost hopes and dreams. Over the centuries, the tradition devolved into the rainbow of feathers now offered for petty desires. Still, it was a vibrant festival, filled with dancing and laughter.

"We can enjoy a meal while they prepare our replacements." Sohar gestured to a large wooden structure. An artistic sign above its door stated its name and purpose—the Token of Kings Inn.

"I'm sorry, we're full. This crazy festival has the town in chaos." The stableman shook his head, shaking free bits of hay from his mussed hair.

"I want to change these two and stable the fresh horses for the hour it takes to get a meal at the inn." Sohar's scowl descended like thunderclouds over the Sea of Turmoil—foreboding.

The stableman pursed his lips, his gaze shifting between Joi and Sohar. "I wish I could, sir. There are stables two streets down. They might accommodate you."

"Very well." Sohar spun on his heel, and she sighed, trailing him. He looked angry, not expression-wise but by the way he stomped the distance to the next stables.

She hid a chuckle. Someone should tell him stoicism needed to extend to his body too. That someone would not be her since she liked seeing him emotional in some way. It meant he wasn't cold and unfeeling.

This stableman had room, and sans horses, Sohar and Joi meandered in the direction of the Token of Kings Inn. The aroma of food assaulted her, and her stomach grumbled. Something other than cheese or duskrats would be wonderful. The noodle stalls called to her and nostalgia struck, spurred by hunger. She would kill for a bowl of Pan's noodles.

Sohar startled her, fisting the front of her tunic to yank her into a dark alley. Her glare faded when three shadows broke away from the walls. Three men followed them into the alley. Her medallion pulsed in eagerness, but she didn't release it. It would be wise to save her power for when she needed it most. With a flick of her arms and shoulders, she disrobed her cloak. Catching it on her foot, she kicked it onto an old barrel. Her travel bag fell to the floor which she slid toward the barrel, as well. Sohar did the same.

"Not messengers then. I wasn't planning on killing anyone today, but fate has decided." She withdrew her sword and pressed her back against Sohar's. "I'll try not to get any blood on you."

He grunted. "Try not to die. Ky won't take too kindly if I return your corpse."

"I'll try to be considerate." She launched herself into the air, high and far, spinning her body parallel to the ground with her sword aimed forward. They deflected her lance, so she brought the blade up to shield her. This move accomplished exactly what she needed—to close the distance and place her two attackers on the defensive. With her braid trailing each movement, she ducked and spun, slicing across one man's thigh. He stumbled but didn't go down. Instead, he whipped his sword in a flurry of movements. She blocked all but one which sliced her upper arm. Her pale and bloodied skin was visible through the cut sleeve, the wound emanating a light sting—it was superficial, at best.

A black sash hid her attacker's face, but with his eyes visible, triumph glimmered within them. A mistake on his part. With a confident smile, she pulled her dagger from her boot then spun it and her sword toward him, both blades extended. The dance was graceful if performed correctly. One blade slashed across his chest, and he clutched his wound. Joi tossed her dagger up high, and as his focus trailed its spinning path, she hit him, palm extended, into his chest, sending him flying backward. His feet dragged trails on the dirty cobblestone before his body crumpled.

Catching her descending dagger, she dropped to her haunches, facing her sole remaining attacker. A quick glance revealed Sohar fought an opponent with two swords. As much as she was enjoying this battle, she was hungry. Crisscrossing her dagger and sword in swift slashes, she charged the third man, forcing him to shuffle backward with hurried, clumsy steps. He bumped against the side of the alley and vaulted upward into the air, defying gravity. She frowned. Only Xiaxan trainees knew how to do that, and it was dishonorable to attack one of their own. She followed him, going higher to peer down at him, and with a solid kick to his jaw, he flipped and plummeted to the ground, landing on his head with a decided crack.

She landed in a cloud of dust and twisted toward Sohar who withdrew his sword from his opponent's chest. Blood ran like a rivulet to the tip of the blade and dripped off. With a flick of his wrist, he cleaned then sheathed it.

"You're getting old, Ozu," she teased, sheathing her own sword.

"Your skills have improved, yet you did not kill them with your blade." He gestured to the crumpled bodies unstained with excessive blood.

"I hate cleaning my weapons. A broken neck is less messy." Dropping her dagger into her boot, she lifted the cut cloth of her sleeve to assess her wound.

Sohar grunted, striding forward to loop an arm around her waist and tug her closer. He nudged her fingers out of the way to inspect her wound. With a yank, he tore her sleeve off and handed it to her as if it were commonplace to rip her clothes off her. He glanced between her eyes and her wound, a frown marring his forehead.

"It's not deep—should be a quick mend." White energy erupted from his palm and fingers before he gripped her upper arm. Ice burned her skin, inflamed her wound, and she bit her lip to smother her moan.

Joi studied his face as a distraction as he repeated the process. Having never been this close to him, she could see every eyelash and the white flecks in his crystal-blue irises. His slashing eyebrows were darker than his hair, but that only drew attention to the vibrant color of his eyes. Were all Greyadians this beautiful?

He glanced up and caught her staring. Heat warmed her cheeks, but she didn't look away. After all, she had done nothing wrong. Silence descended between them, intense and vibrating with an energy she couldn't name. Her breath hitched, expanding her chest like steamed dumplings. His head shot up, and he yanked her to the right, just as a dagger passed over her shoulder to embed in his chest.

She gaped at it, then as a crimson stain grew, so did the anger and fire within her. Wrenching out the blade, she used that momentum to launch it at the attacker. It buried in the assailant's heart. Without a sound, he crumpled to the ground.

"Curse it." She faced Sohar, who pressed his icy-white palm over his wound, now healing himself. It didn't seem to be doing much since blood seeped through his fingers and stained his white tunic. "Let's get you into the inn. Can you walk?" Despite his paler than usual skin, he pursed his lips as if she implied he was a weakling. "Then show me, Mighty Sohar."

Chapter Seventeen

Deceived

In the middle of Naisomian Wood, Rannic bore down on the colorful caravan with his fresh horse eager to stretch his legs. This one he would keep. He liked the line of his flanks, and his ebony coat shimmered like silk. Yes, he was most pleased with this horse. Despite this, every hoof hitting the ground reverberated through his exhausted body. His royal backside and thighs ached, his throbbing muscles demanded a different posture with a lack of stimuli.

Exhaustion beat him down, but he forced himself on. Grit covered his eyes, and a fine layer of dust made his skin itch. His silk tunic and pants were beyond salvaging, travel-worn from sleeping on the hard-packed ground or a prickly forest floor. The soft bed in Misondos had been heavenly, but it was a distant memory now.

"I command you to cease this caravan at once!" He drew the horse to a halt before falling off with as much dignity as he could muster. His knees buckled once. Drawing in a deep breath, he gathered his strength to face the armed men and caravan. He shot a passing glance at his own guards dismounting, their exhaustion mirroring his.

"I seek the princess." His gaze darted from face to face until he landed on one man who looked like an imperial servant.

"Greetings, my prince." The man bowed. "Princess Joi is not with us."

Rannic stiffened in anger, and he smothered a groan as fresh waves of agony coursed through him. "Do you take me for a fool?"

The servant shook his head with his face averted. "I dare not, my prince. Princess Joi and Prince Sohar traveled ahead. The princess wanted to visit the Swamps of Phaendor, and Prince Sohar, who is eager to please her, agreed to the outing. They should have passed through Moury this morning."

"Very well, to Moury it is." With an ill-concealed grimace, Rannic vaulted into the saddle, before commanding his men to follow. "Curse it." He shifted his position, trying to ease the throbbing. Perhaps he should take the time to enjoy a hot bath and a meal in Moury before resuming the pursuit. After all, it wouldn't do to look unprincely when he killed Sohar and claimed the princess.

Pondering how he would kill the arrogant Crown Prince of Greyad and flay the skin off Jenaso's back were the only thoughts keeping Rannic in the saddle. The five hours it took him to reach Moury were the longest in his life. As soon as he entered the small town, he slid off his horse to lead it to the first suitable inn he came across.

The walking helped ease some stiffness of his muscles, but by then, his tolerance was non-existent. Outside the Inn of Dancing Dragons, he tossed a guard his reins and climbed the steps. The wonderful aroma of noodle soup and dumplings greeted him, and he dropped beside a table, not caring about protocol.

He ordered food for him and his guards—wine carafes, as well. When they returned from the stables, he gestured for them to join him. They hadn't complained once on the journey, a skill he gratefully valued.

They ate in silence—their combined exhaustion solidifying the camaraderie. In a moment of rare kindness, Rannic requested three rooms with steaming tubs, then grabbed a carafe and with jerky movements pulled himself up the stairs to the innkeeper's best room.

Sinking into the heated water drew a deep groan of pleasure from him. With his arms along the wooden tub's sides, he leaned his head back and only moved when he drank from the carafe. The laughter and music from the inn's occupants pierced the thin walls, soothing him long enough for him to gather his thoughts.

Something was unbalanced. A subtle nudge he hadn't noticed before pressed his subconscious. Probing it where it sat at the edge of his exhausted mind, he waited for it to formulate. He dozed off, then awakened to recall what he had tried to unravel. Nothing, so he poked at it from another angle.

If he was in Sohar's position, what would he do? Would he whisk her away in the middle of the night? Yes. Would he escort her to Tennaba, or would he head for home, to his father and surround her with legions upon legions of warriors? Rannic sat up so quickly water sloshed over the sides.

They had deceived him.

He rang the bell, and the innkeeper rushed in, bowing every few seconds.

Ice stiffened Rannic's spine, and he scowled, hating that he had been taken for a fool. "Tell me, has a Greyadian passed through Moury today?"

"No, my lord." The innkeeper bowed and shook his head at the same time. "We don't see many Greyadians in little old Moury."

"Curse it." His roar had his guards dashing into his room in mere toweling robes and drawn swords. The innkeeper scurried out, not willing to deal with irate and armed customers.

"What is it, my prince?" A guard scanned the room, focusing on the shuttered window.

"It seems we have run a merry chase." He threw the carafe, and it shattered against the wall, raining clay shards. He shouldn't have underestimated a Greyadian, considering what rumors reached him of Sohar's abilities. "If I wasn't in so much pain, I would congratulate Prince Sohar on this strategic move."

"There is no princess?" The second guard frowned. "We have failed you, my prince."

"No, you two continue to Chaus, and take your time. Stop off at each town for a day. I will fly to Vaeril in the cover of darkness."

"They will not discover this?" The guard's concern arched Rannic's brow. "Will the generals not ask about your location?"

What he loved most about his excursions outside of Manorio was the independence and the illusion of privacy. He had forgotten he would need to report in. "I tasked you to guard the princess's caravan to Tennaba. As to my whereabouts, I escorted her to the Wood of Yellow Suns but stayed for the Festival of Forgotten Feathers in Vaeril."

"Your wisdom is Divine-inspired, my prince." The second guard bowed.

"Take three gold." He gestured to his coin pouch resting alongside his Drem imperial token on the bed. "This should more than cover your expenses."

"We bid you farewell, Prince Rannic." They bowed, hands over their hearts, before leaving.

Alone again, he settled deeper into the tub, planning his next move. He would leave tonight to chase the wind and clouds. If he flew north-west to Dazoche, he would inquire whether a Greyadian passed through. That would reveal which path Sohar planned to take. To go through Orth would be suicide for any traveler, but since the Greyadians battled the Orthians in an endless war, this might not concern Sohar. It would be risky, but no one would think to follow him into the barren wastelands.

Going from Dazoche into Letoura placed the princess at risk. If anyone recognized her eyes, she would need to claim the throne at once. Since the caravan was an elaborate decoy, he had to assume she wasn't ready to rule.

Which meant Vaeril. If he flew without rest, he would arrive in a little over sixteen hours. He might miss them by a few hours, but he would at least confirm that Sohar intended to take her through Bray's Pass and into Orth.

With the plan finalized, Rannic ordered another carafe. After an hour of rest, he rose, braided his hair, dressed in his filthy garments, and from the roof of the inn, he launched himself skyward. Engulfed by his black energy, it coated him in the shadows of night, hiding him from sight.

Chapter Eighteen

New Memories

Sohar's eyes fluttered open. He studied the wooden ceiling, not recognizing it. How had he gotten here, in this carved bed? Forcing his mind to focus, he recalled the attack, then receiving the wound. Fool! He should have made certain the assassins remained incapacitated, but all reason abandoned him at the sight of Joi's bloodied sleeve.

A splash of water drew his attention. He turned his head, testing out his shoulder as he did so. The wound didn't hurt when he probed the burning scar with his fingers. His gaze fell on Joi. He sucked in a silent breath, disbelieving the vision before him. With her back to him, she stood in front of the water bowl without her tunic on. Nude from the hips up, the white cloth she rubbed her body with had traces of her blood, but smears and not spots. That was good. It meant she wasn't bleeding any more.

The curve of her spine, the dip of her waist as it flared into her hips, and the arch of her neck captivated him. She had piled her braided hair on top of her head with escaped ebony wisps caressing her shoulders and the braid slowly unraveling. He had never seen anything as enthralling as her. He observed the sheer beauty of such an ordinary task, trailing her hands with a mesmerizing obsession.

"You missed a spot," he said.

She gasped, and spun to look at him, thankfully having thrown an arm across her breasts. Despite this, they still bounced, responsive in their youth.

"Where?" She twisted left then right, trying to find the spot. Her innocence called to him, along with her beauty and integrity.

"I'm teasing you, Joi-Joi." He slumped onto the bed, shielding his eyes from temptation with his forearm.

She mumbled something he was certain castigated his manhood. She had done so on numerous occasions, forming many of his fondest memories training under the Xiaxan generals. Her mutterings preluded the rustle of clothing and her leaning over him.

"How do you feel?" Her fingers fluttered over his chest and around the scar. She pressed here and there, causing an intense burn of another kind to enter his body, traveling lower.

"Better." He grunted. "You need to teach me this technique."

"Now you're teasing me again." She huffed. "You know more healing techniques than I do."

He lowered his arm to watch the light play across her face, lingering where it warmed her lips. "Yes, but I don't know yours."

"What does it matter? You reacted like an idiot, Sohar. You're the crown prince. Let me take the blade next time." Her cheeks flushed with anger as she glared.

"Your life means more than you think!" he roared, her face paling under his angry gaze. Good, maybe she would take him seriously. Silly girl.

"Huh. I'm Letouran and hunted, Sohar, and I'm sorry I involved you in this. The Drem do not forget." She fidgeted, then rested her palm on his chest.

Warmth seeped from her small hand into his skin, soothing him. "I choose to involve myself, Princess," he whispered.

"During all those years of training, I thought you knew I was a Letouran royal. It's why you challenged me to live up to my legacy." She dipped a cloth in a nearby bowl and rung it between her hands. Then with a gentle touch, she held it to his scar. The cool cloth drew a sigh from him.

"That's not why I challenged you." He closed his eyes against the mesmerizing golden lure of hers. "Take my token and inform Mazza of the attack. He is to expect the same."

She fumbled with the belt of his pants, and the heavy weight of his imperial token lifted. His father had the Greyadian symbol—a shield and sword—cast from gold and not the usual iron or bronze. Gold was their heaviest metal, and as such, was a symbol of responsibility. Cracking an eye open, he watched her petite hand hover over the token with her brow furrowing in concentration.

Affection surged against the hardened walls of his heart, demanding he reach for her, to touch her, hold her. With dwindling determination, he thrust down the silent pleading. His resistance was crumbling, one smile of hers at a time.

Scarlet swirls of energy feathered out from her hand to caress the carved edges of his emblem. He bit down on his lip to hide his gasp. It was the Scarlet Fox, and she wielded it with ease. An illusion appeared, concern evident in the wavy lines forming Mazza's face.

"Princess," Mazza greeted. "Is My Lord well?"

"The idiot took a blade for me, Mazza," Joi said. Sohar cleared his throat as a reminder that Mazza was her subordinate. "We're at the Token of Kings Inn. He's fine, but he's bleeding like a skewered wild boar."

Sohar snorted, but the good humor that rumbled his chest was beyond his control. He flashed a grin. His lips splitting felt unnatural. She blinked, her own smile freezing before she dragged her focus to the illusion.

"I am certain My Lord acted as needed," the poor man said.

"Be vigilant, Mazza," Sohar called out.

"We will be on our guard, my prince. Please, stay safe." Mazza's image blurred as the illusion disintegrated.

"I thought the inn did not have spare rooms." Sohar scowled. Had the stableman deceived them and purposely sent them to their deaths?

She laughed, and joy swirled within him. It was sudden, warm, and exquisite, saturating every arid part of his chest.

"I threatened to burn down the inn if the innkeeper didn't find a room somewhere. I might've violated a natural law by using the Scarlet Fox for personal gain, but here we are. Also, he found our travel bags and cloaks. He'll have our garments washed and ready for tomorrow. Hungry?" She tied his token onto his belt.

He closed his eyes as she bent over him, the scent of jasmine entering his lungs to find residence there. On any other woman, jasmine was too sweet, too overpowering. On her, it suited her. It emanated from her thick black braid falling over one shoulder, the tail of it curling on his bare stomach, caressing him.

"Yes." His voice sounded harsh even to his own ears.

"That's a good sign. Dress while I rush down to see if the innkeeper has anything for us." She jumped up. Her energy levels were high, as per usual. Sohar grabbed at her wrist but caught her fingers instead.

"Take care, Joi-Joi," he said. "The assassins could still be out there."

"Good point." She blessed him with another smile, eagerness splitting it wide. "I'll ask the innkeeper if I can make something in his kitchen."

"You cook?" He winced, realizing his shock was obvious.

"You'll just have to pretend to like it, friend." She freed her hand and left him to his traitorous thoughts.

Chapter Nineteen

Panic

Joi did not want to go through something like that again. Sheer panic had gripped her when Sohar crumpled against the alley wall. Right there, she had summoned her energy, not caring who saw her.

Whispering the words Pan taught her, she had pressed her palm over his wound. Fire burned from her chest down her arm and out her fingers. It drained from her, the tingles lessening in severity. The medallion pulsed a warning, and heeding it, she stopped. Transporting him into the inn became paramount. Ducking under his arm to support him, she was able to rouse him, and he staggered with her guidance to the entrance.

There she had encountered the arrogant innkeeper and singed his eyebrows with a small portion of energy. His servants carried Sohar into a room before leaving them alone. She had stripped his tunic off, trying to focus on the task and not the revealed contours of his taut abdomen. His skin was velvet heat, his chest hauntingly beautiful. A perfect example of a virile man as seen in ancient artwork.

She had cleaned his wound and waited the necessary time for her energy to regenerate before healing him again. In her mind's eye, she saw Pan shaking his head at her. He wasn't here but had he been in her situation, he would also exhaust his power. She remembered not to give her all. Thankfully, the medallion kept her in check.

Running down the steps, she followed her nose to the kitchen. When she entered, the servants greeted her with shock and commands to leave. She waited for one of them to summon the innkeeper. He took one look at her and instructed his servants to allow her access. She smirked. Good.

As she went through the motions of preparing Pan's noodles, her thoughts dredged up the past hour. Heat, not from the pot, spread across her cheeks and down her chest. She had exposed her body to the Crown Prince of Greyad. At least he had the good manners to tease her. Castigating herself for being sensitive, she added meat to the pot. He would see more of her since their journey had just begun. At some point, she would need a bath, be it in a river or at an inn.

She would see more of him too. Curse it. Joi dipped her fingers into a washbowl and patted her cheeks. This wasn't the first time she had seen a man's chest, so why the sight of his flustered her remained a mystery. Shaking her head to clear her thoughts, she scooped the noodles into two bowls and placed them on a tray with a carafe of the local wine. Whether it was good quality didn't matter.

The innkeeper rushed in to see if he could assist her further, and she instructed him to find her two tunics, preferably a small black one for her and a large white for her husband. At the lie, another wave of embarrassment hit her. With her hands full, she couldn't cool her cheeks. And he was to pack a traveling pouch with the best in his pantry. She gave him a look implying should anything be of a subpar standard, she would return and destroy his inn. By his paling complexion, she assumed he understood her.

Nudging the door open with her backside, she entered the room to find Sohar sitting up. His white hair cascaded around him, more disheveled than she had ever seen him. At least he had changed. Placing the tray onto the table, she gathered their discarded garments.

"That smells good. You brought wine. Well done, Meila." His gaze flittered to the innkeeper, hovering behind her conveying they weren't alone.

She handed the garments to the innkeeper. With a nod of thanks from her, the man closed the door and left them alone. She brought Sohar a bowl and placed it into his cupped hands. Then taking up her own bowl, she dropped onto the wooden chair at the table and proceeded to eat. The meal would restore her energy. This would aid her to fully heal him, and she was hungry. The savory noodles settled in her stomach, spreading warmth and nourishment.

"This tastes like Pan's noodles." A broad smile spread across his features with ease as if he smiled often. "You made this?"

Joi ignored his question, focusing on her meal rather than on his smiling lips. Besides, she didn't want to discuss how she managed to learn Pan's secret recipe. "How are you feeling?" She shoved her empty bowl to the side to pour two cups of the burgundy wine.

"Good." He handed her his bowl and accepted the offered cup. "I insist you teach me this healing technique."

"I can't." She pouted, snagging his focus, but she doubted it was in an admiring way. "It's linked to the Scarlet Fox and the medallion." She wiped her mouth on her sleeve.

"*And* the medallion?" He traced the ruby resting on her chest. It was at eye level and easily accessible to his bedridden height.

"The medallion helps with the burden Scarlet Fox places on the Letouran royals. A single royal cannot carry the full power. It would be lethal. The Orthian Warlords created the magical medallion before the Battle of Heaven's Fire."

He nodded, sipping his wine. "I am pleased you killed that man. It was always a concern for me, that when the time came, you'd spare your enemies."

"My enemies? Sohar, their eyes weren't a specific color. One had the green eyes of Seit and the other the black of Drem. With such variety, they had to be from the Temple of the Divine in Raica. Why would the Divine Priestess want me dead? Perhaps they followed you from Greyad?"

As he considered her words, his expression became stoic, hiding his thoughts from her, but the pinching of his lips told her his conclusions were unsavory.

"You may be correct, Joi-Joi. They should have chased after the caravan which left an hour before us. Only the three of us knew of our departure. Unless they waited outside for any suspicious movement?"

She chuckled, shaking her head. He didn't spend much time in Greyad's imperial palace, did he? "The stables would have known about the two horses. The kitchen about the food my maidservant organized. Nothing is secret in the palace, Sohar. You should know that."

His cheeks darkened. "They cannot travel through Bray's Pass and into Orth. We will be on our guard, just the same. We'll leave Vaeril through the same gate we entered then loop back west, crossing the Xysion river between Vaeril and Endon. It will add, at most, half a day to our travel."

The enormity of their journey slumped her shoulders, but she shook off the dread. Such a long time spent in the saddle would impact more than her body. "If you've finished your wine, I'd like to heal your scar. Then it's to rest for you."

"And you." He handed her the cup and laid back. She placed their cups on the tray and returned, sitting on the side of the bed.

Wrapping her hand around her pulsing medallion she whispered, "Source of life, heal through me."

Fire rippled in concentric circles outward, covering her chest in wavering crimson tendrils. It flashed down her arm and out through her palm cupping his wound. He sucked in a sharp breath. It was warm for her but seared him, his skin blushing around her palm. A fine sheen of sweat formed on his brow and upper lip. The fire smothered itself as quickly as it burst into life.

"It's done," she whispered with her palm still resting on his chest.

Focus on his healing, Joi had leaned over him. She straightened her spine, yanking her hand away. Twisting, she bent to wring out the cloth and hold it to his chest. He sighed, his eyes fluttering closed, sparing her from his observant stare. After a few minutes, she folded the cloth, dropped it into the water bowl, then rose to her feet. She didn't make it far when he wrapped his long fingers around her wrist to keep her close.

"Thank you, Joi." His crystal-blue gaze met hers.

"You did save my life, Mighty Sohar," she said.

"And you have saved mine."

She frowned, not liking that he thought the life debt settled. He wouldn't be sporting a wound if he hadn't thrust her aside. When she tugged on her hand but he refused to release it, her eyebrows rose in query.

"There is only the one bed. You best climb in with me." He tapped the bed, making his request clear.

Everything within her stilled as she eyed the length of him taking up most of the bed. There wasn't space for her, and he knew it.

"Blow out the candles, and come to bed. This might be the last softness you sleep on for weeks." He frowned at her hesitancy. Her reticence raised too many questions. He couldn't discover how much she admired him.

She huffed. He did have a point. Last night's sandy bed left her stiff this morning. He released her wrist, allowing her to hasten the darkness. Before she did, she looked at him, finding he had rolled onto his right side and shifted with his back against the wall.

Without the familiar warmth of the candles, moonlight filtered through the shutters, casting a silver glow on all it touched. Flicking her fingers, she tossed a Scarlet spark at the door. "Source of life, safeguard me this night." The Fox shimmered over the door, blanketing it. Her medallion gave off a reassuring hum.

Resigned, she sat on the bed and removed her boots, dropping them next to his before lying down with her back to him. Joi stayed close to the edge with her left hand gripping the side. With a sigh from him, he looped his arm around her waist and pulled her back until the warmth of his length soaked into her.

Her heart hammered at their closeness. She had never laid with a man like this before.

"Now sleep, my Xiaxan Fox." The weight of his arm pinned her in place.

Sleep eluded her as she analyzed the tone of his voice and the new term of—dare she think it—endearment. Castigating herself for her pointless thoughts, she proceeded to list the reasons why he shouldn't show interest in marrying her. Yet despite the extensive list, with some items on there not so flattering, she couldn't help the continued staccato of her heartbeat.

Listening to his steady breathing, she whispered, "Source of life, cleanse me." She hoped it would rid her of these irrational emotions. As the Scarlet Fox slithered through her, it did nothing except solidify in her lower belly for a while before returning to the medallion. With a snort at her own silliness, she realized there was no easy solution for this.

She would have to guard her heart.

A deep sigh loosened from her chest. The warmth of him was soothing, and the weight of his arm on her waist she now found comforting. Sinking into the bed, she allowed solace to find her.

Chapter Twenty

Good

Sohar awoke to find himself staring up at the ceiling again. He was warm, bordering on sweltering, with an unexpected weight pressing on his thigh. The scent of jasmine tickled his nose, and he glanced down, searching for the source.

Joi-Joi.

Her head rested on his chest, her right arm and leg wrapped his body as if to keep him close to her. Sometime during his sleep, when he had, at last, found solace, he had looped his arm around her with his hand cupping her hip. Drawing in a slow, silent breath, he allowed himself this enjoyment. He had never awoken with a woman before. Most of his concubines left him as soon as he fell asleep. The few wanting to stay had hidden agendas that didn't include his happiness.

The sun's rising light bathed the room through the shutters. It was almost time to awaken, but he was reluctant to disturb her sleep. Nuzzling the crown of her head with his chin, he savored the freshly released jasmine. As a princess, she had behaved and performed above reproach on this journey.

Her skill during the skirmish had impressed him. She was an excellent sparring partner, but since their last match years ago, she had acquired confidence. Her techniques were not just Xiaxan though, and he couldn't state their origin. He would ask her about it at some point.

She stirred, and her fluttering eyelashes mesmerized him. Her lips parted on a soft sigh, and still ascending through the depths of her solace, she shifted closer. Her fingertips stroked his skin above his heart, swirling a tingling heat in his chest.

Why did she affect him so? A question he asked himself from the time he had started his Xiaxan training. For a person who endured the loss of her family, she exuded an effervescence that had at first irritated him. It appeared to him as if she didn't take the mentors seriously. He voiced as much, and to his disgust, his mentors paired them. Day by day, she had sparred with him, taunted him, tested him.

She still did. More so now she was older. More so when she rubbed her cheek against his chest, humming in pleasure. Tempted to pretend he hadn't noticed, to feign sleep, Sohar didn't want to embarrass her with their intimate embrace. When she gasped, and her head flew up to meet his gaze, he forwent the opportunity at ignorance. A sleepy-faced Joi was breathtaking.

He drowned in the molten amber of her eyes as her breath fanned his chin. This close he could pull her down and kiss her. He glided his hand from her hip, up her back, as if to do just that. Her fingers flickered where they rested on his chest, her touch scorching hot.

"How...how are you feeling, Mighty Sohar?" She lowered her gaze, breaking the hypnotic connection.

He cleared his throat and drew in a deep breath. "I am well, Joi-Joi."

She nodded, then slid off the bed backward, as if she didn't trust him not to strike. As innocent as she was, she had good instincts. They would serve her well when she assumed her royal seat. When he made no attempt to restrain her, she sighed, the same deep sigh she reserved for Kylen when she escaped punishment. Sohar had heard it many times before, and the sound of it always tempted him to smile. She twisted as soon as her feet touched the floor, and the sweep of her unraveling braid brushed over his arm.

"Sohar, the sun's rising—we need to hurry. I'll dash down to speak to the innkeeper if you need to...um, cleanse?" Color splashed across her translucent skin, and an urge gripped him to test the warmth of her cheeks with the pads of his thumbs.

"There's no need. I did so last night while you cooked for us."

"Good." She rose from the bed, scooped up her boots, then dropped into the wooden chair to put them on. Grabbing his clean tunic, she held it out to him as if she was his servant. He accepted the offered garment, despite having only swung his legs over the side of the bed. The heat of her body still emanated from the bedding, warming his backside and thighs.

He slipped the white tunic on, freeing his hair from under the cloth, then attended to his boots. As she untangled then combed her hair, her jasmine scent permeated the room. She braided her long ebony strands with quick, deft fingers before tying the end with a ribbon.

"Did you pack a comb?" She offered her jade comb as if she didn't understand the significance of sharing combs. His heart leaped to choke him, at the idea of sharing something so intimate and what it meant under Greyadian law.

"You know I cannot, Joi-Joi," he said, sorrow straining his voice. It would be a declaration of his intention to court her. As much as he wanted to be, he wasn't the man for her.

"Sharing a bed isn't a declaration?" she teased, her lips curling in that mesmerizing way of hers. "We're escaping, Sohar. I'm not placing any significance on anything we must endure for expediency. Comb?" She offered it again, and with a sigh, he accepted it. "If I attended to your hair, then *that* would be a declaration." She held out a ribbon from her traveling bag.

He grunted, accepting it too.

"Your coloring is unusual in Meideon. You draw as much notice as I do." She tied on her leather armor. Withdrawing her gold pouch, she counted out two gold coins before pulling on her cloak and flicking the hood over her head. Her mischievous smile remained visible, that and the jut of her stubborn little chin. He couldn't help but observe as she sheathed her sword, slid her dagger into her boot, clipped her token to her belt, and stroked the medallion nestled between her breasts.

Wrapping her bag's strap across her chest, she turned to the sealed door. "Source of Life, return to me." The red tendrils unraveled their intricate patterns and returned to her, engulfing her chest before dissolving.

"I would suggest skipping the morning meal in the common room. We can stop somewhere along the Xysion river." Drawing his sword from its scabbard, he scanned it for bloodstains before sheathing it. His dagger hadn't left his boot, his token hung where she had tied it, and his coin pouch still weighed down his cloak.

Joi bounced on her toes, sharing her eagerness to depart. "I agree, less chance of someone recognizing us or a repeat of yesterday's adventure."

Slipping into his cloak, he settled his bag across his chest, and crowded her to prevent her from going down the stairs first. She halted to glare at him, resting her hands upon her hips as her foot tapped out her frustration.

"I didn't need this last night," she said.

"Last night I was unable to see to your care." Grimacing, he acknowledged how he failed her. "I am well now, and it is, therefore, my duty to protect you."

"Duty, honor, I know what they mean, Sohar, but does everything have to revolve around them?" She pouted, throwing a sad expression at him. "Couldn't it just be because you care?" She shook her head and pressed a dramatic hand to her temple.

He inched closer to soothe her, raising his hands to grasp her upper arms. Her grin was mischievous, and she darted around him, dashing down the stairs with her laughter tinkling off the walls.

Thank the Divine his father and masters weren't there to see him. His smile felt good, the rumble of laughter within him both warm and incredible. Taking the stairs at his leisure, he watched her stare up from the bottom. Her name suited her. Joi—bringing life and laughter wherever she went.

"My Xiaxan Fox, I won't always be so easily deceived," he promised.

She nibbled her bottom lip, her focus distant. "True, but until then, I will enjoy this journey for the adventure it is. Once I become queen, Sohar, such experiences will be rare."

Sorrow pierced him. She would lose her vibrancy, perhaps grow to resent her destiny. "Not if you surround yourself with joyful people, Joi-Joi."

"How many grumpy advisors surrounded Da and now Kylen? How many surround your father? They're unavoidable. It seems rulers are not taken seriously without grumpy advisors at their side." She chuckled. "And old."

"Find young advisors, virile generals tested in battle or those glib with tongue." A vision of her surrounded by handsome young men throbbed pain across his temple.

"Ah, my own harem?" she teased, rubbing her chin as if she considered his suggestion valid.

"That's not what I meant, Princess, and you know it." He strolled past her and into the common room.

"Still a valid suggestion. When last has a queen ruled any of the realms?" she whispered, skipping to catch up to him. The innkeeper spotted them from across the busy room and rushed over. She held gold out for the man to accept. "Are our garments ready? The food pouch?"

"Yes, Mistress, as requested." The innkeeper beamed. Sohar suspected the gold and their departure lightened the man's mood. "I took the liberty of asking the stableman to send two of his best horses over. They await you outside." He bowed as he escorted them down the front of steps to the tethered horses. "Within the food pouch is cold meats and fresh bread for you to break your fast."

Sohar hid a chuckle at the innkeeper's desperate attempt to see Joi on her way. She said she had singed his eyebrows, and judging by their thinness, she hadn't lied. He dropped another gold coin into the innkeeper's palm as if to apologize for her treatment of him. Hooking his traveling bag—now filled with freshly washed garments—and the bulging food pouch onto the leather saddle, Sohar vaulted onto his horse.

Gathering the reins, he nodded at the innkeeper before spurring his horse east. He wanted onlookers to witness them leaving through the same gate they arrived at, and he did this by riding his horse. Doing so elevated him above the crowd, drawing attention. Joi cantered behind him, once again silent.

Chapter Twenty-One

Drained

Rannic's knees almost crumpled when he touched down in the Wood of Yellow Suns east of Vaeril. Too exhausted to form thoughts and too drained to do much more, he stumbled toward the stone bridge crossing the Xysion river. He had traveled vast distances until dawn foiled his approach. Not willing to lose more time, he had used his magic to conceal him. The punishment, if caught flying, would be magic suppression for one year. To do that to a royal would strip his power, his authority. He couldn't recall the Drem chronicles mentioning one disobedient royal across all the realms.

"Did a Greyadian pass through here?" Once the words left his mouth, he smothered a grimace. Too used to demanding, he hadn't thought to curb his tone. When the gate guard glared at him, he pressed his fingertips to his forehead and bowed his head in apology. "Forgive my lack of courtesy. I am concerned. He has abducted my younger sister, and I need to find them." The lie trickled off his well-oiled tongue—a skill learned at a young age in the courts of Drem.

The guard's expression softened. "Yes, a Greyadian did pass here with a cloaked figure trailing him. You'll have a problem convincing her to leave with you, sir. She was a willing follower."

Rannic grinned in delight, pleased he had found them. He shook his head at the guard as if he were the long-suffering brother. "She's too naïve to realize he's poison to her. What time did they pass you? Today?"

"Just after sunrise, heading east." He pointed in the direction of Ethrielle.

East? Rannic's brow furrowed. He ignored his trembling knees and paced in front of the guard. Why would Sohar take her back to Meideon's Royal City? Was she ill? He voiced as much, and the guard informed him that all he had seen was her chin. Ah, cloaked, with her gold eyes hidden? As Rannic had suspected, she did not believe she was ready to rule. He should have expected such a cowardly act from a Letouran.

He was so close he could taste the victory. Imagining her shocked expression spurred him on, filling him with renewed energy. "Is there a stable nearby? I need to procure a horse."

"The closest one is past the Token of Kings Inn, and may I suggest, you see to yourself first before you chase after your sister?" The guard gestured to Rannic's wrinkled garments. "It does no good if you cannot fight for her honor, sir."

He grimaced but refused to slide his palms down the tunic as if they alone could iron it smooth. "Yes, thank you for your concern. An hour's rest would refresh me."

"May the Divine assist you, sir." The guard bowed.

He had never thought kindness could be such an effective tool. Striding toward the inn, Rannic ignored the colorful feathers, not caring what the peasants did to entertain themselves. A meal, rest, and a good horse, and then he would find Jenaso soon enough.

Although, what he would do or say when he did find them had yet to clarify in his mind. The thought of killing Sohar was delicious, but Rannic wasn't a fool. The battle deeds of the Crown Prince of Greyad entertained royal courts and winehouses, having reached Manorio, as well. Sohar should not expect the killing blow. Perhaps poison? No, too unpredictable. A challenge? No, it would place Sohar on the offensive, then every attack Rannic made, no matter how cunning, he would predict. An arrow? Yes, unanticipated, invisible, perfect.

Once Sohar's blood saturated the ground, Rannic would claim the silly princess in the sodden soil. If she behaved, she could keep her horse, but if not, he would toss her over his saddle. To say he had endured enough for the woman was an understatement. He hadn't exerted this much effort for the lesser gender in all his years. They were pawns and needed constant reminders, a chore he found untold pleasure in performing. He had never found a sturdy woman though, one capable of enduring his harsher delights, and Jenaso's weak royal form wasn't promising. Although she had an air of stubbornness about her that he liked. It implied her will was stronger than her body. Breaking her might prove a worthy challenge.

The innkeeper ushered him to a low table and served a variety of dishes. The food was suitable, the wine palatable, but more importantly, the horse and a change of garments would arrive within the hour. Once more soaking in the wooden tub the innkeeper had prepared, Rannic grimaced at finding himself in steaming water sixteen hours after he departed from Moury. At least he found their trail, what little consolation he could derive from that.

Ringing the bell, he instructed the bobbing innkeeper to bring him a variety of bows. From the comfort of his tub, he procured a decent weapon the local bowyer assured him was of the finest yellowwood. The innkeeper, having placed a dark pile of garments on the bed, cast concerned glances at him. Rannic assumed the princess had found solace at this very inn.

"What say you, old man?" he asked the prostrate innkeeper when the bowyer left. "I seek a Greyadian." Rannic gestured to him to rise.

"They left at sunrise this morning, my lord. The woman was generous with coin, but I was most pleased to see their backs." Fear darted across the man's face. Intriguing. What could the weak princess have done to garner such a reaction?

"She harmed you?" Rannic faked concern with a well-creased forehead. His gaze traveled the man's body, looking for injuries but didn't expect to find any.

He shook his head. "She has golden eyes and red magic. An ominous union."

"Red?" His voice rose in alarm, and he sat up to study the truth on the man's face, ignoring the spilling water.

"Yes, my lord." The man bowed and scurried out after Rannic flicked his fingers.

"She has the Scarlet Fox?" he asked the empty room. "What a waste—such power in one so weak. But how did she activate it?" He sank into the water, and his head dropped back as he stared at the ceiling, recalling the procedures to activate energy. Only one possible approach came to mind, one that was the most plausible. "She has the Medallion of Scarlet Mirrors. Oh, this is good."

The smile crawling across his face felt delicious. Once he had her, he had the ancient medallion. According to the chronicles, it was a magical artifact crafted by the Orthians and contained more power than any existing relic. Most of the revered magical artifacts vanished in the Battle of Heaven's Fire. And this pitiful princess had the Fox and the medallion.

He was grateful to have this knowledge, serving as a warning not to underestimate her. It doubled her value. After her death, he would have Letoura and the artifact. Now he understood Sohar's determination to have the princess for himself. The realms would concede defeat, to submit to a higher power. The Greyadian forces with the Scarlet Fox? Invincible...*if* Sohar kept her alive.

Greyad was a sizable realm and merging it with Letoura would allow them to dominate the remaining three realms. Should any of the Greyadian princes marry the Crown Princess of Seit, this world, as he knew it, would alter and not in his favor.

Too energized to remain in the tub any longer, Rannic climbed out, braided his wet hair, and dressed in the cotton garments the innkeeper had brought. It wasn't of the finest silk and without silver threads sewn into them, but they were black and clean.

Dressed, his token secured, his pouch hidden, and his sword at his hip, he clambered down the steps to drop two gold coins into the innkeeper's hand. With a hopeful smile, he leaped into the tethered horse's saddle. He was so close. With a nudge into the horse's flanks, it bolted forward, startling a few peasants. Ignoring them, he galloped down the pebbled street, laughing as Vaerilians dived out of his way.

He burst through the town's gate and across the bridge over Xysion river. If he made good time, he would reach Cour late this evening. He didn't want to think about being in the saddle for that long again. "Curse you, Jenaso."

Despite the coiling dark whispers of hate in his chest, he remained on the road. Within the hour, he drew the horse to a halt to stretch his legs for a few minutes. The Wood of Yellow Suns was on the horizon, the yellow leaves and bark glowing gold under the sun's light. Despite the glimmering beauty of it, something bothered him again. The last time he had this feeling he had realized Sohar deceived him.

Unlooping his token, he held it in front of him and waved his black magic over it. Ebony tendrils unraveled around his fingers to embrace the carvings on it. Black shimmers wavered, forming his father's face.

"Rannic," he said in greeting, his voice as hard as the volcanic stone of the token.

"Father, how far into Orth is the Greyadian army?" He didn't bother with niceties. His father didn't appreciate them, and Rannic didn't feel *nice* toward him.

Rumoc glared, not answering. "You look drained. Your magic is not visible. If you die, I'll have to find another concubine, and you know how I hate inconvenience."

"I don't have time for this. Where is the army now?" He clipped each word in his question for emphasis. "Or don't answer me, and Greyad can have the princess, the Scarlet Fox, and the Medallion of Scarlet Mirrors."

"Truth?" Rumoc's voice softened in awe. He glanced to the side, and the background behind him shifted as he crossed his throne room to the war table. "They are south of the Mouths of Varturg."

Rannic frowned. That was a long journey into the hazards of Orth. "Have they fought any battles, skirmishes, or have they been there for some time?" As if they waited for a certain prince and his package.

Rumoc shook his head, a puzzled expression instead of his usual scowl removed years off his visage. "Approximately a week with no noteworthy reason to be that far into Orth."

"Oh, they have reason. Sohar's taking her through Orth. Curse him." Rannic waved his hand over his token then tied it onto his belt.

He untied the traveling bag from the saddle, one filled with garments and food—a generous gift from the innkeeper. The horse bolted toward its home, Vaeril, after he slapped its rear. Looping the bag over his shoulder, he paused with his arms outstretched. With long calming breaths, he closed his eyes, and sent out his senses, searching for the magical pulse of the land. It was weak for a foreigner, but every ounce of energy would aid him.

He coerced the glowing power into his body, and with his black energy encircling him, he launched himself skyward. West to the Gates of Exted, Bray's Pass, and into Orth. Four hours, at the most.

Chapter Twenty-Two

Affection

The sounds of the winds brushing,
The leaves of their sorrowful sighs,
The memory of longing-filled lovers,
Buried by daggers and cries.

SOHAR SMILED AS HE listened to Joi sing. Her voice carried in the winds, lyrical and husky, evoking emotions on behalf of the doomed lovers. He knew the song well, an ancient one often performed in winehouses, yet never heard at court. It was a pity, for it was such a beautiful story.

The Northern Hokhoun Mountains loomed as they approached. They were snow-capped on the tips, and the temperature cooled the closer they traveled. Taking a more indirect route from Endon bypassed the Forest of the Unloved. The remains of the unclaimed fallen soldiers from the Battle of Heaven's Fire were still present.

The whistling winds sifting through the trees wailed the loss of their loved ones.

Some trees embraced the skeletons, now displaying them in their trunks and limbs. It was a macabre scene, worsened by the gray trees bleeding black, which only the brave harvested. He lost himself in his thoughts as he peered into the depths of the forest. He hadn't realized he had jerked his horse to a halt until Joi stopped alongside him.

Her hood had fallen back shortly after they left Endon, and the sunlight kissed her hair like volcanic rock. That was better than calling it oru. Her pale skin glowed with vibrancy, her cheeks flushing from the sun's warmth. She needed to stay covered when they traveled through Orth. He grimaced, imagining what the harsh winds would do to her soft skin.

"I thought I saw someone in the forests. Do you think they need help?" Her hand rested on the hilt of her sword, conveying she was ready.

Sohar shook his head. "They farm oru, a black substance used to water-seal boats."

"I can hear the wind's sad voice from here. I can't decide if those men are brave or stupid." Joi flashed a smile and steered the horse onto the paved road leading straight to the Gates of Exted carved into the side of the mountains.

The structure had stood for hundreds of years since the battle and served as the only entrance into Orth. There was no access from Letoura through the Hokhoun Mountains, and Greyad had built the Kilryn Wall to keep the banished within Orth.

Greenery from Meideon rolled up to the foot of the mountains, up through Bray's Pass. Once they ventured down the western slopes, arid soil and hot winds would greet them. The burning sunlight bathed the gates' façade. Stone supplied by each realm was discernible in the striated construction. It served as a visual reminder of the unanimous decision to seal off Orth. The Kilryn Wall was of the same donations: black volcanic rock from Drem—shipped while it still cooled, the gray stone from Seit's oceans—smoothed over eons by crashing waves and variegated brown stone from Meideon—mined in the Bowels of Abarat. From Letoura, they had carved snow granite out of the south-facing Hokhoun Mountains. The mortar Greyad supplied, a realm sworn to uphold the hard-fought peace. There was symbolism in that.

> *Oh, ceaseless winds, where is my lover now?*
> *Tell him of my hollowness, tell him of our child,*
> *Whisper to him the words of our lovers' song,*
> *Let the twilight embrace him, so he is not alone.*

Sweet happiness warmed his chest, affecting his stoic features like a disease he couldn't cure. Joi must have felt free of spirit to add her voice to all those who revered the words. This delighted him. She continued to sing as they neared the gates, a siren song calling the guards to attention. The gates were immense, and it often felt that no matter how far or fast they traveled, they would never reach them.

The soft whistle of a seeking arrow was the only warning. Sohar yelled out, but he need not have worried. A bolt of scarlet fire burst out from her, incinerating the shaft. Its singed feathers fluttered around her like the ashes of an erupting volcano. Another whistle sounded, fusing into a whine, and he knew there was more than one this time. He vaulted out of his saddle to land in a fighting lunge. He had drawn his sword, its point brushing the tips of the grass.

Daring a glance to the right, he noted Joi had done the same. Instead of drawing her sword, balls of scarlet spiraled in her palms. Her hair whipped around her as if disturbed by a violent wind when there was not a breeze stirring. She rolled her palms over her forearms and a massive sphere surrounded her and her horse.

Sohar grunted, and threw out a hand, palm facing the hidden foes. A shimmering wall of white formed in front of him. He clicked his tongue at his horse, and it moved closer to him.

"See anything?" She sidled closer, and heat from her sphere brushed against him, coating his body with a fine sheen of sweat.

"They must be in the forest." He pointed with his sword. "It's a strategic attack point."

"I'm lost as to what to do, Mighty Sohar." Even in danger, she didn't cease to tease him with the endearment. "If we turn around and continue to travel, they'll keep firing those arrows. If we go toward them, they might flee deeper into the forest."

"Joi, we ride for the gates, keeping our shields up."

"I can't." Fear darkened the gold of her eyes. "I only know how to create this sphere, not move with it. It might harm my horse."

"Ride alongside me—I'll widen my shield." He sheathed his sword and climbed into the saddle, using one hand to haul himself up. He hadn't wanted to vault up in case the shield shifted. Their attackers would wait for a gap, no matter how small. Once seated, he spun to face the rear of his horse and added his other palm to the shield. It expanded, shimmering above the grass. Sweat drenched his forehead, and his arms trembled with the exertion, his energy draining. He searched for a stray pulse to replenish his stores, but this close to Orth, magic was elusive.

Lunging closer, she smothered her Fox then vaulted into the saddle. She gathered his reins before urging both horses into a canter. Arrows ricocheted off the shield, each strike reverberating up his arms. Now at a full gallop, he prayed to the Divine they would be out of range soon.

"Source of light, heal through me." Joi placed her hand on his upper arm. Scarlet tendrils slithered along her fingers and dissolved into his tunic. A burst of warmth and healing flooded him, lessening his trembling, and replenishing a little of his power.

Grateful, he sucked in a much-needed breath. "Thank you, Joi-Joi. How far are we?"

"We're close enough to see the guards' faces, but Sohar, the arrows have lessened." She peered through the transparent shield. "There's no one trailing us either."

He lowered his hands, thinning the shield to test their unseen attackers. The fresh arrows fell short, confirming they were no longer in range. Sighing, he dropped the shield, then faced forward in his saddle. She tossed him his reins, and they hunkered down for the final few miles to the gates. The two guards rushed forward as they drew to a halt, the horses' hooves clattering on the cobbled bridge.

"Greetings, my prince, my lady." A gate guard bowed, his staff sweeping to the side in the formal gesture—exquisitely performed, as expected of a Greyadian. "We saw the attack, but I apologize, Greyad has forbidden us to abandon our posts to aid you."

"We needed no help, but my thanks for your concern. Any travelers heading to Orth?" Sohar patted his horse's sweaty neck as it pawed the paved stones.

"Not before your arrival, my prince."

"Good. Any missives for your loved ones?" He was en route to Greyad, and it was an expected protocol to offer. Above all his men, as the crown prince, he must adhere to the same standards. Only those men who valued solitude guarded the dreaded gates of Orth. To offer to deliver missives or a gift in parting was a courtesy defined in Greyadian history and still practiced today.

"Thank you, my prince, but it is unnecessary. A missive for you arrived two days ago, from Prince Vard." The guard held out a folded parchment. He bowed as he did so with his hand cupping his forearm.

His brother Vard's white stamp sealed the document. Since it was from a prince, they assumed it held importance, and thus kept it close at hand.

Sohar gestured to his food pouch. "Allow me to offer a carafe from my traveling bag."

"Our thanks, my prince, but we would not wish to deny you the much-needed sustenance for your journey across Orth."

"Then I bid you farewell and Divine-blessed." Sohar bowed, his hand over his heart, and the nod he bestowed upon the guards was well-received.

They followed courtesy, their mannerisms, and etiquette as expected of Greyadian soldiers. He slid the letter inside his cloak and led his horse behind him. They would swap the horses with camels at the Gates of Cytium Va on the western side of the mountains. Once they passed through the steel portcullis, it rattled shut behind them, sealing them between the two gates and trapping them on the mountain. He mounted his horse, and after Joi did the same, he led her through the pass.

The wind was biting, its icy teeth piercing his cloak which he gathered closer. A glance back revealed she had done the same, her hood once more drawn over her face. He smothered a smile for he had a surprise for her, one he knew she would enjoy.

By the time they veered off the path into the hidden grove, the break from the incessant wind was welcome. The grove was as he remembered. Green grass and rainbow blossoms surrounded them. The air was warm and heady with exotic fragrances. He dismounted and hurried to gather her reins in his hands. Her gaze darted around them, delight clear in her sparkling eyes.

"We camp here tonight?" Her eager voice rivaled the delight painting her features with vivid beauty.

He nodded, not trusting his voice. She dismounted, and he led the horses away, careful to tether them in a safe area. As fragrant as these flowers were, a few were deadly.

"Come, Joi-Joi." He offered her his hand, and she accepted it without hesitation, flashing him a bright smile. "I'll fetch our things once I show you where we will find solace."

"It's warm here, Mighty Sohar," she said, breathless in wonder. "These flowers are beautiful, but I don't recognize any of them. Orthian?"

"Yes, the last known paradise." He escorted her through tall lillyspring trees, their silver bark glistening in the fading light. As the moon rose, the trees would come to life, luminescent in the moonlight. Shoulder-high cobaltmists swayed as they passed, their blossoms turning to follow them. The bloodvines stretched knee-high—a dark red grass, as soft as it was strong.

Leading them into a stone-floored clearing, he spied his surprise, gurgling a happy welcome among the wall of flowers. "Bathe. Call if you need me."

He should have expected her squeal of delight and her arms wrapped around him for a crushing hug, but yet, as per usual, she surprised him. Unable to deny the need to hold her, he gathered her against him, but released her sooner than he liked.

As he walked away, the whisper of falling garments and her groan of pleasure disturbed the rhythm of his heart. He wanted to watch her bathe, see the expressions playing across her face, bask in the unfettered joy of her smile. For these reasons, he stayed with the horses, brushing them down with more vigor while she sang.

My ever-yearning arms, my endless tears,
A thousand dying suns and uncaring moons,
Across rivers of ice forming frozen fears,
With no beloved at the eternal gates.

"Sohar," she called. "Please, can you bring my soap?"

He scowled, having not anticipated this. Rummaging through her traveling bag, he found the white bar of soap carefully wrapped in thick cloth. Unable to resist, he brought it to his nose to sniff. Sweet jasmine. He groaned before taking another deep inhalation, as if to memorize the scent of her. Looping her bag over one shoulder, he stomped his way there, announcing his arrival.

There was nothing to concern him, for she had sunk into the water with her chin resting on the surface. There was an occasional glimpse of a pale bare shoulder and the glimmer of her ruby-gold medallion. Her unbound hair swirled behind her, and her face glowed against the dark depths. He lowered the soap onto the rocky edge of the heated pool, her bag farther away.

"Thank you." She smiled.

He nodded, leaving her alone once more. Each step away, he took under duress. A little while later, she shouted it was safe to return. This time she was out of the pool and dressed in her pants and tunic. She was braiding her wet hair, holding the tresses away from her as each flick of her fingers sprayed droplets.

Sohar lowered his bag alongside hers and watched her fling her braid behind her as he removed his boots, dropping them on the floor. Joi stood transfixed when he removed his cloak and undid his belt, his sword and token still attached. With a soft gasp, she hurried, chin-down, toward the pathway, granting him the same privacy he had offered her.

Fear spiked through him. When she bathed, he was between the road and the pool. With him bathing, there was no one to protect her. "No, stay, please. I will be vulnerable in the pool and cannot come to your aid should you need me."

"Stay here?" Her voice squeaked as she glanced at the path, then at him before nodding. She strolled to the opposite side of the entrance and dropped to the ground, keeping her back to him.

He nodded, content with this solution. As he undressed, he caught her brushing her fingers across the bloodvines' blades. They paled to pink under her caress. He shivered, imagining her running her fingers across his skin.

"This is the Hot Pools of Heaven's Fire?" Her voice warbled and wasn't as strong as he had come to know it.

He lowered himself into the hot water and sighed, dipping to wet his hair.

"Yes, fed by the Klakk River and heated by the molten rivers the Orthian warlords summoned." Contentment descended upon him as he allowed the water to loosen his stiff muscles.

Joi didn't say anything but continued to hum, her voice as soothing as the water. She rose to her feet in one fluid motion and faced him. Her sudden confidence surprised him. As she circled the pool, he appraised her body, taking note of certain curves he had no right to look upon.

"Would you like to use my soap, *Ozu*?" She kept her tone light even as she glared a warning.

Sohar frowned. Were they not alone?

Chapter Twenty-Three

An Unpleasant Visitor

Every splash Sohar made shot across Joi's sensitive nerves. The naked man bathing behind her drew her full attention. At least running her fingers over the long, red blades of grass distracted her a little. The red faded to a pretty pink as she touched it. Everything about this grove was beautiful. Her botany studies had been on existing plants, not on those made extinct in the battle. She smiled. Not as extinct as her mentors had believed.

The heady fragrance in the air was overwhelming with the scents merging to form an intoxicating blend. Knowing the flowers' names would have been wonderful. The tall blue ones were disturbing and delightful when they followed her every move. The silver trees stood tall with pride and the swaying red grass was soft to the touch. Other flowers peeked at her from the thick living wall. Little yellow ones and long-petalled pink blossoms. Perhaps Sohar knew their names.

One looked like brown eyes... Fear, sharp and suffocating, froze her when she realized they *were* real eyes. Someone was watching them. This man had seen her bathing...naked. Fury burned through her, inflaming her cheeks, and traveling down her neck as she forced herself to look away as casual as possible. She chewed on her bottom lip, wondering how best to warn Sohar.

Running her fingers across the red blades, she assessed the situation. Her dagger was still in her boot, and her sword still hung on her belt, which was resting on top of her bag. At least she had bathed with her medallion, so she had the Fox with her. The Fox was inside her too, but she hadn't yet grasped the enormity of that. Besides, the heavy weight of the medallion comforted her as if her father was still with her.

She rose to her feet, making sure she didn't glance in the man's direction. Facing Sohar, she hadn't expected his broad shoulders and the silver of his wet hair to mesmerize her. His blue eyes strangled her voice, and held onto it, making her struggle to speak past the lump in her throat. He was breathtaking. Oh, Divine!

But the visitor...

"Would you like to use my soap, *Ozu*?" She dusted off her pants as she circled the pool, trying to convey they weren't alone. Kneeling beside her bag, she placed her cloth-wrapped soap on the side of the pool, then picked up her belt.

"Thank you," he said. His lips flattened to a thin, grim line. He understood her message, and she smiled as joyfully as she could muster.

She strapped on her belt and yanked on her boots, then sat on the stone floor, facing the intruder, halfway between him and the pool. He would have to move past her if his target was the Prince of Greyad.

"These flowers are beautiful. Do you know their names?" Joi brushed her gaze across the wall of blossoms. The question was an excuse to keep her focus on *him*. She had wanted to ask Sohar anyway. A movement and a flicker of light on metal stiffened her muscles. The intruder held a weapon. The light reflection wasn't off a polished metal as expected of a dagger or sword. It was a duller metal—iron, perhaps? A javelin? A crossbow?

Telltale splashes and droplets splattered against the surface of the pool when Sohar rose out of the water. Bare feet slapped the stone as if he jumped up and down to shake off most of the water. Whispers of fabric, followed by grunts and huffs, meant he struggled as she had when she pulled her pants over her wet legs. Envisioning him dressing distracted her, but at the sound of the arrow's release, she sprung up and cried out, "Source of life, protect me."

The surge of fire gripped her as the Fox raced to engulf her. The arrowhead pierced her chest—just the tip—before it splintered into a thousand pieces. The force of the strike was enough to send her stumbling backward. She clutched at the minor wound—the pain was sharp, breath-snatching, but not as crippling as the Fox healing her. She dropped to a crouch with a groan. The sound of another arrow leaving the bow made her burst forward, firing bolts of red toward it and the bowman.

The incinerated arrow brushed past her cheek, a burning, scarlet dart doomed to fail. The yelp from the visitor rushed her forward as Sohar materialized beside her, a white mist forming into his familiar shape. He sliced his hand with his dagger and flicked his blood at the man hidden among the flowers. A squeal penetrated the silence, followed by violent cursing, then a thump as the intruder hit the ground. Seconds later, there was no movement except desperate mumbling.

"What—?" Joi's curiosity won out. She curled her fingers to smother the tendrils still forming balls in her palms.

"Bloodvines attack anything bleeding." He strode into the living wall. Tall, bare-chested, and with his long commanding strides, he dazzled her.

She shook her head, trying to dislodge the strange hold he had over her. The fading light highlighting the rippling muscles on his back prompted her to squeeze her eyes shut, as well.

"But he's not bleeding." She popped an eye open before deciding if it was safe to follow behind him, unsheathing her sword as a precaution.

"Blood is on his body. That is all that matters." He crouched down alongside the bloodvine-entombed man. Sohar healed his hand before caressing the vines across the man's face until they receded. The man sucked in a desperate breath, his face dark and mottled yet somehow familiar.

"Prince Rannic, I cannot say I'm surprised."

At Sohar's calm tone, she leaned forward to study the bundled man's features.

Yes, burnished hair, darker skin, brown eyes...Rannic. Her stomach coiled.

"Curse you, Sohar! Release me." He struggled against the tightening vines.

Sohar's chuckle was cold. "Why would I do that? You attempted to kill me—and poorly."

Rannic met Sohar's mirth with defiance, his jaw clenched. "You have the princess, the Scarlet Fox, and the medallion...what else was I supposed to do?"

She bit her lip to keep her focus, horror solidifying in her chest at the thought of Sohar dying because of her. Moreover, Rannic thought of her as a tool, powerful yet only worthy as a pawn.

"He does not have me. I am not a possession, Drem." She spat, her fingers gripping the hilt of her sword. One kill and she would be free of him. The whisperings in her head were incessant, demanding she kill him. Pain shot through her temple, and she gasped, dropping her sword to grab at her head. She fell to her knees, fighting the agony, the screaming voices drowning out her own logic.

"Source of life, cleanse me," she mumbled as Sohar scooped her off the ground and against his warm body.

"Joi-Joi, listen to my voice. Focus on me, my Xiaxan Fox." His breath brushed her cheek and ear as he held her in a velvet-soft steel vise. The strength of it was comforting as if he would keep her safe even from herself.

"If I kill him now, I'll be free. The Scarlet Fox whispers this, Mighty Sohar." She twisted to look at him. He was so close her face reflected in his cerulean-blue eyes.

"There's still Rumoc." His gaze darted down, resting on her lips before meandering back to her eyes.

"True." She raised her hand to rest on his chest, above his heart. It pounded fast, tapping an erratic rhythm against her fingertips. The jasmine scent of him brought a smile to her lips, the humor in that silencing the whispers. "You can release me now. They're quiet."

"The Scarlet Fox remembers, Joi-Joi. The souls of your family, of your ancestors, they remember." He helped her to her feet before standing, as well, but kept her within the circle of his arms. She suspected he did so to ensure she found her balance.

"Thank you, Sohar." She cupped his cheek. As one, they faced a trapped Rannic.

"I travel to Greyad while Kylen selects my husband." She gritted her teeth. It angered her to have to explain it to this Drem. He didn't deserve the courtesy.

"Truly?" Rannic peered up at her, his arched brow implying he didn't trust her words.

"Why would I lie, Drem?" She squeezed and released her hilt, a dull ache forming at her temples. "You should have stayed in Ethrielle for Lord Aoni is most determined to win my hand."

"Lord Aoni?" He scoffed. Even Sohar's smirk curled his upper lip.

"He is without family, without obligations, and can devote himself to Letoura. You cannot say the same." She sucked in a shuddering breath before revealing her intentions. "I would release you from this revenge cycle, Rannic, lest we trap our descendants in an endless war."

"Revenge?" He narrowed his eyes.

"Yes, *my* revenge. Your father destroyed a city, slaughtered my family and my people, all for unrequited love. I have a right to seek revenge, to kill you where you lie." The medallion pulsed in agreement, and she covered it with her palm, stroking it to calm it. "Do I not speak the truth? Is your version of events different from mine?"

His forehead creased, his expression calculating, but then it softened, and he nodded. "My version is the same."

Rannic admitting to the truth surprised her, and she smiled at him. This was progress. If the two of them could breach the chasm between Drem and Letoura, it would usher in a time of peace.

Wait. Then why was he here? She frowned. "Then why do you seek me still?"

He shrugged, but it was slight with the strength of the bloodvines confining him. "At first, it was for my father. He still burns with hatred for all things Letouran. Then Sohar revealed what marrying you would bring to *me*, not my father. I believed, as he implied, he planned to marry you and conquer the known world, a Letoura-Greyad realm."

Joi couldn't help herself—she laughed at the absurdity of it. Yes, she would love to marry Sohar, but she had never hope he would consider it since she was like a sister to him and a fellow Xiaxan trainee. Purposely deceiving the Drem was worthy of a laugh though.

"It's called strategy, Drem." Sohar's chest swelled as if he was proud of his deception. "I wanted you to think I was taking her to Tennaba, thus granting us the time to escape to Greyad. I couldn't trust that you wouldn't continue on your father's murderous path."

"You don't realize the realms might force you two to marry regardless." Rannic snorted. "The princess has been in your care, unchaperoned, and at your mercy."

"I will demand an innocence assessment." She winced at the thought of an old woman probing her.

Both men's eyes bulged, and she smothered another laugh. This wasn't a casual meeting of friends. These were serious matters they were discussing, yet humor bubbled inside her. Her cheeks split wide in a constant smile.

"Sohar, one of these flowers wouldn't affect my mood, would it?" She chuckled at the idea of a giggling flower.

"Yes." His broad smile was as mind-numbing as always. "The cobaltmists release a variety of essences that affect a person's mind. We have been here long enough, I think."

He brushed his hand along the bloodvines, asking them to release Rannic, who lay there smiling with a dreamy expression on his face. Pulling him to his feet, they trailed her into the clearing. She gathered their things, including their boots, and followed them back to their horses. The crisp air was a welcome relief, since the hot pool heated the air around it, and she suspected, had intensified the strength of the cobaltmists' essences.

Sohar collected his boots from where she dropped them. She snuck peeks of him donning his tunic. Rannic collapsed on the ground, exhaustion rolling off him. She would offer to heal him if she could trust the Fox to do just that.

"Hungry?" She opened their food pouch to see what she could put together for a meal.

"Starving." Rannic hesitated, her unexpected kindness forming wariness in his eyes.

"Bread and cheese, as usual. I could kill for noodles." She placed the items on her spread-out cloak.

"The Token of Kings' innkeeper packed a food pouch, but it's back there." Rannic gestured to the pool. Sohar disappeared along the path to collect it. "He wasn't fond of you, said your red magic and golden eyes were ominous."

"Did he now? I should singe his eyebrows again, the old goat." Joi laughed at the memory. "During a skirmish, Sohar took a dagger for me, and the innkeeper had the nerve to claim he was without spare rooms."

"Skirmish? With whom?" His startled expression and stiff posture stilled her hands. She studied him for any signs of deceit.

Since it had been the Divine's disciples, she couldn't distrust his astonishment. "We suspect the Divine Priestess sent her disciples."

"It *is* odd." He frowned. "I assume it isn't Sohar they want since he is accessible so close to the temple in Raica, but why would she want you harmed?"

"My question as well." Sohar entered the clearing, handing Rannic his traveling bag.

A quick rummage, and Rannic rose to offer her the wrapped cold meats. "Not noodles but better?"

"Yes, thank you," she said.

"As I see it, you have two choices. Wait in Ethrielle with Joi's suitors, if that's still your intention, or return to Manorio." Sohar lowered himself next to her, his sword in one hand and a cloth in the other. His long, sure strokes of the cloth along the blade with the moonlight glimmering off the polished steel, were threatening yet comforting.

"Both are unacceptable to me." Rannic withdrew his own sword to "polish." "I cannot return to my father empty-handed. My death would be certain. It would anger him to find me in an Ethrielle without Jenaso."

Sohar paused, his hand tightening around the cloth. "I can't take you with us, and I don't want to. Crossing the barren wastelands is hazardous enough for a Greyadian, but the Orthians despise Drem more. They'll kill you on sight."

"You need not cross Orth now that I am with you. Surely this was all to deceive me?" Rannic said it without arrogance and for that, grudging respect grew.

She scowled at that thought—respect a Drem? Well, she supposed stranger things had happened.

"Some of her suitors are overzealous." Sohar arched a pointed brow. "Crossing Orth is the fastest route to Greyad. My second brother Vard is waiting. He has crows stationed at Bray, and when I deploy them, he will move my army east toward the Ruined City of Zugba. If Sister Luck is with us, we will remain unchallenged by the Orthians."

Rannic raised a clenched jaw, his eyes narrowing. "I will remain with you then."

"I don't trust you, and I will not keep a viper at my back, not when Joi's life is all that matters," Sohar roared, jumping to his feet to glare at the Drem, the tip of his sword an inch above the ground.

She knew that pose—it was a blatant challenge. Joi huffed, folding her arms across her chest at his usual only-her-life-matters nonsense.

"I say he comes with." She dropped her chin to her chest to hide her surprise. What in hell was she thinking? It was insane to keep an untrustworthy Drem royal with them. Sohar had the right of it. "He'll follow us anyway, Sohar. At least we can ensure he doesn't have an arrow pointed at your back."

She rose to hand him his bread and cold meat, forcing him to sheath his sword then offered Rannic his portion too before resuming her seat. She ignored their silent stares, hating that neither of them revealed their thoughts to her.

She threw a twisted smile at Sohar as she chewed on a bite of bread. "Then he can see you have no intention of having your way with me. He can give his father progress reports, keeping that side happy, and we can cross Orth with just the Orthians to worry about."

Rannic's face was a mask of confusion as if she had grown a dragon's tail. She laughed at his stunned expression, loving it. Sohar was angry with her, his stoic features hardening as he silently conveyed his disapproval. She laughed again, unable to resist teasing them both, preferring to blame the cobaltmists for her wicked behavior.

She rested her gaze on Rannic. "Perhaps, through marriage, you and I could form a bond strong enough to merge Drem and Letoura."

She loved their reactions. Rannic's held interest and dare she say excitement? Sohar's face had flushed, then hardened with fury. She had wanted to see him lose his unbreakable control, and he had. His stiff posture, white knuckles, and the pulse ticking at the base of his jaw told her he was ready to kill something. She almost snorted.

As if Kylen would match her with a Drem. They were both fools for taking her seriously.

Chapter Twenty-Four

Control

SOHAR DISBELIEVED HIS EARS. Had she said she would forgive the Drem? That she would consider marrying the deceitful viper? And she watched him with those large mesmerizing golden eyes of hers, looking innocent and logical. Yes, her reasons made sense, but it didn't *feel* right. He wanted Rannic as far from her as possible.

Her suggestions pleased the idiot. His expressive eyes rested too long upon the beautiful woman he had no right to breathe near, never mind marry. Choosing to kill Sohar with a bow was either cowardly or cunning. Rannic had to know a face-to-face would result in his untimely death. That alone was evidence of his untrustworthiness. And curse it, to have such a man travel with him—he would have two souls to protect through Orth. Not knowing the Drem prince's fighting abilities, he had to assume he was but a child. Should the man die during the journey, Drem would forever be at war with Greyad.

"I hear Manorio is a beautiful city when the sunlight glistens off your dark volcanic rock palaces," Joi said around mouthfuls of bread.

Sohar clenched his jaw, fighting the anger coursing through him. She acted as if she had settled the matter. It wasn't, not unless he said so.

"Curse Manorio—he *is not* coming with." He met her gaze then sighed when she raised her chin in defiance.

"Then I will stay here with him unless you plan on throwing me over your saddle?" She arched a smooth brow, challenging him.

He trembled with the need to punch something. "What I will do is throw you over my knee, Princess." He ground his teeth, taking a step toward her to do just that.

"Now, Sohar, you can't be serious." Rannic chuckled, but his eyes were wide in disbelief and an underlying delight.

He nodded, he had been right—Rannic was a viper. "She is under my authority as decreed by King Kylen, her brother. More than this, she acquiesced to my authority."

Rannic stilled. "You did?" His voice had lowered, surprised.

"Yes, Kylen is my king until I return to Tennaba." She nodded.

Sohar hated the implication, that he would lie about such matters. He gritted his teeth.

She focused on Rannic, and the slight pursing of her lips, noticeable to one who knew her well, meant she didn't trust the Drem either. "I am a naïve, untutored princess, and through me, my husband will reign as King of Letoura. It is wise that this decision rests upon Ky's shoulders."

Sohar glanced up at the dusk's sky to hide his smirk. She was playing the pawn the Drem prince believed her to be.

"Of course, Jenaso, but to grant Sohar full authority over your life and the direction of it?" Rannic tore off a chunk of black bread and popped it into his mouth.

"I am also stubborn and impetuous." Joi giggled, as if she were too youthful to understand the intrigues at court. "It is why Lord Nateo served as my constant shadow. My brother guards me, as does Sohar."

"Lord Nateo, King Buro's personal guard?" Rannic looked impressed, not that it mattered to Sohar. He needed this settled, but she spoke before he could.

"Sohar has decreed you cannot journey with us, Drem, and so, I must concede." She jumped up, dusted the crumbs off her pants, and slid on her armor, tying it in place. Her ruby token glistened in the dusk light as she wrapped her cloak around herself. She gathered their traveling bags, handed Rannic his, then blessed Sohar with a graceful bow. "I am ready, my prince."

He had meant to camp here for the night, but sleep would be elusive with a Drem nearby. They would have to find rest at the Gates of Cytium Va.

"Wait with the horses. I'd like a word with Rannic." Sohar used his imperial tone, hoping to appear the draconian guard she portrayed him as.

She skipped away on light feet, dutifully following his directives. He let a smile escape, since no one of worth could witness it. He had never seen her this obedient, the sly fox.

She was up to something. Once she was out of sight, he yanked Rannic to his feet and slammed a fist into his face. The man had little time to react.

"For trying to kill me," he growled, fisting Rannic's tunic as he swung another without hesitancy despite his knuckles stinging. The crack of bone was loud and satisfactory with blood gushing out amid the Drem's howl. "For harming Joi." He threw a punch into the man's gut, doubling him over. "And this is so you think twice about following us. I *will* kill you, Rannic, and conquer Drem if you come near her again."

He released the man's tunic and allowed him to crumple to the ground, shaking his hand to ease the throbbing and to flick off the blood—both his and Rannic's. Luckily for him, the bloodvines weren't on this side of the clearing.

"I'll get you for this," Rannic moaned, smearing his blood across his mouth.

"You can try. Just make sure Joi is nowhere near me or else you will die a swift, but painful, death." Sohar untied Rannic's token. He waved his hand over it and allowed his white magic to saturate the volcanic rock.

Rumoc's face formed, the shimmer not hiding his shock. "Prince Sohar, this is a surprise."

"Rein in your dogs, and the ships I will deploy to guard your shorelines will serve as a reminder. Continue pursuing this hatred, and I will task them to decimate Drem." Sohar met Rumoc's dark gaze. "Greyad has had enough of your selfishness."

"You threaten me? How dare you?" Rumoc's face mottled, noticeable through the wavering illusion. "You would start a war over a Letouran?"

"I will finish the war you started—a childish man with too much power. You chose this path, Rumoc, and by the Divine, I will end it." He closed the connection and flicked the token onto Rannic's chest. "Stay in Ethrielle, and perhaps Kylen will spare your life."

With a bounce to his step, Sohar left the prince and returned to Joi, who waited astride her horse, with his horse's reins gripped in her hands. She tossed them to him and steered her horse onto the path.

"You weren't serious about wanting him to travel with us?" he asked when they reached the main road and headed west. It wasn't wise to travel with the dying sun's light, but three hours from now, they would reach the gates into Orth.

"No, he expected a pawn, a girl lacking intelligence. I tried to keep him guessing, to underestimate me. I also wanted to assess his character, whether he is loyal to Rumoc or

Drem, and how committed he is to destroying Letoura." Her tone was cheeky. "Did it work?"

He grunted. "If I had agreed to his inclusion?"

"My reasons remain valid, but as you said, the Orthians hate Drem. If he died by their hands, that absolves us of his death, does it not?" She smothered a yawn, garbling her words.

"True and false. Taking him with would have led to his death, and knowing this does mean we are responsible. One Drem dead by our hands versus the thousands killed by Rumoc? Do forgive me, Princess, if I'm indifferent." He swirled his white magic over his knuckles, healing the lacerations. He could feel her stare pressing on him, but when he glanced up, she was facing forward. The wounds healed, but the blood smears remained.

"I am excited to see Orth, Sohar." Joi's face now hid in the shadows. The early-Orthian magic-hewn walls on each side of Bray's Pass meant there was no need for light. They could not plummet to their deaths on either side of the path. The horses would continue westward without needing direction. "The blue flowers are cobaltmists, and the red grass are bloodvines?"

"Yes." Her childlike curiosity warmed his heart. "The trees are lillysprings, and they glow silver in the moonlight. The little yellow flowers are sunbursts. When they first blossom, orange dust sprays out. The pink ones are cherrynettles—their fragrance was once in high demand as the main ingredient in Orthian love potions. And the tall bamboo-like plants are firthorns, prickly and unwelcoming."

A comfortable silence descended between them. The night's choruses marked their passing with silence and burst once more into life upon their departure. The stars twinkled brightly, but the moon formed a tiny smile, not illuminating their way.

Sohar didn't like not seeing her face, having to use her breathing and her horse's gait to gauge her direction. The shape of her was a mere outline of black against the darkness. Yet he could see when she slumped forward then righted herself. He sighed, urged his horse closer, and scooped her from her horse onto his saddle in front of him. She gasped, but snuggled against him, her head lolling back to rest trustingly on his shoulder.

His Joi-Joi.

Chapter Twenty-Five

Fury

They said anger could manifest as erupting sores. Or was that hatred? Rannic could believe either for his blood boiled. Soaking in the Heaven's Fire pool wasn't helping. He had healed his wounds, but the humiliation haunted him, a phantom throbbing in his once-broken nose.

Bypassing the singing princess had pleased him. He had waited with surprising patience to ensure Sohar did choose to find solace by the pools tonight. It had gone better than Rannic could have planned. The hiding spot within the cobaltmists—with a cloth over his nose to limit its effect on him—was well-chosen.

Jenaso's beauty had delighted him, revealing how exquisite she was with each garment she had removed. Her form wasn't as soft as he expected from a princess, but the strength rippling through her had excitement rising within him. Stubborn and strong, she would suit his tastes well.

Then she had shifted to face him—now fully clothed—close enough for her gold eyes to mesmerize. Her graceful movements and inane chatter lulled him. Her standing up to offer Sohar her soap, even calling him *charmer*, hadn't alarmed Rannic. When she had strapped on her belt, that hadn't aroused suspicion either, for what did it matter if a child held a sword?

She sat down again, closer to the pool this time but still facing his hiding spot. This did not please him for she obscured the arrow's path. When Sohar returned to the clearing, then sank into the pool, Rannic notched the arrow and strung his fingers for a pre-draw.

He need only wait for the perfect timing. Shifting to the right to open the shot, he drew the arrow back and anchored it just below his jaw. Taking careful aim and a deep breath, he exhaled, and released the string, following through to ensure his arrow stayed on target.

Jenaso launched herself into the air with red tendrils wrapping around her chest as the arrow struck her. She landed in a perfect Xiaxan lunge. Scrambling to act through his shock, he notched another arrow, aimed, and released it only to have her set it and him on fire. Her Xiaxan training showed with every gravity-defying leap, but that she could use the Scarlet Fox as well? Her skills surprised him and fired his blood, snatching his breath. She would make an excellent queen.

Thwarted by a princess and bloodvines? How humiliating. His cheeks were still inflamed from the incident. Thank the Divine that no one had observed his dismal failure. She had revealed much during the meal. Her offer to release the Drem from revenge? How noble of her, but unbelievable. From when the bloodvines immobilized him to when Sohar left her alone with him, she had his thoughts darting from one revelation to another.

The Scarlet Fox spoke to her, demanding vengeance. Her eyes had turned an eerie rose-gold color with hatred twisting her graceful features. So much power in the hands of an insignificant female. A naïve princess led to believe this marriage nonsense by the deceitful, pompous Sohar. She had handed her authority over to a Greyadian! He could have her imprisoned, and Kylen could do nothing.

Jenaso had tried to break free from this authority, her status that of a pawn as she accused Rannic of assuming. She had wanted him to travel with her and Sohar. Rannic doubted she was aware that her logical reasons were a subconscious effort to justify her imprisonment.

He shook his head, intrigued by it all. Buro and his sons had convinced her she was nothing but a token queen, one who would have no power.

Rannic would take that power for himself. Curse his father, a man mired by bitterness to the point that only darkness spewed from his mouth. Despite Sohar's beating—one he hadn't been able to avoid no matter how he tried—and subsequent warnings, Rannic planned to trail them to Greyad.

Using the night's darkness, he would fly along the Hokhoun Mountains, away from Orth. Resting during the day, he could reach Corough within three days.

An uneventful trip through Orth would take five to six days, so he would recuperate in an inn and await their arrival. His token shimmered, and he glared at his furious father's wavering face. Rannic had long ago ceased caring about pleasing the man. If he wasn't the only child born to Rumoc, his father would have killed him years ago, accidentally, of course.

"I am most displeased," he said.

Rannic didn't respond. His father's opinion didn't matter. Besides, the shifting wilds behind his father had him wondering where the man was rushing to. Could it be Greyad, as well?

"About?" He sighed. His father would say nothing more until he, at least, participated in his game, one he had played numerous times.

"That arrogant pup for thinking he can threaten Drem. Not to mention, your inability to resolve this without my involvement and your lack of results despite your assurances otherwise. Where is the princess, Rannic?"

"With her husband." He splashed water on his face to hide his smirk, trusting his father's thirst for vengeance to bolster the lie. "This marriage-matching was a ruse. Kylen awarded her to Prince Sohar before I arrived in Ethrielle."

"What? A Greyad-Letoura realm would be too powerful for the three remaining realms to control. What was Buro thinking?" Rumoc's face mottled red again. His eyes darkened and narrowed into a glare. "You must kill him now."

"I tried, twice. Since you denied me Xiaxan training, for political reasons, of course, I am no match for him." He didn't mention the princess' skills—he intended to portray her as a weakling. The less his father knew, the less he would connive and meddle in Rannic's affairs. "She threw herself in front of my arrow. The naïve thing believes he loves her."

"You wounded her?" Rumoc roared, the image rippling under his emotional strain. "Her death must not point to me. A war with the realms would annihilate us."

"The Scarlet Fox protected her. It burned my arrows as if they were paper dragons." He flicked petals off the surface of the pool, growing bored with this discussion.

"Poison him with Ilutar venom. She'll use up her life essence to heal him, killing herself in the process." The glee on his father's face stirred nausea in Rannic's belly. Had his father always been this bloodthirsty? How many people had died at his hands? Did Rannic want to end up like him? Bitter and hating everything good?

"I am following them into Orth and to Greyad." He met his father's gaze, lying with the skill Rumoc taught him.

"I will be in Greyad by the time you arrive at Corough." His father's face shimmered out, and with a sigh, Rannic let his head loll back. He had three to five days to decide his destiny, one uninfluenced by his father's presence. A sense of peace drifted over him, as rare as it was precious.

Many questions swirled in his mind. The Scarlet Fox healing Jenaso without her command. Her need to forgive Drem and rebuild Letoura—that had rung true. What was the disciples' involvement? Whether Sohar was aware he cared for her more than he should? What the plan was when they reached Greyad?

He chuckled. All these thoughts were futile if they didn't survive Orth.

Chapter Twenty-Six

Breathe

Joi moaned at the person shaking her awake. She was having a lovely dream where Sohar smiled at her over a bowl of steamed dumplings and noodles. When she fluttered her eyes open, searing torchlight blinded her, and a full groan escaped past her lips.

"Joi-Joi, we're at the gates. Come, you can rest inside." Sohar's deep voice penetrated her lethargy, but only enough to spark warmth in her chest.

She grumbled under her breath about the comfort of his arms and it being the best place to rest. Her breath caught as he lowered her feet to the ground. Grateful he hadn't heard her mutterings, she ran a hand over her face and removed her traveling bag from her horse. The gate guard gestured to her to follow him into the tower, and after casting a glance at a Sohar, she nodded at the guard to lead the way.

Climbing the stairs on weary legs, she trailed her fingers along the cool stone, needing its strength more than she was willing to reveal. They spiraled upward, the tiny windows nothing but darkness. The guard scraped an iron door open and entered to hold it for her. The circular room contained a daybed, a table with two chairs, and a stand. A bowl of water and cloth awaited her. She thanked the guard and placed her bag on the chair just as Sohar entered.

She was not about to bemoan the loss of privacy, and to endure another night alongside him was worth it. As a bed partner, he was accommodating. Not that she had known any before, only Ayo when thunderstorms had frightened Joi. Stripping off her cloak, armor, belt, and boots, she clambered onto the bed to face the wall and allowed exhaustion to lull her into the sweet depths of sleep.

On the peripheral of her consciousness, he thumped his boots around the room and to the basin. Water splashed against the stone as he washed, then the bed dipped as he sat, blessing her with warmth at her back when he held her against him. She mumbled a greeting.

His arm tightened around her waist, and his breath fanned her nape. Her braid moved as he draped it over her shoulder with the ends brushing her forearm. Then, with the barest of touches and in her sleep-addled mind, she swore she felt the brush of his lips on her neck. That was when she knew she was dreaming.

THE SHARP STING WHEN he slapped her backside caused her to sit up to glare at Sohar who dared to arch an innocent brow at her. A glance at the shuttered window showed an absence of sunlight, and the lit lantern did nothing to ease the grittiness in her eyes. The air was dry and at an uncomfortably warm temperature.

"Come, Joi-Joi." He hopped on one foot to yank on a boot. "We must leave for the Ruined City of Zugba before it's too hot."

"Before?" She shifted to the side of the bed to swing her legs over, grabbing her boots, yawning as she did so. He placed her cloak and armor on the bed and draped his cloak over his shoulders before opening the iron door.

"I'll check on the camels. The water closet is downstairs in the guard room." Sohar dropped both bits of information without waiting for her response.

"Camels?" She knew what they were and their purpose, but she never thought, not in a thousand years, she would find herself on one. "And I have to pee where guards can hear me?" Joi tightened the straps of her armor, checking her coin pouch, her token, and her sword.

Finding her comb, she unraveled her braid, combed the knots out, then braided it again. With a sigh, she scooped up her traveling bag, tossed her comb inside, then trundled down the steps. The rumble of voices drew her, and she followed the sound, along a narrow passage and into the guard room. They bowed and left through another door, granting her privacy. Heat splashed on her cheeks adding to the fine layer of sweat that coated her skin. When she pushed open a wooden door, the cleanliness of the closet surprised her, and she released a pent-up breath.

Hurrying through her ablutions, she bolted out the tower's main door and into the pre-dawn light. Against one wall was a line of cages. Sohar had donned a handling glove on which a crow rested, its claws embedding in the leather. He was feeding it something in between strokes of its head. With a flick of his arm, he launched it skyward. It cawed and circled twice before heading west.

"Ready?" Stripping off the glove, he handed it to the guard.

"A message for Vard?" Her curiosity piqued. He nodded. "Why can't you use your token?"

"Magic is unstable in Orth. It damages the wielder and is unpredictable, often acting opposite to what the wielder intended." He waited in front of the portcullis and strode forward when it had risen high enough for him to do so. As soon as they passed under, the guards lowered it, not wanting it to stay up longer than it needed to. If it remained open, it might lure those exiled in the wastelands.

His long strides carried him through the towers' stone archway and into dry heat which sucked the air out of her. Joi gasped at the sudden rise of temperature, dragging in breaths with stars forming before her eyes.

"Slow and deep." He gripped her shoulder, his touch hot through her tunic. "The air quality is poorer than you are used to, and the heat doesn't help."

She nodded without looking at him, drawing in slow, dedicated breaths until the stars faded. Only to gasp again. Sohar stood alongside a camel twice the size of a horse. And she could smell it. She wrinkled her nose, twisting it at the abuse. There were two of them, and one must be hers. Swift panic suffocated her, and she thrust it down with a growl before stomping forward. She wouldn't let a camel ride break her. Pausing alongside Sohar, she held up her arms, arching a brow in expectation.

He clasped her waist, the heat of his hands burning her through her armor. Then with a grunt from him, he tossed her up. Her squeal of surprise covered his laugh, her arms flying out to grab onto a saddle, a hump, anything. Hanging on for dear life, she shot him a glare that melted at the sight of his smile. Oh, Divine. She had yearned to see it, but hadn't realized how it would devastate her senses, leaving her scrambling to gather her wits around her.

"Next time, get yourself up, Princess. Xiaxan training has taught you how to manipulate gravity." He swaggered away, *swaggered*. The arrogant man. Adjusting herself around her tight grip on the camel's hump, she slid into the saddle with a sigh of relief.

"Princess Joi?" A guard held up a small water pouch. She took it with a smile. He glanced at Sohar then at her before whispering, "This is Velvet, and if you want to get on or off, just rub her behind her ear." He scanned his surroundings to make sure his words hadn't traveled, then with a formal bow, he scurried off.

She grinned. Oh, she couldn't wait to see Sohar's face when Velvet did her thing, whatever that was. Leaning down to pat the camel on the neck, she ruffled the tuft of hair on her head. Unable to resist, she crooned at her, delighted to know her name. "Just the two of us against the desert, Velvet."

The camel released a loud growl as if in agreement, but when Sohar broke into a gallop, Velvet grunted as she galumphed after him. Joi clung to the hump while placing the water pouch into the traveling bag hooked onto the pommel. She settled into Velvet's gait, her hips undulating from side-to-side in a seductive dance.

Yanking her hood down over her face for shade, she stared at his cloaked back. Hunger pangs gurgled in her stomach, and her mouth was dry, but she wouldn't assuage either need until he said so. She had no idea when they would stop to rest the camels or whether there was water in this forsaken place.

It was desolate. As far as she could see there was sand—curving, rippling valleys of sand. Far in the distance, a brown smudge shimmered in the heat, melting the surface. What the Divine was it? A fine layer of dust formed on her face, but she dared not rub it and make it worse.

Sohar gave the village of Bray a wide berth. Not that it offered much to a traveler. Dotted on the horizon, and in the foreground, stood crude houses built from stones and rocks, semi-sunken, giving the appearance of ruins. The closest structure was a stable for camels. There was no other evidence of life with no squeals of playing children or squabbling women. An ominous sign of what awaited them in Orth.

Chapter Twenty-Seven

Wastelands

Three hours later, Sohar drew his camel to a halt. By then, Joi's tongue had sealed itself to the roof of her mouth, and Velvet verbalized her displeasure with a continuous grumble. They had neared jutting rocks casting shade in the mid-morning sun. The darkness called to her, tempting her, for she hoped it was a few degrees cooler.

Under her cloak and armor, her Xiaxan tunic and pants clung to her damp body, absorbing as much of the moisture as it could. The heat had baked the cloth onto her, suffocating her, and now a thin layer of perspiration lay beneath the sand coating her skin.

As Velvet drew to a halt alongside Sohar, Joi decided this would be the perfect opportunity to stroke her camel's ear. She would relish the look of surprise that would surely grace his features. As soon as she rubbed Velvet's ear, the camel bucked forward onto her knees and tossed her out of the saddle. Her Xiaxan training kicked in, and Joi spun in the air to land in a lunge facing the now prostrate camel.

His rumbling laughter drew her startled glance despite the additional warmth now conquering her chest. His shoulders shook, and there were perhaps tears glistening his eyes, but she couldn't be certain. He had turned away to pour water in his hand for his camel. At least, she had experienced his laughter—a rare occurrence and worth almost burying her face in the sand.

She drank from her water pouch before pouring some into her hand for Velvet to lap. The camel grumbled when the water ran out, so she added more to her hand and held it out for her. When her water pouch was half-empty, she stowed it and sat down beside Sohar in the rocks' shadows. He had splashed water onto his face, washing away any potential evidence of tears. A sweet sigh of relief escaped her despite the heat rising off the sand a foot from her boot where the shadow ended.

"We will be camping just outside the Ruined City of Zugba tonight. It will be cold, but the warmth from the camels should help." He handed her chunks of bread and cheese. Despite her preference for noodles, she was too hungry and too grateful for the meager fare.

"Sleep with Velvet?" Looking at the kneeling camel, she sighed before nodding. Yes, sleeping with Velvet might wiser than having Sohar as her bed partner. Once they arrived in Rendar, she would no longer be his responsibility. Nothing bound them together despite her fondness for him, so adding a little distance now might spare her heartache later.

The thought of reigning as Queen of Letoura overwhelmed her, a vise squeezing her chest circling spots in her vision. Her people would rely on her to lead them into health and prosperity. She had to rebuild Tennaba as well, and a man with undivided loyalty to her would aid her. Sohar would reign as King of Greyad one day—she wouldn't tear him from his birthright. He too had a realm relying on him. Therefore, a future as a couple was impossible.

Jeiram would reign over Letoura if she could find him. That didn't mean she could abandon her duty to her people. There was too much to do for it to fall on her brother's shoulders. Like the Scarlet Fox, they shared the burden, the consequences, the responsibilities.

"You named it?" Sohar asked from between bites of cheese.

She shook her head to rid herself of her heavy thoughts. "Hmm? Oh, the camel? The guard told me her name." Saying no more, Joi peered into the distance, the shimmering heat making her eyes water.

What was Jeiram like now? Teaching her how to fly a kite was one of her fondest memories. It had been a gift from her mother's people—a beautiful asoquay bird in vibrant purples and blues. Her last memories of him were of her first magic lesson.

"Why the sudden sadness, Princess?" He offered a carafe of wine.

She accepted and took a sip, grimacing at the taste of heated wine. On the edges of Orth, the white-peaked Hokhoun Mountains looked cool and refreshing, a vast difference to the desert's oppressive temperatures. "I pestered Jeiram to teach me a spell. I used it when my handmaiden and I escaped. Had I been stronger, she would have survived." She met his gaze, hoping he knew something. "Where is he now? To which king did Father send him?"

He shook his head, and disappointment slumped her shoulders. "You said you knew he was alive?"

"Pan said the Scarlet Fox was different, that it retained the Letouran magic, passed on from generation to generation, growing in strength. It shares itself across all living Letouran royals. I contain half of the power." She wrapped her fingers around the medallion, stroking her thumb across the flame-shaped gem.

"Half?" He appraised her body as if he doubted her. She huffed, resisting the urge to fire a red bolt at him. "Pan? As in Pan's noodles?"

"Yes, he was once known as Lord Panzan, and he served as my Cento mentor for three years." Joi handed him his carafe then chewed on another bite of her bread.

Sohar stilled. "Lord Panzan, the renowned Letouran General and your father's most trusted advisor? *That* Panzan?"

"Jeiram has to be with King Velisand." She ignored his question with a pointed look.

Sohar's lips twitched, and she held her breath, hoping for a smile no matter how small. He arched a brow, instead. "How do you know my father doesn't have him hidden?"

"You looked at the Scarlet Fox with surprise, Sohar." She jumped up, tired of this discussion, of the heat, and this whole cursed journey. Patting Velvet's neck, she glanced at a brown smudge on the horizon, suspecting it was an abandoned structure, and sighed. "Damn you, Rumoc."

Climbing into the saddle, she rubbed Velvet's ear and clung to the pommel when the camel rocked back and forth as it rose.

Sohar stared, his face inscrutable again. He stowed his carafe and vaulted into his camel's saddle, his Xiaxan skill coming into play. The reality of her situation was settling in her heart—they would reach the smudge, then travel to wherever, landing in Greyad at some point. More traveling to Rendar where she would await news of her chosen husband. Then she would travel back, perhaps through Letoura this time, to marry a man she didn't know.

As excited as she had been about this *adventure*, it now seemed pointless. Why couldn't she find a hut somewhere and stay there? Somewhere in the mountains would be wonderful.

"Rannic's correct. I don't need to run." At her shouted words, Sohar spun in his saddle to look at her. "I could hide in the mountains. Curse it, Sohar. You'd think I was defenseless the way you and Ky are behaving."

"Do you think Rannic will abandon his desires because you asked him to? How naïve can you be, Princess?" Anger flitted across his face, and the ease with which it appeared showed he too was feeling the heat's irritability.

"Let him come. Let Rumoc come. I'll sink my blade into his black heart." Fire burst through her veins, and Joi gasped. Why was she so angry? Why now in the middle of nowhere? The medallion pulsed, and she shot a pleading look at Sohar, scared her volatile emotions might trigger her magic. He had dismounted his camel and hurried to her side.

Grabbing her arms, he dragged her down, pressing her back against Velvet's underbelly. "Breathe, Joi-Joi. Look at me, keep your eyes on mine, and mimic my breathing. Slow and deep."

"I'm furious. I could kill everything, anything. I...*hate*." She vibrated with rage, her limbs trembling as the Fox tore through her. She clenched her fingers into tight fists trying to calm herself, the Fox.

"Residual magic infests the sand, the stones, and the wind. The Fox reacts to its presence. The trapped souls bring the loathing. I'm sorry, I should have mentioned this but foolishly hoped we would be in Zugba before it affected you." He crushed her to him, pressing her face into his shoulder, the cloth scratching the sand off her cheek. "Ky considered a hut, but a moving target is harder to find. Please, trust us to keep you safe." He leaned back to meet her gaze. "Your brothers love you. They have been protecting you since you were eleven. Whoever they choose as your husband will die should he so much as frown at you." He lifted her onto Velvet, gentler this time, and as soon as she was comfortable, he returned to his own camel, vaulting up.

"Thank you, Sohar," she said, loud enough for him to hear.

He waved without looking back. "I thought you wanted to see Rendar?" The scorching breeze carried his question.

Joi forced a chuckle, hoping to smother the anger lingering in the recesses of her mind. "Travel through Orth? Escape a Drem? Marry a stranger? See Rendar? Have I thanked you for these wonderful experiences, Mighty Sohar?"

"You did want an adventure," she thought she heard him say.

The arrogant bastard.

Chapter Twenty-Eight

Failure

Fear was an unpleasant emotion, slithering under Sohar's guard, consuming his heart and mind. He needed her home and surrounded by his armies. Danger in a physical form he could handle, but the residual magic toying with her soul, that he could not fight nor protect her from. He should have told her, warned her what dangers awaited them in these lands. What an arrogant fool he had been to assume he was all she would need.

In many of the planning sessions with Kylen, Sohar suggested they seclude her in the mountains. He would have surrounded her with soldiers and powerful safeguards. Her youngest brother, Mion, pointed out the success rate of assassins.

Sohar raised his gaze to the horizon where the Ruined City of Zugba loomed. The midday sun beat down without mercy, his cloak barely sheltering him. Within a few hours, they would reach the first sunken buildings. He would choose one in which to rest—his preference would be for the outskirts of the city—less chance of an ambush.

Glancing back at Joi, he sighed, seeing only her plump lips and a stubborn chin. Why did she plague him so? From the moment they had met, her life force called to him. It wasn't as if his father disapproved of such a match. Her lineage was more than suitable. It was the level of emotion she invoked within him, indicative of his Final Contest.

That wasn't what kept him from her. It was that he liked himself more when she broke through his resolve. His life wasn't an endless obligation when she was smiling at him. Fool that he was, he had agreed to Ky's plan. Sohar had agreed, in his selfishness, to days alone with her before she married another man.

The wind whipped his hood back, and sand stung his skin. He grimaced as he peered into the darkened midday sunlight. His camel brayed a warning before the brown clouds around the city and on the horizon took on a more ominous tone. Cursing, he leaped off the camel as it drew to a halt on its own. He jerked on the reins and led it toward her. She had flipped her hood down, holding it in place against the sand's barbs. The cursed wind was hot and unforgiving.

Closing the distance between them, he called out her name, taking the reins from her as she jumped down. Sohar scowled, seeing no available shelter from the impending sandstorm. He had the camels kneel alongside each other with a narrow gap between them. Unhooking both their traveling bags, he tied them to his feet so he wouldn't lose them in the shifting sands or if a camel bolted. Then he gestured for her to lie down.

"Wait." He shuffled closer, trailing their bags in the sand. Grasping the hem of her cloak, he pulled it up behind her. Holding it above her waist, he nudged her to sit. She did. He gathered the cloak over her head, creating a cocoon. "Take the edges from me, then lie down between the camels. They can endure the storm and should bear the brunt of it."

One last glance at the obscured landscape, Sohar took the food pouch and positioned himself over Joi's sprawling body before ducking under her cloak. Their combined weight sank them into the hot sand. She held her cloak's edges at his hips, sealing them in. The roaring wind dampened, but the heat became more oppressive, almost suffocating. Sand splattered and whipped at the cloak. She shifted, tightened her hold, and crushed him against her body.

"Am I too heavy?" He placed the pouch to the side of her head, adding another barrier to shield her. They might be there for hours which meant water would be crucial.

"No." She spread her legs to accommodate him. Her cheeks flushed, and her breathing came in shallow gasps. He didn't know if it was from the intimacy or the unbearable heat. Sweat trickled at his hairline, tickling him. "How long do you think the storm will last?"

Her gaze darted everywhere before meeting his. He grabbed this opportunity to look upon her. This close, the gold in her eyes swirled, and her long eyelashes fluttered shadows onto her pale cheeks.

"I don't know." He traced his thumb along her jaw. He hadn't meant to touch her, unaware of his actions until he already made contact.

Despite the thin layer of sand coating it, her skin was soft to the touch. Her breathing hitched at his caress, her golden eyes almost glowing.

When he spoke, his voice had roughened. "Tuck your cloak ends under you and rest. Once we reach Zugba, we will wait for darkness before traveling by moonlight."

She nodded, her tilting hips nestling him deeper as she followed his instruction. Not that she noticed how she affected him, nor said anything. She brought her hands up to rest on his upper arms, but he assumed it was a more comfortable position for her.

"Now that I have your undivided attention," she teased, the gold in her eyes sparkling with humor. "Why did you leave without saying farewell? You reprimanded me for sending my maidservant with the noodles then left Ethrielle the next day." Despite the smile curling her lips, her expressions hinted at sorrow, regret, and disappointment.

He chose honesty since he didn't know how else to answer her. He took a deep breath. "You make me feel, Princess."

Her smile faltered as her eyebrows arched, almost touching her hairline. "I know—anger, frustration, impatience. I'm sorry, Sohar. I'll try harder, I'll try to hold my tongue and not disappoint you." She closed her eyes and bit her lip to hide her pain.

How could she believe she was at fault? He had failed his mentors, his father, and his Final Contest, the latter when he had first seen her after all this time. All his denials and attempts to avoid this had been futile. And now he had failed her by his abrupt departure so many years ago.

"Don't..." he rasped, fighting the intense wave of emotions erupting in his chest. One emotion he could deal with, but this many all at once? Divine, she had such a hold on him. "Don't change who you are, Joi-Joi. Not for me." Her gaze flew open as her mouth parted. Curse those plump lips, pinkened by her nibbling teeth. "I like your smile," he said then she smiled for him, a slow curling of her lips into a breathtaking visual delight.

He leaned down, waiting for her to turn away from him. She didn't. Dammit, she was so innocent and didn't realize what he was doing until it was too late to stop him. When his intention dawned on her, her eyes widened in surprise, their golden depths drawing him in, intensifying his need to kiss her. He brushed his lips over hers, moaning at their softness, then pulled back to regard her.

Before he lost his courage, he slid his fingers behind her neck and kissed her again. Many things penetrated his mind—her clasping fingers embedding into his arms, the hitch of her breath, the sweet taste of her hot mouth, and her thundering pulse under his thumb. Sohar deepened their kiss, and her sigh of pleasure brought unneeded warmth to his overheated body.

His conscience beat at him as he continued to kiss her, to drown in her. He might never indulge again—this might be the last time he could kiss her, and by the Divine, he would enjoy it. He had sacrificed his honor, his principles, his duty, for this one chance to simply be a man in love with a woman.

He jerked away. The full realization of his feelings solidified within him as he stared into her hooded eyes. He loved her, had always loved her. That was why she had such an effect on him. He couldn't prevent the smile from forming, despite the sadness hovering on the edges of his mind. If only her destiny was free—no obligations, then he could marry her. If he claimed her, who would rebuild Letoura? Her realm needed her as Greyad needed him. Marrying her would crown her as the queen apparent of Greyad, thus splitting her loyalties and responsibilities. He couldn't place her in such a situation, not when her heart longed for Letoura and her people.

"Rest, Joi-Joi. I'll wake you when the storm's over."

"But..." She paused, nibbling on her kiss-swollen lips as she studied his face. He didn't know what he revealed to her, but she squeezed her eyes closed.

Her breathing slowed from ragged to peaceful. Sohar watched her sleep, his fingers brushing her jaw with what he hoped was a soothing manner since he couldn't make himself stop touching her. As soon as the wind settled, he would resume the role of her friend, her Xiaxan brother, her guard, but he would never forget the kiss.

Chapter Twenty-Nine

Captured

Sohar's sudden grunt startled Joi awake. Buried beneath his solid form, with her cloak sheltering yet smothering them, she had enjoyed a pleasant solace. His sleepy eyes showed he too had found rest. With her still in his embrace, he vaulted upward, taking her with him. Levitating in the air, she realized they were not alone before gravity won out, and she descended to land in the soft sand. The food pouch thudded at her feet as her cloak swirled up little dust devils.

"This is a treasure, indeed. Viggu will be pleased," a swathed man said, his voice smothered by the cloth covering most of his face. Only his gray eyes were visible. The color was mesmerizing, so pale of a gray, like old snow. A glance at the other men gathered around them revealed the same eye color. Orthians.

"Taking us to Viggu will waste your time," Sohar said, ignoring their drawn, curved swords.

"That is for Viggu to decide," the man said, and with the sharp tip of his blade pressed to the underside of Joi's chin, he raised it, forcing her to meet his cold gaze. "Beautiful. She will please him." The man laughed, glancing at his men before lowering his blade. "Mount your camels, my dear captives, the sun waits for no one." With a flick of his fingers, his men closed the distance, their wicked swords driving Joi and Sohar to their camels.

He crowded her, trying to shield her from harm, a pulse ticking at his jaw revealing his unease. He grabbed her waist, gave her a squeeze as if to reassure her, then tossed her onto Velvet—this time, she gripped the pommel, landing in the saddle with a grunt. On his camel, he fell in beside her, despite these bandits forming a line. As one, the bandits sheathed their swords, and they set off for this Viggu in a southern direction, presumably toward the Uncursed City of Ta.

Both traveling bags and their food pouch now hung off the leader's pommel. Joi grimaced, longing for the water pouch. Two men each they could fight, but seven and under the midday sun, she wasn't as confident. She flicked her hood over her face and leaned down to console a grumbling Velvet.

For the next twelve hours, she learned to appreciate one thing—water. Without stopping the caravan, a man would dismount and offer her a drink before clipping a water bag over Velvet's head. Joi's lower half ached, her muscles spasming from undulating her hips for so long. A few times, she had glanced at Sohar, but his stoic features had returned, and the man who kissed her passionately mere hours ago was no longer present.

At last, the sun set, and the blessed coolness of night breathed life into her heated body. The stars dotted the sky like a tapestry of stories, the moon absent for the telling. The breathtaking sight drew her attention repeatedly.

Exhaustion drummed in her mind, liquified her body, and she struggled to remain upright. During this quiet time, she relived Sohar's kiss, analyzed its effect on her, her obligations, and her friendship with him. More than this, what truly bothered her, was the reason behind it. *Why* had he kissed her? She shouldn't place too much value in it—after all, winehouses contained many stories of men who were liberal with their kisses.

He must have realized the error mid-kiss when he jerked away, looking startled. She settled on the thought the heat had driven him mad driving him to kiss her in the first place. Not that she would complain. Kissing was an amazing experience. Yet another thing to be thankful for on this adventure.

Someone lifting her off Velvet awoke Joi. She must have slumped forward to sleep. How amazing the body was to find solace anywhere. They had arrived at a formidable structure carved into the northern face of the Hokhoun Mountains. Torches illuminated parts of the fortress, higher than she could see.

Snuggling in Sohar's arms, she let him carry her, too tired to argue with him, and infinitely grateful. She lingered her hooded gaze on his chiseled jaw, and the blue of his eyes as he peered at her, his face unreadable. Her attention flitted to her surroundings and the multi-layered garments of the people gathering around them. The vast cavern they entered was well lit, a welcoming warmth after the cold darkness of night. Children darted around their mothers' draped gowns, their fathers hovering behind them, armed and tense.

Joi understood why they were curious. A Greyadian among them, with his white braid falling down his back and his cerulean-blue eyes, was a marvel to behold. Her ebony hair would also draw notice against the Orthian coloring of bronzed skin and blond hair in various shades of sand.

A robust man awaited them at the end of the procession. Gray streaked his sandy hair, and his eyes were white. He had broken his strong nose at some point, but for now, he clenched his lips together, his expression calculating. One hand rested on the hilt of his sword at his hip as if their presence threatened him.

"What is this, Xudag?" His voice reverberated off the rock walls and creviced ceiling. He strode toward them, casting a disdainful glare at Sohar.

"The wastelands provide, my chief," Xudag said.

"Yes, it does. The Crown Prince of Greyad." Viggu's announcement was met with outcries and cursing.

He held up a hand, stilling the rising demands for justice. He settled his sharp focus on Joi, still clasped against Sohar's chest. She gripped his shoulder, silently asking him to release her. With gentle care, he lowered her feet to the rough-paved path but kept his hand on her back for balance.

The Orthian chief grabbed her by her arms and yanked her off the ground, his face aligned with hers. This close, silver flecked his smoky-gray eyes. They widened, then he crushed her to him, engulfing her within his bulky arms. A hug was not what she expected. He was too huge to fight, so she endured it. Perhaps it was their custom? Although, her studies hadn't mentioned it.

"Joi-hin? Is it truly you?" He held her back to stare into her eyes, disbelief and delight easy to read.

She was beginning to feel like a straw doll, but this man seemed to recognize her, calling her by a name she hadn't heard for fourteen years. She pressed her hands to his cheeks to keep him still. Her fingers recognized the familiar stubble and the tiny scar below his left ear which she traced with the pad of her thumb. An image, long forgotten, shimmered out of her faded childhood memories.

"Ker-hin?" she asked, uncertain if she remembered correctly.

Her father's most trusted friend, Ker. The smile he bestowed upon her was bright, bold, and forgiving. Years melted off his face, and the one she had long ago cherished formed. With a gasp, she flung her arms around his neck and hugged him, the same way she used to do when he visited the palace.

His bombastic laugh vibrated through her, and at the sound, something hot engulfed her heart. His beloved face from her past tore a sob from her, and she drenched his tunic with her tears. He patted her back as if she was still the little girl he had comforted, carried around on his shoulders, and brought gifts to from afar.

"I'm pleased to see you, Joi-hin. Though, not with this *khonu*." He glared at Sohar, nudging her to the side in case he needed to draw his sword.

Panic gripped her, sharp and mind consuming. The fury rippling off Ker-hin meant he could kill without regret. Sohar had saved her so many times on this journey she had to act, had to do something.

"Sohar's my husband, Ker-hin," she said, surprising herself. To hide this, she wriggled out of Viggu's hold to loop her arm around Sohar's waist. She trusted he would hide his shock at her announcement and not call her out as a liar. "He's taking me to Rendar to keep me safe since Rumoc hasn't forgotten his hatred."

"Wise to marry one so strong, Joi-hin, but I'd have preferred a Meideon," Viggu grumbled before turning to address his people. "Fellow Tans, this is Princess Jenaso of Letoura."

The crowd responded in a mass bow. She gasped, stunned by the progression of reverence across their audience like a dance performed by hundreds of people.

"The princess from the *Devil in Drem*, my chief?" a man asked.

Viggu chuckled. "Firelight stories," he said to her in explanation. "Yes, and her husband is General Sohar." The crowd roared their displeasure. "Would you mind, Joi-hin, if I killed him?" The hope on his face was comical.

She shot a glance at Sohar to find his gaze resting on her.

"If you promise to keep her safe, I will die for her." Sohar's words silenced the crowd, his expression, for once, not that of a Greyadian. Adoration covered every sharp angle and line of his face.

"Yes, I would mind, Ker-hin. It's hard to find a good man these days," she teased, amazed at Sohar's mastery over his expressions. Perhaps, while she was in Rendar, his tutors could train her? "To kill him is to war with Letoura. As the future queen, I would bridge this mountain between us and forge a new future with Ta."

"What?" Sohar growled, his question drowned out by the crowd's cries of happiness and hope.

Joi cupped his cheek, keeping his focus on her. "Are you not tired of war, Sohar? How long will the realms punish these people for the sins of their ancestors?"

"The realms agreed on this punishment." He trapped her hand with his larger one.

She huffed, wishing she could smack some sense into him. "As I recall, your distant ancestor killed his daughter. Does that mean you…you are a danger to your children?"

"No." Horror molded his features. He grimaced then nodded, conceding she had the right of it.

"We cannot continue punishing for our ancestors' mistakes. Look at these people, Mighty Sohar, look. I don't see criminals. I see families trying to survive in a world that has cast them aside. Open the gates, free them, forgive them, and for the love of the Divine, forget their fathers' sins. As I would forgive Rumoc his."

"What?" Viggu roared. "Forgive the devil himself, Joi-hin? Why? What would your father say?" Disgust and shock warred with his anger.

Her shoulders slumped. This was how everyone, even the hated Orthians would react to her decision. What lay ahead for her drained her, the insurmountable hatred they shared for Drem. "My people are all that matter now, Ker-hin. To rebuild on hatred and vengeance is an unstable foundation."

"I was as displeased when she told Rannic this, Chief Viggu." Sohar gripped her hip and tugged her closer to him. "Perhaps you could talk some sense into her?"

Viggu grunted before capturing her hand in his then pulling her away from Sohar. Viggu's large hand engulfed hers, and before she could say anything, he led her deeper into the cavern. Carved into the bedrock were houses with stairs spiraling upward to cater for more houses. What Ker-in had accomplished there was beautiful and massive in scale.

"You will be my guests for as long as you need. Ta is as safe as Rendar." He threw out his arm in a sweeping gesture. "No Drem dare show his face here."

"Two days." Sohar raised his chin as a show of determination.

Viggu stared at him for a while then nodded. A few children followed their path, but the crowd had dispersed, thankfully no longer intending to kill Sohar anymore. Judging by the stony expression on her *husband's* face, she would have some convincing to do when they were alone.

145

Chapter Thirty

Disbelief

Sohar trailed an arm-in-arm Joi and Viggu leading the way. Things had taken an unexpected turn—one he was torn over. Curse it, when was he not torn? The Orthians capturing them hadn't factored in his plans. Viggu knowing Joi, blindsided him, but more than this, having her announce their marriage? Oh, Divine.

Sohar knew why she lied—to save his life. Viggu wouldn't hesitate to kill a Greyadian and a general more so. Her golden eyes and sweet smile hid a strategic mind. He should have known Buro would educate her, would equip her with knowledge and skills to survive the Drem. Sohar had been a fool to believe otherwise. Kylen would have known though. What was his excuse?

What made Sohar tremble was that he had promised himself the kiss would just be the one. That another need not occur. Yet here he was, her *husband*, and closely observed by the Tans. One wrong move, one wrong impression would unmask their subterfuge. Yet he was looking forward to playing the role. His time with her was lessening, and soon he would have to bid her farewell.

"Borba will show you to your chambers. Until the morning." Viggu drew Joi into a hug and kissed her temple. He threw a glare at Sohar before striding off.

A young woman bobbed and led them to a room with a cloth as a door. Sohar didn't like the lack of privacy, but it also meant they weren't prisoners. Borba held the cloth back, gestured them to enter, and with a smile left them alone.

The square room had a low stone shelf for the bed, a stuffed roll as a pillow, and folded blankets at the foot. Carved alcoves held candles, a jug with small drinking bowls, and thin folded garments. Simple and clean. He wrapped his fingers around Joi's wrist and ushered her to the farthest corner of the room.

"This lie will kill us both," he whispered then raised his head to project his voice. "I'm tired, Joi-Joi. How are you feeling, my blossom?" He peered at the shadows flickering under the cloth door. If he was Viggu, he would place spies everywhere, not trusting a Greyadian amid his city.

"It's for a few days, Sohar. Someone with your amazing control should be able to pretend to love me. Truly, I wish to learn such a skill. Would your tutors agree to teach me?" She untied her armor with slow, mesmerizing movements that only frustrated him further.

How could she remain calm? And to *pretend* to love her? Divine, if she only knew the truth.

Facing the door, she said in a too-loud voice and a wide smile just for him, "I'm exhausted too, my sweet Sohar. Who knew sleeping on a camel would be so uncomfortable?"

"What skill?" he asked, trying to follow the pendulum swing of her thoughts.

"Your vacant expressions mixed with adoration, silly." With a flick of her fingers, her cloak slipped off. She caught it and draped it over the bed before peeling off her armor.

His amazing control hadn't been present when he removed the mask to reveal how he felt. She had taken it as an act, a skill she needed to master.

"Are you calling me stupid?" he teased, unable to resist doing so.

Her gaze flew up to meet his, then she laughed. "I dare not...well, not to your face." She untied her sword to place it alongside her armor then crossed the room to undo his cloak, flicking it off his shoulders. This close, the sunbaked scent of jasmine teased his nostrils.

"What are you doing, Joi-Joi?" he asked, as she added his cloak to her things.

"Preparing you for bed?" Mischief danced in her eyes.

A tap near their "door" drew his attention, and he yanked her into his arms, his hands splaying out at the base of her spine. The embrace was intimate and convincing, his body reacting as it should. He stiffened, not wanting to release her, wanting to keep her against him indefinitely.

"Enter," Joi said, her voice breathless.

Sohar's focus fell on her lips, unable to resist the temptation. He allowed it since it would appear as if his *wife* captivated him. Anyone could see how she enchanted him.

"Greetings. I am Shelur, Ker Viggu's first daughter."

Sohar glanced at the woman but returned his attention to Joi. The one look was all he needed to assess the intruder. As he admired Joi's profile, he listed Shelur's appearance and skills. She was tall and dressed as a man. Tight leggings hugged muscular thighs with knee-high camel-hide boots. A pale tunic wrapped around her, showing off her curves, and multi-braided silver-sand hair cascaded around her. Her bronzed skin drew attention to the smoky-gray eyes, coal-lined. A striking woman for an Orthian.

"Greetings, Shelur." Joi smiled, disarming the woman who relaxed a little. "This is my husband, Sohar. We trained together, and he would beat me in every sparring match. I loved that. The other trainees treated me like a woman."

"Believable since Greyadians cannot show mercy," she spat, her body stiffening again.

He forced himself to remain relaxed, despite the furious fire in his gut rippling up his throat. The Orthians were the butchers, choosing to return to their ancestors' vulgar and barbaric behavior.

"It is true," he said. "To show mercy to the merciless is a fool's road."

Shelur huffed, anger darkening her cheeks.

He smothered a chuckle. She was easy to rile, this woman. "Is there a purpose for this intrusion? As you can see, all we need is within each other's arms."

"Sohar." Joi groaned, her eyes widening in dismay. "My apologies, Shelur. He's not usually this boorish."

Shelur shrugged. "He is a man. Father has suggested a visit to the Pools of Renewal. A meal awaits you there."

"A bath?" Joi flashed a bright smile.

Divine, how he loved her smile.

"Thank you, Shelur, for the opportunity. We are grateful." Sohar blessed her with a formal bow, incongruent with his earlier words and behavior. If he could not charm his enemy, then he failed his father and his teachings. Besides, a bath *would* be wonderful. "We do not wish to waste such a precious treasure. You should save your water."

"The Pools of Renewal are Ta's secret oasis. They lie deep within the Hokhoun Mountains, and we believe they are the last untainted magical gardens in Orth." She twisted her lips as if she thought sharing this with a Greyadian wasn't wise.

Lacing his fingers through Joi's, he gestured to Shelur to lead the way. Down narrow passageways she took them, venturing deeper into the bowels of the mountain. The air grew cooler and the lit torches fewer, casting ominous shadows. After a while, he was beginning to suspect this was a trap, to lure them away from the main cluster of houses. He had tried to remember the twists they had taken. Tightening his hold on Joi's hand, he considered running but where? Though this action might endanger Joi further.

Shelur entered a large cavern, the air warm and inviting. She paused to let them pass, and with a gasp, Joi knelt to cradle the petals of a Gyqio orchid. Hundreds spread around them, all blossoming a soft pink in the pale-yellow light. Sohar glanced up at the cave's ceiling that had no obvious origin for the light. Since it was dark outside, he did not expect to see sunlight.

"How is this possible? They bloom only once in their lives." He stroked the length of a Gyqio petal.

"We don't know. They have bloomed for all the years we've lived here. Come." Shelur darted around them to usher them to the rear of the cavern.

As he followed, the air thickened with an intoxicating fragrance. Jasmine. He paused to inhale, dragging in the deepest breath he could, hoping to trap it within his chest.

"Oh, it smells like you, Sohar." Joi rushed to wrap her arm around his waist. "Sunbaked, spicy, and exotic."

He admired her upturned face and the sweet smile curling her plump lips. Looping his arm around her, he cupped her neck, holding his thumb to her jaw. He leaned down, his lips almost touching hers.

"Joi-Joi, now is the time to show them how married we are," he whispered, flicking his gaze across her face, unable to settle on a single feature. She stilled, and her breath hitched before she released it on a long sigh.

"So-so, not while Shelur is watching." She giggled, gave him a quick kiss on the lips before darting around him.

He smiled, unable to help himself, wondering why the Gyqio smelled like jasmine while Joi scented something different. Embedded in the rocky floor were pools worn smooth by centuries of the water's ebbs and flows. Steam spirals rose off the surface, a twirling and dancing enticement. In one rocky wall, an alcove held toweling cloths. Alongside the pool was a bar of soap and a carafe of wine.

On the back wall, a thick vein of gray crystals glimmered in the torchlight, a contrast against the warm browns of the cavern's rock-hewn walls. They were natural and beautiful. He strode toward it and touched one jutting piece. It shimmered, changing its color to white, then it rippled outward until white crystals covered the entire wall.

"The Wall of Light and Serenity. It reveals a person's energy." Shelur paced in front of him. The crystals returned to their original gray color. "See, Orthians no longer have magic. It's our curse to bear."

"May I?" Joi hesitated, holding out a hand to the wall before lowering it. The gray crystals formed red swirls, as expected.

"Your medallion is magical, is it not?" Shelur ran a fingertip along the golden chain. "Perhaps have your Greyadian hold it for you."

Joi looped off the medallion, offering it to Sohar. He accepted it, wondering why it would affect the magic within a person. Surely the Fox was inside Joi? The crystals pulsated red but blue swirled within its depths, forming purple. He swallowed his startled grunt. She brushed the wall, the purple streaking across where her hand hovered.

"Blue? I created a blue protection spell before the Drem killed my handmaiden. I wasn't strong enough to hold it," Joi said to Shelur. "I can use magic here? In this cavern?"

Shelur's lips twisted into a rueful smile. "Only in this untainted garden, although we cannot test it."

Joi smiled—this time it was one of sadness. Sohar's heart leaped in response to it, not liking her in such a state. She stretched out her hand, palm forward, and swirled her other hand over her forearm with her eyes closed in concentration. Blue magic swirled around her fingers and up her arm, mingling with the Fox to form a purple layer of protection around her. He had never seen the like.

"Jeiram, I haven't forgotten." Tears trickled down her cheeks unhindered.

He didn't know if it was from happiness or sorrow. She flicked her fingers with the spell dissipating, then she walked into his arms, burying her face against his chest.

"Joi-Joi." He didn't know what else he could say to comfort her.

Rubbing his hand up and down her back, he rested his cheek on her temple. When her sobs dwindled into hiccups, she broke away, and only then did he realize Shelur had abandoned them. Looping the medallion over Joi's head, he laced his fingers through hers, wiped her tears with the pad of his thumb, then led her to the pool.

Bending to her feet, he removed each boot with her balancing on a foot at a time. He undid her belt and placed it next to her boots. With trembling fingers, he unwrapped her tunic. As tempted as he was to lower his gaze, he kept his neck stiff, his focus above her shoulders. He gave her his back, taking his time to fold the garment. Amid the pool's gurgle, the soft slither of cloth, followed by a splash, told him she had pulled off her leggings and lowered herself into the pool. Releasing a deep shuddering sigh, he folded those too before undressing.

She rested along the side, with her back to him. He nodded, appreciating this token of privacy. Once naked himself, he approached the pool. Joi splashed water on her face then, affording him the dignity to slide into the hot water without embarrassing her. He didn't know if she had seen a naked man before but seeing him so would compromise her future marriage.

Sinking into the water until chest height, he found her smiling with her eyes closed. Pink traveled from her flushed face to the surface of the water, but he couldn't tell if it was from her thoughts or the heat rising off the pool.

"Why the blush, Princess?" he asked, finding he needed to know the cause.

"My torturous thoughts remind me at inopportune moments how I bathed in front of Rannic." She chuckled and splashed water over her face again, her bare shoulders rising above the water's dark surface. Sohar scowled—yet another reason to flay the skin off that Drem's backside. "To marry him might have been the wiser solution, Sohar."

"Rumoc would never accept you. He would have you dead within the Season of Delight." He tried not to think of Rannic and Joi sharing their first intimate year. Once the allotted season was complete, then the official marriage ceremony would occur, and all royals would travel to them to bless the union.

"Surely he would wait until after the ceremony? Besides, I might have the Divine's blessing within the first year." Her expression softened, as if the thought of children, no matter who the father was, delighted her.

Sohar's breath hitched, and he smothered it with water, almost blinding himself with the force he used to wash his face. Joi blessed with a child? She would look beautiful, her cheeks rosy, and her eyes glowing with happiness. Just not with Rannic's child—*that* he wouldn't allow.

"Wine?" She uncapped the stone carafe then held it out to Sohar.

He accepted and drank deeply before offering it to her in return. After quenching her thirst then capping it, she placed it on the side. Shifting closer, she held a bowl between them, and they feasted on strips of spicy meat. She shoved the last morsels toward him and rinsed her fingers in the water.

"Turn, I'll wash your hair," he said and sleepy-eyed Joi did as commanded.

She sank deeper into the water the longer they stayed there. Gathering her hair into his palm, he rubbed the soap along the gleaming strands, before massaging her scalp. She moaned, the sound of her enjoyment spiking his heart rate. Rinsing off the soap, she faced him, and he offered her his back. Having a woman wash his hair implied a more personal relationship, one of commitment of the heart.

Sohar had offered for two reasons. He was certain they weren't alone and anyone knowing the Greyadian custom would understand the significance. And, as Joi mentioned, there were some situations where necessity would win. This was one of those times. As soon as he rose from the water, having ducked under to rinse his hair, she pressed her forehead to his shoulder.

"Do you think you could find our way back to our chambers?" She had slurred a few words, but he knew her well enough to understand.

"No." He chuckled, spinning to catch her against his chest, her skinner softer than he imagined. "Come, let us dress, and perhaps someone will escort us?"

With a long sigh, she climbed out of the pool. He glanced away, but not fast enough. Her pale form would remain imprinted on his mind. The curve of her hip, the indent of her waist, and the delicious contours of her backside.

After climbing out the other side, he jumped up and down shaking water off him before accepting the toweling cloth she offered him. She toyed with her medallion, silently conveying she wouldn't look away from it until he was ready. Sohar dressed then gathered their things in one arm, her hand in his, and went in search of a guide.

Chapter Thirty-One

Revelation

"You can't expect me to trust a Greyadian simply because he is your husband, Joi-hin," Viggu said over the morning meal in his home.

His two daughters, Shelur and Nyry, served fresh bread, bowls of milk, and sweet strips of meat. Having met Shelur last night, feminine Nyry drew Joi's attention. She was shorter than her older sister but more curvaceous and as beautiful. Woven into her dark sand-colored hair were beads and leather strips.

"He is the ice to your fire, the white to your black, stone to your joy—a wise choice. No man adores you more. He will deal with the Drem, of that, I have no doubt." Viggu sipped his tea.

Joi nodded, keeping her face relaxed and her posture unchanged. Her heart leaped into her throat—for Sohar was all those things. Relief flooded her as well. They had convinced Viggu theirs was a real marriage which meant Sohar's life was safe.

"I'll deal with the Drem. King Buro made sure I could. What concerns you, Ker-hin? I know that look." She smiled her thanks, accepting the offered stone bowl of tea.

She sought out Sohar, needing to know he was near. He sat behind her, at his own table, a sign of Viggu's continued distrust. Sweet and courteous Nyry served him, a stark contrast against Shelur's aggressive stance who leaned against a stone wall, unwavering in her regard of Sohar's form. Her hand on her hilt revealed her thoughts.

"Tell me, have you encountered the Divine's disciples on this journey?" At Viggu's question, silence descended upon the chamber.

Joi shot a nervous glance at Sohar before meeting Viggu's gray eyes. She nodded, releasing a long sigh. "Yes, we were set upon in Vaeril."

His face was grim, forming the strong visage of a leader. She couldn't read the myriad expressions behind his eyes, but his clenched lips said he wasn't pleased.

He cupped her hand, trapping it between his. "It is as your father suspected. The priestess must have seen the attack on Tennaba in the Well of Tomorrows, and in past attempts, when the realms were on the brink of war, she intervened. Yet, when your father visited her, she claimed she foresaw no impending attack. Not trusting her, Kura planned according to his instincts." Viggu dropped her hand to pull out a cloth-wrapped object from within his tunic. "He left this for you. He placed his faith in the Divine himself and not in the priestess. I believed him to be a fool to leave it with me...yet, here you are."

She accepted the object with trembling fingers. In the crucial minutes before Da's death, he had given her three things: the token, the medallion, and her life. A tear escaped as she imagined him wrapping the scarlet cloth, determination furrowing his brow. Worn and faded now, the cloth still held the fiery emblem, the same one carved into her token. The Letouran Crest. She traced the pattern with a fingertip before unraveling the braided ebony hair binding the cloth. Her father's?

Her breath shuddered out of her, and she stifled a sob as she gathered the braid to hold against her cheek. After tucking the braid inside her tunic, she unwrapped the object. It was a leather-bound parchment, edged with lion fur and sealed with her father's mark. The same one he let her play with when she was six, wasting red wax and parchment under his amused watch. Breaking the brittle seal, she unrolled the parchment and gasped. Two inscriptions awaited her.

> *The power of soul, of the Divine,*
> *Of heart and light,*
> *Mind and plight,*
> *Judge now, the guardian of thine.*
> *—You will know when to you use this, little one.*

She handed it to Viggu to read before passing it to Sohar. He read it, rolled it, then rose to his feet to bring it to her. She gave him the cloth instead, and he returned to his table to wrap the parchment, placing it inside his tunic for safekeeping.

"I cannot say what it means, Joi-hin, but if the Divine Priestess wants your life, then she is not of the Divine." Viggu shook his head. "For though He takes life, it is not by trickery."

"I foresee a trip to Raica to resolve this, Joi-Joi," Sohar said. "And you thought traveling to Rendar was a waste of time. The Divine has revealed His will."

"Will you visit me when I'm in Tennaba?" Choosing to change the subject, she leaned across the table to squeeze Viggu's hand.

"You spoke truth about ending this war, our solitude?" Viggu's eyes widened in delight.

"Of course. The Divine grants authority. To sit and do nothing while people suffer? Da and Buro did not raise me so." Joi glanced at Sohar, knowing her words would hurt.

Although he was a man of principles, continuing the path of war without contestation simply because the realms decreed it? That was dishonorable. His clenched lips showed her words displeased him. Or perhaps, displeasure at the truth behind them?

She wouldn't apologize, but she was sorry she had harmed him—pain lingered in his stiff shoulders. "I will speak to Jeiram."

"Jei-hin is alive?" Viggu slapped his thigh as laughter erupted out of him. "Kura, you old devil. Yes, Joi-hin, I will visit you both when you return to Tennaba. Now, Shelur tells me your power is purple? Eria was a forest maiden, her energy was blue, and I suppose, merging with the Scarlet Fox would make purple. It's rare though since the Fox overpowers the lesser power within."

"I haven't tested my energy since I escaped from Tennaba, focusing instead on my Xiaxan training." Joi sighed. No one in Ethrielle had thought to teach her the use of her magic, although it would have been weaker in a realm not of her birth. "I should have before Pan activated the medallion."

"Panzan?" Viggu slapped his thigh again for another round of chuckles. "The Divine has been busy. Did you enjoy the Pools of Renewal?" His gaze sharpened, warning her there was significance to the pools she wasn't aware of.

Not knowing what he was seeking, she chose honesty. "I loved it, especially the blossoming Gyqio orchids. I've seen paintings of its beauty, but the annals hold no other information. They don't blossom long enough for the scholars to study."

"Their fragrance is of particular interest," Viggu said, his focus darting between her and Sohar, searching for something.

"Yes, Joi-Joi did not scent jasmine, as I did." Sohar nodded in thanks at Nyry for his refilled bowl of tea.

"For each person, it alters to what they love the most in this world," Shelur said, cleaning a fingernail with the tip of her dagger.

Joi's eyes widened, and she glanced down, trying to hide her surprise. She should have smelled Pan's noodles or her father, but she hadn't. Instead, she had smelled Sohar's sunbaked scent and a hint of spiciness remnant of cinnamon. Shelur's words rang truth in her heart, a loud knelling of a bell. It had a finality to it, and the weight of the revelation smothered her confidence.

"My chief." A man intruded, bowing to Viggu. "The *Phader* has arrived."

"Vard is here?" Sohar bounded up, revealing his excitement.

"Yes," Viggu said, rising to his feet, as well. Shelur flanked her father with a white-knuckled grip on her hilt. "His division awaited your arrival west of Zugba. Harm none of my people, Greyadian, and I will grant the second prince access to Ta."

"Harm your people?" Sohar gaped. "Chief Viggu, my wife has announced her intentions. To scorn your hospitality is to disgrace her. You must know this?"

Viggu nodded before leading the way down various passages to the paved stone road that brought them inside the Hokhoun Mountains and Ta. Just outside the massive gates, a division of mounted men awaited them. Three broke away, riding their camels with a skill Joi envied. Viggu approached them by foot with Shelur to his left. Sohar laced his fingers through Joi's hand, and they trailed behind.

"Greetings, Prince Vard." Viggu's voice boomed a welcome.

"Greetings, Chief Viggu. I see you have my brother and Princess Jenaso. Since they are not bound, am I to assume they are not captives?" Vard vaulted off the camel, landing on the paved stones without disturbing the sand encasing them.

Shelur's gasp was soft—Joi wasn't the only one impressed. The Greyadian strode forward, his white cloak billowing behind him as he flicked his hood back. A jawline as chiseled as Sohar's, a wide forehead, and a tapering nose—these features highlighted their relationship.

"Welcome, second brother." Sohar dragged Joi closer. Despite liking her hand in his, she didn't need him to drag her around as if she was unwilling.

"If Sohar would release my hand, you will see I too am not a captive." She peered around Sohar's bulk to look at Vard.

A flash of humor crossed his face as he gestured to his two men. They retreated, then with precision, his division dismounted as one. It was breathtaking to observe.

"My apologies for resting on your doorstep, Chief Viggu, but I assume by Sohar and Joi's freedom that our wait will not be a lengthy one." Lightning quick, Vard stood before Joi, staring at her.

Scowling, she castigated herself for her distraction. She gave him a formal bow with the wrong hand since Sohar refused to release her. Glaring at him revealed he was laughing at her.

"I thought carafes of Redanta had addled your mind, Sohar. I see now you spoke the truth. She is beautiful." Vard flicked his attention at his brother, a small smile twitching his lips.

"She's standing before you." She squared her shoulders despite shyness fidgeting her fingers. It warmed her heart that Sohar considered her so. She thought he tolerated her and found her, in general lacking—despite the kisses.

"And spirited, disrespectful, stubborn, mischievous? Weren't those your words?" Vard's laughter was a warm sound, and with such ease as if he did so often—an unlikely Greyadian trait. "When you said her eyes were mesmerizing, I consulted with the royal physician."

"Sohar, is he toying with me? I can't tell with you Greyadians," she grumbled, dipping her head to hide her embarrassment. A grin split her cheeks as she considered setting fire to Vard's silver eyebrows. The imagined shocked expression on his face had her chuckling.

"How touching," Shelur said, derision dripping from her tongue. "Take your men and leave, Greyadian."

Viggu's grunt showed his displeasure. "Shelur."

Joi twisted to gape at the woman. Did her hatred run too deep? She frowned, seeing what she could have become had she not chosen a better path. Bitterness infused Shelur's posture and contorted her Orthian features.

"I've tolerated their presence long enough, *Ker-hin*," she spat, mocking Joi's familiarity with her father. "Visit your *Joi-hin* in Letoura. Here in Ta, we have one constant—no one mourns the death of a Greyadian." She stomped around them to confront Vard, her face so close to his she almost kissed him. "No one gave you permission to enter Ta, *khonu*. Your arrogance does not mean Orth belongs to you. The sands remember."

The crowds murmured repeating the phrase, as if the spirits Sohar mentioned were in attendance.

"Viggu, I invite Shelur to travel with us. As an Orthian ambassador, she is more than suitable to negotiate an end to this war." Sohar's suggestion was a surprise, and the slight curling of his upper lip said he had a plan, a cunning one.

"I agree," Viggu said without hesitation.

"But..." Shelur growled, facing her father. Anger darkened her striking features, and the gray swirled in her eyes like an ominous storm. Joi pitied her. To be thrust among her enemies would not be pleasant.

"I am chief, daughter-of-mine," Viggu roared. "A fact you forget when it suits you. Disobey me and you'll be *ashilé* and no longer welcome in Ta. Prince Sohar, since you have your hands full with your wife, Prince Vard has my authority."

Shelur gasped, and both father and daughter missed Vard's arched brow. Joi smothered a smile against Sohar's shoulder. She almost pitied Vard too.

Viggu didn't back down. "Do you submit? Will you pack your things for a journey or bid farewell to Ta?"

Instead of answering, Shelur stomped off. Viggu watched her, sadness softening his face. "You are wise as well as blessed, Prince Sohar." He addressed dutiful Nyry. "Gather their things and prepare them for travel." She nodded before scurrying off.

"She is young, my chief," Sohar said, showing Viggu great respect with the use of his title.

"Joi-hin." Viggu opened his arms for a hug, and at last, Sohar released her. She wrapped her arms around Ker-hin's waist, clinging to him. "I'd hoped to spend more time with you, but I see the Divine has other plans."

"It was wonderful to find you, Ker-hin. I love you, you know that." Here stood a connection to her da. Tears stung her eyes, and she blinked them away, not wanting to show weakness.

"As the birds in the sky and the fish in the sea." He chuckled.

It meant more to her than she could express that he remembered her childish declaration at his last visit with her father. Despite her efforts, her tears trickled down her cheeks, and she rubbed at them in anger. A princess did not cry, especially not in front of so many.

"Take care of her, Prince Sohar. And my daughter, Prince Vard. I place into your hands treasures which are without measure."

Within half a day, they had nourished the hundred soldiers forming the Greyadian *Phader* and their camels. Sadness lingered when Joi snuck glances at Ta, shrinking the farther they traveled. She hoped to catch one more glance of Viggu. The link to her father and her history was bittersweet.

Facing forward to lean down and ruffle Velvet's tuft of hair, she pondered the next leg of her journey, feeling as if it was never-ending. According to Ky's plan, they would travel to Rendar, to while away the time until he revealed her chosen husband.

The Divine Priestess's assassins steered her along another path with Viggu confirming her destination with his revelations. In a way, traveling to Rendar, via the Temple of the Divine at Raica, was possible, if one could stomach the delay. She needed to confront the priestess, Divine willing.

As the sun baked Joi in her cloak, with the heat shimmering along the arid wasteland, she closed her eyes against the depressing horizon. Traveling the exotic realms in her world was best kept to her imagination. She would blame sweltering Orth for her disillusionment.

Yes, seeing the Wood of Yellow Suns outside Vaeril, the Forest of the Unloved with its eerie skeleton-infested trees, and the Festival of Forgotten Feathers as they traveled had brought her inexplicable delight.

A sunbaked gust swept her hood back and assaulted her face with stinging sand. She shot a glare at Sohar's back. Could they not have traveled at nighttime?

Chapter Thirty-Two

Explanations

Vard drew his camel alongside Sohar's, and the repeated glances thrown his way said his second brother wanted to talk. He knew what question plagued Vard. Looking back, Sohar sought out Joi's face, finding her riding alongside Shelur, both women united in silence.

"She lied to Viggu about our marriage to save my life." He faced forward, keeping his voice low in case his words traveled.

"I see." Vard frowned. "And with his daughter on the journey, the ruse must continue?"

"We will reveal it to Shelur once she has developed a fondness for Joi." Sohar lowered his hood. "It shouldn't take long."

Instead of speaking, Vard's gaze rested on the Orthian woman, lingering on her longer than required. What was Vard thinking? She was a striking woman, strong, passionate, but Sohar knew not his second brother's preferences, Sohar erred on the side of impossible. Proud and stubborn Shelur would never consider a Greyadian attractive, even if he was the second prince.

A union between Orth and Greyad would smooth the transition from war to peace. History showed many such unions, but Father would not force such a match on his sons. King Codin's own marriage was a political union with no love lost between them. Their estrangement was so extreme his father hadn't mourned his mother's death.

"She's as prickly as a firthorn, but I will admit her passion is intoxicating." Vard's voice deepened.

Sohar nodded—yes, a union between Vard and Shelur might resolve decades of hatred between the two realms. *If* he could charm the Orthian firthorn. Sohar sided with Joi on the abolishment of the war. This would surprise his father since all the princes were devout warriors. They had spent their time honing their fighting skills, studying past battles, forming war strategies, and visiting their favorite brothels.

"You haven't said anything about Joi's promise of peace." Sohar watched his brother's face. He knew him well with the slightest twitch revealing more of Vard's heart than a full sentence might have. The twitch was a hopeful one.

"I'm tired of fighting. Father doesn't know I've dismantled a few weaponsmiths, converting those towns into silk farmers or wine growers. I'd like to have children too. The thought of tormenting my daughters' suitors brings me great joy."

"You'd make an excellent father, Vard." Sohar smiled, allowing it to conquer his face. Having to be the strongest, fiercest, most honorable man in all things, soul-deep exhaustion dogged him. It was dishonorable to fight a pointless war. Joi's words had hurt. More so since they echoed his own thoughts.

"Does she have the Scarlet Fox?" Excitement sparkled in Vard's eyes.

Sohar nodded then pinched his lips. "And she has my heart, not that she asked for it."

"This is wonderful news, first brother." Vard bounced in his saddle. "A union between Greyad and Letoura would strengthen us."

"And weaken the other realms which they would not tolerate. I will not endanger her further, increasing Letoura's enemies. Besides, if Jeiram doesn't come forward soon, she will reign."

Vard stopped fidgeting to gape. "Jeiram's alive?"

"She says she has half the Scarlet Fox's power, proving he's alive." He stole another glance at her. "King Velisand must have sheltered him."

"If he does reign over Letoura, would you claim the princess?" Vard patted his camel's tuft.

This question had haunted Sohar since she revealed Jeiram's existence. Sohar didn't take the Gyqio orchids as definitive proof she loved him. The flowers and their effects were unknown, the Orthians untrustworthy, but it felt good knowing she might think of him as more than a brother trainee.

"She hasn't revealed how she feels, Vard."

"She cares for you. Wait until Father hears you married without following protocol." Vard chuckled.

Sohar glared at him, his hand resting on his hilt in a silent warning.

Vard threw up his hands in surrender. "Three days? I don't know if I can survive the journey." He peeked at a fuming Shelur. "When we stop to water the camels, would you mind removing the daggers from my back?"

"Her animosity is understandable, Vard." Sohar sighed.

He too glanced back, but his attention lingered on Joi. Again. She wasn't tense—her plump lips relaxed as she once again disappeared into her thoughts. She was exuberant, true to her name. Then times like now, she was serene, mature. Divine, he loved both sides of her.

She caught him staring and flashed him a bright smile. Gesturing with her hands as if she drank wine, she reminded him of his promise to a night at a winehouse in Corough. He chuckled, nodded, then faced forward again. He would keep his promise to her, for such an evening spent in each other's company might be their last.

Chapter Thirty-Three

Finality

"I can't believe you married...that. Father praised you often—he never once hinted that you lacked intelligence." At Shelur's spiteful words, Joi twisted in her saddle to look at her before peering at Sohar and Vard as if she was giving her response solemn consideration.

"Tall, handsome, powerful, battle-honed, and wealthy, hmm, yes, you are right. There's nothing to attract a woman. What was I thinking?" Joi grinned. She couldn't help comparing the two princes though. Both were regal in their bearing.

"Mock me, Princess, but I have seen what Greyadians can do."

"As they have seen Orthians slaughter villagers. How are your actions justified and theirs not?" She raised her hand to silence Shelur. "The Divine Priestess and five kings decreed the punishment Orth would receive. You blame Greyad for fulfilling that decree. They blame you for forcing them to do so. Take a leap of faith, Shelur, and accept this opportunity to end this hatred, the bloodshed. If you choose not to leap, then think of this as an adventure. When last did an Orthian travel through Greyad?" She leaned down to pat Velvet's neck before picking at her armor to create air movement in the hopes of cooling down.

"They killed my mother," Shelur ground out.

Joi addressed the closest Greyadian soldiers. "Tell me, have you lost loved ones in this war?"

"A brother and many friends, Princess." A soldier glared at Shelur.

Joi arched a brow at another soldier.

"My two sons, my princess." Despair hunched his shoulders. The Greyadian and Orthian men around her yelled out their loss, startling Shelur. Her posture stiffened as she straightened her spine against the combined weight of their hatred and loss.

"We all have suffered, Shelur. Death is unavoidable and birth a gift. Choose rebirth and let the dead rest." Joi squeezed her thighs, and Velvet trotted forward, ending the depressing conversation. "That woman," she gasped in greeting as she drew alongside Sohar's camel. "I thought *you* could drain a lemon of its bitterness, Mighty Sohar."

"Oh, he can, and he's an excellent tutor if you wish to learn." Vard flashed a smile.

"Continue down this destructive path, second brother. You have to sleep at some point," Sohar teased.

"Princess Joi will protect me. She's had years of experience surviving your *bitterness*." Vard laughed at her nod of agreement. "I have missed you, dear brother." He slapped his brother on the shoulder.

"As I missed you." Sohar nudged his chin ahead. "Where's third brother Neha?"

"I left him in charge of the Corough encampment and to await our return."

"He can handle the responsibility." Sohar nodded as he dug out a water skin to offer to Joi.

She smiled her thanks. The hot water was vile, but it was better than nothing. She capped it then returned the pouch to him.

"It might have been wiser to await night." Joi picked at her armor again, giving Sohar a pointed look.

"A division of Greyadians outside Ta was asking for trouble. The quicker we left, the better for all," Vard said.

"True, we cannot abolish lifetimes of hatred in one day." Sohar leaned across and tugged Joi's hood down, shading her face.

She frowned. Why was he so attentive? Was he still pretending to be her husband? She glanced at Shelur to find she was reading a thick parchment and paying them no attention.

"She's not looking, Sohar," she said, keeping her voice low.

"So I should let you burn? Turn you into an Orthian? Kylen would kill me." He looked horrified then ruined it by chuckling.

He was doing that more often. Chuckling. She had succeeded in her goal without even trying. Who knew a trip through the fires of hell, also known as Orth, would call forth his humor?

"Ha, you've never feared Ky. Of the two of you, your swordsmanship is better." She laughed, but it felt insincere. Something bothered her, like a darkness lingering in the back of her mind that she couldn't name.

"Princess, did you compliment me?" He clasped a hand over his heart and made shocked gasping noises in his throat.

"You're being silly." She halted Velvet and turned to ride alongside Vard instead. "Tell me about yourself, Vard. Why did you not come for Xiaxan training?"

"Sohar chose Ethrielle, Berandaros was my burden to bear, and Neha remained with our generals."

"Ah, Berandaros. Would your decision have something to do with three lovely princesses?" Joi teased. She suspected it was their molten curls that drew attention. Glancing at Sohar, she wondered if he found them as magnificent. Rannic had almost shoved her to the side to reach them.

"I didn't see the princesses enough to form an opinion on their personalities, but they *are* lovely. Then again, all Seitians have the same coloring. In Ethrielle or Rendar, their vibrancy would be hard to miss."

"In Greyad, your coloring will be as spectacular, Joi-Joi," Sohar said, but he didn't glance at her. He kept his focus on the shimmering horizon, granting her the perfect opportunity to study his handsome profile.

"Did you see Jeiram there?" she asked Vard, desperate to change the subject.

He shook his head. "No, my apologies, Princess. He must have received private tuition."

She sighed. Any news of her brother would be welcome. Until she saw him with her own eyes, she dared not hope he was alive. Pan said half of the Fox was with her, then claimed Jeiram had to have the other half. Only the Divine knew who of the Letouran royals were still alive.

"What are you thinking, Joi?" Sohar asked.

She met his gaze and shrugged, biting hard on her lip to focus. Long stretches of time with her thoughts rattled her. She would travel to Raica then to Rendar to await the name of her husband. From there she would return to Tennaba for her Season of Delight.

At some point, she would need to deal with Rumoc and Rannic. She might have to stop hoping Jeiram survived. And, glancing up at Sohar, she would have to learn how to live without her heart. Why had she fallen in love with him?

She poked a mental finger at her heart and realized she had loved him for years.

"Princess?"

Instead of answering a now-concerned Sohar, she halted Velvet, cast a last longing look at him, then steered her camel back to Shelur. She kept her face down, hiding the tears.

Horror, joy, and despair mingled, stirring nausea in her stomach. Loving him, though wonderful, meant split loyalties, meant Greyad above her, meant Letoura above him, meant busy lives and only seeing each other at solace—if they shared chambers. It meant combining Letoura and Greyad, the Scarlet Fox, and Greyad's formidable armies.

How could she fall for him? She drew in a shuddering breath, fighting the rigidity in her chest. Oh, what a fool she was.

Chapter Thirty-Four

Anger

"It's been three days," Sohar ground out, burning Vard's ears with yet another whispered tirade. He huffed at Sohar in irritation. "We're *married,* but she hasn't smiled at me, nor spoken to me. Nothing."

"Perhaps it is for the best if you won't marry her by the Divine, Sohar." Vard nodded at his soldiers standing guard outside the ZinYi communication post.

He tasked a soldier to ride ahead and notify Neha of their impending arrival. The Kilryn Wall loomed before them, a marvel of Greyadian ingenuity. All the realms donated staggered slabs of stone that were longer than his height and thicker than his waist. Soon they would journey through the Corough gates. In three hours, this blasted heat would be behind him. Then more traveling across green fields before they dismounted in the Corough encampment.

Vard understood what Sohar was feeling. Shelur was driving him senseless. Vard's emotions tossed like a ship crossing the Sea of Turmoil. Curse women. Each evening he had met her under the darkness of night, and she talked to him, sharing her thoughts and life experiences. The vivacious woman was a delight. By daylight, she hated him, but peppered him with unguarded moments when he would catch her looking at him. He drew in a quivering breath. No wonder he preferred the dancers at the brothels. Having coin was communication enough.

"What's the first thing you'll do when we see Neha?" he asked Sohar. It was a game they played whenever they approached a well-situated encampment.

"Bathe, then I will escort Joi to a winehouse. I made a promise to her at the start of the journey."

Vard glanced at the princess and wondered if she would agree to join Sohar for an evening of overindulgence. She looked unhappy, and if he didn't know better, he would say broken-hearted. His mother used to have the same look when Father hadn't visited her in a while. As a high consort, she had no rights. After the queen's death, his mother found happiness again.

He smiled, imagining the battles fought within the harem. Why did men believe they had the knowledge of warfare? Truly, concubines would be victorious in any battle since they strategized daily. They fought their battles, not by the sword but by their words.

"I assume you'd prefer to be alone with her?" He glanced at Shelur, wondering if she would enjoy a few carafes of wine with him.

Sohar stared off into the distance, frustrated and distracted. "You are most welcome. Joi said she could drink her weight in wine."

"Since she doesn't weigh much, it would only be a few carafes." Vard chuckled. "I'd suggest we reserve rooms as well. Once we sit down for the evening's storytelling, I do not want to ride another animal."

"You wouldn't be saying that if it was a brothel instead of a winehouse." Sohar smiled.

The dark circles under his eyes concerned Vard. Did Joi not care? He had been under the impression she did, which was why she saved Sohar's life repeatedly—if the stories were true. Vard glanced at her; she had lowered her hood over her face, revealing only her chin and lips. Those were bright red as if she had drawn blood with her teeth. With a shake of his head, he halted his camel and waited for Shelur to reach him.

"Ride with me," he said, his tone brooking no argument. She followed, and he suspected it was more out of curiosity than obedience. He would deal with that another time. Once they were far enough away from the division, he slowed his camel to a walk. "Has she spoken to you? Mentioned why she's sad?"

Shelur huffed. "Yes, but why does it matter to you?"

"Shelur," Vard growled. "He's my first brother—why do you think it matters?"

She studied him in silence, her gray eyes swirling with her inner turmoil. Divine, they were magnificent. Drawing in a deep breath, she nodded.

"She fears Jeiram isn't alive. A future rebuilding Tennaba alone weighs heavy on her heart. She revealed that Sohar isn't her husband, that she lied to save him because he is dear to her. You can tell him to stop acting as if her silence devastates him."

"He loves her, Shelur," he said. "It's no pretense, but yes, they're not married."

She stared at him again, her gaze traveling his face, searching. "I assume he doesn't want to burden her further? As queen of Letoura, to be the Greyadian queen might be too much for her."

Vard nodded, pleased she understood the ramifications. "That's my assumption, as well."

"Jeiram still alive would free her and delight my father." Hope blossomed on her beautiful face before fading. "If he lives."

"I asked Sohar, but he didn't answer me. This evening, we plan to drink to our safe return. Would you care to join me?" He tried not to hold his breath. Why did it matter so much if she agreed? Curse it, she tied him in knots, and by the looks of it, without even trying. "If you'd prefer to remain in your tent, I'll have my men deliver a few carafes."

"I will join you. My thanks for the invitation." Her soft words made his chest tighten, as if under a vise. He met her gaze and smiled, keeping it small and not too wide. Because, Divine, he wanted to yell his delight.

"Should we intervene?" He gestured to Joi and Sohar.

"What do you have planned?" A mischievous smile curled her lips.

"Reserving all the rooms at the winehouse, bar one?" He arched a brow.

She shook her head. "They spent a night together at Ta which made no difference."

He rubbed his jaw, not coming up with anything worth mentioning. "What do you suggest?"

"Your father—convince him of their suitability." Her strategic approach stunned and disappointed him since he imagined them being mischievous together.

"Ah, shake Sohar's foundation?" Vard studied her, respect growing. His father wouldn't force a union, but if Sohar loved her, then perhaps Father could apply his wisdom to devise a solution. "In a few hours, we'll be soaking in a hot bath, then en route to Corough. Chilled wine does sound delicious."

She offered her pouch. Wrapped in many layers of cloth and leather, it was ungainly to hold, but as he tipped it to his lips, cool Naferian wine coated his tongue. Sweet, rich, and spicy. He held the pouch out, twisting it from side to side. An ingenious idea.

"Thank you." He smiled, returning the pouch to her. She pressed her lips to the opening. His joy faltered. In a way, they just shared their first kiss of some sort.

"A bath sounds wonderful," she said as she stowed her pouch.

He sighed, dragging his focus elsewhere. "Have you given thought to the peace negotiations?"

"I don't hate Greyadians, I hate their actions. I'm as surprised at this revelation as you are. It will take me a while to rein in my antagonism, though." She gave him a small smile. "For the good of my people, peace would bring relief, perhaps prosperity?" She leaned down to pat her camel's neck. "The problem I foresee is relocation. Many of my people will choose to abandon Orth for the richer realms and what they could provide for their families. Animosity is sure to follow with what the realms might call an invasion."

"Not if Letoura, Meideon, and Greyad offer land for your people to settle on." Vard hummed under his breath as he considered such a solution. "All three realms are rich with land. I suspect Joi will welcome all your people since she wants to rebuild her realm. The additional support and guidance of your father will be of great use to her." He called to the closest soldier. "Ride to the ZinYi communication post and have them travel to ZinEr and ZinSa. I want the Varturg encampment dismantled and returning to Corough. All posts, as well. It's time to go home."

"Peace, my prince?" The soldier gasped and bowed formally. "Forgive my outburst, my lord."

"Peace? Would you want it?" Shelur asked him.

The soldier bowed again, displaying no anger toward her. "It is my right to protect my loved ones, but if there is no need, then that is a good life."

"True. We will have to find another way to deal with our exiles," Vard said as the soldier left to do as bidden. It had become custom to banish lawless people to the barren wastelands. Opening the gates would invite them to continue their deceitful ways.

"Grant all amnesty and turn homeless soldiers into subprefects, prefects, and judges, based on your hierarchy. Any further lawlessness, then exile them to Orth, but seal the gates. Or enforce harsher penalties for repeat offenders." She ran a fingertip over an eyebrow as if she warmed to the subject. "The alternative would be to keep your exiles and put them to work, improving the realm. Farming, building roads, or schools. An unpaid workforce."

"Slavery? No, not slavery, a punishment for a predetermined time based on their offense." He grinned. He couldn't help himself. She was amenable during daylight and hadn't once thrown hatred at him. Despising Greyadians must be a habit for her with a hardened shell encasing her heart and perspective.

"If we abandon Orth, perhaps nature will restore the balance, strip this land of its residual magic, and over time the trapped souls infesting the stone and the wind will forget." She scanned the ruins in the distance.

"I do believe we are reaching an accord, Shelur. I thank you for your wise counsel."

"Don't thank me yet, Vard. You still need to convince King Codin and his advisors."

"*We* need to convince them." He snatched her hand resting on her thigh and kissed her palm. "You will delight and impress my father."

She yanked her hand back, glowering at him as her cheeks darkened but her eyes tipped at the edges with barely suppressed humor. This time, it was from embarrassment and not anger. She returned her hand to her thigh, but her fingers fluttered. Oh, she challenged him, this Orthian woman. Fired his blood and mind with her boldness.

After a comfortable silence, he chuckled, drawing her attention. "Joi plans to drink her weight in wine."

"No more than two carafes." Shelur grinned.

"Four," Vard said.

She arched her brow, her smile still lingering on her lips. "So you wish to wager with me, Greyadian? I am Orthian—we may not have magic, but we do have luck."

"A wager? What would you like if I lose?"

"Your dagger." She didn't hesitate.

He nodded. It was a worthy prize. The bejeweled Meideon steel dagger was a gift from Mion many years ago. "Agreed." Facing forward, he waited for her to ask what this wager might cost her, but she remained silent. "Why haven't you asked what I want?"

"Orthians do not lose." She smirked then shrugged. "Very well. What would you like if I lose?"

"A kiss," he said.

Her eyebrows shot up, and she laughed. "I will give you a kiss now for your dagger. A fair trade, but as part of a wager, it must be of equal value."

"Marry me," he said, surprising himself.

Her gasp, and the anger in her narrowed eyes said she wasn't pleased.

"Orthians have different protocols to follow. My father has to agree, an offering of gifts to my family, an unarmed fight with any who wish to challenge your request, and a night of passionate abandonment to ensure we are compatible."

At the words "passionate abandonment," Vard jerked the reins of his camel to ride in the opposite direction. Shelur did the same, galloping after him with her braided hair trailing her like the tail of a celestial star. He liked everything about her. Throwing a grin at her, he looked ahead, laughing as he encouraged his camel to gallop faster.

"You cannot be serious. You will not travel back to my father, Vard," she yelled.

He drew to a halt and spun in his saddle to stare at her. He had never been more serious in his life. Gone was his usual jovial attitude, replaced by a fire to claim this woman by all and any means necessary.

"I see that you are," she said, a little breathless. "Let us negotiate peace then return to my father. If he says no, I will have, at least, done as he commanded."

She wasn't outright denying him. He grinned. "Very well, but know you are mine, Shelur."

"You are not following Greyadian customs either," she grumbled.

How could he out here in Orth's blazing sands? "I will once I see my father. I will marry you."

She met his gaze without flinching, but by the press of her lips, she had smothered her response. As they returned to the division, grumbles from under her breath sounded something like "it's been three days," and "arrogant fool doesn't even know me" followed by "let's see how determined he is when he has to fight my father."

Vard chuckled. He had gotten under her skin and won this battle, but with Shelur, there was no guaranteed victory.

Chapter Thirty-Five

Waiting

Rannic stood immobile on the wooden wall surrounding Corough. He had been there for days, impatiently waiting for Joi to arrive. Not for the first time did he consider that something might have happened to her. As a Drem, his darker coloring drew unwelcome attention wherever he went. All treated the Drem with suspicion and at worst, hatred. Only the dancers were eager to see him for his coin. The past two days he had taken to standing guard at the wall, watching the Corough encampment for messengers.

His vigilance had at last paid off in the past hour—a messenger had arrived. The camp was a hive of activity. The Greyadian soldiers had erected two additional tents, both of royal stature. He appreciated the excitement bubbling inside him. The joy was a stark contrast to the dark thoughts plaguing him. He had come to an unpleasant decision. The sight of Joi was the final step. Whatever emotions she evoked would determine the path he chose.

So he remained on the battlements, watching, waiting. The dust cloud on the east horizon heralded her arrival. Camels crossed the green fields. Based on the height differences, he could judge which rider she was. A wagon trailed behind, carrying trunks and servants. Odd. Joi and Sohar had only their traveling bags. Who in the procession required these items?

Another hour or so passed before five riders on horses in Greyadian livery left the encampment, heading for Corough. Rannic didn't hurry down. He kept his focus on them in the setting sunlight. Joi and Sohar he recognized, even from this distance. The other three riders must be Greyadians. As they galloped alongside the Laugar River, westward to the Isahere bridge, he caught the pale braided hair and dark skin of an Orthian woman.

Well, now, that was interesting. Since there were no bags strapped to their pommels, they weren't planning on traveling far. He leaned over the battlement wall to watch them cross the stone bridge. A slow smile curled his lips as a plan formed. There were only three inns in Corough, all at capacity since they catered for the visiting families of the Greyadian soldiers. There were two winehouses, which made finding Joi easy.

He strode along the battlement to the ladder closest to his awaiting horse but spotted another horse leaving the encampment. This rider was as small as Joi but why she trailed the princess he didn't know. As she too drew alongside the river's embankment, her dark chin peeked out from her hood. Another Orthian? They were growing bolder. With a nod, he vaulted down, landing beside his horse. Time to face his *nemesis*, again.

As he rode his horse along the main road, he searched for the horses or Joi's ebony hair. Either would tell him which inn or winehouse they were at. A sliver of fear slid along his spine. He needed to see her alone, but Sohar had been explicit—approach her and die. Rannic would have to risk it.

Outside the Inn of Dawn Blossoms, snorted five horses saddled in Greyadian martial custom. Dismounting, he tossed his reins over the railing and strode to the entrance. Then halted. It would be bold of him to walk up to her and ask for an audience. It would be wiser to assess the situation first. He scuttled to the side of the building and peeked through the unshuttered window. The Greyadian princes, Vard and Neha, sat opposite the Orthian woman, but there was no sign of Joi. He continued to walk along the building's perimeter, scanning the common room as he passed each window.

"Speak, Princess, or so help me, I will beat you until your tongue loosens," Sohar roared, the sound a beacon to Rannic's searching gaze.

"You can try, Sohar. I've never feared you."

Rannic smiled at Joi's defiance. He rounded the corner of the building where Sohar pressed her against the inn's wall. Their faces were whispers apart. His hands gripped her shoulders, but she remained calm. It was almost as if their roles had reversed—Joi stoic and Sohar passionate. Many runners and passersby cast curious glances at them in the crowded alley.

"Speak to me, please," Sohar begged, his fingers feathering along her jaw, the caress surprisingly intimate. "Your silence worries me."

"I have many concerns and unknowns." She dipped her head. "You know this more than anyone."

"Share them with me." His voice was a whisper.

Rannic strained to hear him above the cacophony of the crowd. She bit her lip before looking away, and her eyes closed as a tear slipped down her cheek. It shimmered in the lamplight and the last vestiges of sunlight.

"I cannot, Mighty Sohar. Please don't ask me to." She placed her hands on his cheeks, staring into his eyes. "I will treasure our time together. I will never forget you."

She ducked under his arm and strode in the opposite direction from Rannic. He scowled, turned, and broke into a run. He would catch her at the entrance. What he did not expect was to collide with someone also spying. As they tumbled, and their limbs entwined, one thing became clear: he had tackled a woman. Wrapping an arm around her waist and his other around her head, he protected her as they tumbled.

Settling on the paved ground with a grunt, he stared into the smoky-gray eyes of an Orthian woman. Her pale gold hair against her bronzed skin and white eyes was breathtaking. She moaned as she struggled under his weight with her soft curves merging with his harder edges. Unable to resist her tantalizing fragrance, he dipped his nose into her hair. She scented of untamed freedom, sand, sunlight, and honey.

"Drem," she said in greeting.

"Orthian." He smiled at her impudence. "My apologies, but I am seeking someone. I don't have time for this." He bounded up, taking her with him in one fluid motion. With a hand gripping her hip under her cloak, he ensured she regained her balance before rushing off. Only to bump into the armored chest of a prefect. Rannic drew in a sharp breath, his patience running thin.

"A Drem and an Orthian? Well, we can't have that in Corough." The prefect gestured for them to follow.

Rannic scowled, taking a step to the side as if to bypass the irritating man. The woman sidled closer to him, hiding behind his back. Truly? He needed to reach Joi now and not deal with whatever this was.

"Oh, no, kind sir," The Orthian leaned around Rannic to address the prefect. "Please let us go. My father...he'll kill me if he finds me."

Her fingers wrapped around Rannic's arm, too familiar in their caress. Her implication was clear. After the dearth of entertainment in Corough, he was enjoying himself. The coin-hungry dancers didn't count.

"He hates Drem, and since Elinan was raised a Greyadian from birth, it made Father more violent."

"Keep your stories to yourself, Orthian. You two were loitering around the inn." The prefect pointed to the inn's windows. "Loitering is bad."

"I saw the horses and thought my father had arrived. Please, kind sir, look inside the inn and you'll see an Orthian." She skipped in front of Rannic, gripping his cloak as she clung to him.

She had positioned her body in an intimate pose. Oh Divine, how he liked the feel of her. The prefect gestured to one of his three subprefects to peer through the window. Knowing who they would see, Rannic hid a smile by pulling her snug against his body and hiding his face in her braided hair. She gasped but smothered it with a small cough.

"She's your sister?" the prefect asked, confirming the presence of another Orthian.

She nodded, burying her face against Rannic's chest as if she awaited the prefect's decision to return her to a cruel and unforgiving father. He wrapped her within his arms, appearing as if he would protect her from the world. What he wanted to do was applaud her performance.

"Come, we'll hide you two in our office."

"But..." Rannic growled. He had played along, hoping the prefect would release them. Rannic had not anticipated a kind-hearted and gullible man. "Beloved, face her. It can't be as bad as you imagined." He tilted the woman to gaze at her upturned face.

The prefect shook his head. "That I cannot allow. Releasing you guarantees a disturbance in the inn. To our office it is."

Following the prefect, Rannic scowled at the woman beside him. He was not pleased. He could use his token, his magic, his sword on the four men, but that would ruin the days he had spent remaining hidden. Hiding in a brothel had helped. Besides, to deceive the prefect, she claimed he was a Greyadian. Revealing the ebony dragon on his Drem imperial token would find them both arrested.

"How long do you plan to detain us?" he asked instead, lacing his fingers through hers. She twitched as if she wanted to struggle. This he too found amusing.

"I will release you before the judge arrives in the morning."

Rannic bit his tongue, his body trembling with the effort to restrain himself. He had a new appreciation for the authority a prince held. He didn't like the helplessness of the common man.

As soon as they entered a windowless room and the door locked behind them, he spun on her, gripping her by her upper arms to shake her. "I had plans, Orthian, plans I have been waiting days to implement."

"You're after Joi-hin?" she asked, startling him.

He jerked, his fingers tightening reflexively. At her wince, he released her and backed away. "Joi-hin?"

"I know why you hate her, Drem, but nursing you're the king's evil will taint your soul."

He scowled, not needing a lecture from a child. Stomping over to the small bed, he sat down, resting his elbow on his knee, his face in his hand. He had lost out on the opportunity. Tomorrow he would need to be bolder. Sneak into the Greyadian camp and her tent? Risky but doable if he used his magic. The dark tendrils of Drem magic were weaker here, in Greyad. He didn't want to deplete his stores if it wasn't necessary.

"So, what's your excuse?" he asked, using his full authority on her—a straightening of his shoulders, the deepening of his voice, and the regal stare refined in the bowels of the Drem court.

Her shoulders slumped, and despair cloaked her. "The Orthian woman *is* my sister, Shelur."

"And?" He added impatience to his voice.

"She's on one of her adventures again, leaving me at home, the only woman in my father's house. If I don't do something, I fear I will die alone having lived half a life."

"Orthian, doesn't—"

"My name is Nyry," she said cutting him off.

No one dared to interrupt him. She lacked a healthy respect for royalty. Made evident by her sitting on the bed next to him without asking permission. Then she kicked off her slippers to fold her legs beneath her. Rannic blinked, fighting a forming smile. A woman's feet were an intimate sight, but he doubted Orthians considered it as such.

"Nyry, is there no father chasing after you?"

She laughed, the sound a delight in the dull confines of the prefect's office. Nyry pulled a thin braid forward to unravel and rebraid, her nimble fingers moving swiftly.

"Yes, Father will not be proud of me. I wanted to wish Shelur farewell before I start my journey, but I doubt I will get a chance. She and Joi-hin shared a tent, so I couldn't sneak in."

"Joi-hin? Why do you call the princess that?"

"It's Father's name for her. He knew her when she was a little girl." Nyry shrugged. "Tell me, Drem, why do you want Joi-hin?"

How to explain this to a girl? He pursed his lips. "To marry her. I've decided to align with Letoura and thus rejoin the other realms. My father will die, whether by his own doing or by old age, it matters not, and I will reign over Drem, as well."

"Who are you to believe she's within your reach?" Nyry's gaze traveled his form, her pale brow arching in query.

"Prince Rannic of Drem," he said.

Her mouth fell open then she laughed. He scowled, not used to women finding him humorous. "She's married to Sohar, you fool."

"No, she hasn't. My father has not heard of this, and a royal union requires the approval of the realms. Joi suggested marrying me five days ago. She would not have if she had married Sohar."

"And how would they notify the realms? Communication in Orth is crow reliant. Besides, why would a Letouran princess choose you, Drem?" Nyry chuckled, shaking her head. "Even if, by a Divine miracle, she loved you, I doubt the kings would bless the union."

"My name is Rannic." He pinched the bridge of his nose, fighting for calm. "I was intending to speak to her this evening." He didn't need to say more but leveled a glare on her. "They had better be here tomorrow, Nyry. I'll blame you if she's left Corough."

"Blame away. I seek my own fortune tomorrow. What you do and whose lives you destroy have no impact on me."

Rannic clenched his jaw. Her disrespectful attitude irritated him. She didn't notice or care that his anger simmered under the surface. Instead, she leaned in to braid his hair. Startled at her audacity, he almost knocked her hands away.

"Father hopes Shelur can negotiate peace with the Greyadians." Her words froze his hand, which hovered in mid-air. Had she said negotiate peace? She captured his hand with hers and lowered it to his thigh before resuming the braiding.

"Your father is Chief Viggu?" He frowned. That would make her royalty of a sort.

She nodded, flashing a small smile. "Peace with Greyad and Letoura will allow our people to leave Orth."

"All hate Orthians as much as the Drem." He let his gaze travel her pretty features.

Her shoulders slumped, and she released his hair mid-braid. Crawling onto the bed behind him, she turned her back to him. "Good solace, Rannic. Perhaps tomorrow you will receive resolution."

He sighed and sprawled alongside her, resting his head on his hand for comfort. Warmth emanated off her little body as if she carried the heat of Orth wherever she went. It called to him in the cold room. No matter where Nyry traveled, because she was Orthian, animosity awaited her. For a strange reason, this angered him. A wealth of emotion churned his belly, the need to protect her forefront. Calling himself a fool, he curled around her, accepting her warmth and sweet solace.

Chapter Thirty-Six

Joyless

Joi stared at Shelur and the Greyadian brothers around the table. Five empty carafes littered the wooden surface, and partially filled bowls awaited her unquenchable thirst. She agreed to this because of the promise, but sitting opposite Sohar made her desperate for relief. Her thoughts plagued her: doubts, longings, plans, and unconfirmed conspiracies. A headache shot darts of pain and unease behind her left eye.

The Divine's disciples occupied other tables in the common, their unity confirmed by their constant focus on her actions. After she emptied the first carafe, she had noticed the growing number of customers fascinated by their party. The three princes were well-known, and Shelur drew attention with her coloring. Letourans were a usual sighting in Greyad with their black hair and dark eyes which was why Joi knew no one should be staring at her. But she counted nine non-drinking, dedicated worshippers, their hands hovering near their swords.

Whispering to the innkeeper, she asked him to water down her wine carafes, but she struggled to appear intoxicated. Sohar watched her, his blue gaze not missing anything. She should have known he would notice their growing audience, as well.

"Two behind you, Joi-Joi, watching you too intently," he whispered, throwing a charming smile at her. She wished he would stop doing that, no longer wanting to see it or to feel its effects on her.

"Nine I can see, all gripping their weapons." She poured wine into his bowl before cupping it and offering it to him. He placed his hands over hers, trapping her, then leaned forward and drank from the bowl. His lips brushed her fingertips. His gaze remained fixed on her face, showing his actions were deliberate.

"You can't avoid me forever, my Xiaxan Fox." He winked.

"You truly want me to share?" She huffed. "Fine. I spoke to Kylen today. He mentioned a few possible suitors, Aoni being one of them. I asked him to add Rannic to the list."

"You what?" Sohar roared, his hands releasing hers too fast for her to prevent wine from spilling onto the wooden table.

"His inclusion will appease Rumoc, for now." The pain and fury on his face was a balm to her despair. "Considering what my goals are for Letoura then marrying him will ensure this."

"You cannot be serious, Princess," Neha said, sipping from his own bowl. "No one trusts the Drem and for good reasons."

"Better the devil I know." She smiled at the younger man. His softer features reminded her of Sohar when she first met him.

"This is what you've been thinking about? This stupid plan?" Sohar's palm slammed onto the table, shaking the bowls. "No wonder you didn't want to share this with me. I'll kill him if he comes close to you, Princess. I promised him that."

She frowned, unable to handle this emotional Sohar. What did it matter who she married? Or was it just Rannic he objected to? "Then sharpen your blade. He's here in Corough. It's not hard to spot him among your silver-haired people. As I said, he'll follow me, and since the Divine hasn't intervened, then I assume we share intertwined fates. I mean to take him with me until the Divine reveals our destinies."

"What can he do if she's surrounded by Greyadians?" Shelur asked, proving she was paying attention to their conversation despite the sweet words Vard must have been whispering in her ear. Her cheeks had flushed after every intimate interaction, and her glare had softened. "Unless you doubt your skills?" All three men scowled at her. She laughed, throwing her head back in joyful abandonment. "Fine, then you doubt Joi's skills?" Shelur raised her bowl, a smile lingering on her lips. "Or perhaps she should have no say?"

"Your words cut deeply." Vard's lips dipped downward.

"As they should." Shelur shrugged. "Marry the Drem if it will save your people, Princess, but remember, such a life will not be a smooth one."

"A royal's life is never smooth. Stolen moments of joy are all I can hope for." Joi dipped her chin to hide her tears. "While my husband grows his harem, I will grow mine."

"Well said." Shelur chuckled. "I wonder if Father will grant me my own harem."

"As a reward for negotiating peace? I don't see why not," Joi said, ignoring the thunderous look that burst across Vard's face. Shelur had revealed he wanted to marry her. Now, that had been a surprise.

Joi shot a glance at Sohar and found herself smiling at him, as wide and as bright as her cheeks would allow. He didn't like the idea of her own harem. His furious glare evidence enough. Like she cared. Yes, she did. Her smile faltered, and she sighed. Rising to her feet, she tossed a few coins onto the table, bid them good solace, and skipped down the stairs into the cool night air.

Sohar and eleven men rose, as well.

"You're insane to leave alone," he said, his long strides catching up to her, with his attention switching between her face and the disciples trailing them.

"My techniques are easier to use without you here. I don't need your help to save me. I wish you and Kylen would realize that." With one show of power, she could end the Divine Priestess's hunt for her and force Sohar to realize she was no longer a child. Determination squared Joi's shoulders, and she strode into the quiet street as balls of scarlet flames burst into life on her open palms. "I don't need my sword or my dagger. I don't need yours either."

Scarlet tendrils raced up her forearms as she undulated them in precise clockwise movements. With a soft burst of sound, a sphere of blinding red light engulfed her. Sohar jumped back as Pan had done, the heat of the Fox too intense or so Pan had said. She stopped in the large courtyard—a central point for everyday commerce. Abandoned at this time of night, it would suit her needs.

The disciples trailed her, their swords drawn with determination and fear masking their faces. They encircled her, their intentions clear.

"Why do you wish to kill me?" she asked, but they did not respond. "Leave now or die." Still no response. Sadness gripped her as she cast a glance at Sohar, making sure he was far away. Then raising her hands upward, above her head, she pressed her palms together. "Last chance?"

They answered by leaping forward, swords raised. With a downward swing of her hands, she sent out a ring of fire. Eleven men combusted, their screams of agony reverberating through her, each wail striking a black mark across her soul. Ignoring the disciples' charred corpses, the blackened walls, and stone paving of the courtyard, she faced Sohar.

Drawing in any residual Fox and flames, she smothered her energy until the tendrils receded into her palms, taking the intertwined scarlet markings with it. Self-disgust settled like day-old dumplings in her stomach.

"Joi, I didn't know," he whispered, his eyes large as he surveyed the circle of death she had caused. "My energy doesn't work like yours. I can't decimate en mass." He wasn't horrified by her skill, though she hadn't expected to see it on his face.

"Still believe I need you?" She placed a palm on his cool cheek before once again striding away from him.

She vaulted into her saddle, ignoring the curious glances from her party. A desperate need drove her to flee from Sohar as fast as possible. When the road twisted from his view, she slumped over the horse's neck, allowing nausea to rise. Joi fell off and staggered to the verge, throwing up the inn's lovely fare and undigested wine.

Her body trembled, shivers racking her limbs as cold sweat drenched her face. She had never used so much energy before. Had never killed this many men at once. She crumpled to her knees and spilled her stomach onto the unforgiving pebbled ground. As she wiped the back of her hand across her mouth, she grimaced. The energy expenditure was necessary. To prove to him she was strong enough and more than capable to be a queen. The Divine's disciples forcing her to kill, angered and saddened her. Emotions warred within her, coiling her stomach tightly, bile rising again as if she hadn't just tossed out her meal.

"Why?" she asked the shadows. A tear trickled down her cheek, hot against her clammy skin. "Why do you hate me so, Priestess?"

She clambered to her feet. Using the horse's reins to guide her, she grabbed the pommel and pulled herself into the saddle. She didn't have the strength to vault into it, to challenge gravity. She let the horse lead, let it return her to the camp, and only when she neared her tent, did she take control.

Tossing the reins to a waiting soldier, Joi slid off the saddle, her limbs liquid and unstable. The Divine himself must have blessed her for she made it inside her tent. Collapsing onto her bed, she peeled her armor off, letting it fall where it may, and allowed exhaustion to claim her.

Chapter Thirty-Seven

Blinded

Sohar stared at Joi's sleeping form. The gray tinge to her skin, her discarded armor, belt, and imperial token revealed what he expected. Sitting next to her, he raised his hands and allowed his white tendrils to embrace her, healing her with as much of his magic he could spare. Testing his own limits to heal her might be too much for him, yet he would pay for it, whatever the cost.

Silly girl. As enthralling as it was to watch her use her energy in such a powerful strike, she had risked her life—and to what purpose? Now she wanted the viper to remain close to her? His fingers trembled, a visual evidence of his emotional turmoil. He drew in a deep breath to calm himself. If he could not focus on healing her, then he shouldn't even bother. Disciples surrounding her, a Drem at her back? What was she playing at?

He flicked her silky curls off her face, exposing the little color that had returned to her cheeks. The softness of her skin beckoned him to run a forefinger along her jaw and to sweep his fingertips across her petal-pink lips. With a sigh, he pulled the blanket over her before spending a few minutes tidying her tent.

"How is she?" Neha asked as soon as Sohar exited the tent into the cool night.

"Better." He raised his face to the star-dusted sky. The weather was pleasant, a marked difference from the desert. The heat awaited anyone stupid enough to cross the wall. Magic from the realms infused the stone wall, separating Orth from Greyad and preventing energy transference. The sky remained the same though, engrossing and humbling.

"I never knew that was possible." Neha mimicked Joi's hand motions including the sounds the fiery wave had made. "Sorry, when you two bolted out of the winehouse, I followed. Best decision ever. I mean, history mentions such a power, raising Letoura as *the* formidable realm. Centralized, any decision they made was well-respected. Makes you realize Rumoc's insane."

"Love can do that to a person," Sohar said, heading for his own tent. "He killed all with the authority to launch a counter-attack. Rumoc may be insane, but he's a brilliant strategist."

"You admire him?" Neha stilled before hurrying to catch up.

Sohar nodded, patting his third brother on the shoulder. "Not why he did it, but the way he did it, yes. The massacre reveals who he is, and it is wise to understand such a king. To strengthen our guard."

"Yet Joi would marry Rannic?" Neha shook his head. "I cannot understand this, first brother."

Sohar tossed his youngest brother a glare and grimaced at Neha's arched brow. Drawing in a deep breath, Sohar gestured to his tent before striding in, assuming he would follow. How to explain how Sohar had failed his Final Contest? He would begin the tale from when he first met her.

The minimal time it took to reveal his failure was disappointing. He expected Neha to spew harsh judgment for his emotional turmoil. He expected wise counsel to help him rid himself of this weakness, to distance himself from Joi. What he did not expect was laughter.

"I am not advising you on this, Sohar." Neha chuckled. "You know your heart better than I do. I'd like to know what the point of all this was. It doesn't make strategic sense to move a queen to another realm. Was it to lure out her killers? Did Kylen expect suitors to abduct her? Did he feel she was in danger?"

"*I* knew she was in danger. When Rannic saw her for the first time, the look on his face was one of hatred. Later, he confirmed his intention to kill her. It's why I cannot trust his deference now." Sohar sighed and lowered himself onto a pile of embroidered silk cushions. "Then Aoni snuck into her palace to force her to choose him. Kylen's request was logical." Everything Neha said was a dart of light in a tunnel of darkness. All his points were valid. Why hadn't he, the Crown Prince of Greyad, thought of them?

"Surely keeping her in the palace would have been safer for her?" Neha's puzzled expression didn't soften. "Surrounded by Xiaxan generals and trainees?"

"A stationary target is easier for assassins." Sohar poured a bowl of wine for each of them. He clung to Mion's observation, clung to the belief it had been wise to travel to Greyad.

"Assassins?" Neha scoffed. "Who besides the Drem would kill her?"

"The Divine's disciples, as you witnessed. This is the second attempt." Sohar threw the wine back and poured another, the taste of it doing nothing to calm his erratic emotions.

"Ah, that explains this evening's events." Neha sipped from his bowl. "Why would the priestess want Joi dead?"

Sohar scowled. Despite his better judgment, they headed for an island instead of Rendar. "That is unknown, which is why we'll travel to Raica, straight to the source."

"Intriguing. Not knowing of the priestess's involvement, you escorted Joi from Ethrielle, from the safety of the Meideons? Using her as bait for the would-be assassins and the Drem, who now forms part of the caravan to your new destination, Raica?" Neha laughed again, a calculating look settling in his blue gaze. He pressed the bowl of wine to his lips before tipping the contents back. "Truly? Your emotions have affected your mind, first brother."

"In what way?" Sohar stiffened, as if his subconscious knew the words Neha would speak, words his heart embraced like reunited friends.

"Kylen hoped time spent with the princess would make you realize your affections for her are more than that of a fellow trainee."

At the truth in Neha's words, Sohar jerked, spilling wine onto his fingers. He put the bowl down harder than he needed too. Curse it. He had known Kylen's hope, known and hidden it from himself. But, Divine, he had wanted this time with her, needed it to the very marrow of his bones.

"What do you advise I do?" He slumped his shoulders under the weight of his heavy heart.

"You gave your word—complete this mission, see her to the safety of Rendar and Father's court. Since you are adamant you cannot marry her, then live by your decision and accept the consequences." Neha refilled his own bowl then raised it to hover before his lips. "If she chooses Rannic, you cannot command her otherwise." He drank from his bowl and lowered it, a brow arching, as if he expected another volatile reaction.

Sohar clenched his jaw, fighting for stoicism. He hated that his emotions were easy to read. Curse it, when had he lost the skill to remain impassive? "Until Rendar, I do have a say. She is under my authority as if I speak for Kylen. If I allow her to marry Rannic, then I have violated the intention of this journey."

"The intention was to invoke your love for her. But yes, should she choose Rannic while in your care, this would displease Meideon. Once she reaches Rendar, Kylen will reveal the candidates he has selected. All you have spoken about Kylen indicates that he dotes on her, which means the final choice of husband will be hers. Between Rendar and Tennaba, your authority falls away." Neha rose from the cushions to grip Sohar's shoulder. "Be careful, first brother. The wrong word from you could push her to have done with this and marry the easiest or closest man. The realms need her to choose wisely."

"Who would you choose for her?" Sohar asked, the words barely escaping his clenched lips.

"I'm a romantic soul. I'd choose you, of course." With that, Neha abandoned him to his torturous thoughts.

Sohar refilled his bowl and drained it. He abhorred Rannic and all he stood for. Allowing Joi to marry him was to reward him for his father's sins. Everything within him roared over how wrong that was. But if Rannic wasn't her husband? How would Sohar feel if she married Aoni? A rage, bold, hot, and blinding, consumed Sohar, setting his hands trembling. That worthless boy would *never* have her. Then who could be her husband? Frowning, Sohar drained his bowl and threw it. It hit the carpeted ground with an unsatisfying thud.

If he had his way, he would march across to her tent and demand she choose him. A breathless peace swept through his heart as his mind settled on a plan. What if he could have her? What if he need only be patient? Then he could not tell her how he felt, not until the time was right, not until she was free to choose him. Could he abdicate his throne to Vard? Would he? Yes, because he no longer cared for his beloved Greyad, for his obligations, not if she wasn't with him. Joi was all that mattered to him now.

He needed her safe. Whatever decision or plan he made must not endanger her further.

Chapter Thirty-Eight

Surprises

The sweet sound of birdsong awoke Rannic from his solace. He could not remember when he was last this well-rested. Staring up at an unfamiliar ceiling, he squinted, fighting the fogged thoughts to recall all that had transpired. As time passed, a soft hum disturbed his train of thought. A foot rested between his calves. The heated weight of another body pressed along his side, and a feminine musk assailed his nose.

The silky, pale blonde braids cascading across his chest in wild disarray, implied more had occurred than was the reality. Nyry shifted in her slumber, and a gasp escaped her parted lips. Her skin glowed like smooth honey. He didn't resist the urge to stroke a fingertip along her cheek. She had sprawled her arm across his stomach, her embrace possessive. It felt good, too good.

He didn't allow the concubines to share his bed—this was a new experience for him. If he had to be honest with himself, with any other woman, he would push her off him, off the bed, and command her to leave. He couldn't with her, not only because it was wonderful having her beside him, but because they were prisoners still. There was nowhere for her to go. Wrapping his arms around her, he gathered her closer to him. Affection? Is this what it felt like?

Something unfurled in his heart—a strange feeling he couldn't identify. It made his breath hitch. He rubbed his jaw along her temple, marveling at her softness. The breathless feeling crushing his chest intensified. With a frown narrowing his vision, he kissed her temple, as light as a butterfly's wings.

Bright life burst in his arid soul. The urge to thrust her away gripped him, but he curled his fingers into her flesh and clung to her. His self-preservation demanded *he* run, but he fought it before ignoring it. He had nowhere to run to either.

"Is it time?" She mumbled her words, her heavy-lidded, pale gray eyes peering up at him.

"I've heard no movement." He tightened his arm around her, conveying that he didn't want her to move.

She didn't scramble off the bed—instead, she shifted closer, rubbed her cheek along his tunic-covered chest, and sighed. "Good. I'm tired." Exhaustion saturated her voice.

He stroked one of her silver braids, nudging it in place. "I will wake you when the prefect arrives."

"I shouldn't abuse your consideration, Rannic. Not on the day I bid farewell to my old life." She rose to lean on her elbows, meeting his gaze.

He frowned. "Are you determined to follow this path?"

"I'd love to see more than the cavern walls of Ta." She nodded, her fingertips trailing a crease in his tunic. "Greyad is beautiful. I imagine the other realms are more so."

"And you have sufficient coin? Defense skills in case of bandits?" He didn't lower his focus to her arms, resisting the temptation.

"Coin yes, skills no. I can shoot a bow better than I can wield a dagger." Nyry cast him a small smile before sitting up. "I'll find a caravan and travel with them."

"Where is your weapon?" He rose to grip her upper arms. He wanted to shake her, the naïve girl. Didn't she know it was dangerous out there? She would be at the mercy of anyone stronger than her. A harsh pain gripped his chest, rising to claim his throat. He bared his teeth at its intrusion.

"I left it behind." She shrugged. "Taking it would've revealed my intentions."

He grunted. "We'll get you a new one this morning. You need to prepare for a journey. It's not a stroll through a garden."

"I don't know why you feel you need to bother with me. After the prefect releases us, we part ways. If I die, I promise not to hold you responsible." Her teasing smile infuriated him further, and he gave her a little shake.

"Don't be a fool, Nyry. Your father and sister would have to mourn you." Rannic released her and slid his legs off the side of the bed.

He trembled with anger, the sudden onslaught blinding. She was right, curse it. Why should he care? But he did, and therein lay his dilemma, his confusion. She was a stranger, someone who cost him time and opportunity. She was young and naïve too—for that he blamed her father.

Running a hand over his face, he reined his thoughts in, focusing on where he needed to be shortly after release. "You're correct. I hope you have a wonderful journey filled with beautiful memories."

"Thank you, Rannic." She ran her nimble fingers through his hair to weave a braid.

"You violate cultural protocols by doing that. Best keep it to Orthians." He didn't pull away though. There was something peaceful about this simple action.

She paused her nimble fingers then continued as if he hadn't spoken. "Oh? What protocol would that be?"

"To braid a man's hair is to imply an intimacy beyond friendship, and in Greyadian custom, to marry him."

"Marry?" She laughed. "You're not Greyadian."

"True." He couldn't hold back a smile. "For Drem, it is still intimate."

"Orthians cannot be idle." She ceased, gently scraping her nails over his scalp, and finger-combing his hair, only to unravel her own braids. He mourned the loss of her touch. "My gratitude for the warning. May I ask you a question?"

He nodded.

"Why are you kind to me? All the rumors I have heard about Drem say you're a barbaric and uncouth realm." She held no judgment, no recrimination in her gaze.

He blinked at her, taking the time to ponder her valid question. Since Sohar spared his life, something within him had shifted.

"Being barbaric and uncouth is exhausting." He allowed a genuine smile to form. "Joi doesn't hold me accountable for my father's sins...that was a remarkable revelation. To be able to choose my own path? I've had time to consider what I want in this life. Yes, marrying her would grant me power, but it's a power I can use to free myself from under my father's tyranny."

"An army could do that too." She removed a few of her beads and wove them into his hair. "If you'd chosen friendship with the other realms, they might have supported your reign."

"I knew only the Drem life, having not considered other possibilities. When I was young, Father taught me that the Letourans loathed the Drem and that they would kill me on sight." He paused, an aching pressure pushing on his chest. "There are many untruths my father taught me."

"I'm sorry, Rannic. Your life sounds horrible. I had my father's love even though I lived in my sister's shadow."

He frowned, his thoughts flitting back to his earliest memories. Love? He didn't know love. Allegiance was all his father demanded of him. His mother had appeared doting when the court was in session, and he supposed, his aunt Nina had loved him when she visited. He could still recall the joy burning through him when she would sneak into his playroom. The scent of the sea when she engulfed him in unceasing hugs. The many gifts and scrolls she had brought him, and the wide and patient smiles she had shared with him.

When he started martial training under his father's incompetent generals, she stopped visiting him. Not for the last time did he wonder where she was and whether she was well.

Nyry wrapping her arms around him drew him back to the present. She squeezed, crushing her soft form against him, burying her face in his neck. He reacted without thought and circled his arms around her waist.

"I'm sorry you didn't know love, Rannic." Her whispered words jolted him—he hadn't realized he had spoken aloud. Heat splashed his cheeks, so he buried his face in her cool hair to hide his embarrassment and his appreciation of her gesture.

"Come, you are free to leave," the prefect said as he swung open the door. Judging by his frazzled appearance, he had one hell of a night. "Have the dead collectors arrived yet?" he asked a subprefect who hovered behind him.

"No, sir, but we have a witness. Said a young woman glowed with red fire. Killed the eleven disciples at once."

"Drunk Mershor is not a witness," the prefect said. He faced Rannic and gestured with his hands, his impatience clear. "Drem, if I didn't have you locked up, I'd blame you. You don't count, young lady. All know Orthians are magic-drained."

"What happened?" Rannic lifted Nyry to her feet as he rose off the bed.

"Eleven disciples burned to a crisp. Oh, the priestess will have my head for this." Under his fine sheen of sweat, his skin was pale.

"If the priestess sent them, she can't hold you accountable for their deaths. Where can we find the weaponsmith?" Rannic grabbed Nyry's hand and hurried her toward the door. "He should have a bow for you, for extra protection, my blossom."

"Very well, Elinan." She glanced down to the floor as if she was shy. He almost snorted.

Once the prefect explained the weaponsmith's location, Rannic led his "wife" out of the office. Within the hour, he had procured a decent bow, one that fit her shorter arms and was light enough not to tax her untried muscles.

"A morning meal and then I will escort you to the encampment to bid your sister farewell." He was hungry, but the factor driving the suggestion of a shared meal was his wish not to part from her just yet.

She laughed in that untamed way of hers, breathless and endearing, then laced her fingers through his. "Don't you mean *I'll* escort you to camp? You, they would capture on sight, but yes, a morning meal sounds wonderful."

Hand in hand, he allowed himself this enjoyment as if he wasn't the Crown Prince of Drem. He imagined a pleasant life, strolling down the street with his beloved wife. On the outskirts of his mind, the truth bombarded him, and it required valiant effort to keep it smothered. Nyry was just a woman needing his protection and company, nothing more. It was silly to read anything deeper into such a magnanimous gesture on his part. Silly.

Chapter Thirty-Nine

Cowardice

"I'm doing well." Joi faced a shimmering Pan. His face hovered above her imperial token; the edges of the image was tinted with scarlet.

"Doing well? You've never lied to me before, Princess."

She scowled then ran a trembling hand over her face, revealing how ill she was. Having thrown up her morning meal, the lack of nourishment meant she would need a longer time to regenerate her energy. It wasn't like her blue magic; she couldn't call on the earth, the sky, the air. No, the Scarlet Fox was tied to the medallion and the souls of her ancestors. It needed time and sustenance to replenish.

"The disciples attacked again last night. Their determination is unparalleled." Attempting to shrug only fired agony along every aching muscle. Faking a cough smothered the whimper but brought tears to her eyes when her ribs spasmed.

"So you drained your energy to within a whisper of your life?" Disappointment twisted his features.

His admonishment across the miles between them made her wince. "I used the Nova of Luminous Scarlet." Her voice was soft, fresh tears pressing behind her eyes, unable to endure the expected chastisement.

"How many were there?" His face filled the rippling illusion when she hesitated. "How many, Joi?"

"Eleven." She toyed with her medallion. It pulsed a dying greeting, yet more evidence she had overdone it.

"You killed eleven?" Pan boomed, and his face flushed the same color as the Fox. "Where is Sohar? Get me the prince now."

"We're not talking." Casting a worried glance at her tent's entrance, she expected him to stride in as if Pan could summon him out of the ether.

"Curse it, Joi."

The image dissipated, and she crumpled onto the bed. Talking to him drained what emotional energy she had gathered. How he knew she disappointed him, almost killed herself, and was still with Sohar, she couldn't say. There was much about Pan she didn't understand.

A sob escaped her, and she buried her face in her bedding. Her tears sizzled, and the stench of burnt linen perfumed the air. She clambered off the bed to find the bucket and emptied…nothing, there was nothing in her stomach. Feeling miserable, and sorry for herself, she wrapped her body around the bucket, holding onto is as if it were her salvation.

A cool hand pressed to her forehead, and she moaned, turning toward it. A blanket of cold embraced her, and she clung to it. Someone held her, but she couldn't draw the energy to open her eyes to find out who. Later she was airborne, floating on a cloud of chilling zephyrs. Then lowered into icy water, sizzling as she submerged. A sigh of pleasure escaped her. Words reached her through her dazed mind, *stubborn* and *Divine, please save her*. There was pain in that voice, so much she wanted to rouse herself to offer comfort.

Darkness called to her, and she succumbed—its painless promise a temptation she couldn't resist. Time passed, and she surfaced to sounds, blessed coolness saturating her body, bone-deep, only for darkness to claim her again. At some point, cold soup slid down her throat. She tried to convey it was no use, that she would toss her stomach, but the person ignored her.

When shivers racked her body, someone scooped her out of the water and wrapped a toweling cloth around her. They placed her in the bed and covered her with blankets. Her teeth chattered for a while, but she found warmth at last. It wasn't darkness that awaited her this time but restful solace.

Cracking an eyelid open, she blinked against the minimal sunlight peeking into her tent, telling her it was either early morning or late afternoon. There at the foot of her bed was Sohar, leaning against the bedpost and fast asleep. Shadows of exhaustion nestled below his eyes. Vague memories intruded, reminding her of the past hours. Or was it days?

Joi couldn't recall how long she had languished in blessed darkness. Sitting up, she bit her lip against the weakness gripping her limbs.

"Sohar?" Her voice broke, and she licked her dry lips.

With a jolt, he lunged for her, his fingers clasping her upper arms. "Joi-Joi, how do you feel?" Before she could answer, he yanked her in his arms, crushing her against him. "You had me worried, Princess."

"How long was I asleep?" Nuzzling his shoulder, she settled into his embrace, drawing on his strength and warmth. "Did I delay our trip to Penk Gove?"

"Delay?" He released her to glare at her. "You've been unwell this day. As to the delay, Penk Gove is not going anywhere. Pan was most insistent you do not use your energies to such an extent again."

"Pan? He spoke to you?" She groaned. Well, that explained why Sohar helped her.

"No one has dared to reprimand me as Pan did this morning. Joi-Joi, do you hate me so much that you could not send for me?" His voice cracked, and he cleared his throat. "You wound me, Princess."

"I didn't want to need you, Sohar." She chose to be honest with him. For once his stoicism was gone, replaced with the pain she caused.

"Need me?" He bounded to his feet, his fingers flexing as if he wanted to punch something. "How would I explain to the world that you died? Under my guard? How would I face Kylen and Mion? King Buro? What you did was selfish, Princess."

"Selfish? Is it selfish to guard my heart? Cowardice, yes, but selfish, no." Tears of fury and frustration stung her eyes, and she wiped them away. Curse him, she had revealed too much. "Thank you for healing me, Prince Sohar. You can inform Pan I won't be this stupid again."

On trembling limbs, she rose off the bed to rifle through her traveling bag, using her shoulders to dry her cheeks. Inside the bag she had a spare set of garments.

He stood there staring at her, not leaving her as she expected him to do. Well, she had dismissed him, but he was choosing to ignore that fact. With a sigh, she faced him, giving no sign of her impatience. Why couldn't he just leave? Why continue down a path neither of them intended to bolster?

"Guard your heart?" he asked in a voice above a whisper. Was his face paler?

"I don't want to care for anyone. It's not fair to promise my life to someone if I don't know my destiny." Promise to someone? She almost snorted at herself. There was only one man she would swear her allegiance to.

"You would marry Rannic." Anger coated his voice. How could he fluctuate between sadness and fury so easily?

"Our lives are intertwined. I will return to Tennaba, and he will follow." She palmed her medallion, its bright pulse welcoming. "If he tries to kill me, at least I'll see it coming."

"That's a senseless reason to keep the viper with you." Sohar shuddered.

"So you've said numerous times." She flicked a dismissive wrist, done arguing about this. "How often must Rannic and I meet before you realize the Divine has His own plan?"

Sohar folded his arms across his chest. "He can cross your path until Orth regenerates to its full glory, and I still won't accept this, Joi."

"You're stubborn, Sohar. Keep him close, test him, and if he betrays us, kill him. It's not as if you or I are defenseless." She slipped behind opaque screens crafted in bamboo and silken strips to peel off the stiff pants and tunic and don clean ones. Unraveling her hair, she glided from behind the screens and accepted the comb he offered her. "Please, trust me on this, Mighty Sohar. If I can connect with Rannic and end this feud, the children of Letoura can live in peace. It is pointless to continue this hatred, and if I need to be the better person, then so be it."

Sucking in a deep breath, he held it, clenched his jaw then gave her a curt nod. "I'll have a few of my men escort him to you." He ran a hand over his face as if he was striving for control.

At last. Joi offered him a small smile as compensation. "Thank you, Sohar."

"On one condition." Crowding her, he peered into her upturned face. "Promise me you won't marry him."

"But..." Her face flushed hot then cold, and she gasped. Part of her was amazed at his audacity, and part of her wanted to rage at him for daring to interfere in her life.

"Promise me," he growled, grabbing her upper arms as if to shake her.

"I promise if it's not the will of the Divine." Her words were a test of his conviction. "Who are you to decide His will?" On impulse, she looped her arms around him for a hug. "Something tells me everything will have resolution once I leave for Tennaba. I'm hoping Jeiram reveals his existence, and the Divine Priestess explains her determination to kill me," she said into his silk-encased shoulder.

"Prince Sohar." A soldier burst into the tent, keeping his head down as he bobbed. "Orthians are at the Corough gates demanding your head."

She pulled away to peer at the soldier. Orthians? Had Ker-hin changed his mind about Shelur negotiating the peace treaty? She tossed the comb onto the bed and dusted off her boots before wiggling them on.

"Is Viggu at the head?" Sohar strode toward the tent's entrance. "Princess, come with me."

Jumping up, Joi rushed after him. As she braided her hair, she doubled her steps to match his strides.

"Joi, did I hear correctly? My father is here?" Shelur ran up to her and grabbed her wrist. Joi didn't halt. Instead, she dragged Shelur with her until she fell into step beside her.

"Orthians are at the gates, that's all I know." Alongside a saddled horse, Joi paused, staring at Shelur's hand still gripping her wrist. With a sheepish smile, the Orthian released her. Grinning, Joi vaulted into the saddle, marveling at how good she felt. Who knew arguing with Sohar was such a good healing technique?

Chapter Forty

Accusations

Sohar faced forward, resisting the demanding need to seek out Joi. How was she feeling? Perhaps bringing her along wasn't wise, although the ride to the eastern gates wouldn't take long. If anyone could calm Viggu it would be Joi-hin.

Sohar's heart pounded hard enough to vibrate his throat. Why had she said that she needed to guard her heart? The pleading in her eyes—for his empathy, and the implication in her voice, set his senses aflame. But, no matter how much he wanted her, he had to set her free. He didn't want to be the reason she would regret not following her destiny and not bringing peace to her father's spirit. Although, marrying Rannic would disturb her ancestors for an eternity.

Sohar shook his head, curling his fingers around the reins in a white-knuckle grip. The Divine wouldn't have such ill-conceived plans to marry a Drem to a Letouran, would He? He jerked—he had twisted in his saddle to ogle Joi.

Clenching his teeth at his lack of control, he forced himself to look away, catching a glimpse of Shelur's face in the process. She wasn't concerned or nervous which meant she knew not the reason for her father's visit and demand.

He leaned back into his saddle, one hand resting on his thigh. The Corough gates opened on well-oiled hinges, the massive iron doors swinging as if made of light bamboo. Each door's thickness was the length of his forearm. They parted in a slow reveal of the impressive Orthian army awaiting him. His men had mentioned that Viggu's power and influence had grown, but the true extent of it was visible today. Thousands of armored men and women sat astride their camels, tense as if expecting a battle.

Sohar kicked his horse's flanks, and it bolted. Unafraid, he cantered to Viggu, his posture relaxed with his hand remaining far from his sword's hilt. A blatant display of fearlessness in the face of Viggu's fury. As Sohar neared, fear and concern warmed in Viggu's pale gray eyes.

"Chief Viggu," Sohar said as a greeting.

Viggu launched himself off his camel, landing beside Sohar's horse. With surprising speed, he dragged Sohar out of his saddle. Despite having Viggu's face a whisper away from his, Sohar held up a hand to stop his soldiers from drawing their swords. Not at all intimidated by this, he marveled at a man who had traveled across the planes of hell yet still managed to smell of mint.

"I want my daughter and none of your tricks, Greyadian *khonu*." Viggu's hands tightened on Sohar's tunic, twisting, and crumpling the silk.

He frowned, casting a glance at Joi with Shelur alongside her. "Shelur has yet to speak to my father. She may return to you as and when you please."

"Shelur?" Viggu roared. "I'm referring to my youngest, Nyry."

"Father, are you saying Nyry isn't home?" Shelur slid from her saddle to rush toward her irate father.

Sohar wished she had come forward sooner. This tunic was one of his favorites. Viggu's hefty hands ruined the delicate fabric and crushed the exquisite embroidery. From behind, she wrapped her arms around her father, clinging to him as she tried to break the hold he had on Sohar's throat. His tunic tore in the struggle.

"She was last seen before your departure. You didn't see her on the three-day journey?" Viggu asked, his brow furrowing as dismay claimed his face.

"You know I don't pay attention to the servants." Shelur released her father but did not move away. She kept her hands on his shoulder, and it seemed to calm him.

"My apologies, Sohar." The chief released him. "I was certain it was your doing."

"No apologies necessary. Did she follow Shelur, or did she travel toward the Gates of Cytium Va?" Sohar asked in a casual manner, as if the abuse of his person was a usual occurrence for him. He backed away to create distance between them, taking the time to right his ruined tunic.

Viggu shook his head. "No other footprints mar the sand, none but your caravan."

"Then she must have hidden in the wagon?" Joi called from her saddled position.

"You, go, gather the Orthian servants," Sohar commanded a captain. "Use as many men as needed." He faced Viggu, only to see a rider galloping toward their small party from the direction of Corough. It was Prince Vard, and judging by his tense posture, he bore critical news. He leaped off his horse before it halted.

"Greetings, Chief Viggu. I apologize for this intrusion." Vard bowed to the man as if he were a visiting king. In a way, he *was* the last remaining royalty of Orth. But bowing? Sohar glanced at Shelur and fought the temptation to smirk. Ah, showing respect to Shelur's father? How cunning of his second brother.

"What is it, Vard?" Sohar asked.

"Father has arrived. Our youngest brother, Neha, is setting up his tents. Looks like he's staying for a while." He nudged his head toward Joi while meeting Sohar's gaze. "And he's not alone."

"Chief Viggu, welcome to Greyad. I invite you and your people to camp alongside the Corough encampment. I advise, though, that you remain within your camp with no unescorted excursions to the town of Corough. News of the peace treaty has yet to reach the towns and villages." Sohar vaulted into his saddle, gathering the reins in one hand. "Vard, see to it. Present the Orthian servants to Chief Viggu as soon as they arrive. Joi, you're with me." He galloped back to the camp with her horse thundering behind him.

Less than an hour later, they entered the Greyadian encampment. He halted his horse, releasing a sigh of disappointment. His quiet, well-disciplined camp was a bustle, with soldiers on various errands. They had erected his father's tent alongside his with another royal tent north of this one. How odd—two additional royal tents. Had a consort traveled with his father?

Sohar didn't waste time, urging his steed forward until he was close enough to dismount. He tossed his reins to the first soldier he saw and strode into the tent unannounced. He glimpsed his father then realized he abandoned Joi outside. With a scowl, Sohar spun on his heel to find her hovering alongside her horse. Gathering her hand in his and cupping her elbow with his other hand, he ushered her into the tent.

King Codin was as regal as Sohar's memories portrayed him. Months had passed since he had last seen his father, and it was wonderful to see court life hadn't aged him. He was the tallest among the royal men, his hair more silver than white. As his father explained, each silver strand was a sliver of moonlight from the number of moons he had witnessed across his lifespan. His dark gray silk garments swayed as he wrote missives, the embroidered bell sleeves hiding more than one weapon. Such garments were the norm for Greyadian royals.

Sohar would make certain Joi received such garments with their clever pockets and the weapons to match. Codin scooped up a missive from his desk and stood still to read it. Lost in thought, he spread it out on top of ancient texts while his favorite incense perfumed the air.

"Father? I thought to meet you in Penk Gove." Sohar rushed forward to bow. With Joi's hand in his, he could not bless his father with a formal bow, and he was reluctant to release her hand to do so.

"That was my intention also, but my guest insisted this was urgent—a matter of life and death," King Codin said without looking up. His focus was on the brush in his hand as he wrote out orders.

"Guest?" Sohar glanced around the tent with the usual servants present.

Without raising his head, his father spoke. "Tell me, is it true Chief Viggu is at our gates?"

"Yes, Father. I have invited him to camp alongside ours. Before I take the necessary time to explain the situation, please allow me to present to you, Princess Jenaso of Letoura."

At this, his father's head shot up, and he lowered the missive and brush. He strode across the rugs to Joi, his arms extending in front of him as if to gather her hands in his. Sohar scowled and released her hand, ushering her forward too. The smile spreading across Codin's lined face was brilliant and the widest Sohar had ever seen. It was a rare sight to see such intense emotion on his father's features.

He loomed over Joi, but she didn't cower. She bowed, instead, her hand pressing over her heart. This brought a chuckle from his father, startling Sohar, who could count on one hand the number of times he heard humor from him.

"King Buro said he would train you as a son." Codin laughed when she blushed. "Never mind, little one. Let me see if you have the look of Eria."

"Or the look of me?" A Seitian ducked into the tent as if he had a right to.

Sohar spun to challenge the man's audacity and faltered.

Chapter Forty-One

The Fox

Joi stared at the man, wondering why she would look like him. Was he Letouran too? If so, he and Pan were the only Letourans she knew. Long, black hair fell down the man's back, unbraided, and disheveled. An unhealthy pallor coated his skin, as if he wasn't well. He wore Seitian garments: loose, brown trousers tucked into knee-high, leather boots with a sea-blue, embroidered waistcoat over a long-sleeved, white tunic. There was something familiar about his features, though. His forehead was wider than his cheekbones, but the same width as his angular jaw, and his nose tapered into narrow lips which curled up on one side. An image of her father blurred across this young stranger's face.

And his eyes were golden.

A lump formed in her throat, but she strangled out one word, "Jeiram?"

"Dear one." He opened his arms wide.

Her breath hitched, and a shudder tore through her. Her brother was alive and stood before her. A sob escaped her, and she bit her lip hard, fighting the tears pooling on her lower eyelashes. She took a tentative step and found herself in his embrace, crushed against his chest. He had rushed forward to gather her close, burying his face in her neck. She held him back, staring at him in disbelief. Tears streaked his cheeks with joy burning behind his eyes.

"I hoped." She fluttered her fingers over his face, his cheekbones, his jawline before she wrapped her arms around his neck and hugged him. "Why didn't you find me sooner?

I wouldn't have had to run or travel through oppressive heat. Wait!" She shuffled away, wanting to see his expressions. "Have the Divine's disciples attacked you too?"

"Disciples?" Jeiram shook his head. "No. Just legions of Drem. Rumoc found me sooner than expected."

"Prince Jeiram." Sohar greeted him with a formal bow. "Perhaps you would speak to Joi-Joi about her silly idea to keep Rannic near her."

She glared at him, biting her lip again, but this time to prevent herself from chastising him in front of his father and her brother. Her medallion pulsed and healed her lip. Wrestling between sadness and fury, she flicked a glance at Sohar, letting the fury win. "I've explained my reasons. Why can't you accept this is my decision to make?"

"I see more than an explanation is needed," King Codin said. "Come, sit, let's start this at the beginning." He gestured to his table with silk cushions strewn around it.

Joi looked down, hiding her heated face. She had forgotten about the king. For this, she would smack Sohar later.

"Include the hundred ships you deployed to guard Drem and end with Orthians camping on Greyad land." The king arched a brow at Sohar—he wasn't pleased with this development. There wasn't an expression that hinted at his displeasure. It was something she sensed.

One hundred ships to guard Drem? When had Sohar deployed those, and why?

The four gathered around various wines as he detailed the past week's endeavor. He didn't leave out much, just little moments she treasured, such as the sharing of beds and the Pools of Renewal. Mentioning their fake marriage had the king's brow furrowing, followed by a nod when Sohar explained why. Codin stiffened at her plans for peace but didn't speak. No flicker of anger or surprise marred his face. He was better at stoicism than his eldest son.

An hour had passed when Sohar ceased talking. Joi sipped her wine and listened, often closing her eyes, and letting his baritone vibrate through her. Silence descended, and the king sat there staring at his son while drumming his fingers on the wooden table. A rumble sounded, like distant thunder, and unexpected laughter erupted out of Codin. It was loud and robust, coming from deep inside him, and it filled her chest with warmth. She smiled, licking wine off her hand from when he startled her with his good humor.

"As I understand this, you escorted Princess Jenaso to Greyad to save her from the Drem and instead, discovered another enemy? Across the sands of hell, the princess brokered peace with a belligerent chief and has formed a truce with Prince Rannic of Drem? You are on your way to confront the Divine Priestess then what?"

"Launch Vard's Season of Delight," Sohar said. "I suggested he marry Shelur to finalize this treaty."

"He agreed to this?" Codin's expression flattened, once more unreadable. No trace of his earlier laughter remained. So this was where Sohar inherited his fickle moods.

"Yes, she has his heart." Sohar smiled as he refilled their bowls. "Prince Jeiram, Father said you insisted on traveling to Corough. That it was life or death." He eyed Jeiram, raising his bowl with two hands as a sign of welcome before pressing it to his lips.

Joi smiled, staring at her brother with such joy she couldn't contain it. She stretched across the table to squeeze his arm, almost disbelieving that he was here. He looked so like her memories of Da. She dipped her chin to her chest, to hide the tears forming on her eyelashes.

"Last night, my Scarlet Fox drained from me, and I knew Jenaso was in danger." Jeiram layered his fingers over hers still gripping his arm. She no longer mourned the loss of her parents. Yet having a breathing replica beside her had a vise gripping her lungs, inhibiting her breathing.

"Last night you killed eleven disciples?" King Codin asked.

She and Sohar nodded.

"I drained you? Is that why you look unwell?" She freed her hand to lace her fingers through Jeiram's, raising a teary gaze to meet his. "I didn't know that was possible. I mean, Pan did say we share the Fox, but he didn't mention we could use each other's energy."

"Pan as in Lord General Panzan?" King Codin chuckled again. "Oh, this is better than the boring sagas told in court."

She smiled through her sorrow. "Pan's my Cento mentor. He taught me how to use the Fox, my king."

"And scolded me just this morning for your recklessness. If he couldn't control you—I'm uncertain as to how *I'm* supposed to." Sohar sighed and refilled his bowl.

"Where were you before Greyad?" she asked Jeiram before sipping her wine.

"Hidden among the Seitians." A mysterious smile spread across Jeiram's features. By his expression, he had enjoyed growing up in Seit. Was it the realm, its people, or one person in particular? "News of your identity reached Berandaros. I left for Ethrielle at once, but it seemed as if I was doomed to miss you. A long sea voyage followed, and thank the Divine, the Sea of Turmoil was kind to us." He drew in a deep breath. "I docked at Seave and traveled by barge to Penk Gove to meet with King Codin. There we heard of your arrival in Corough. It was en route that I became ill."

"My invitation was waylaid? Did the servant you sent ascend to heaven? Die from a dragon attack?" Vard said, striding into the tent then dropping onto the closest pile of cushions. "Father." He bowed then accepted the bowl Sohar offered him. "You must be Prince Jeiram—an honor." Vard bowed again before pausing with the bowl to his lips. "Those Orthians are thirsty work." He took a mouthful of wine and swirled it around as if he washed away sand.

"You should become accustomed to it if you wish to marry into their family," King Codin said.

Vard spluttered and choked on his wine. Sohar wasn't sympathetic as he pounded his second brother on the back. "You know?"

"Of course I know. I'm the King of Greyad." He straightened his bearing as a smile twitched his upper lip.

"I told Father," Sohar said. "To secure the treaty."

"For the treaty? Yes, yes, that's my plan." Vard nodded with too much eagerness.

Joi laughed. Did he like Shelur that much? Enough to marry her? Did giving her his heart mean a marriage was imminent? She settled on Sohar and lowered her gaze, trying to hide her futile hope. The dream of having his heart was a marvelous one.

"Please excuse us, my king. I wish to spend time with my sister." Jeiram pressed their clasped hands against his chest.

King Codin dismissed them. She rose with Jeiram but snuck a glance at Sohar. He watched her, but his thoughts remained hidden. She nodded, wishing him a good solace even if she couldn't speak the words.

As she followed Jeiram out, they ran across Shelur pacing in front of the tent's entrance. She was twisting her hands in agitation, and each spin on her heel arced her braids around her. When she saw Joi, she rushed toward her.

"Have you found Nyry?" Joi freed her hand to grab Shelur's trembling one. She tilted her head at Jeiram's tent and nodded, a silent promise to her brother that she would find him soon.

"No." Shelur sobbed, her voice breaking. "The servants say there was a fourth girl, but they never saw her face."

"Are the soldiers scouring Corough?" She hugged Shelur.

Shelur freed herself to rub her cheeks. "Yes, but the waiting is killing me."

"If she's in Corough, they'll find her." Joi tucked a stray silver curl behind Shelur's ear. "An Orthian girl will stand out—someone might have seen her. Go wait in Ker-hin's camp. They'll head straight to him if they find anything."

"You're right." Shelur held her wrist to her nose to hide her sniffles. "Thank you, Joi-hin."

As she scurried off, Joi reflected on the state of her life. The last few days, traveling across Orth to the Corough gates, had been dull—the only highlight was watching Vard woo Shelur. Joi managed to avoid Sohar without offending him. But the nights were uneventful, with the only conversations being between her and a grumbling Velvet. Now, having reached Greyad and the Town of Corough, she couldn't turn a direction without stumbling upon an intriguing event or person.

Excitement coursed through her when she faced Jeiram's tent. She bounced where she stood, the energy too much to contain. Anxiety churned her stomach, for she had been away from him longer than she had known him. What if he didn't like who she had become? What if her actions, skills, mannerisms displeased him? Joi didn't know how she would survive disappointing him. Drawing in a shuddering breath, she hurried to his tent and ducked through the draped entrance. In her heart, she was once again an eleven-year-old girl.

Chapter Forty-Two

Victory

Joi stumbled into her tent, more exhausted than the previous night. The hours flew by with her and Jeiram reminiscing, mourning, and planning a new Tennaba together. He had agreed to the invitation she wanted to extend to Ker-hin's people and that keeping Rannic close was wise. Overall, her brother had been magnanimous.

He had also found his future wife, the Third Princess Tuyra of Seit. She would become the next Letouran Queen. Joi was delighted for him, but more than this, the direction she imagined her life would take had altered.

Relief flooded her, slumping her shoulders. She wanted to pool at his feet in gratitude. She wasn't the direct heir to the throne and future queen of Letoura anymore. Of course, she wouldn't abandon Jeiram in case he needed her.

A lone lantern cast shadows across her carpeted tent, but she paid it no attention. Instead, she hopped on each foot as she yanked off her boots. Climbing onto her bed, she flopped down, uncaring that it was a graceless action. Warmth emanated from the middle of the bed, and she smiled, rolling toward it without thinking.

Her eyes flew open, and in a single motion, she shoved the man off her bed. Falling into a fighting stance she loaded her kick, ready to attack if he charged her.

Cursing and grumbling followed as he clambered to his feet, sweeping unbound brown hair out of his face. Rannic? Here in her tent? She laughed, lowering her leg before dropping onto the bed again.

"I'm glad you found me. I've convinced a stubborn Sohar to let you travel with us. If you're still interested." Her words wiped the grumpiness off his face, replacing it with surprise then satisfaction. "We can discuss this later. It's too late to get you settled, so sleep on the floor." She scooped up the blanket from the foot of her bed and tossed it at him. He caught it just before it hit his chest.

"Thank you, Joi." He lowered himself to the rug. She nodded before leaning back onto the still-warm bed and pulled the blanket across her. "I hear Jeiram is in camp."

She grinned. "Yes. It was wonderful to see my brother again."

He flicked out the blanket and lay back. "I wanted to marry you to gain the might to defeat my father, but that's no longer valid with Jeiram here."

She allowed the Scarlet Fox to ripple along her fingers, glowing brightly in the darkness. "You try to harm him, and I'll kill you, Rannic."

"I believe you, Princess." He shifted. "I won't risk your wrath, not after you killed those disciples."

"You know about that?" She huffed. Of course, he did since he mentioned it. "Never mind. So why travel with me?"

He took a while to answer. "Why not? I must return to Drem at some point, and the longer I'm with you, the more time there is to plan."

"If you convince Sohar of your good intentions, perhaps he will aid you. You might not need Letoura at all." She wished he would keep quiet. She was so tired her eyelids refused to open.

Hope spliced his voice when he said, "Do you believe so, Joi?"

She yawned. "Rannic, if you don't let me sleep, I *will* kick you out of my tent. You can find solace with the horses, for all I care." Silence met her outburst, and with a snort, she rolled over, giving him her back with a soft command to her medallion to guard her well.

Minutes later, a hand rested on her shoulder, and with a flick of her wrist, she flipped him onto the bed. It wasn't Rannic, and it wasn't dark outside. Shelur groaned, and Joi released her twisted hand.

"Sorry, Shelur. I thought you were..." Joi nudged her aside to find Rannic still asleep.

With a deep sigh, she stroked the medallion, grateful that it hadn't considered Shelur a threat. She didn't want to harm the woman she had come to value as her friend.

"I see you had a visitor last night." Shelur gestured at Rannic's snoring, blanketed bundle.

"Have you found Nyry?" Joi swung her legs over the side of the bed. Scanning the tent, she searched for her boots. One was near Rannic's head. Laughing, she splashed water onto her face from a large bowl.

Shelur polished her dagger with her braid. "No, they've scoured Corough. The prefect mentioned keeping her and her husband for the night."

"Husband?" Joi dried her face on the cloth supplied.

Shelur shrugged. "Strange, I know. Father's in a state."

"She said she wanted to bid you farewell first. Have you been to your tent?" The blankets smothered Rannic's sleep-soaked voice.

"What?" Shelur crouched beside him to yank the blankets down. He squinted as he met her gaze. "You know where Nyry is? Tell me now or die, Drem." She flicked her dagger in front of her.

"You women and your death threats." He sat up to rub his face. "Nyry doesn't want to live in your shadow anymore. She said she would rather die on an adventure than from boredom. I came here with her, but we couldn't sneak into camp until late last night."

"She's in my tent?" Shelur didn't wait for him to respond but bolted out. The tent's flap whipped in cool air and the early morning sunlight.

"Here I thought you pined for me," Joi teased. "Married to an Orthian—I didn't see that coming." She tied her belt on, still with her imperial token and sword attached, indicative of how exhausted she was last night.

"It was a farce. The prefects caught us spying on your party." He clambered to his feet and splashed his face from the water bowl she just used.

"Not according to an irate father. You spent a night in a room with his innocent daughter. I doubt you'll slither your way out of this one." Joi laughed as she held out the drying cloth for him to use.

He glared at her for her observation. "No Orthian chief would bless his daughter to a Drem."

"Let's hope for your sake he will." She scooped up her boots and lowered herself onto the closest chair. She wiggled them on while watching Rannic straighten his sleep-wrinkled garments. "My comb is in my traveling bag if you want to tackle that bird's nest."

"You're one to talk, Princess." He rummaged through her bag before standing behind her to unravel her hair and drag the comb through her tresses. The unexpected intimacy of this action snatched her voice. Heat burned her face at his audacity.

"Rannic." She twisted to reclaim her comb, but he dodged her grasping fingers. "If you think I will return the favor…" On a growl, she allowed the Fox to inflame her palms, spiraling the now-familiar markings up her bare forearms.

"No need for anger." He handed her the comb.

"Just use the cursed comb." She leaped to her feet and rushed out of the tent, uncaring that her hair swirled around her. That man infuriated her.

Raising her palms, she studied the intricate markings as she crossed the camp to Jeiram's tent, but he wasn't inside. This did nothing to calm her. With another growl, she spun on her heel and stomped to Sohar's tent. If neither of them was there, she would burn his tent down.

"Joi-Joi. Good morning. Hungry?" Sohar, seated around an overladen table with Jeiram and his second brother Vard, greeted her as she stormed into his tent. He patted the cushions beside him, and she huffed as she dropped onto them. She took the time to focus on her palms to snuff her Fox. "Not a good morning then?"

"I'll kill Rannic." She shoved a dumpling into her mouth. Stealing it from Sohar's bowl didn't matter.

"He's here?" Jeiram took his bowl and piled food into it before sliding it across the table to her.

She swallowed the too-large mouthful, slowing when she thought she would choke on it. "The cursed fool just tried to comb my hair. At least he knew where Nyry was—I hope Shelur has found her."

"An appeased Viggu would aid the peace negotiations." Sohar added dumplings to her bowl. "We shall leave that in Father's hands while we travel to Raica."

"Is this farewell?" She paused to point at a bowl of wine with her chopsticks. Jeiram sighed and offered her his bowl, grasping it within two hands.

"It is. From Corough, we'll take the barge to Lesowey and a ship to Terpor." Sohar gestured at the traveling bags she missed upon entering. "The barge is awaiting our arrival."

"Today? But I just reunited with Jeiram. Sohar, your arrogance sometimes makes me furious!" Joi slammed her utensils onto the table, rattling it.

"Little one, find out why the Divine Priestess wants you dead. I'll stay for the negotiations. As King of Letoura, I need to represent the other realms." Jeiram captured her hand to lace his fingers through hers. "After we have resolved all matters, I will return to Tennaba and await you there. Tuyra will join me for our Season of Delight."

"I'm truly happy for you, brother." She cupped his hand still holding hers and squeezed it. "You said you presented yourself to Kylen. Will he still be sending the names of my potential husbands?"

"He said so, but the choice remains yours." Jeiram freed his hand, and his Ring of Bloodless Dawn pulsed a greeting. Father gave her the medallion and Jeiram his ring. Both magical relics aided the Scarlet Fox.

"You better take this then." She untied her imperial token and held it out to him with a bow. "My king," she said then peeked at him. Jeiram brushed his fingers over it before accepting it.

"I thought it was lost in the massacre," he said, his voice rough with emotion.

"Very well, brother. I'll join you in Tennaba." She rose to kiss his cheek, then scooped a few dumplings into a bowl. "I'll bring Rannic, and we'll meet you by the horses." She rushed out of the tent, ignoring Sohar's thunderous scowl.

Rannic waited for her at her table when she strode in. She handed him the bowl before racing to braid her hair and put on her armor. "We leave for Corough, then to Lesowey to set sail for the Temple of the Divine." She fondled her hidden coin pouch, making certain it was still there. After the last few days, many events had occurred where she could have mislaid it. "Or would you prefer to participate in the peace negotiations?" She stroked the gold links of her medallion.

"I'm with you, Princess," he said between mouthfuls. "Thank you for the food."

"Good, ready when you are." She nestled her comb beside her coin pouch, planning to leave her traveling bag behind since Sohar had another one packed for her. She hoped it had more than one spare set of garments.

Rannic jumped up, a dumpling in hand as he gestured for her to lead the way. She strode out of her tent, crossing the awakening encampment with the Drem trailing behind her. She had expected him to draw attention because Drem loathed Letourans, so to see two together without bloodshed was a miracle.

Sohar waited alongside three saddled horses. His thunderous scowl hadn't lessened, but he gave Rannic a small nod in greeting. She accepted the reins for a dark gray horse and vaulted into the saddle. The three of them, and a soldier, galloped out of the camp, heading west to the bridge. They didn't make it far when two horses followed behind them. She twisted to look, and the trailing sandy hair forced her to a halt. Her party did the same, and they waited with impatient mounts for Shelur to reach them. Alongside her rode Nyry.

"Please, take Nyry with you since she's so eager for an adventure." Shelur squeezed her sister's arm, sadness drooping her smile. "Father and I would be at peace if she travels with you to Tennaba."

"Ker-hin agreed?" Joi jerked in surprise. The way he raged, she didn't think he would let Nyry out of his sight again.

Shelur sighed. "This was his suggestion. Will you agree to her company?"

"Of course. Nyry is more than welcome." Joi shot a glance at Sohar who didn't reveal whether including Nyry delighted or angered him. "We're traveling to Raica, if a sea journey excites you, Nyry?"

"We are?" She gasped then clapped her hands in excitement. "Orthians don't travel by ship. To see such a large body of water would be my fondest wish."

"It's settled," Sohar said before bowing to Shelur.

"On the voyage, we will practice your archery skills." Rannic winked.

"Thank you, Drem." Shelur smiled. "Prince Sohar, Joi-hin, you have my eternal gratitude." With a wave, she galloped back to camp.

"I promise not to be a nuisance." Nyry dipped her head to hide her embarrassment.

Sohar chuckled, leaning across to pat her shoulder. "You can never be more of a nuisance than Joi-Joi."

"What?" Joi gasped, then shook her head. He was teasing the girl to put her at ease. Sometimes he was a sweet man—when he wasn't infuriating.

The party of five rode into Corough, where the barge waited. In a matter of minutes, they were rolling west down the Laugar River. Joi handed her traveling bag to Sohar and meandered to the bow of the barge. There she found a comfortable spot on top of wine barrels to watch the passing scenery.

The earthy and somewhat primal fragrance of the water scented the air, with hints of grass and fish. Other barges passed them, going in both directions. One had children on it, waving with boundless enthusiasm. The sun was merciless, but she didn't mind, choosing instead to drop down to the deck and lean her back against the barrel. It cast its shadow over her and shielded her from the sun's heat. Nyry sat by her for a while, sharing the shade and the wine she had brought with her. When the sun found their hiding spot, Joi rose, pulling Nyry to her feet. It was time to venture inside. Besides, Joi was starving.

Chapter Forty-Three

Hope

Sohar stared through the unshuttered window of the barge, his focus fixed on a quiet Joi. He preferred to watch her than speak to Rannic. No matter what the viper said, there was no way he would trust him. A cool breeze tossed her braid across her back, her ebony locks glowing once more like oru. She twisted his innards and shook his control. Only the Divine knew how she did it.

"I vow to you, I won't harm her," Rannic said from beside him. They had not spoken once—why did he choose now to do so?

"I'm to trust you?" He snorted. "They're mere words to you, Rannic."

"Here." Rannic held out his imperial token. "Take it and return it to me when you bid her farewell."

Sohar stared at it for a long time, disbelieving the valiant gesture. To be without his token would render Rannic powerless. He wouldn't be able to speak to his father—or anyone for that matter—unless they contacted him. Rannic ignored his hesitation, grabbed Sohar's hand, then dropped the token onto his open palm. Curling Sohar's fingers around it, he forced him to accept it. The black volcanic rock held its own warmth as if the fiery depths that forged it remained within the dragon-carved token.

"I will protect this with my life," Sohar said, unable to convey how such an act of faith affected him. Perhaps there was something in the Drem's character that was salvageable, something Joi-Joi had seen days ago.

"I'll find out if the captain plans on serving a meal." Rannic bowed and bounded away.

Tying the token to his belt, Sohar's thoughts drifted back to the private discussion he had shared with his father and brothers. Third brother Neha joined them later, for he had much to say. Not all of it Sohar wanted his father to know.

"Death does not guarantee the successful completion of one's Final Contest, and not every Contest requires such a solution," Father said. "You have not failed in choosing to spare her life. You passed by making the right choice. That is all the Contest is, created by the Divine to test your morals. I can see she means the realms to you, first son. Why is it that you hesitate to marry her? Do you think me displeased with such an alliance? Does my approval count in this matter of the heart?"

Sohar hadn't disappointed his father and hadn't brought shame upon Greyad. Warmth exploded in his chest—his father approved his claim. When it was time, of course. "She has much to accomplish, Father. I cannot steer her off her chosen path and demand she chooses me instead of Letoura, jeopardizing her chance at peace. Should we marry now, she may come to regret and resent our marriage. I have thus decided that if she loves me, she will wait for me."

"What nonsense!" Vard slammed his empty bowl onto the table. "Could you not aid her on her path?"

"You speak as if I haven't considered all strategies. Joi-Joi is stubborn. In the restoration of Letoura, she wishes to play an important role. I cannot expect her to divide her time between Jeiram and me."

"From my perspective, I'm hearing excuses," Neha said in that calm way of his. "What I'm perceiving is that you don't know how she feels." Sohar glared at him, hating him for his insight. "She adores you, by the way, but she too doesn't know how you feel."

"Go now and tell her." Vard jumped to his feet before swaying.

"Sit before you hurt yourself, second brother." Neha tugged on his pant leg to bring him down to the safety of the cushions.

"How do you feel?" his father asked Sohar. He sipped from his bowl with a casual air, but his focus was intense.

"There's a fluttering where my soul resides. Thoughts of her rip aside my control and call forth potent emotions." Sohar rubbed at the strange sensation in his chest.

"The fickle heart wants what it wants, but it will follow the mind. Decide and live with the consequences." Harsh words from a benevolent father, but Sohar agreed, so did Neha.

Vard's hiccups didn't count. He wanted to marry Joi, but how could he and also give her what her soul needed—to rebuild Letoura, to free her people?

"The captain will have a meal prepared," Rannic said, intruding on Sohar's reverie.

The question remained, haunting him with a solution beyond his grasp. If one did not present itself soon, he would have to bid her farewell, forever. "Thank you. Where's Nyry?"

"She joined Joi on the bow. Tell me, Sohar, what do you expect the Divine Priestess's reasons are? Isn't it against the Divine's ordinances to cause another's death?" Rannic caught a thin braid of his brown hair, woven with leather strips that looked like the ones in Nyry's hair. He fondled it with more reverence than it should have evoked. Intriguing.

"Perhaps we should leave Nyry on the ship. The temple could place her in danger," Sohar said in a casual manner. He couldn't reveal that he suspected Rannic had feelings for the Orthian woman in his care.

He jerked, his dark eyes widening. "Danger? Why...? Oh. You expect the disciples to attack as soon as we disembark. Then I agree, but it's best the command comes from you."

"She has your heart, Rannic. This could prove a dilemma for you both." Silence met Sohar's announcement. If he didn't know better, the man's skin had paled.

"My heart?" His hand slammed down on the window's frame as if he was unstable on his feet. Rannic's other hand flew to his temple then fluttered to his chest. He drew in great shuddering breaths. "I hadn't realized." He faced the unshuttered window to stare at Nyry. "How can it be so rapid? Losing one's heart?"

"It took a while for me to realize it. In hindsight, I suspect Joi-Joi had my heart the moment I saw her. I was so young then. She's my Final Contest—one I thought I failed." Sohar's lips curled with self-mocking humor, for he spoke the truth. No longer did his passing or failing bother him. He recalled Mazza's wise words. A longing for his servant twisted his heart, and he fondled his token. He would speak to him once they boarded the ship awaiting them at Lesowey's port.

"You hide it well," Rannic said. "I thought you were protective out of a filial obligation. I apologize, Sohar. I didn't mean to throw salt on your wound when I mentioned my intentions to marry her."

Sohar frowned. "My wound?"

He nodded, the action tossing his beaded braid. "If she's not yours, then yes, your injured heart."

"Well, there's no need to apologize. As I said, it took me a while to realize she *is* mine." Movement on the bow drew his attention, and with a relieved sigh, he strolled to the table.

Lowering himself onto the cushions, Sohar awaited Joi and Nyry's entrance. Rannic remained by the window. From the other door, a man scurried in with a laden tray in his arms. The aromas of chicken, dumplings, and noodles tickled Sohar's nose, reminding him of his hunger. There was something about the scent of water, be it ocean or river, that moistened the tongue and awoke the ravenous beast within.

"Princess, Nyry, please join us." Rannic gestured to the table's aromatic offerings just as the man placed the last bowl.

Joi chose the cushions beside Sohar. He focused on the steaming bowls and platters before him, not wanting her to know how he longed to gaze upon her sun-warmed face. He slid a few gold pieces to the servant then scooped a dumpling into Joi's bowl. She blessed him with an eager smile before pouring wine into his drinking bowl.

Tightening the grip he had on his utensils, he cleared his throat. "Joi-Joi, after this meal, would you care to join me for a stroll on deck? The final stretch of the journey before we dock in Lesowey is breathtaking."

At his invitation, her cheeks flushed red, and her eyes twinkled with delight. He wasn't certain it was time spent with him or the visual delights of the ocean that excited her. Sohar was grateful regardless. She was mesmerizing when she glowed with happiness.

"I'd love to see it, Sohar. Thank you for thinking of me." She served him a bowl of wine with both hands and a small bow.

If he could keep her joyful for the remainder of the journey to Rendar, he would consider that a gift from the Divine.

Chapter Forty-Four

Voyage

The *Dawning Sun* was a two-mast ship, its bow curled and arched like a wave's crest. As Sohar had stated, it awaited them in Lesowey's port with small cabins reserved for comfort. The heady scent of yellowwood assaulted Joi's senses until it overpowered her. Opening the little window didn't help the burning in her nostrils. The sway of the ship, as it sailed out on the high tide, was soothing, and the Xiaxan training she received aided her balance.

A timid knock echoed through the small space, and when she commanded the person to enter, a slim man opened her door. He held out her traveling bag. She smiled a welcome and hurried to take it from him.

At the glint of a steel dagger, she jumped back, missing a sweeping slash. The cabin was too confining to manage a backward flip or an aerial vault. Calling forth the Fox, she commanded the medallion to protect her as he thrust forward.

Unable to dodge his attack this time, she trusted the Fox to save her. Striking the scarlet smoke must have broken the bones in his hand. The dagger clattered to the floor. He screamed, grabbing his limp wrist and distorted fingers to cradle against his chest. Stumbling away from her, he darted a look behind him, seeking to escape.

She lunged, striking him on the knee with a booted heel. Crying out, he collapsed to the floor. Not hesitating, she knelt to punch him in the throat. As he fought for life, he gurgled, clawing at his throat with his good fingers. His blue eyes were fearful and haunting as Death tore him from this realm.

This was the fourteenth man she had killed in nine days. Scowling, she mourned the necessity, but the underlying emotion claiming her was fury. They had placed her in this position, forcing her to take lives. With a muffled scream, she curled her fingers into fists, wanting to pound on the dead man's chest. Trembling, she gritted her teeth and rose to her feet then left her cabin to search for Sohar.

Close to the bow, he stood gripping the wooden railing. The wind tossed his hair like finely-spun spiderwebs that glistened in the fading sunlight. The sight of him brought her unexpected peace, and her stiffened shoulders slumped. A sob threatened to escape past her pinched lips. Killing people wasn't normal for her, and she doubted it was something she could become accustomed to. Those men had hopes and dreams. Now they were but gray wisps of a dying candle, dissolving and forgotten.

"Sohar?" Her voice cracked, so she kept quiet as she hurried over to him. He turned to her with no hesitation in his actions.

"What is it, Joi-Joi?" His long strides crossed the distance between them, and he slid his hands along her forearms to cup her elbows. She wrapped her fingers around his arms, as best she could and clung to him.

"May I find solace with you tonight? Maybe Nyry could share a cabin with Rannic?" She chewed on her lip, wondering about the impropriety of Nyry finding solace with a man.

Joi doubted an assassin would fear or spare an Orthian woman, and she couldn't face Ker-hin if Nyry died because of her. She would rather explain to him why his daughter married a Drem. The cabins weren't large enough for three people, which meant this was the only solution. Short of tossing the crew overboard.

"Joi?" Sohar cupped her cheek, and she shifted closer, needing his comfort, his warmth.

"An assassin is in my cabin," she said.

With a jerk, he peeled his body away from her then bolted. Cursing his long strides yet dreading his reaction, she ran after him. But there was no body when she entered the cabin. "I vow, Sohar, I killed a man." There was no sign, no blood, not even a fallen dagger.

"If you missed sharing my bed, you only had to say so, Princess," he teased, a smile gracing his lips.

Growling, she stamped her foot, and considered smacking him for his ill-timed humor. "He had a dagger. Is this lying?" Through her sliced tunic, she stuck her finger and wiggled it.

He swiped her tunic out of her hands to see for himself. "Curse it. I should've anticipated that the civilian crew might belong to the priestess. Removing the body means there's more than one assassin on board. It is best we keep to our cabins and don't venture on deck alone."

Thankful he believed her, her anger deflated, and she closed the door to grant them privacy.

"He didn't hurt you, did he?" Sohar stroked across the torn fabric, a formidable scowl hardening his features.

"No, I have the Fox, remember." She frowned. He hadn't answered her about the cabins. "I could share Rannic's cabin, but I didn't think you'd agree." The image of Nyry and Sohar married twisted something sharp in her chest, and Joi looked away to hide her gasp. What was wrong with her? He had to marry at some point. It was best for her to accept that fate.

"You'd be correct. I'm beginning to see the merits in his personality, but it doesn't mean I trust him with you." He scooped up her traveling bag and ushered her out onto the deck. He crossed to his cabin and held the door open for her. "I asked the barge captain to pack a food pouch for us in case we suspect the poisoning of our meals. I assume you're starving?"

She rubbed her belly where a hollow pit resided. "Ravenous. I don't know what's wrong with me."

"You *have* gotten shapelier." His lips curled upward.

"Did you just say I've grown fatter?" Joi smacked him across his upper arm.

He erupted into laughter, the sound breathtaking even if he annoyed her. Fending off another smack, he looped his arms around her and crushed her against him.

"Be calm, Princess. The Fox demands more energy, and you did kill eleven men at once. Your increased hunger might be a symptom of that." He kissed her temple. His explanation and embrace mollified her. So, starving all the time was healthy for her?

A chuckling Sohar rubbed his cheek across the crown of her head. "It's a good thing the captain thought I was the ravenous one. He packed more than enough food."

She struggled in his embrace, showing him she wanted him to release her, but he tightened his hold instead.

"Tell me, Joi-Joi, what plagues you? You haven't been the same, not since Ta." His serious tone stilled her wiggling and held her breath.

She intensified the struggle, needing to escape more than she needed food. Why was he so stubborn? Why couldn't he leave it alone? "I'm not discussing this anymore, Sohar."

"I don't believe your last words on this matter were the truth. They make no sense." He pulled away, freeing her, at last.

She dipped her head, flicking a few escaped tendrils to hide her face even as she peeked at him. "Why would I lie?"

"Why are you guarding your heart?" His serious expression made her huff.

She wasn't about to tell him how she felt. He was an honorable man, and should he know she loved him, he would feel obligated to marry her. It wasn't that their marriage wouldn't be good, but with the right woman, his life could be wonderful. A vision appeared, of her confessing her love for him, hearing him repeat the words to her. Scene after scene flitted: the Season of Delight with Sohar, helping her rebuild Letoura, spending her solaces in his arms, what their children might look like. It had warmth flooding her, removing the stain of the assassin's death that lingered in her soul. Yes, their Season of Delight would be Divine-blessed.

Then what? She couldn't see him sacrificing Greyad and his obligations for her. He wasn't a man to shirk his responsibilities and marrying her would place more onto his broad shoulders. Her enemies became his just as his enemies became hers. Either way, their union didn't bode well for their realms.

Fighting this attraction for him took all her focus. Sometimes, in his unguarded moments, she caught fleeting expressions of affection, perhaps love, and even though it snatched her breath at the possibilities, she had to strengthen her resolve. If she truly loved him, she needed to place his interests first, even if it cost her heart and a lifetime of happiness. Until Drem was no longer her enemy, until Letoura was free and thriving, she could not commit herself to a carefree life with Sohar. It hurt to give him up, to not try, like a vise gripping her chest, stealing her breath.

He grunted, drawing her back from her sad thoughts. In the struggle, her hand slid down the straps of the food pouch, and she wrapped her fingers around a chunk of something soft. Yanking it out revealed a small wheel of green cheese. The aroma of herbs and garlic hit her, and she twisted in his arms to bite into the soft goodness. Joi moaned at the explosion of flavor now coating her tongue. He released her and snatched the cheese out of her hand. She almost cried at the loss.

"No food until you tell me why." His jaw clenched, and a pulse ticked at an alarming pace.

She sighed, then swung a punch which he dodged with ease, leaping back out of her range. She swung another, and he ducked, chuckling as she stamped on his foot to hold him in place for a rising knee. He stepped into her kick, catching her under her thigh. His grip sent a shiver through her. He yanked her against him, trapping her. Then, with blatant satisfaction, he bit into the cheese wheel, making exaggerated noises of delight.

She released a scream of frustration and shot her hand out to grab it, but he bent back. Impatience and hunger drove her, and she burst forward. With his hand clasping her leg, he was unbalanced, and she forced him to stumble backward. He did so but didn't release her leg. He took the brunt of the fall with a groan as she landed on top of him. He rolled over, pinning her beneath him with far more ease than she liked.

"Why are you guarding your heart?" He brushed hair out of her eyes. His breath scented of garlic and herbs, and her stomach twisted with its unrepentant demand for food. She considered kissing him for a taste of cheese. Divine, what was wrong with her?

"I can't tell you, Sohar." She looked away, not wanting him to read anything in her eyes. "Please accept that."

He shook his head. "We have an open relationship, Joi-Joi."

She whipped her head back to glare at him. "Fine, I'll lie then. I'm deeply in love with Mion. I've longed to marry him since I was eleven."

"Mion?" He chuckled.

"Would you believe Kylen?" She arched a hopeful brow. The foolish man laughed. "Aoni?" Again, no. "Rannic?"

His humor evaporated, and a scowl descended. "You so much as press your lips to any part of him, I'll gut him, Princess."

"Not Rannic either?" She drew in a deep sigh and opted for a little honesty. "Would you believe I'm scared I'll fail my people? I'm just a girl, Sohar."

She hoped to never forget the look on his face as it softened with compassion. When he revealed his emotions, he did it with devastating effect. All fight and teasing left him, and he leveled his face on hers, ensuring she could not look anywhere else.

He abandoned her hair to caress her cheek, his touch trailing sparks. "You may feel redundant with Jeiram to rule, Joi-Joi, but you're Letoura's heart. Jeiram will rebuild your realm—you will rebuild your people."

"I am? I will?" Warmth marched across her face and crept down her throat. She hadn't known he thought her so capable. With a sigh, she nuzzled his hand cupping her cheek. His scent engulfed her, potent and masculine. There was something addictive about it.

He nodded. "I have faith in you, Joi."

"Thank you, Sohar." Her stomach clenched. "I don't want to disappoint anyone."

He rolled over, and she was, at last, free. His arms wrapped around her, crushing her to him, with her cheek resting against his tunic-covered chest. His one hand splayed against the base of her spine which he slid up and down, presumably to soothe her. It did not. Instead, it invoked intense coiling in her stomach, warring with the ever-constant hunger.

His pulse leaped and settled in an audible beat, deafening her. In the Token of Kings Inn, his heartbeat soothed her—now, it excited her. She drew in a slow, silent breath, trying to assuage her sudden breathlessness. Was this what being with him would feel like? Oh, she would have preferred not to know than to have this memory haunt her.

"May I eat now?" Fear lanced through her, that he might see how much she adored him. She dipped her head again, hiding her eyes from his vigilant gaze.

"Of course, Joi." He bounded up, taking her with him. He took a second to steady her with a hand on her hip before offering her the half-eaten cheese.

"What else is in the pouch?" She pinched off a chunk from the soft, aromatic cheese.

He yanked her hand closer to steal her piece of cheese. "Now, keep in mind it must last three days, but I do believe I spotted a large roasted ham."

Her stomach gurgled on cue. Chuckling, he shoved his traveling bag aside, along with the parchment Viggu had given her. She was happy to see he guarded it well. When he tipped the food pouch's contents onto the bed, all thoughts of reading the inscription again dissolved. She grinned at the sight of black-crusted brown bread, fresh fruit, the roasted ham, a variety of dried meats, and more cheese. He knelt to sort the bounty, and with another laugh, snatched up a small cloth-wrapped bundle. He twisted to hide it from her, but she didn't care as long as she could eat.

Unraveling the braided bread, she nibbled on a piece before lifting the ham. The aroma of the succulent meat tempted her. A blissful sigh escaped her as she opened her mouth to take a bite. With a wicked gleam in his crystal-blue eyes, he popped something into her mouth instead. An explosion of tart sweetness saturated her tongue. The exquisite sugary taste drew a moan from her, and her eyelids fluttered closed as she savored the flavor.

"What is this?" She licked her lips in search of a stray morsel.

He smiled, chewing on one too. "Candied dates from Raica. It's rare and only available to the family of the Divine's disciples."

"Do you think I have killed the barge captain's son or daughter?" Horror penetrated her mind and heart. Each person she killed was someone's child. Bile rose to choke her, and she whimpered, lowering the bread and the roast ham.

"No, and if you did, they grant the Divine Priestess full control over their destinies. If their death serves the Divine, then they die happy." He waved another date under her nose.

"Their deaths didn't serve the Divine," she said before holding her mouth open for more. He obliged, and she closed her lips on his finger. Her eyes widened in disbelief, and she hurried to free him.

"You don't know whether their attacks served the Divine or not." Sohar's voice was odd, deeper, and rougher.

He glanced away from her, staring at the strewn food for a long time. Pulling the bread closer, he broke off a piece. His cheeks darkened, but he said no more. She wondered at his withdrawal. Breaking off a strip of ham, she offered it to him. He accepted it with a nod, yet kept his face downcast. Shoving the meat into his mouth, he bounded up, surprising her. He nodded at the bed as he scooped up an apple. The candied dates—still in their wrapping—lay discarded alongside the bread.

"Try not to eat everything, Princess. I'll inform Rannic and Nyry regarding the assassins and your solution." The door slammed on his way out.

Joi blinked at it, her mouth agape before she sank her teeth into the ham again. Had she said something offensive? Thinking over their last words, she couldn't find what made him leave as if an irate dragon were on his backside. Then a thought gripped her—did he know she loved him? No, that was impossible. She hadn't exposed her heart to him, not by word or deed, of that she was certain.

A heated shiver rippled over her skin as sheer humiliation washed through her. His open affection had her believing he might reciprocate, but his rejection confused her. Or he did love her but knew it was futile to pursue this? Over analyzing this wouldn't help her. It would place thoughts and ideas in her chaotic mind, ones she would wish were true.

With a shrug, she packed the food back into the pouch, rewrapping the dates with care. Whatever bothered him, she was certain he would share with her, if it were important.

Chapter Forty-Five

Storms

Two days passed with ease. The crisp blue skies and the fragrance of the seas settled peace into her soul. Each second on board was a blessing, a cherished experience. The captain kept the coast on their left, and the weather treated them well. Sohar had returned guarded, once more encasing his emotions. He had chosen to seek solace during the day to protect her at night. It was an unusual arrangement, but he couldn't see the stupidity of it, no matter how she argued.

Joi struggled to find solace knowing he stared at her. Rannic and Nyry didn't leave her side until Sohar relieved them of their duty. This too made no sense since she was more than capable of defending herself. She suggested separate cabins to protect Nyry. Having her as company still endangered her.

The sunset on the second day was minutes away, not that Joi could see it. A turbulent wind had risen, tossing the ship like an autumn leaf in a river's churning current. The gray clouds were dark and ominous. When it rained, it did so without warning. She raced to the bow and gripped the railing, thrilling in the dipping ship, the violent wind, and the thick droplets drenching her.

Laughter erupted at the sense of freedom that consumed her soul. The Divine's creations were exhilarating. An arm looped around her waist and pinned her against a warm chest. Lifting her face, she met Sohar's furious blue gaze.

"What are you doing, Princess?" he asked, as if it wasn't obvious. His roared words in her ear made her shiver, the warmth of his breath against the cool rain affecting her. "Anyone could push you over the side."

"Mighty Sohar," she greeted him, not willing to let his dour mood ruin this moment. She couldn't keep the smile from her face. The sea's tantrum called to something primal within her. "Isn't it breathtaking? Raise your face to the heavens and honor the Divine for such a blessing." She spun in his arms to watch him do so, but he didn't. He stood there, as soaked as she was, staring at her as if she were insane, and perhaps she was. Forced to yell at him above the thunder, she said, "You look intense. Was your solace not good?"

Something sad lingered on his face. "As good as yours, Joi-Joi."

She scowled. Did he know she didn't rest well, and that she pretended to sleep until exhaustion claimed her? He gripped the railing with one hand and his arm—still looped around her—tightened, crushing her against him. She splayed her hands across his chest, peering at him. An emotion she couldn't read burned in the crystal depths of his gaze. He slid his palm up her back, along her clinging wet tunic, to nestle between her shoulder blades.

"What's bothering you, Sohar? You're acting strange," she said—a lull in the wind meant her yell was louder than it needed to be.

"Strange? No." He shook his head. "Mad? Yes. You drive me mad, Joi."

She gasped, a sharp pain twisting in her heart like the plunging of a knife. "I don't mean to anger you, Sohar, you know this."

"Anger?" He chuckled, but it lacked humor and was self-deprecating. "I can deal with anger, Princess."

What was the matter with him? He wasn't his usual, dominating self. They said sea voyages could drive men insane. Not him though. She couldn't see a three-day journey across the Bay of Faith as the cause of his current behavior.

"You're speaking in riddles." She shook her head to dislodge the raindrops running rivulets down her face. The refreshing cold of the wind and rain didn't chill her. The Fox and Sohar kept her warm.

"Do you like me holding you like this?" He leaned in to ask her, his warm lips brushing her earlobe.

"Hugs are wonderful. Ma used to hug me all the time." She knew the protocol for physical affection within royal courts, but Buro had shown her grace.

"During Xiaxan training, I would long for a hug, but you never blessed me with one." His lips brushed her ear again, and she shivered.

"I never hugged you?" She chewed on her bottom lip as she sifted through her memories. He was correct. Shame burst through her, and she clung to him, to beg him for forgiveness. "I'm sorry, Sohar. I thought you tolerated me on the best of days. I'd never force a hug on you." She squeezed him, giving him a big hug. "There, a long hug to make up for my negligence."

"I don't want a hug, Princess."

"Oh." She jerked away, dropping her arms as the heat of humiliation warmed her face.

She glanced down, trying to hide her embarrassment. What did she think? A few days in her company would soften him? The sting behind her eyes warred with the ache in her throat as she fought the rising tears. She was making such a fool of herself, adrift in a relationship she didn't recognize and couldn't navigate.

"The time for hugs has passed." He trapped her against the railing using his hips.

With the violent waves behind her, she should feel fear, but she didn't. He spread his legs wide for balance, released the railing, and captured her chin in his firm, cool fingers. He held her there, ensnared by his smoldering gaze.

"You're a woman now, Joi." He dipped his head, his face whispers away from hers. His warm breath fanned across her chin and mouth.

What was he doing? She frowned. "I still feel like the eleven-year-old girl running for her life."

"I remember the day I met you, the day you emerged from your fountain, as drenched as you are now. I remember a storm like this one." His lips claimed hers.

The suddenness of it made her gasp. The heat and taste of him were better than candied dates. Joi ran her fingers up his arms to cling to him as he deepened the kiss. The Divine created Sohar as wild as the chopping waves and the roiling gray clouds above. Her heart leaped into her throat, and she tightened her hold, not wanting this experience to end.

A flash of lightning, too close for comfort, broke the kiss. He glanced at the sky before he rested his gaze on her face. Clenching his jaw, he scooped her into his arms and carried her across the deck to their cabin. Depositing her alongside the bed, he grabbed his traveling bag then left. The burn of anger rose within her, and she stared at the closed door. Stomping her foot and pummeling her bed did nothing to relieve the tension inside her. Loneliness settled on her shoulders, sinking deep into her soul. She felt...abandoned.

Hopping on each leg, she yanked off her boots, throwing them across the small cabin, hard enough to bounce off the walls. Ducking to avoid the rebound of a flying boot, she laughed. Breaking her shoes wouldn't help either. Drawing in a shuddering breath, she stripped off her wet garments and pulled on fresh ones. With her wet tunic and pants hanging on the hooks provided, she gathered her shoes. Her braid was sopping wet, but there was nothing she could do about that.

Dropping onto the bed, Joi rummaged through the food pouch for a strip of dried meat. She chewed and sucked on the piece until it softened enough for her to tear at it with her teeth.

This was the second time he kissed her. It was senseless to do so when they couldn't marry. Then again, what did a kiss mean to a man? The winehouses and brothel dancers she had met attested to kissing meaning nothing. She clung to that as a reason. It was silly to dwell on the why and to simply enjoy the experience, but her heart ached—a constant throb in her chest. With their journey ending, each precious kiss, she feared was her last. Sighing, she curled her fingers over her medallion, using its pulsed greeting to ground her.

Jumping off the bed with the dried meat dangling from her mouth like a blade of grass, she needed to rid herself of the excess energy coursing through her. She moved through her Xiaxan morning routine, incorporating her Cento training, as well. With controlled steps, she slid her feet back, to the side, into a low lunge, before dropping into a crouch. While her hands and arms twisted and entwined as red tendrils unraveled up her forearms, she repeated each technique until her limbs trembled and sweat dripped off her chin. Sohar's delayed return was indicative of his feelings regarding Joi and being with her in close confinement.

With a long-drawn-out sigh, she pressed her damp tunic to her face before rehooking it. She hoped she could find solace with ease, and she had better do so now before crystal-blue eyes arrived to stare her awake.

Chapter Forty-Six

Closure

T HE WHITE STONE OF the temple glimmered on the horizon long before the ship neared it. Joi gripped the railing in the exact spot where Sohar kissed her. She shook her head, not willing to drown in the morass of her thoughts. Remembering the kiss was the trigger. Yet, he was a horse length behind her, his intense gaze burning her back.

"We'll have to fly," Rannic said, startling her, as he drew up beside her.

"Fly?" She squinted between the ship and the island. "You can fly?"

"Only those born with magic can, Princess. After the Battle of Heaven's Fire, the reigning kings forbade the use of such an ability. That is why you never had the training." A wicked gleam in his eyes told her he had received training and had often broken that rule.

"I can fly?" She flashed a bright smile at him, prepared to break the rule too if it meant she could soar like an asoquay. "Show me, please."

"There's no time. Come, Joi. Stand on my toes." Sohar held out his arms. Pouting, she squeezed between them, using his forearms as leverage while she placed her feet with care. "Now hug me and don't look down, Princess."

She scowled. How had he learned to fly, and why wouldn't he share this with her? With the way she felt toward him, she would rather have flown with Rannic. Since the kiss, Sohar's behavior had been cold and stoic. One would think she had confessed her undying love and forced him to kiss her. The wind whipped her escaped whisps of hair and tossed her braid, as well. She buried her nose against his chest, wondering when they would fly and laughed at the thought of it. To fly like a bird would be such a blessing.

"You can release me now, Joi-Joi," he said, and she jerked out of his arms to look around. They were on the white stone steps of the Divine's temple. Nyry waved from the ship's railing, farther away than Joi realized.

"Will you teach me to fly, Sohar?" she asked.

He stared at her before nodding, as if unsure of their future friendship. Sadness seeped into her soul. He would never have hesitated before the kisses. She faced the steps, hiding the tears threatening to fall. Rannic joined her as she climbed to where two disciples guarded the temple's ornate entrance.

"Greetings, travelers." A guard angled across their path. "I am Imlamir, a humble servant of the Divine. What brings you to our fair island?"

"I seek answers." She gave him a small bow.

"Do we not all seek answers, young one?" His tone was gentle.

"I have but one question, Imlamir." She drew in a deep breath. "Why does the Divine Priestess want me dead?"

Imlamir jerked as if she slapped him. Confusion furrowed his brow, and his gaze skirted along her black hair before peering into her golden eyes. His shoulders slumped, and he nodded. "Answers you shall receive this day. And you, Prince Rannic? It is strange to find one of your reputation seeking the Divine."

"I go where Joi goes," he said.

"You have married?" Imlamir asked, both eyebrows touching his silver hairline.

"No, my wife is safe and awaits my return," Rannic said.

They must have spoken their vows to each other in the privacy of their cabin. A year of bliss was now theirs to enjoy before they held an official wedding ceremony. To see him and Nyry married was more than worth the long journey Joi had traveled.

"This is wonderful, Rannic. I'm so pleased for you." Smiling, she hugged him but hurried to release him when Sohar cleared his throat.

"And you, my prince?" Imlamir addressed Sohar.

"I guard the Letouran royal," he said as if that was all she meant to him. An obligation, a chore.

Ice drenched her face and squeezed her heart, and she glanced at her boots. Loving him meant every deed and word from him might wound her. This was a harsh lesson to learn.

"Then remain here, guard." She met his gaze, letting him see how his words hurt her. "If Imlamir promises not to kill me within the temple, you may stay behind."

"On my life, Princess," the disciple vowed.

With a glance at Rannic, she passed the two guards. Whether Sohar followed or not, she did not care.

The temple's interior seemed larger than the exterior had suggested. Massive pillars supported a carved stone ceiling depicting the Divine creating the five realms. There were no benches to diminish the immense feeling of the nave, and toward the dais, upon which the Divine Priestess waited. Her white robes draped her diminutive form, her headdress appearing too heavy for her. She was a beautiful young woman which was surprising for someone with this much power and responsibility.

Joi strode toward her, admiring the intricate tapestries lining the blank walls. The air scented of herbs and spices, some warming her heart with their familiarity, others teasing her nose with their exotic fragrances. Torches lit the vast chamber with flickering light, inviting yet ominous.

"Divine Priestess." She blessed her with a formal bow. She had decided to approach from a point of courtesy before accusing her of attempted murder. Behind her shimmered a large pool, images visible in its blue depths. *The Well of Tomorrows.*

"Princess Jenaso, this is a surprise." The Priestess's voice was melodic yet aged with wisdom.

Joi almost laughed at the lie. With the well, nothing should surprise the priestess. "As is seeing your disciples with daggers in hand." She winced. So much for civility.

The priestess stared at Rannic before gliding toward Joi, keeping her hands tucked inside her billowing embroidered sleeves.

Joi whispered words to her medallion, preparing it for an attack.

"Why could you not die? I'd planned everything with such care. Your death would free me, free my son." Her brown eyes darkened, along with the tightening of her jaw. "Can you not see how the realms are better without your existence?"

"How would killing me free anyone?" Joi frowned at the woman. "Even if I die, my brother will reign, and Letoura will return to its former glory."

"Jeiram lives?" The priestess gaped, then pinched her lips. "The Well of Tomorrows has been silent regarding your fates." She forced a smile. "It matters not. I will send my disciples after your brother."

"Priestess, does she speak the truth?" Horror stained Imlamir's voice and face. He stumbled forward, kneeling to embed his fingers in her robes. "To take a life is forbidden. Why? Why would you do this, my love?"

The priestess ripped her garment out of his hands and veered around him, intent on reaching Joi. "Despite my attempts to end your life, you seek me out?" The woman threw back her head and laughed. "Oh, you are a fool to trust that I will not kill you myself."

As she lunged for Joi, Rannic leaped between them, and the priestess jerked to a halt as if she hit a wall. Joi shot a surprised glance at Rannic. Before she could summon the Fox to take the offensive, Sohar's voice echoed in the hall as if he recited a poem. Irritated and delighted that he followed her, she struggled with the conflicting emotions, choosing to glare at him for his intrusion. He had unraveled her parchment to read the written words her father left her.

> *The power of soul, of the Divine,*
> *Of heart and light,*
> *Mind and plight,*
> *Judge now, the guardian of thine.*

The priestess screamed—a mixture of rage, fear, and pain—as a ball of blinding white light burst out of her chest to hover before her. It did nothing else, except dodge her grasping fingers before dropping to skitter along the floor to where Imlamir kneeled. It circled the man before darting into his chest. His eyes widened, and he roared, his body convulsing. The priestess cried out his name and rushed to him. By then, he had stilled.

As she stretched out a trembling hand, he caught her wrist and shoved her away. Rising to his feet, with more grace than his old bones should have allowed, he turned to Joi. Years melted off his face, and he was once again a young man. The priestess was the opposite—wrinkles lined her skin, her lips dipping. Her wise eyes remained the same though.

"What happened to you, Imlamir?" Joi asked, sneaking amazed glances between the priestess and the rejuvenated disciple.

"I am the manifestation of the Divine. Through me, He shall speak. The inscription is as old as time, dear child, its purpose and thus its hidden powers forgotten. By speaking it, Prince Sohar has invoked the promise the Divine made. Should His chosen one fail His people, He will choose another, and so He has." Imlamir held out his hand, and without hesitation, Sohar placed the parchment in it. "Know this, your family is at peace, Jenaso of Letoura. So shall you be for the remainder of your days. As for you, Rannic of Drem. I present to you your mother."

"My mother is dead," he said but scrutinized the priestess.

Imlamir shook his head. "Rumoc of Drem deceived you. The priestess, Ninlassa, is your mother, someone you once considered your beloved aunt."

"Ninlassa? Nina?" He grabbed the priestess by her shoulders to peer into her eyes. "It is you. Why did you abandon me? How did I drive you away?" He tore off her headdress to stroke the silver-streaked burnished brown of her hair. His touch was gentle, and reverent. "My mother?"

She nodded, tears flowing down her cheeks unhindered. There in her eyes was an expression Joi recognized. The same had been on her father's face when he kissed her one last time.

"She was weakening you. Turning you soft," Rumoc said, stepping from behind a pillar.

Joi gasped, studying the man responsible for the deaths of her parents and the turmoil in her realm. He was thinner and shorter, with less stature than she expected. Did she hate him for what he did? No, for his evil and selfishness touched everything, even those closest to him. She wanted no part of such a corrosive emotion.

"Does your hate not have limits?" Rannic pushed Ninlassa behind him.

Backing away, Joi granted the reuniting family a little space, but drew Rumoc's stare.

"What do you know of hatred, boy?" The elderly king marched into the clearing. His gaze remained on Joi, and she straightened her shoulders, running a bold appraisal over him. "I see your skill at deception has improved. She is as beautiful as Eria." His sigh was one of a disappointed parent. "You could not kill her or marry her? Why am I not surprised?" He tsked. "You are incapable of ruling, as I suspected."

Rannic's mocking laughter reverberated off the stone pillars. "My hate was like yours, Father—all-encompassing, but now I feel hate toward one person. A man who has no capacity for forgiveness or kindness, or Divine-forbid, love."

Her heart twanged, sharp and incessant as she imagined a young Rannic desperate for love or, at least, some affection. The way he protected Ninlassa meant he found some comfort, but Rumoc had ripped it away.

"Words cannot harm me, boy." Rumoc chuckled, a cold and rehearsed sound as if he imagined this scene many times. "I'll kill her myself." He drew his hands up and released two bolts of black energy at Joi. His face contorted as dark evil consumed him.

Sohar bellowed something from the side as he darted toward Joi, dissolving into his white mist. The Scarlet Fox burst to life, swirling around her in eager expectation. Rannic dove in front of her, catching the brunt of Rumoc's black energy, and two voices screamed his name. Where he landed, he remained, unmoving. Ninlassa dropped by his side, her twitching hands hovering over his body, as if she didn't know where to touch. Rumoc hadn't expected his son to sacrifice himself—he too called out his name.

"You killed him, just like you promised to do." Ninlassa's sobs shook her frail body. "Why did you let hate *rule* you, Rumoc?" She rose onto her feet as Sohar materialized in front of Joi, wrapping an arm around her to shield her with his body. She wriggled and twisted in his arms, not wanting to miss the altercation.

"I didn't mean to..." Rumoc sounded broken.

Sohar lifted Joi into his arms to carry her away from the scene. She pummeled his chest, demanding he release her.

"Didn't mean to?" Ninlassa's laugh was manic, bouncing off the pillars and rippling the fountain's surface. "I thought the princess would be his downfall, but no, you were the entire time."

Rumoc screamed, and Sohar spun to look. Ninlassa had used her black energy to rip out the king's heart. She stared at the beating, scorched organ, dripping black and red blood through her fingers. Rumoc collapsing at her feet meant nothing to Ninlassa.

Flipping her hand over, she let the organ fall to the floor before wiping her palm on her robes, the blood a bright stain against the white silk. She returned to Rannic's side and held her hand over him, summoning her energy to heal him.

Joi vaulted out of Sohar's arms, landing next to Rannic's sprawled body to ask the Fox to heal. As soon as her red tendrils entwined him, she knew it was bad. The sudden drain on her power was strong.

"Jeiram, please," she begged, pulling more energy through their link.

The medallion pulsed warnings at her, but she ignored it. None of it mattered. Rannic had saved her and such an act of honor shouldn't go unrewarded. When Sohar knelt beside her, sending his white magic spreading over Rannic, the warmth of relief and gratitude swept through her. Together, they could save Rannic.

She didn't know how long they pushed their energy into Rannic, but it was only when Priest Imlamir joined them that she believed there was hope. It was too late for her though, the Fox having drained her completely. She dared not take any more from Jeiram lest she kill him outright, and Letoura deserved a ruler more than her people deserved a heart.

Facing Sohar, she kissed his cheek—a silent farewell. Then with a smile for a blinking Rannic, Joi allowed death to claim her.

CHAPTER FORTY-SEVEN

BITTERSWEET

RANNIC'S EYELIDS WERE HEAVY, more so than usual. That was odd. It felt as if he had slept for days, yet rest eluded him. Moaning, he struggled to sit up. At the sight of his *mother* leaning over him, the past day came flooding back. He darted a glance to the side where Sohar cradled Joi to his chest, deep sorrow marring his face.

Tears fell unheeded with silent sobs racking his body. How had she died when Rannic spared her from his father's hatred?

A bloody lump of something sat beside his father's lifeless body. Sohar killed him? Rannic should've been furious, but in hindsight, every decision Rumoc had made led to this point. Yet, in the end, his father won. Joi was dead.

Rannic struggled to his feet with the aid of his mother and the Divine Priest Imlamir. The man radiated peace, a true reflection of the Divine himself.

"What happened?" Rannic stood still to let the dizziness pass.

"She healed you," Ninlassa said.

The full impact of those words hit him. He had killed her anyway, fulfilling his father's request. His lip curled in self-derision. This couldn't be true.

"No," he said. "She can't die. Not Joi. Letoura needs her to undo my father's deeds. I'm so sorry, Sohar. I didn't expect her to sacrifice herself to save a Drem."

"You don't know Joi then, Rannic." Sohar wiped one side of his face on his shoulder. "She's not dead. The Divine Priest healed her."

"She's not?" Relief flooded him then confusion furrowed his brow. "Then why the tears?"

"He loves her but must let her go, my son, as he did his mother," Priest Imlamir said.

"His mother?" Rannic asked. The one rumor he could recall about the death of Sohar's mother was that it was sudden. No other news had reached Drem.

"She died in childbirth, her daughter a few hours afterward," Ninlassa said. "I saw it in the Well of Tomorrows, but there was no avoiding it."

"He lost his mother and sister in one day?" Rannic winced, surprised to feel compassion for a Greyad.

"*He* is sitting right here, and yes, I lost both that day. Rannic, I have a task for you." Sohar vaulted into the air to land beside him with Joi clasped against his chest. "It will take days for her to regain her strength. I place her in your care. See that she arrives in Tennaba."

He gaped. "You're not coming with?"

"No, if I do not let her go now…" Sohar sucked in a deep breath. "Should anything happen to her, I will kill you."

Rannic flicked a dismissive hand. "Yes, yes, I've heard the speech, but I still don't understand why you'd abandon her now?"

"Abandon?" He passed her limp body to Rannic, his fingers trembling as he tucked an ebony curl behind her ear. "She needs to fulfill her destiny—only then will she be free to choose a new path, a life with me."

"In matters of the heart, you are a coward, Greyadian," Rannic said, his voice rasping as he imagined the look in her eyes when she awoke to find Sohar gone.

Sohar's hands stilled as he untied Rannic's imperial token before placing it on top of Joi's stomach. "Please, tell me how she's fairing and as often as you can, King Rannic."

He ignored Rannic's insult. Instead, he placed his hand over his heart and bowed before doing the same to the Divine Priest.

"Get your things, Mother." Rannic flashed her a smile.

Her gasp of surprise brought warmth to his chest. He had a mother. She had been there for him in his younger years in the role of an aunt, and he had often wished she were his true mother. Life was strange sometimes.

"I have no things," she said.

With a small bow to the Divine Priest Imlamir, Rannic strode out of the temple. Nyry waited at the ship's railing—her sunlight-kissed hair waved a greeting in the cool ocean breeze. She had confessed her feelings with her Orthian boldness, asking him to cease wasting time and claim her.

He had done just that. He had never known a woman like her. Despite the dire situation in his arms, heat exploded in his heart.

"Shall we, Mother?" he asked the woman trailing him.

She grinned, and with a nod, they took to flight. He landed on the deck and carried Joi to Sohar's cabin. Spreading her onto the bed, he stared at an unconscious Joi. Sohar's abandonment would devastate her.

At the thought of leaving Nyry, his heart constricted like a painful fist squeezing the life out of his body. Never. He wouldn't leave her to suffer no matter how much her destiny demanded it. Nyry was his wife. To abandon her was to lose his soul.

Yes, he had to convince her father to trust a Drem, but in his heart, Viggu's blessing mattered not. Only that Rannic had Nyry's love. How far had he fallen? He chuckled, but it was a cold humor. He had hated all the realms with a fiery passion that consumed his every thought. Now he loved an Orthian with a consuming passion that inflamed his heart.

"What happened?" Nyry wrapped an arm around his waist, peering around his shoulder at Joi.

He spun to capture her in a full embrace.

"I love you," he said, desperate for her to know.

Her cheeks darkened as she gaped at him. He wanted to kiss those lips until there were no more tomorrows.

"It was *that* bad?" She rose on her toes to plant a kiss on his chin, stroking his cheek with a gentle touch.

"Yes. My father is dead, and Sohar has left Joi in our care. We're to see her to Tennaba en route to Manorio." He snuck in a quick kiss. "Perhaps we should stop off at the Underground City of Callisor so I may extend a full apology to the Selions?"

"Your father? I'm sorry, Ran-hin." Nyry frowned. "Did you say Sohar left her? But he loves her." She pressed her forehead against his chest. "This will break her heart."

"Yes, but there is some good news." He twisted, searching for his mother. She stood outside, a small figure in her stained robes. "I'm reunited with my mother. Ninlassa, this is my wife, Nyry of Orth."

"Your mother? Oh, how wonderful." Nyry tore from his arms to embrace Nina. This startled the older woman, but she succumbed, hugging her back.

"My dear child, I see why Rannic values you. Your heart is pure, and your soul is a blinding light." She glided into the cabin and sat alongside the bed. "I'll stay with Joi. Rannic, set the destination for Rendar. Let us fulfill Sohar's request and see this young woman home."

He hesitated—not an hour ago his mother wanted to kill Joi. He wasn't sure he could trust her not to harm her.

"Be at ease, my son." Ninlassa brushed a curl off Joi's temple then summoned her magic to heal her. "She sacrificed herself for you, and there is nothing I can do that will ever repay her for such a gift."

Since the pink returned to Joi's cheeks, he nodded. He laced his fingers with Nyry's smaller hand to lead her out of the room. Rannic wasn't an idiot, but a Drem raised by Rumoc.

He placed a Greyadian guard at the door.

Epilogue

Peace

Joi smiled as she lifted the toddler onto her hip. He clapped his pudgy hands, pleased with the attention. She surveyed the orphaned children and the house her people had finished building. The children melted her heart for the few hours a day she spent here. But when she rode home, the darkness would once again enshroud her.

As usual, her thoughts flitted back to that fateful moment when she had awoken to find herself alone in the back of a caravan, days away from Raica.

Rannic and Nyry were there, along with a division of Greyadian soldiers but no Sohar. The weeks following were the hardest. Joi had cried herself to sleep every night, mourning her broken heart. She still did. The Greyadian obligatory gift arrived for her birthday, but she could not bear to open it. To her, it was a token, nothing more. If he cared for her, he wouldn't have abandoned her.

"It is time, Princess," her maidservant said.

Joi kissed the little boy's sweaty forehead before handing him to his carer. She left the building, stepping out onto the busy street. Tennabans bustled with excitement on their tongues and hope in the air. Seven months ago, she had arrived in Tennaba, and the restoration began. Her people had welcomed her with such love the memory of it often brought her to tears.

Her horse awaited with a traveling bag on the pommel. This morning, she had bid Tuyra and Jeiram farewell. No matter which way she turned, there were Seasons of Delight. Despite being happy for her friends and family, she remained alone, and soon she would have to attend any number of marriage ceremonies. She dreaded this, expecting to see Sohar at one of them, at least. Jeiram said he asked after her, but she didn't believe him. Even if he did, it was a courtesy and lacked true meaning. As she had suspected, his kisses, his open affection meant nothing to him. They were but words for a winehouse saga.

After hugging her maidservant, Joi vaulted into the saddle. Hope blossomed within her, a bright spot on her darkened soul. If she headed north, then traveled northwest, she would reach her cabin. A place of her own away from the demands of court life. Letoura didn't need her anymore, and she wasn't ready to commit her life nor her heart to another man no matter how much Aoni pestered her.

The journey to the southern mountains of Hokhoun took her seven days. One day longer than needed since she stopped at every village to enjoy their hospitality. She reveled in each decision she made that didn't require a council or permission from Jeiram. That was true freedom.

Taking the winding path through the mountains excited her, and with a squeal, she spurred her horse on. As she crested the rise, the sprawling house came into view. It was breathtaking to think this was hers. Her sanctuary. A relieved sigh escaped her. Constructed of bamboo and Selion wood, the estate was small enough to clean with ease. Behind it, the royal gardener had created a waterfall paradise.

She dismounted and led her horse around the back to the stables. The chorus of birdsong and trickling water greeted her. No other sounds disturbed the peace. The tiny waterfall was the reason for this location, which the gardener had transformed into a small oasis with a large, rocky pool. Bamboo bridges crossed the waterways flowing under her house. The variety of plants were vibrant, their fragrances intoxicating.

Smiling, she slipped off her boots, dropping them in a haphazard manner. Stripping her remaining garments, she dove into the pool. She laughed in delight when she burst out of the water, flicking her braid out of her face. This was better than her fountain in Ethrielle. She could swim the day away or run around her home naked, if she so chose.

"Greetings, Joi-Joi."

She squealed and ducked her shoulders under the water. That voice? Sohar? Spinning in disbelief, she faced him, not caring that he had her at a disadvantage. The eagerness to see him outweighed the pain piercing her shriveled heart. How long had he been there? Had he seen her naked? Oh, Divine.

"Sohar? What are you doing here?" Her voice cracked. The sight of him was Divine-sent, although he was thinner with dark shadows under his eyes. She didn't like seeing him so, as if he had been unwell. She tamped down the bolt of concern shooting through her.

"Are you coming out, or am I diving in?" He strolled along the stone path toward the pool. His feet were bare which implied he had been there a while.

"Neither. I don't understand why you are here of all places. You can just leave, however you traveled." She darted a glance at her horse in the stables—the only horse.

"I flew." He pulled off his tunic, baring his chest.

He was a beautiful man. She stared, allowing herself the enjoyment of admiring his body, then realized he watched her do so. She dipped her chin to hide her face, pressing her wet hands to her burning cheeks.

"We need to talk."

Trailing her fingers across the surface, she created ripples to hide her nudity. When his presence remained, she squinted at him. She wouldn't cower, not after the way he had broken her heart. "I asked you to leave, Sohar. Please do so."

His sigh was loud, discernible above the waterfall. "Did you read my missive?"

"What missive?" The pool reflected the sun's rays, mesmerizing her, distracting her from the temptation to ogle him.

"The one I sent with your gift." He inched closer to the edge, and she glared at him.

"I didn't open your gift." She huffed. "I don't want your gifts. You can instruct your servant to cease sending them."

He folded his arms across his bare chest, his muscles rippling. Curse him. "I select each gift, Princess. I always have."

She wanted to snort. Did he think her a fool? What prince had time to choose gifts for a woman he didn't care about? "It doesn't matter anymore. You made your feelings known."

"I have?" He chuckled. The flash of his white teeth stunned her, and she splashed water on her face to break the enchantment. "I doubt that, so let me start with...I didn't abandon you."

Joi gasped and turned her back on him, wiping at the tears and water droplets spilling down her cheeks. How had he known? His words struck her heart, triggering a waterfall of tears, the pain of his abandonment *still* tender.

"You needed to focus on rebuilding Letoura, and if I left Raica with you, I wouldn't be able to set you free."

Had his voice roughened? What did it matter? Deeds meant more than words.

A splash followed, and she spun in a circle, shocked that he would dare to join her in the pool. With her naked. He resurfaced before her, and she folded her arms across her chest, hoping to hide as much of her nudity as possible.

"What are you doing?" She tried to keep the panic from her voice, but the urge to yell at him, to pound his chest with her fists made her tremble. He had made this worse. She couldn't leave and expose herself for perhaps the second time today. If he left, he would expose himself, for on the wooden bridge lay his discarded pants.

"Confessing if you'll let me." He smiled, with stoicism nowhere on his face. Her heart fluttered before dancing at the intensity in his blue eyes. "I loved you from the moment I saw you. Kissing you in the desert made me realize just how much. I fought these emotions, fought the temptation of you until I couldn't anymore."

Her mouth fell open—she wasn't certain she heard him correctly. Did he say he loved her? That she tempted him? Her chest constricted, shooting butterflies up her throat, squeezing off her air. She couldn't breathe, but she was afraid to try anyway for fear of disturbing this beautiful mirage. Tears prickled behind her eyes, and her nose burned.

His gaze dipped to her lips and lingered there, starting a spark across them, a tickle until she licked them. He sucked in a sharp breath. "Joi-Joi, you must know, across the five realms, there is nothing as enticing as your soft lips."

She shuddered, but blinked at him, a little dazed. "What?" She had to have imagined this, these words, his presence, and his mesmerizing crystal-blue eyes promising happiness. The water painted his hair silver, and it clung to him. He was the boy and the man she loved. Yet, there was a vulnerability in his eyes as if he feared her response.

He lifted his hands out of the water to cup her shoulders, but she was too stunned at his confession to berate him. His touch seared her, and she wanted to drop her guard, to throw herself into his arms and cling to him.

"These seven months have been hell. Every cursed day I wanted to come for you, to claim you. Only the Divine knows how I survived." He shifted closer, the heat of him warming her arm across her chest. She shivered, the goosebumps confirming she was awake. This wasn't a dream. "Then Pan told me you were leaving for your mountain home, and I knew it was time."

First, Sohar said he loved her, had always loved her. She struggled to absorb his words, to believe him. Then he revealed Pan's duplicity, the conniving old wart. She would give him a tongue lashing when next she saw him.

"Time for what?" She frowned.

His expression intensified, as if what he would say next was important to him. "Marry me, Princess. Let my heart claim yours as it longs to do."

As his words sunk in, a fire burned through her. He had known he loved her, yet he let her leave, and didn't confess any of these emotions during their journey? She shoved away from him, uncaring if she exposed herself.

"You chose to abandon me, knowing you loved me? Sohar, you told me I was Letoura's heart, yet you ripped mine out and sent me here without it. Well, it's encased in ice." The cold of despair drenched her, sliding down her spine from her head to deep within her soul. Her voice spiked, and she forced herself to breathe, hoping to calm her erratic heartbeat. "I don't know if I can love you again, love anyone for that matter."

Part of her screamed and cursed for not seizing this opportunity to be with him. The stubborn part of her refused to succumb, not when he hurt her because he loved her. That made no sense, when she endured bone-aching pain at his abandonment.

"Again?" His voice deepened then he lunged across the gap between them and wrapped his arms around her, crushing her against his chest.

His heat engulfed her, and she opened her mouth to scold him. He took advantage of her parted lips to kiss her. She moaned, succumbing to his assault on her senses. She had missed his kisses, missed the taste of him, and the feel of his velvet skin under her fingers. Her heart melted as if his lips were the key to unravelling her anger.

Desperation, happiness, and desire poured through his kisses and his touch and sheer presence solidified his confession in her mind. Never had she thought he would confess his love, nor that she tempted him, or that he couldn't resist her allure. All the things she had never thought to hear, he had confessed as if instructed to.

When he brushed kisses along her jaw, she mumbled what her body, and her soul demanded she grab with both hands. "Yes, I will marry you, Mighty Sohar." Speaking those words let the unforgiveness melt off her, freeing her for every wonderful second with him.

He stilled, his heart thundering under her fingertips. Vaulting out of the water, he took her with him. She squealed, torn between clinging to him or hiding her nudity. In mid-air, he flipped her so that he scooped her in his arms, a hand at her back and one under her thighs, before landing on the path. Pausing to brush his mouth over hers, he carried her into her new home, his lips not leaving hers.

"I guarded my heart against you, Sohar, but it was too late." She sprawled on the bed.

His gaze traveled her naked form, but she kept her focus on his face, trying to ignore the flush of heat descending her throat. Her fingers twitched to cover herself, but she held firm.

"I hoped you'd confess this to me, Joi-Joi. I needed to know your true feelings." Sohar climbed onto the bed to lay alongside her. Despite the cool waters of the fountain, his bare skin was hot where it touched her—along her thighs, at her hip, and across her chest. "I have you now, my exquisite and breathtaking Xiaxan Fox. Nothing else matters."

He proceeded to show her what was so wonderful about a Season of Delight.

About the Author

Sevannah Storm is a fiction writer who immerses herself in fantastical worlds both magical and science fiction. She has a flare for the creative, having studied art and interior architecture, and spends her time drawing, oil painting, and writing. An avid reader from an early age, Sevannah finds her inspiration from various sources: games, novels, music, and the land of make-believe. The unique versus the practical has brought on numerous debates.

In her spare time, she does CrossFit and Krav Maga and rereads novels that snatch her breath away. Having embraced the social media world, you can find her on most platforms.

Her home is a land south of Wakanda, where animals roam free. Born in Zimbabwe, she grew up in South Africa. The crisp blue skies with cotton-candy sunsets expand her heart and soul, encapsulating a sense of freedom.

Words she lives by: "Know your pothole and dodge it. Don't work in a pencil factory if you're a vampire."

Sevannah loves to hear from her readers. You can find and connect with her at the links below.

Website/Newsletter:

https://www.sevannahstorm.com/

Facebook:

https://www.facebook.com/sevannah.storm

Instagram:

https://www.instagram.com/sevannah.storm/

Twitter:

https://twitter.com/sevannah_storm

Thank you for taking the time to read Xiaxan Fox. If you enjoyed the story, please tell your friends and leave a review. Reviews support authors and ensure they continue to bring readers books to love and enjoy.

Stay tuned for sample chapters.

Ire of Silver

As the bastard daughter of an orc chief, Thugari is nothing more than a slave. After her last beating, disguising herself as a stable-boy, she escapes, stealing as she runs. Unfortunately, her victim is the orc Rukk Knaraugh, a lawbringer from the Council.

When Rukk finds her, she tries to run, fearing for her life, but he's skilled in tracking her. Claiming she is in his debt, he takes her with him, heading north as he hunts wild witches stealing babies. He agrees to release her from the debt in the dwarven city of Dussoum, where, for her, magicless people are welcome. Yet, he fascinates her, awakening something addictive within her along with the claim that she's not without magical powers.

In the sinister Chaosthane Mountains circling Dussoum, it is not shelter she finds. Despite discovering the reason behind the stolen babies, a magic blossoms within her as does her love for a lawbringer.

Chapter One

Fiery agony burned across Thugari's shoulders, setting her senses alight. A grunt from the castle torturer preceded the next lash. Pinching her lips around her protruding tusks helped smother the scream tearing her throat. Another blow split her threadbare tunic and seared her skin. She lost count after her back burned, bombarding her mind with silent pleas to stop. Warm liquid dribbled to her collarbone, the stench of iron stinging her nostrils.

"Enough." Frukag, the captain of the guard, pierced the pregnant silence with a barked command. With blessed mercy, the next blow didn't fall.

Fresh pain ripped through her with each jarring breath.

"Tell us where you hid the locket, Thugari." He grabbed her hair and yanked her head back.

The violence of the gesture clattered his ethnic beads against each other and swayed them across his bare chest. Sharp darts tore at her scalp, calling forth tears, which she blinked away before he could see them. He dipped to meet her gaze, his breath stinking of old ale.

His tribal-marked face mottled red when she remained silent. "Fine. Summon the spellbinder."

She shut her eyes, dreading the soft footfalls of the ancient ether spellbinder serving her father's clan. Despite being human, Uzul was as merciless as Frukag. A breeze stung her bare back. Shivering, she tightened her arms around the stake, clinging to it as if its solid strength could pour into her. The sun began to set, ushering in cooler temperatures.

She wouldn't have to wait long for Uzul, not when he had a prior arrangement with the village healer in Bire before the evening meal.

Uzul's hem dragged on the paved stones. His impending brand of torture stiffened her shoulders, sending a renewed rivulet of blood along her collarbone to the front of her tunic. Sweat or blood stained what garments she owned. The rich, royal-blue velvet of Uzul's robe brushed her knees as he stopped beside her. Cold anise-scented air shoved her braid aside and stroked along the rune carved into her nape without his physical touch.

Activating the rune with his air magic summoned her body's memories of past lashings. Blinding agony spasmed through her, and she whimpered, not having the strength to smother the sound. As she slumped against the pole, Uzul's oily mind slithered along hers, probing her recent activities. She didn't fight him, unable to gather the will to do so.

"She's innocent," he said.

The pain ceased, and she bathed in the blessed relief like the sweetness of water after days of thirst.

"Lady Arob witnessed Thugari taking her locket." Frukag kept his voice low.

"I assumed you searched the tower?"

"Of course I did, Uzul." Hatred dripped off Frukag's tongue.

"Mmm, then consider justice served, and release the slave." Uzul's voice dwindled as he glided away with his robe trailing dirt and leaves.

Her ropes loosened, and she slumped then collapsed onto her side to coil around the base of the stake. A breeze fanned her chest. She didn't care if her torn tunic gaped, having exposed herself to the warriors before. As the illegitimate daughter of Chief Varthug, none dared to touch her. Nor was she fit for polite company.

The inner yard emptied. The darkening skies and rumbling thunder heralded a storm and left her without an avid audience. No one came to her aid, not that she expected any. As the rain splattered the sunbaked stones beneath her, she tilted her face to savor the cool droplets on her cheeks. Through those catching on her eyelashes, she gazed at the changing sky from blazing oranges to a haunting dark blue. If she lay still, her back didn't throb, and she could convince herself she didn't ache.

She whimpered, rolling onto her knees. The evening meal and her chores awaited her. Clambering to her feet, she clutched her tunic to her chest and raised her gaze to the impressive white stone façade of Haraton Castle, once a human bastion. Peering through the stained glass window, Lady Murzush curled her lips downward and narrowed her.

The fading sunlight touched on her clan markings across her bare stomach and behind her guda covering her breasts. With a flick of her gold-beaded braids, she abandoned Thugari to her suffering.

She staggered to the kitchen, hoping to slip through and up the spiraling steps to the broken-down northwest tower. It served as a room of sorts, where the wind pierced the splintered roof and missing mortar to cool her in summer, but freeze her in winter.

Belen the cook wasn't present when Thugari hesitated at the door. Tempted to drop her shoulders in relief, she caught herself in time and wove through the kitchen. Other maids shot her nervous glances as she passed them. Each step jolted her back, but there was nothing she could do and no one to tend to her.

Anger no longer settled in her soul, forcing her to react or vow vengeance. She fast learned it worsened her fate. Numbness claimed her emotions, nor did she fear losing her life. Frukag bemoaned her stoicism, that he couldn't discipline someone with whom he couldn't bargain. There was nothing more he could do to her besides kill her. She snorted. Death was a kindness he wasn't prepared to bestow upon her.

She climbed to her room like a decrepit elder, but the breeze sweeping down the steps cooled her damp skin. She shut the splintered door, granting herself a fragile privacy. At the task ahead, she held her temple to the coarse wood while she fought for strength. Peeling the tunic off without skinning her back took all her concentration, with each fiery twinge slowed her movements. Once free, she left the tunic where it fell on the straw-lined floor.

She crushed lavender, rosemary, and mint into her broken pewter jug, swirling the concoction to mix the herbs. On bare feet, she paused in front of the window, missing its glazing. While holding the jug to her chest, she released a slow breath then tilted the concoction over her shoulder to trickle the water down her back. Renewed fire sliced through her. She clamped her hand across her mouth to muffle her screams. Her nostrils flared, and she slammed the chipped jar on the stone windowsill, grabbing the stone to steady her.

Crimson-stained water dripped through the splintered floorboards to the abandoned guard room below where she slept in winter. The kitchen fires penetrated the southeast wall, granting her some warmth. Taking an old but clean cloth, she wrapped it around her shoulders. Biting on a scavenged black root, she rolled her back against the wall. A moan shredded her throat, and she bit harder until her teeth ached.

Not an apology crossed Frukag's wet lips. No healer did he summon. Nor could he take to task the lying bitch who accused Thugari of this theft. They believed her, for they must. The same fate awaited anyone who questioned the word of Varthug's legitimate daughter. Thugari had no rights. Her mother, Nerinai, had arrived on Haraton Castle's doorstep with her dark-skinned child. One look at Thugari's eyes and all knew who sired her.

Chief Varthug Nehrakgu's lineage sported silver-gray eyes, as it had done for thousands of years. His people were once masters of moon magic. None of her father's ancient power or her mother's human heritage had seen fit to bless Thugari with magic. Though, what knowledge she had of magic was meager.

A strange sickness took her mother when Thugari was but five summers old. Varthug welcomed her for appearance's sake but could do no more. Not without his mate, Lady Murzush, giving her permission. As constant proof of her father's blatant dalliance with a dark human, Thugari would die before receiving Murzush's kindness. Over the years, whatever obligation her father may have carried for Thugari had dwindled. Whatever love she might have had for him, he destroyed.

She peeled the cloth away from her lacerated skin and draped it over her rickety bed. After pulling on a clean tunic, she crawled under her bed, nudged a stone out of the wall, and stroked the locket lying there. She smirked. She may not have taken the locket her silly half-sister accused her of stealing, but she had stolen jewelry from Murzush. Frukag and his males never found Thugari's treasure whenever they searched her room. Only the dumbest males served her father.

The soft pad of feet on the wooden bedframe warned her she was no longer alone. She lunged for the intruder, snatching him into her arms, and crushing him against her chest for a cuddle.

Gnash, her rat, squirmed, and she giggled, releasing him. He clambered up her chest to curl into the curve of her neck. She ran a gentle finger from his gray head to his bulbous backside.

"Mmm, you've grown fat." She scratched him under his chin, and he purred, but the moment she dropped her hand, he chirped. "I'm hungry too, little one."

One more moon and she would slip out of the castle, past the gate guards, and into the southern village of Bire. She would travel through the eastern forest, circling around Haraton to head north to Chaosthane. The dwarves might shelter her for a while. They too were powerless and welcomed any creature with the same affliction. The city of Dussoum, south of the Chaosthane Mountains, might serve as a new home. The journey would take eight days, but she could do it.

The accusations were becoming more frequent, and her punishments harsher. Only a fool would remain here and court more suffering.

Chapter Two

Rukk Knaraugh swung his legs off the side of the bed with a swallowed groan, rising from the mattress to tug on his breeches, a black tunic, and a thick leather overcoat. No beads proclaimed his heritage. No war markings announced his allegiance. He was an orc without affiliation, except to the law as indicated by his black ensemble, despite the dark leaf-shaped markings along his wrists. He'd earned those during childhood trials.

As a fully clanned orc, it had taken a while to grow accustomed to garments, but now a sense of vulnerability, as if he were unarmed, claimed him when he was nude. With a soft command, white tendrils rose from his skin to sift through his hair, unravel and re-braid it. He didn't care how.

"Stay," Elanil whispered.

He grimaced. Hope poured from her blue elven gaze. He chose not to lay with a female more than once for this very reason. Not that he had found a female worthy of repeat samplings. They were a predictable and tiresome lot. Elanil had made herself available, and he was too tired to seek out another. Elves were preferable to humans, who were too weak to handle an orc at full vigor.

"Farewell." He scooped up his sword as he left her room. Once he had rutted, he never remained charming. Then again, the act itself blunted his magic and drained what energy he could muster for niceties.

She cursed his name, but that didn't bother him either. As a wood nymph with basic magic, her curses wouldn't harm an insect.

In the passage of the brothel, an Atrarian human male leaned against one wall, flicking and catching his jeweled dagger. His mannerisms conveyed impatience. His unkempt, gold-streaked brown hair fell across his dark-skinned brow, yet his vigilant gaze rested on Rukk. Tarid Inaris and he had trained together since childhood. The Council encouraged the forming of close bonds across races.

"I've summoned the healer," he said by way of greeting, sheathing his dagger into a knee-high boot. "You must be ill to have rutted with the same female twice."

Rukk scowled but ignored his fellow lawbringer otherwise.

Not needing a response, Tarid gestured at the bedroom door. "Her magic isn't powerful enough to enchant you. I considered mischievous intent, but that didn't ring true. Rukk, the imperious lawbringer, wouldn't succumb to the weak will of a wood elf."

Rukk trudged down the stairs. Exhaustion weakened his knees, and the urge to sleep on his feet bombarded him. He continued to ignore Tarid, forcing his partner to scamper after Rukk.

"Oh, ho! The silent treatment?" Tarid barked out a laugh, loud enough to echo off the narrow wooden walls of the passage. "Now that you've appeased the demands of your loins, the Council is sending us south to the bowels of Thoraval."

Frustration froze Rukk's next step, and he faced Tarid, granting him, at last, the attention he sought. "No knights available?"

Tarid leveled a serious gaze on him. "Vanishing bairns, my dear Rukk."

"Rumors," he said with a dismissive flick of his wrist.

"The cries of forlorn mothers say otherwise. Haraton Castle awaits." Tarid swept out his arm, whacking his knuckles on the wall.

"Anything south of here is unpleasant, but Haraton is hardly the bowels. It's the hours spent in the saddle, dodging ill-kept humans and orcs alike, I detest. Find another lawbringer." Rukk pulled an ebony-leather glove out of his cloak pocket to slap against his palm before gliding it on.

"The Grand Lawmaster selected you for this quest." Tarid tapped his heels against the wall. He palmed a black root and clamped it between his lips. His jaw worked as he chewed.

Inhaling in a calming breath, Rukk stared at his lawbrother, studying their differences. Tarid's more natural look contrasted with Rukk's obscured origins. Browns and golds comprised Tarid's palette, but Rukk's grays and blacks hinted at racial mix in his ancestry, if his protruding tusks and pale skin didn't. He settled his gaze on Tarid's brown eyes, forcing his friend to look away first. He did, but only for a second.

When he lifted his face, his grin brightened the dimly lit passage. "Come now, Rukk, when last have we traveled for something this intriguing?"

"Are the mounts readied?" Rukk resumed his strides along the passage and out into the quiet road, wishing he could bury his fingers in his soil pouch from his homeland. He needed a portion of his magic restored.

Rutting emptied his overflowing energy, yet laid him low for at least a day. Sleeping beside Elanil hadn't been an option. Now, he must suffer en route to Haraton.

"Of course!" Tarid bounced beside him, all joyful and excited, as if every day was a marvel and not a chore. He gestured to the local stables, built behind the tavern. "The page will meet us at the trading post with our satchels."

"How long have you known about this task?" Rukk studied Tarid's face.

Guilt twisted his features, confirming Rukk's suspicion. Tarid had hours to prepare, by the sound of things. Strolling toward the stables, darting his gaze around, Rukk was careful to hide his annoyance from his friend. He slapped his other glove against his thigh as he walked, grateful for the thick coat shielding him from the dawn mist. The locals believed its icy fingers brought more than shivers, that curses and plagues clung to it, and any exposed skin would feel its wrath. Foolish, yes, but it was cold after the sweet warmth of Elanil's curves.

"The Grand Lawmaster summoned you after the witching hour."

Fire burned through Rukk, and he spun on Tarid, grabbing him by his fur-lined cloak. "What?"

"I couldn't find you!" Tarid raised his hands in surrender.

"Did you scry?" Rukk's voice slipped through tight lips, his jaw clenching and softening as he fought for control. Hours lost! What must the Lawmaster Janar think of him? Curse Zetar!

"You're immune to scrying!" Tarid lowered his hands as a scowl marred his forehead.

Rukk's hard-earned patience evaporated. "Not me, the female, idiot!"

Tarid snorted. "You never rut with the same female twice. How was I to know she would be so blessed?"

"Fair enough." Rukk released him without offering an apology. His friend stank of ale, which meant a dalliance at every tavern he had 'searched.' "Any further information on these bairns?" He picked off a strand of auburn hair from Tarid's cloak before marching to the stables.

He flashed Rukk a sheepish grin. "Same across the lands. Taken at dawn, burn marks on their blankets or mangers, and never seen again."

Rukk nodded. A vague memory teased his thoughts, something from his studies. It remained elusive, so he focused on the moment. "Any missing livestock? Reports of fires in forests, fields, or farms?"

"No more than usual." Tarid snuck glances at him, as if he had solved the mystery of the missing bairns.

Rukk smothered a snort. Did everyone think him the Arch-Magus? "Let's see what Haraton Castle has to offer. Lord Nehrakgu's hospitality is legendary."

"At least there will be a fresh batch of females for you to plunder."

Rukk shook his head, accepting Tarid toyed with him. All knew Rukk kept a strict schedule. Every thirteenth day meant an evening spent attending to his baser urges. To miss such an event made his magic unpredictable, his focus carnal. If his instincts were right about the cause of the disappearances, then they should return before he next needed to rut.

Tarid, however, kept no such schedule, finding any female worthy of plunder. He believed his magic lay within the rutting, despite their archives stating otherwise. Rukk envied his jovial friend's ability to deal with the energy drain. Not once had he been on the verge of losing control as Rukk had. Perhaps more frequent rutting would ease the aftermath. Or Tarid had hidden the size of his energy pool, and it would never overflow.

According to the magi, magic came from the soul—the purer the body, the more powerful the magic, no matter the energy pool's size a wielder was born with. Hence why neither of them could aspire to more powerful positions on the Council. Tarid had no inclination of mastering the art, and Rukk had declined joining the magi. He far preferred merging his powers with combat training.

"A four-day journey through the Forests of Anduia. Oh, joy!" Tarid hoisted his great bulk into the saddle. For Atrarians, Eslaniel retained warhorses—more than suitable for a male of Tarid's size.

Unsheathing his iron sword, Rukk sheathed it in the scabbard fixed to the saddle. Taking a moment, he patted Harpax's neck, whispering orcish words of encouragement before ruffling his mane. The ebony gelding with white socks on three of his feet had been with Rukk for six years. His sleek lines, the ripple of power in his legs, and his stubbornness reminded Rukk of the first horse he had ridden. His mother gifted him with Telayi when he was but five.

Harpax nickered a greeting, pawing the ground to show his eagerness. Rukk vaulted into the saddle. From hours of traveling, the curved leather had molded to the exact shape of his backside.

The morning crowds parted to grant them free passage, avoiding the clumps of mud the horses' hooves flung up. Lanterns offered the illusion of warmth—the last dismal light in the gloom of the mist. He tightened the cloak around his neck, flipping his hood up to hide his pale hair, since the silver of it announced his identity.

A page waited in front of the message board outside the trading post. His gray hood was easy to discern in the lantern he held out at face-level. The lone roan to the left of him, with the Council Magus Sharn Tandagh astride it, drew a mumbled curse from Tarid. Rukk chose not to respond to this development. He didn't want his words twisted out of proportion.

The page attached their satchels to their saddles then snuffed the lantern. The gray mists shifted, lifting enough to illuminate Sharn's pristine beauty—the pale skin of her elvish heritage, but the bronze eyes of her orcish mother. Her pink lips pursed in a practiced pout around her tusks as she watched him. He met her gaze, assuming an expression of boredom.

"The Arch-Magus insists I travel along. Something about needing a female's touch." She fiddled with the reins with her delicate fingers.

Rukk shifted his hood lower, hiding his face from the observant magus. He wished she would forsake her supposed affection for him. Even if it was true, he preferred not to rut with anyone from the Council.

"*She's a spy.*" Tarid projected his thoughts across their bond, made possible by their proximity. Neither were powerful enough to master greater distances.

"*I am aware.*" Withdrawing his dagger from his boot, Rukk pricked his thumb and cast the blood upward. His gut wrenched as he used magic he couldn't spare. "Shield me, oh, blessed life." An expected swirl of mist carried the whispered words. The glowing droplets shot outward, slicing the air in search of vigilance. Cries in the distance confirmed the intended targets reached.

Sharn slumped forward, clutching her stomach and the pommel as a soft whimper escaped her.

"*Well done*," Tarid said.

Rukk acknowledged his praise with a smirk, delighted to have thwarted the creatures of the night she coerced to spy for her. *"It buys us time, but she will summon more as we travel. What worries me is the Arch-Magus has never sent a magus on a mission with a lawbringer. This is an odd occurrence."*

"Mayhap the stolen bairns are more than we anticipated?"

Rukk grimaced. *"That would mean the Grand Lawmaster hasn't divulged everything. He would never send us on a task ill-informed. My allegiance is to the lawbringers and not the magi."*

The Council comprised of two factions with equal power. The magi ruled by an Arch-Magus and the lawbringers governed by a Grand Lawmaster. Within the Tower of Eslaniel, magi trained those powerful enough in the use of magic. The resolution of problems fell to the lawbringers, tasked to guard the Council and the land from unlawful or abuse of magic. It mattered not why magi rebelled, unsanctioned covens formed, or an untrained magic wielder lost control and killed their cows. Such were the norm for lawbringers, and most were resolved with the lethal use of a sword. What was unusual was the Arch-Magus involving herself in lawbringer business.

Perhaps Sharn traveling with was beneficial. Rukk would take the opportunity, so sweetly afforded him, to explore her mind in moments of weakness. After all, not even a magus as skilled as Sharn could guard her thoughts all the time. At some point, she would reveal why the Arch-Magus had thought it necessary to spy on Rukk at all.

Tɦe Lady and Tɦe Assassin

For sheltered Lady Ruvona, visiting Devenmere Manor to investigate her father's disappearance is a chance to escape her dull life. In Netherbury, the nearest town, the malevolent Lord Emil is taxing and starving the people, and a mysterious dark force is draining the land. Determined to help the townsfolk and save her father, with her magic and the skills her guardian taught her, Lady Ruvona disguises herself as the lad, Robbin.

Assassin Warric masquerades as the new Sheriff of Netherbury and is tasked to thwart Emil. What he did not expect to encounter was beautiful Lady Ruvona bathing in a moonlit river. Nor did he expect an ally in the outlaw Robbin. Aiding the lad is in line with Warric's task, but it doesn't take him long to realize who Robbin is.

Together, with magic and swords, they try to save her father, take on Emil, his ancient amulet, and the plot to destroy all they stand for. While trying not to fall in love.

PROLOGUE

Warric closed his knee-length coat against the chilled wind sweeping across the campsite as it stirred up smoke, reignited embers, and lifted the lingering stench of gunpowder. The sun set on another day with the skirmish unresolved. Soldiers, in dark-blue and gold uniforms, gathered around small fires. Great cannons, mounted on formidable wagons, glowed red as they cooled from the day's barrage. Metallic gyros bobbed, tiny white lights flickering on each ball—no doubt soldiers communicating with loved ones.

How the gyros worked wasn't something Warric could wrap his mind around. Slowly, weird contraptions powered by magic had begun to form part of his life. He grimaced and fingered the pouch of iron balls hanging off his belt alongside a pistol. A dagger or an arrow was silent and the best way to assassinate. No matter his skill, he couldn't beat the speed of a pistol.

General Jacut Devenmere of Bennedor strode out of the tent, then paused to run his hazel gaze over the campsite while donning calfskin gloves. His dark-blue coat piped in gold flickered in the wind. He glanced at Warric, tossed his blond hair off his temple, and grinned. "He is in a foul mood this night, Assassin."

"Perhaps I will soon find out why." Warric smirked.

"Aye, he seems...troubled. I head northwest to tackle the Brivela." Jacut grimaced.

Warric offered a nod in condolence. "A tiresome tribe and quite barbaric in their practices."

"Or so I have heard." Jacut stomped his foot, shaking a fleck of mud off the polished leather. "Imagine claiming a woman as wife by stealing her?" He scoffed. "There have been a few I wished I could silence but none worthy of a good kidnapping."

Warric chuckled. The idea of stealing a woman to wed was ludicrous when most gave out their favors for a kind word. "Are they not all too much effort?"

"Spoken like a man who has never known love." Jacut gazed at the unscalable stone wall as it snaked west for miles. "My sister is quite special. Mother and Father sacrificed much for her, and the little minx knows nothing of it." He squared his shoulders. "We pray she never learns the truth." He forced a smile after delivering that cryptic bit of information. After dusting his wide-brimmed hat in matching beige calfskin across his thigh, he marched off.

"Assassin." The voice, thick, educated, and filled with authority, belonged to Warric's lord, Baron Gregory of Kenningthain.

Only those in the baron's confidence knew Warric's true name. In private, the baron used it, but anywhere else, Warric was known as 'Assassin.' He flipped the tent flap back but halted. Awareness rippled across his skin, raising the hairs. Someone lurked, watched, their intentions ill.

A quick scan of those hovering nearby showed no one glancing in his direction. He ducked inside the massive tent, then let the flap fall, waiting a moment to ensure the guards didn't encroach. With a side glance, he located the baron and crossed the burgundy and periwinkle blue Eryssian rug to stand beside the war table. A detailed map sprawled across it, littered with iron figurines representing the wildemen from the north or the baron's soldiers.

While sucking air through his teeth, the baron ran a finger along the rim of a gold goblet. Warric remained still, expectant, patient for his lord to elaborate on why he'd been summoned. The wind shook the tent, yanking on its supports. From outside, the incessant murmur of camp life, along with sharp clashes of metal, penetrated the crackle of the fire pit inside the tent keeping the chill at bay. The magical flames fed on nothing. A standalone clock in gilded bronze ticked as each second passed. All this was noted in a cursory glance. Once he'd settled, he didn't shift, didn't focus anywhere but on Gregory's rugged face, half-hidden by a sculpted beard.

Yet, Warric's senses prickled.

The tent trembled with what he might have attributed to the gusts whipping across the campsite. Rolling his hand, gesturing to Gregory to talk, Warric cast out his magic—air and darkness. He searched for the void among the noise and dusky light.

Stiffening, Gregory nodded and droned on about his favorite horse as a boy growing up in Kenningthain.

Instincts snapped Warric's gaze to the side of the tent, mere feet from where the baron sat on a bench. No movement, sound, or shadow warned of an impending strike. In an instant, the shape of a man flickered to life, glowing like a lantern at the center of Warric's senses, despite not being visible through the tent cloth. He grabbed Gregory by the forearm and yanked him off the bench. At the same time, he unsheathed his dagger then plunged it downward, sinking it into the attacker.

Had he been wrong, the worst was a hole in the cloth.

"Hell's teeth," Gregory spat and bolted out of the tent.

Warric scowled, pulled the bloodied dagger from the man, leaving crimson stains on the tear. Cursing under his breath, he followed the baron. Sprawled in the gap between tents writhed a 'servant' clutching his chest. Blood saturated his cream garments.

"Who sent you?" Gregory roared, grabbing the man's tunic and bringing him off the ground to within an inch of his face.

The man smirked. Blood dribbled over a bottom lip. He slumped, his head falling to the side.

"Shit, Assassin, you could have stabbed him somewhere less lethal. I need answers." Gregory hooked a finger at a nearby guard, then pointed at the dead servant. With a glance at Warric, the baron stomped into the tent.

He withdrew a bottle from a wooden chest. "Wine?" He uncorked it with his teeth, poured a healthy amount, then held out the goblet.

Warric had just saved the baron's life, again. Something he'd done many a time. Yet the baron didn't bark out commands? No, he seemed...resigned. "So, the dead servant is not up for discussion?"

Gregory met his gaze and wiggled the goblet. "This is the last in a line of attempts on my life. This you know."

"I was here for a few of those, milord." Warric wrapped his fingers around the warm metal, drew the goblet under his nose for a deep inhale, then twitched. Sickly sweet almonds infused the fruity and not-yet-matured wine.

"As I expected." The baron ran a hand through his pale-blond hair. A military man in every aspect of his life from discipline to routine, it showed in his physique, as honed as if he was decades younger. Unlike his brother, whom the baron had often lamented being forbidden to kill.

"The wine is from your brother, Emil, milord?" Warric couldn't bring himself to call that child-man a lord.

Only Emil was cowardly enough to use poison. Then again, if it was said he'd killed the baron, the Conclave would deny him the right to rule. Should Gregory die on the battlefield—a hero's death—then the Kenningthain holdings and all its fiefdoms would become Emil's duty. Warric smothered a snort. Duty? The man knew not the meaning.

At Gregory's nod, Warric lifted the bottle off the table then angled it into the light. Dregs of some sort of powder lay at the bottom.

"I hoped to have his name from the dead servant." The baron took the bottle and poured the contents into the piss pot. "My little ass of a brother is stirring up mischief. I was tolerant when he wasted gold to find some lost amulet. That futile search kept him out of my hair. Now, he's taken over the Netherbury seat, and the rumors...well, you know." Gregory closed his eyes and inhaled, then slowly exhaled. He opened his brown eyes to meet Warric's gaze. "That is where you come into this, Warric. This is a personal matter, and for that, I apologize. We are at war, and yet, I must deal with—" He grimaced. "You are the only one I can trust. I need you to replace the new Sheriff of Netherbury en route to his post. Become Emil's right-hand man by all means necessary. Thwart every vile act without revealing yourself and send me regular updates."

He yanked open a drawer and placed two gold discs on the table—intricate patterns were carved into them. In the center of each was a needle. "State of the art, or so I am told. Will allow two-way messaging." Gregory pursed his lips while staring at the discs. With a squaring of his shoulders, he pressed a thumb over the needles. On each, a drop of blood sank into the grooves. White light burst outward. "Newfangled gadgetry powered by wind and air magic? The pistols and cannons, those I can grasp, but these?"

Warric followed suit, pricked his thumbs, and watched as his blood merged with Gregory's. Still glowing white, he palmed one metallic disc then slipped it inside his coat. "I agree, but adapt we must, milord." He gestured to the baron's plated armor—riveted, curved metal sheets, strong enough to stop a pistol, never mind an arrow.

"If these blasted Northerners would quit attacking my lands..." Gregory wiggled his fingers at the tent flaps. "The sheriff leaves Lorden in two days."

With a bow to the baron, Warric strode out of the tent to his horse tethered nearby.

He grabbed the bridle and rested his temple on Serenity's forelock. "We have been tasked, my dear boy."

Serenity snickered and stomped a foot, as if to say he was prepared for anything. Two pistols slapped Warric's thighs when he mounted. He threw a hand back to check the placement of his shotgun on the right. To the left was his freshly oiled crossbow nestled in its holster. Pulling his hood up, he nudged Serenity, spurring him into a trot. They veered around small tents, campfires, and wagons carrying anything from boom cannons to cannon balls to rations. It would take a day to reach Netherbury. He might camp along the Olion river or perhaps find a tavern close to the Conclave Way and await the sheriff's passing.

Out of all the assignments, this one irritated Warric. He clenched his jaw, rolled his shoulders, and urged Serenity into a gallop as soon as they breached the camp's perimeter. Infiltrate a northerner's tribes? Happy to do it. Kill a deserter or betrayer? What a pleasure. Seduce a fair maiden to reach her father? Whatever Baron Gregory needs, but this? Bow to lazy-as-shit Lord Emil? Warric grimaced. He'd rather lick sweat off a bull's balls.

Chuckling at his thoughts, he hunched his shoulders and faced ahead. If Gregory hadn't chosen Warric's scrawny ass decades ago, where would he be? Stuck in a brothel? Babysitting a sop of a lord? Days wasted guarding a treasured library? He shuddered. No, as a sentinel, he served the baron. If he could ease one of those frown lines etched into Gregory's brow, then Warric had served well.

Chapter One

The air shifted beside Vona's ear, giving way to the precise swing of a sword. She ducked while raising her weapon. Blades struck. The force reverberated up her arms, but she gritted her teeth and parried. Darkness filled her vision, her breathing loud and labored in the courtyard. Only her senses could guide her, and of course, her magic. In water, she was unparalleled. In air, her weakest, she was a sitting duck.

Still, Yrsa of Chalimar insisted on testing this as if magic could be improved with practice. Vona huffed. Many a Conclave noviciate had tried. Each child, known as the untested, was born with the five elements—fire, earth, air, water, and darkness. Though magic could be replenished from its element, the size of the 'jar' deep within each individual couldn't be increased. So, when Vona stated air was her weakest, it truly was, and no amount of blindfolding could help improve its power.

A blade bounced off her knuckles. She cried out, leaping back while swinging her sword wild.

"Channel the pain," Yrsa commanded from Vona's left.

"You say that every cursed time, Yrsa. Injuring me only drains my magic." Vona focused on her hand, the tickling of blood as it trickled down her fingers, making the grip she had on the sword slippery. A warmth swept along her arm, honeyed sweetness that brought instant relief. High in earth and water, she could heal and replenish.

"Wasted magic," a man said, his deep voice bouncing off the stone walls—Uldane Tellalouise of Harvet, Head of the Conclave's military division known as the Sundowners, and dear friend to Mother and Father. Before the blindfold, Vona had admired the forest-green of his jerkin catching the sunlight streaming from the massive windows set high in the vaulted arches.

She tilted her head in his direction.

At the same time, Yrsa nudged her.

Having not expected it, Vona tumbled to the side. She halted her sprawl across the stone-carved floor. Glaring in the direction of Yrsa's voice, she held up the sword just in case.

"Talking to me is not helping, Uldane," she sang.

"No battle is without distractions, sweet one," he chuckled and snapped a scroll closed.

Yrsa remained silent. When she spoke to Vona, steel hardened her voice. "Focus. Recite the levels of magic and their purposes."

A blade cut through the air, forcing Vona to leap aside or lose a limb.

Uldane's steps led to the door to the inner house.

Yrsa muttered a curse.

Vona frowned. "What is it about Uldane that angers you so?"

"I am aware he is a friend to the Devenmeres, to your mother, but he is still Lord Sundowner and as such, has power over me."

"You are stronger than he, Yrsa."

Yrsa laughed. 'Tis good you think so." She tapped Vona on the shoulder with the blade. "Recite."

"Again?" Vona whined, thrusting more earth magic into her limbs. They'd been at this for hours. What she wouldn't do for a goblet of brandy.

"Again." Yrsa was a harsh taskmaster but one of the best Sundowners the Conclave had ever seen.

Striking with her shaved head, she towered over all in the Conclave's hallowed halls. Her muscles rippled with each movement revealed by the furs and armor she wore, that of her heritage from the east of Sagua, in the Osiree Mountains of Chalimar. On her right upper arm, inked into the skin by the magic of darkness, was the Sundowner mark. A griffin and a lion guarded a pentagonal shield. All recognized the symbol and feared the bearers.

"Fine. First are the untested, as of age seven. Their magic and natural power are assessed." Vona lunged, thrusting her sword forward then cursing when she met nothing.

"Second level are the guided, their primary magic identified." Swish, slash, and still, she hit air.

"Third are the noviciates, having mastered elementary spells." She ducked, grateful she'd done so when the air stirred above her head. Sure, she could heal minor wounds but a beheading? There was no coming back from that.

"Fourth are the surpassors, learning to focus their magic on noble pursuits in music, weaponry, or exploration." A tap of blade along blade had Vona spinning toward it. She grimaced, having not heard the woman move.

"Fifth level are the proficient, skilled in their chosen fields. Most do not venture past this level." Like myself. Gasping for breath, she willed the sweat droplets dripping off her chin to sink into her skin. Coolness swept over her, a trail of goosebumps in its wake.

"Level six?" Yrsa's voice hardened.

Vona instinctively leaped back and again, avoiding the swish-swish of another strike. "They're the sentinels, masters in their craft. They may choose to educate the lesser levels or make their mark across Sagua."

"Good." Yrsa grunted. High praise, indeed. Vona knew better than to let it go to her head. "What am I?"

"You, my dear tall one, are an envoy—a level seven assigned to guard a Conclave member. In this case, my mother." Vona lowered her sword, assuming they were done for the day. But the slap of the blade across her upper arm had her crying out. She lifted the sword again.

"Level eight? Why do you forget?"

"An empyrean is legend, Yrsa." Vona gritted her teeth while glaring through her blindfold. "There has not been someone at that magic level for centuries."

The older woman snorted. "Because 'tis legend does not mean 'tis forgotten."

The blindfold unraveled and flew across to Yrsa, who caught and slid it into a pocket. Vona blinked at her and pouted. She hadn't worked up a sweat while Vona wasted magic re-absorbing hers. As an envoy, Yrsa's inner well was massive, her magic extraordinary.

"Come, we have...more guests." Yrsa tilted her head, then scowled. "Bringing bad news."

Vona gave her a token smile. "Not every guest is—"

"I am a level seven in air, Vona. Piers natters like a simpleton, sharing news with each breath he spills." Yrsa stomped toward the foyer, crossing through marbled arches three-men high, her boots thudding along the stone floor. Vona hurried to keep up, tripling after the giant of a woman.

The great doors opened. Vona trailed Yrsa down the circular steps to the pebbled road. Clinking like the tinkerman he was, old Thack slid off his horse.

A skinny runt of a man with a swath of golden hair, Piers of Ruarden bobbed on his donkey. When it brayed and bucked, he clambered off, jangling the qitary in his hand. He juggled the musical instrument to rub his ass in purple, velvet, brocaded breeches. Even his boots had bells.

While waving parchment, Thack wheezed past Vona, offering her a dusty kiss on the cheek before disappearing into the estate's library—her mother's domain.

"I swear, either that donkey is losing weight or I am," Piers grumbled. Raising his deep blue gaze to Vona, he beamed. "Lovelier than the sunset across the Somerto Sea." He sniffed then sobbed into a red silk kerchief. "You've grown so much since we last saw you, my pet."

"Missed you too, Piers." She hugged him, then stepped back to hitch a thumb in the library's direction while he blew his nose.

"Do not glower at me, Yrsa the Great. 'Tis been a while since I last saw Ruvona. She is as breathtaking as the moon and stars, as the sky after a storm..."

Yrsa muttered when his face crumpled, "Do not start—"

He threw his arms around her and wailed. His qitary clanged across her back with each jarring breath he took. Instead of shoving him aside, she patted his shoulder and let him have this moment.

Vona danced around Yrsa to peek at Piers. "Is it bad news?"

"Aye," he sniffed.

Vona chewed on her lip while frowning. "My father—?"

"Best to ask your mother," Yrsa said, then with a gentle hip thrust, nudged Piers off her. "Come, to the library we go." She strode ahead, but a side glance didn't put Vona at ease. If Yrsa was worried, then so should she be.

Piers dabbed his eyes with a delicate touch, straightened his purple and gold jerkin then holstered his qitary to his back. He offered Vona his elbow. She accepted and allowed him to escort her to her mother, like a gentle maiden. Giving into his gallantry was far easier than arguing with him while dodging his hand. He was as stubborn as his donkey, Kit.

The library always took her breath away. Books lined the walls as high as the arches. Artifacts served as bookends. Stacks of rolled manuscripts filled shelves behind the great wooden desk dominating a handwoven circular rug from Isamölk. The rich gold, azure, and forest-green threads complimented the dark wood of the desk and shelves. Sconces with flickering flames lit the vast room. Not an inch of sunlight was allowed entry. The windows, visible from the outside, were covered with more bookshelves. Mother took her sentinelship seriously, spending weeks hunting a specific artifact or the lure of a magical fountain purported to expand inner wells.

The main topic at this year's Conclave moot was the search for the fabled manuscript, Whispers of the Lost Ones. Mother had obsessed over this adventure for the last ten years. She'd narrowed the possible locations to two, or so Vona had overheard.

A thump snapped Vona's gaze to Thack who was waving his arms as he paced, danced, and jumped up and down. His mouth opened and closed as he ranted, but no sound escaped him. He stamped his muddy boots, spraying dirt onto the rug and polished wooden floor, then paced in front of Mother. She didn't glance up from her work, her focus clear in her furrowed brow.

"Ailith, listen to the poor man." Uldane laughed. Under his arm, he'd tucked a few scrolls and balanced an open book on his palm.

With a sigh, Mother placed the quill into its inkpot and flicked her wrist at Thack.

"—in danger, and all you can do is shut me up. He is missing, I tell you. One night, we bid each other 'sweet dreams,' and in the morning, he was gone, taken from his bed. Not a peep I heard."

"Not a peep," Piers sang in a croaking voice. He was a self-appointed bard who couldn't sing, but none of them had the heart to tell him.

Thack's great barrel chest shuddered on an exhale. "I found Hayworth's study ransacked and this letter tucked in his favorite boot."

"How uncivilized to take him without shoes." Piers patted Vona's hand. "We came as fast as we could."

Mother snatched the letter, rising to run her gaze along the scrawled words. She pursed her lips as she studied the document she'd been working on. Uldane dropped the book and the scrolls onto the desk to read the letter over Mother's shoulder. He stiffened.

"What did Father say?" Vona tried to step away from Piers, but he drew her back.

"Some darkness has taken over Netherbury." Mother met her gaze, glanced between Yrsa, Piers, then settled on Thack. "I cannot leave, not now. Uldane and I are so close to— The Conclave is about to meet for the annual moot. Can you return to Devenmere, Thack?"

He nodded.

"Good." Mother handed the scroll to Uldane, veered around the desk and grasped Vona's hands, breaking Piers's hold on her. "You, my dear, must go in my stead. Head to the northern border and locate your brother." Her grip tightened. "We cannot wait for his weekly call. He will speak to Baron Gregory to ask for a leave of absence."

Her brother? Vona jerked back. "But—?"

"Uldane is with me, so Yrsa will guard you." Mother shook her head. "A girl alone is always an easy target."

Vona winced. Girl? Like she hadn't spent every morning in the last four years mastering her weaponry.

"Of course, Piers must accompany you." Mother flashed him a smile. "Without his gallantry, the trip would not be a success."

Grinning at Mother's blatant flattery, he dipped in a flourished bow, waving his hand wide and almost smacking Yrsa in the chest. Mother opened a drawer in a tallboy nearby and dug out two discs and a bag of gold. She dumped them on the desk, careful not to touch her documents.

After bleeding into the discs, she shoved them at Yrsa, who stepped forward to press her thumb to the needles. Vona froze, blinked, then gritted her teeth when her mother didn't ask her to bleed. This said it all. She was to journey to find her brother, but under the supervision and command of Yrsa. How her mother saw Vona was the same as her opinion of Piers—pointless.

"We leave within the hour." Yrsa shoved the disc in the back pocket of her breeches and grabbed the gold.

Without a word, Vona turned on a heel and marched to her chambers. She wasn't about to plead with her mother about this lack of trust or how sadness squeezed her heart. Perhaps on this journey she could prove herself?

"Oh, so now you return?" A voice came from her leather satchel. She ignored it. "Or do you plan to punish me some more? Huh?"

She undid the buckle. As soon as the satchel gaped, a gyro slipped out, rolled across the wooden floor then shot into the air. It twirled into a stop in front of her to shine a light into her eyes.

"Quit it, Orv. You are a distraction during training, and you know it. Not that Yrsa has ever harmed you, but you shy away from her and act as if every swing of her sword will kill me." Vona flopped onto her bed and threw an arm across her face. "Hell's teeth," she cried out, slapping the bed. Tears stung behind her eyes. She missed her father. Her mother was a ball of ice that only melted when Father was home. That had been months ago.

Vona was a disappointment. Her well wasn't more than a five at best. She would never be a sentinel like her brother, Jacut, who'd chosen to serve Baron Gregory of Kenningthain. Which meant she couldn't bring honor to the Devenmere name except through marriage. What family wanted a worthless level five? No, she would go on this quest and earn her honor, her place in this world.

"You seem upset? Did Fearless Yrsa best you again?"

Vona ground her teeth. Even her personal gyro revered Yrsa. How could Vona compete when the odds were against her? "Listen here, you worthless ball..." What could she say? He was an it, an inanimate object made lifelike through her frequent blood donations. A gift from her father when she was six, Orv was supposed to be her biggest champion and protector.

"Milady, we must pack." Mags hurried in, heading for the double doors of Vona's wardrobe.

"Why?" After casting a glare at her now-silent gyro, Vona fell back onto the bed. "I will go as is."

"Do not be silly, milady." Mags removed breeches, tunics, leather jerkins, a coat, a hat, pistols and their holsters. She draped a blue silk gown over the pile.

Vona kicked, dislodging the objects covering her shins. "Mags, we will not be traveling by wagon."

The serving girl pursed her lips. "The silk will crease in your saddle bags. Perhaps the linen gown instead?"

Vona shrugged then folded her arms behind her head to stare at the ceiling. "Whatever my horse can carry."

While Mags darted around the room, muttering and cursing, Vona ventured onto the balcony to watch the grooms saddle the horses and tend to Kit and Thack's warhorse, Baston.

Orv trailed her, and in privacy, it whispered, "So, what happened?"

"The usual." She didn't need to go into detail. The poor gyro had endured many a rant at the injustice of it all. Still, as she shared her attention between the grooms and Mags, she had to admit, her life was preferable to a level four or lower.

"Will you change before you depart, milady?" Mags held up a cream-colored tunic. Vona frowned.

Mags tugged on the fabric of the tunic Vona was wearing. "Your sleeve is bloody."

Slumping, Vona tossed a glance at the horses then entered her chambers to whip off the tunic she wore. First, she slipped on her chest holster, tucking in the tiny pistol between her breasts. While she dressed, Mags tried to brush her hair. "Braid it, Mags," Vona snapped, then grimaced. "Sorry, it...has not been a good day."

Once again, she had failed to best Yrsa at weapons training and under Uldane's watch. No doubt, something her mother was more than aware of. Vona curled her lip. Perhaps it was time. At the age of twenty-two, she was old enough to no longer need her mother's approval. Still, it hurt. Each failure dug into her heart like the piercing of a dagger, twisted when her mother revealed her disappointment or said nothing. Releasing a long breath, Vona tapped her foot while she waited for Mags to finish braiding.

"Piers is at the door," Orv whispered a second before the knock.

"Come in, Piers," Vona called.

The door creaked open, then he popped his head around it. Seeing her standing there, he pushed the door wide to saunter in, his boots jingling. "You all right, my pet?" He cupped Vona's cheeks and held her still for a long perusal.

"I am, why do you ask?"

He smiled. "You know me, your personal empath."

Vona smothered a snort at that little bullshit. "I am well, Piers." She forced a smile. "Excited for our little adventure. When last did we travel anywhere together?"

He hummed. Releasing her to lean back, he folded his arms across his chest and gripped his chin. His thin mustache quivered like a golden caterpillar wiggling to escape. "I do believe it was on a trip to Devenmere when you were ten."

She pinched her lips, having not realized she hadn't left her home for twelve years. Her days had been filled with tutors and training. Father had been there for most of it. She'd spent afternoons in his company. His office, to the rear of Bennedor, their Lisbay estate, was filled with artifacts, weapons, and trinkets. If he needed a manuscript or book, he would visit the library.

"I hope Father is well, wherever he is, Piers." She blinked back tears, not wanting to appear weak.

Without saying a word, Piers yanked her into a crushing hug, then engulfed her in some sort of scent—a mixture of mint and sugar. She sniffed, pressed her temple to his shoulder, and let him hold her.

"You are packed, milady. Will there be anything more?" Mags wrung her hands.

Vona pulled away to glance at the satchels at the foot of the bed. Her dagger and pistols sat on top of the pile. "Thank you, Mags."

"I shall send a groom to collect your things." She dipped into a curtsey and darted out, leaving the door gaping.

Piers bent to catch Vona's gaze. "Meet you downstairs?"

He left before she could respond. Alone, she added bags of gold to the satchels, preferring to be prepared for the worst scenario. After a deep pull, in went her favorite flask holding Brederburg brandy, the finest this side of the northern wall. The smoky flavor coated her tongue then set her throat and innards on fire.

"Orv," she called.

The gyro shot up from behind a velvet arm chair in the corner of the room. "Aye, milady?"

"Ready for an adventure?" She chuckled when it bobbed. "Come on, then." Marching through the door, she skipped and danced down the stairs. Even though she would be under Yrsa's thumb, she was away from her mother's vigilance and disapproving stare.

The horses and donkey were waiting, fed, brushed down, and re-saddled.

"Should we not let them rest?" she asked while stroking Kit's beard.

"Sir Thack stated 'twas not necessary. Said they spent the night in Lisbay."

She flicked a glance at Bent, Mag's brother. "Here I thought Thack and Piers had slept on rocky ground and suffered all manner of hardships."

Bent chuckled. "Perhaps on lumpy beds? Those can do a person's back some harm."

"With plump partners, no doubt." She grinned.

"A lady does not banter," Mother bit out, sashaying down the circular steps, her arm looped through Uldane's. Resplendent in a ruby-red gown, her hair pinned up, she had never looked more beautiful.

Vona dipped her head but not before smirking at Bent. He wisely sidled away.

Mother snagged Vona's hands and steered her around. "Now, take care, my girl. Do as Yrsa instructs."

Uldane broke Mother's hold on Vona. "You are acting as if Vona is unskilled and unguarded, Ailith. Trust that you have raised her well." He glanced over his shoulder at Yrsa marching toward them. "If you have further instructions, now is the time." When Mother hurried away, he grabbed Vona's shoulders, holding her in place. "Enjoy this adventure, my dear. Find your voice and inner strength." His green eyes narrowed. "I pray you find what completes your soul." He brushed a curl off her temple, then gripped and released her chin.

What an odd thing to say. It had an old-world feel so she smiled her thanks and let him draw her into a stiff hug. "You keep Mother safe, Uldane," she commanded, her voice smothered by the fabric of his jerkin.

"For as long as I am able." He helped her mount her horse, Honey.

Thack clanked as he hoisted himself on his warhorse. Piers, however, needed two stable hands to climb onto Kit, his qitary strapped to his back, his boots jingling when he forced his toes into the stirrups. He was huffing by the time he held the reins.

Yrsa's glower couldn't dampen Vona's spirits when they finally set off.